The highwayman with the dagger watched me with wide eyes and lowered his blade. He lowered it only a moment—but a moment was all the time I needed.

My muscles burned with the Nightmare's strength. I struck the highwayman's chest with brutal force, knocking the dagger out of his hand and propelling him backward onto the road. His head slammed heavily onto soil just as the highwayman behind me reached for his sword.

But the Nightmare's reflexes were faster. Before the highwayman could free his blade from its sheath, I caught him by the wrist, my grip so tight my nails dug into his skin. "Don't come here again," I said, my voice not entirely my own.

Then, with the full force of the Nightmare's strength, I pushed him off the road into the mist.

Branches snapped as he struck the forest floor, a curse echoing through the moist summer air. I did not wait to see him get back up. I was already running—running full speed for my uncle's house.

Faster, I called over the drumming of my own heart.

My legs strained with effort, my steps so quick and sure my heels hardly touched the ground. When I reached the yellow torchlight, I threw myself against the brick wall near my uncle's gate and forced myself to take long, burning breaths.

I peered over my shoulder down the road, half expecting to see them chasing me. But the darkness was punctured merely by trees and mist.

The Nightmare and I were alone once more.

ONE DARK WINDOW

Book One of The Shepherd King

RACHEL GILLIG

orbitbooks.net

Cover design by Lisa Marie Pompilio
Cover images by Trevillion and Shutterstock

Author photograph by Rachel Gillig

Orbit
Hachette Book Group
1290 Avenue of the Americas
New York, NY 10104
orbitbooks.net

First Edition: September 2022
Simultaneously published in Great Britain by Orbit

Orbit is an imprint of Hachette Book Group.
The Orbit name and logo are trademarks of Little, Brown Book Group Limited.

Library of Congress Control Number: 2022940802

ISBNs: 9780316312486 (trade paperback), 9780316312585 (ebook)

Printed in the United States of America

LSC-C

Printing 13, 2024

To the quiet girls with stories in their heads.
To their dreams—and their nightmares.

PART I
The Cards

Chapter One

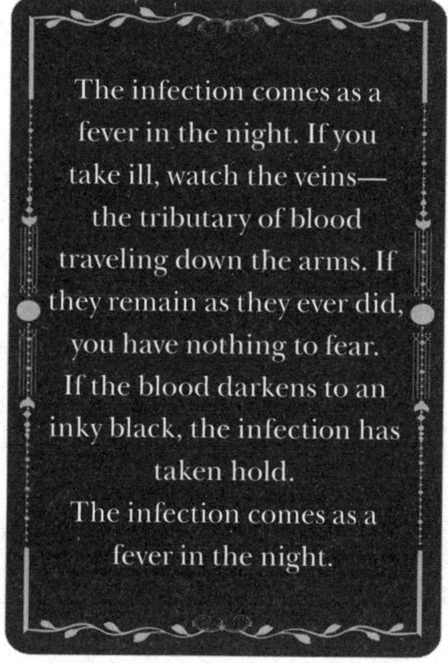
The infection comes as a fever in the night. If you take ill, watch the veins—the tributary of blood traveling down the arms. If they remain as they ever did, you have nothing to fear. If the blood darkens to an inky black, the infection has taken hold.
The infection comes as a fever in the night.

I was nine the first time the Physicians came to the house.

My uncle and his men were away. My cousin Ione and her brothers played loudly in the kitchen, and my aunt did not hear the pounding at the door until the first man in white robes was already in the parlor.

She did not have time to hide me. I was asleep, resting like a cat in the window. When she shook me awake, her voice was thick with fear. "Go to the wood," she whispered, unlatching the window and gently pushing me through the casement to the ground below.

I did not fall onto warm summer grass. My head struck stone and I blinked, dizzy nausea casting dark shapes across my vision, my head haloed in red, sticky warmth.

I heard them in the house, their steps heavy with sinister intent.

Get up, called the voice in my head. *Get up, Elspeth.*

I pulled myself to a rickety stance, desperate for the tree line just beyond the garden. Mist enveloped me, and even though I did not have my charm in my pocket, I ran toward the trees.

But the pain in my head was too great.

I fell again, blood seeping down my neck. *They're going to catch me,* I cried, my mind lost to fear. *They're going to kill me.*

No one's going to hurt you, child, he snarled. *Now get up!*

I tried. Fiercely, I tried. But the damage to my head was too great, and after five desperate steps—the edge of the wood so close I could smell it—I fell onto the dirt in a cold, lifeless faint.

I know now what happened next was not a dream. It couldn't have been. People don't dream when they faint. I didn't dream at all. But I don't know what else to call it.

In the dream, the mist seeped into me, thick and dark. I was in my aunt's garden, just as I had been a moment ago. I could see and hear—smell the air, feel the dirt beneath my head—but I was frozen, unable to move.

Help, I cried, my voice tiny. *Help me.*

Footsteps sounded in my mind, heavy and urgent. Tears slid down my cheeks. I winced but could not see, my vision blurry, like trying to see beneath seawater.

A sharp, angry pain ripped through my arms, my veins suddenly black as ink.

I screamed. I screamed until the world around me disappeared—my vision tunneling until everything had gone dark.

I woke under an alder tree, shielded by the mist and deep greenery of the wood. The pain in my veins was gone. Somehow, my head split open, I'd managed to make it to the tree line. I'd escaped the Physicians.

I was going to live.

My lungs swelled and I let loose a happy sob, my mind still fighting the ebb of panic that had threatened to overcome me.

It wasn't until I sat up that I felt the pain in my hands. I looked down. My palms were scratched and tattered, blood soaking my fingers where my nails, now embedded with soil, had broken. Around me, the earth was upturned, the grass disturbed. Something, or someone, had flattened it.

Something, or someone, had helped me crawl to safety through the mist.

He never told me how he'd moved my body, how he'd managed to save me that day. It remains one of his many secrets, unspoken, resting listlessly in the darkness we shepherd.

Still, it was the first time I stopped fearing the Nightmare—the voice in my head, the creature with strange yellow eyes and an eerie, smooth voice. Eleven years later, and I don't fear him at all.

Even if I should.

That morning I walked the forest road to meet Ione in town.

Gray clouds darkened my way and the path was slippery—thick with moss. The wood held its water, heavy and moist, as if to challenge the inevitable shift of season. Only the occasional dogwood stood in contrast to the emerald sheen, its red-orange hues bright against the mist, fiery and proud.

Birds fluttered beneath a box shrub, startled by my graceless gait, and flew upward in a flurry, the mist so thick their wings seemed to stir it. I tugged my hood over my brow and whistled a tune. It was one of his songs, one of many he hummed in the dark corners of my mind. Old, mournful, soft in the quiet din.

It rang pleasantly in my ears, and when the final notes trilled out my lips onto the path, I was sorry to hear them go.

I pushed into the back of my head—feeling in the dark. When nothing answered, I pattered on down the road.

When my route became too muddy, I stepped into the wood and was delayed by a bramble of berries—black and juicy. Before I ate them, I took my charm, a crow's foot, from my pocket and twisted it, the mist that lingered at the edge of the road clinging to me.

Ants became ensnared in the sticky juice along my fingers. I flicked them away, the sharp taste of acid burning my tongue where I'd accidentally ingested a few. I wiped my fingers on my dress, the dark wool so black it swallowed the stains whole.

Ione was waiting for me at the end of the road, just beyond the trees. We embraced and she took my arm, searching my face beneath the shadow of my hood.

"You didn't step off the path, did you, Bess?"

"Only for a moment," I said, facing the streets beyond.

We stood at the lip of Blunder, the web of cobbled streets and shops more fearsome to me than any dark forest. Folk bustled, human and animal noises loud in my ears after so many weeks at home in the wood. Ahead of us, a carriage hurried by, the sound of clacking hooves sharp against ancient street stones. A man three flights above splashed dirty water out his window, and some of it sprayed onto the hem of my black dress. Children cried. Women shouted and fretted. Merchants hollered their stock, and somewhere a bell chimed, Blunder's crier chronicling the arrest of three highwaymen.

I sucked in a breath and followed Ione up the street. We slowed our pace to peer into merchant stalls—to run our fingers across new fabrics pulled out from behind shop windows. Ione paid a copper for a bundle of pink ribbon and smiled at the clerk, revealing the small gap between her front teeth. The sight of her warmed me. I felt great affection for Ione, my yellow-haired cousin.

We were so different, my cousin and I. She was honest—real. Her emotions were mapped on her face while mine hid behind carefully practiced composure. She was alive in every way, proclaiming her wants and fears and anything in between out loud, like a spell of gratitude. She carried an ease with her wherever she went, attracting people and animals. Even the trees seemed to sway in accordance with her step. Everyone loved her. And she loved them back. Even to her own detriment.

She didn't pretend, Ione. She simply *was.*

I envied her that. I was a spooked animal, so rarely calm. I needed Ione—her shield of warmth and ease—especially on days like this, my nameday, when I visited my father's house.

Far away, in the recesses of my mind, the sound of clicking teeth echoed, slow to stir. I ground my own teeth and clenched my fists, but it was no use—there was no controlling his comings and goings. A boy pushed past me, his eyes lingering a bit too long on my face. I gave him a false smile and turned away, running my hand over the taut muscles of my brow until I felt my expression go blank. It was a trick I had spent years perfecting in the looking glass—molding my face like clay until it bore the vague, demure look of someone who had nothing to hide.

I felt him watching Ione through my eyes. When he spoke, his voice was slick with oil. *Yellow girl, soft and clean. Yellow girl, plain—unseen. Yellow girl, overlooked. Yellow girl, won't be Queen.*

Hush, I said, turning my back to my cousin.

Ione did not know what the infection had done to me. At least, not the extent of it. No one did. Not even my aunt Opal, who'd taken me in when I was delirious with fever. At night, when my fever had burned, she'd muffled the doorjamb with wool and kept the windows shut lest I wake the other children with my cries. She'd given me sleeping drafts and covered my stinging veins with a poultice. She'd read to me from the books she'd once shared with my mother. She'd loved me, despite what it meant to harbor a child who'd caught the fever.

When I'd finally emerged from my chamber, my uncle and cousins had stared, searching me for any sign of magic—anything that might betray me.

But my aunt had been firm. I had indeed caught the fever so feared in Blunder, but that was an end to it—the infection had not granted me magic. Neither the Hawthorns nor my father's new family would be found guilty of associating with me so long as my infection remained a secret.

And I would keep my life.

That's how the best lies are told—with just enough truth to be convincing. For a time, I even found myself believing the lie—believing I had no magic. After all, I bore none of the obvious magical symptoms that so often accompanied the infection—no new abilities, no strange sensations. I grew giddy with delusion, thinking myself the only child to survive the infection unscathed by magic.

But that was a time I tried not to remember—a time of innocence, before Providence Cards.

Before the Nightmare.

His voice faded to nothingness, the quiet shadow of his presence slipping back into darkness. My mind was my own again, the clamor of town swelling once more in my ears as I followed Ione past merchant shops onto Market Street.

Sharp echoes met us at the next bend. Someone was screaming. My neck snapped up. Ione reached for me. "Destriers," she said.

"Or Orithe Willow and his Physicians," I said, quickening our pace, scanning the street for white robes.

Another scream sounded, its shrill notes clinging to the hairs along the back of my neck. I turned my head toward the crowded cobbled square, but Ione pulled me away. The only thing I saw before we turned another corner was a woman, her mouth opened in a wordless wail, the sleeve of her cloak pulled back to reveal her veins, dark as ink.

A moment later she disappeared behind four men in black cloaks—Destriers, the King's elite soldiers. The screams followed us as we hurried up Blunder's twisting streets. By the time we reached the gate at Spindle House, Ione and I were both out of breath.

My father's house was the tallest on the street. I stood at the gate, the screams still rattling through my mind. Ione, pink in her cheeks from the steep walk, smiled at the guard.

The great wooden gate pushed open, revealing a wide brick courtyard.

We entered, Ione ahead of me. At the center of the courtyard, crowded by sandstone, grew an ancient spindle tree planted by my grandfather's grandfather. Unlike our crimson Spindle banner, the courtyard tree still clung to its deep green color, its narrow branches heavy with waxy leaves. I reached out to touch a leaf, careful of the row of small teeth around its edges. It was not a tall, regal tree, but it was old—gallant.

Next to the spindle tree, still small, unmatured, was a whitebeam tree.

On the north side of the courtyard stood the stables, and to the south, the armory. We ventured to neither, our path straight. When we reached the stone steps at the front of the house, I took a breath and fixed my expression once more, knocking three times on the great oak door.

My father's steward greeted us. "Good afternoon," Balian said, his brown eyes narrowing as they crossed mine. He, like the other servants in my father's house, had learned long ago to be wary of the eldest Spindle child.

It had been a year since my last visit. Still, the dull colors of the house were familiar, the tapestries and rugs unchanged. Balian lit a candle, and Ione and I followed him past the dark cherry staircase with the long, winding banister. I did not reflect on how I had loved sliding down that banister as a girl, nor how the house had remained the same since then.

I did not reflect on much at all.

Balian opened the rounded door to the parlor. I could smell the hearth before I felt it, the rich scent of cedar tickling my nose. Inside, my stepmother, Nerium, and my twin half sisters, Nya and Dimia, rose from cushioned chairs.

The twins had the decency to smile, identical dimples carved into their rounded cheeks. I could see my father in their faces, particularly because their mother, Nerium, did not have a face made for easy smiles. My stepmother looked down her delicate nose at me, twisting the ends of her waist-length white hair around her thin, gnarled fingers.

She had all the appearance of a beautiful vulture, perched in her favorite chair. She sat, watching me with keen blue eyes, measuring whether I was worthy enough to consume.

Ione stepped into the room first, blocking Nerium's view of me.

I embraced Nya and Dimia, my half sisters careful not to press their bodies too close to mine. When Balian closed the door, Ione and I took our seats upon the richly upholstered chairs near the fire, my seat nearest to the hearth.

It was so routine it felt rehearsed.

A vase of deep violet irises sat on the small table beside my chair. I ran my fingers over the petals, careful not to bruise them. There were always irises in the parlor.

"Such a lackluster flower," Nerium said, watching me, her

eyes narrowing as they slid over the irises. "I can't understand what your father sees in them."

My insides knotted. Like most things Nerium said to me, there was an undertone of malice in her soft, well-chosen words. My father kept irises in the house for a simple reason.

Iris had been my mother's name.

"I think they're lovely," Ione said, offering me a smile, then shooting my stepmother a venomous glance.

Dimia, who often laughed when she had no idea what was happening, let out a nervous giggle. "You look well," she said, leaning close to Ione. "Is that a new dress?"

Across the hearth, I felt Nya's eyes on me, as if I were a book she had been instructed not to read. When I challenged her gaze, she turned away, her expression guarded.

My half sisters did not love me. Or, if they did, they were long out of practice. At thirteen, born seven years my junior, Dimia and Nya were identical in almost every way, indistinguishable but for the pale birthmark just below Nya's left ear. They'd watched me all my life with mirrored expressions of cautious curiosity, reserving kindness only for each other.

I exchanged empty words with Dimia, heat from the hearth hardly touching me. She told me they'd been invited to celebrate Equinox at Stone, the King's castle.

"I love Equinox," Dimia said, her voice louder than her mother's or sister's. She took a buttered biscuit from the end table, her blue eyes dreamy. When she spoke, crumbs flew from her lips. "The music—the dancing—the games!"

"Not all the games are enjoyable," Nya said, wiping a crumb from the corner of her twin's lip. "Remember what happened last year?"

Nerium's nostrils flared. Ione frowned. Dimia picked at the hem of her sleeve.

I stared blankly. I did not remember—I had not attended.

"High Prince Hauth likes to play games of truth with his Chalice Card," Nerium explained, not bothering to look at me. "A fight broke out between him and one of the other Destriers—Jespyr Yew, I believe. Though why the King has a woman in his service, I cannot understand—"

Your father is coming.

So abrupt I jumped, the Nightmare's voice slid from the darkness, moving directly behind my eyes—urgent. *Can't you see it?*

I held completely still, letting my eyelids fall. There, in the darkness, growing brighter, a royal-blue light: a Providence Card—the Well Card. It looked like a sapphire beacon, floating above the ground, no doubt stowed in my father's pocket. Like other Providence Cards, the Well was the size of any playing card, no bigger than my closed fist. It was hemmed by an ancient velvet.

It was the velvet that gave off the light, a light only I could see. Or rather, a light only the creature in my mind could see.

The Well Card had been my mother's dowry, worth as much gold as all of Spindle House. It was one of twelve different Providence Cards that made up the Deck. Chronicled in our ancient text, *The Old Book of Alders*, Providence Cards were not only Blunder's greatest treasures but also the only legal way of performing magic. Anyone could use them—all it took was touch and intention. Clear your mind, hold a Card in your hand, tap it three times, and the Card was yours to wield. Pocket the Card or place it elsewhere, the magic would still hold. Three more taps, or the touch of another person, and the flow of magic would halt.

But use a Card too long, and the consequences were dire.

They were exceptionally rare, Providence Cards, their number finite. As a child, I had been afforded only glimpses at them.

And I'd only ever touched one.

I shivered, the feel of velvet tickling my memory. The blue light from my father's Well Card grew stronger. When the door opened, the light spilled into the parlor, a beacon glowing from the breast pocket of his doublet.

Erik Spindle. Master of one of Blunder's oldest houses. Tall, severe, fearsome. Most grievous of all, he had once been Captain of the very men called to hunt down those who carried magic—like myself.

Destrier, down to his very bones.

But he was more than a soldier to me. He was my father. Like Spindles before him, he was a man of few words. When he chose to speak, his voice was deep, sharp, like the jagged stones that lingered in shadow beneath a drawbridge. His hair was streaked with silver, fastened at his neck with a leather strip. Like Nerium, his jaw did not lend to easy smiles. But when he glanced my way, the sharp corners of his blue eyes softened.

"Elspeth," he said. He pulled his hand from behind his back. There, painfully delicate in his calloused fist, was a bouquet of wildflowers. Yarrow. "Happy nameday."

Something in my chest tugged. Even after all these years—the death of my mother, my infection—he always gave me yarrow on my nameday. "The fairest of all yarrow"—that's what he called me as a child.

I stood from the bench and approached him, the blue light in his pocket glaring at me. When he slipped the yarrow into my hand, the smell of the woods touched my nose. He must have picked it this morning.

I tried not to look him in the eye too long. It would only make us both uncomfortable. "Thank you."

"We were going to meet you in the hall," my stepmother said to my father, a pinch in her voice. "Is something the matter?"

My father's expression gave nothing away. "I came to say hello to my own daughter in my own house, Nerium. Is that all right with you?"

Nerium's jaw snapped shut. Ione covered her mouth to hide her snicker.

I almost smiled. It felt better than it should, hearing my father stick up for me. But stronger than the tug at the corner of my lips was a dull, aged pain, knotted deep in my chest, reminding me of the truth, ever present, between us.

He hadn't always stuck up for me.

Balian poked his balding head into the parlor. "Dinner is ready, my lord. Roasted duck."

My father gave a sharp nod. "Shall we go into the hall?"

My half sisters quit the parlor, followed by my father. Ione went next, and I a pace behind.

Nerium caught me at the door, her slim fingers digging into my arm. "Your father wishes you to attend Equinox with us this year," she whispered, her *s* coming out a hiss. "Which of course you will not."

My eyes lowered to her hand on my arm. "Why 'of course,' Nerium?"

Her blue eyes narrowed. "Last time you attended, as I recall, you made a fool of yourself with that boy, whose mother, I'll have you know, came calling more than once, hoping to meet you."

I grimaced. I'd almost forgotten about Alyx. It had been years. "You could have told her where I really lived."

"And have people asking why your father sent you away?" The wrinkles around her lips deepened. "We have a happy arrangement, Elspeth. You stay away from court, quiet and out of sight, and your father pays the Hawthorns—handsomely, I might add—to keep you."

Keep me. Like I was a horse at my uncle's stable. I ripped my arm out of her grasp. Whatever appetite I had was gone. I looked over my stepmother's shoulder for Ione, but she had already gone into the great hall.

"I suddenly don't have the stomach for duck," I said through my teeth. I pushed away from my stepmother, slamming the parlor door on my way out. "You'll give my excuses, I'm sure."

I could practically hear the smile in Nerium's soft, wicked voice. "I always do."

I kept my composure until I was out of Spindle House. Then, only once the great doors were closed behind me did I let myself cry.

I kept my head down, eyes hot with tears, and traveled on hurried step all the way to the old church on the cusp of town, granting respite to my ailing lungs only once I was alone on empty streets.

Bent over my knees, I coughed, anger and hurt banging loud discord across my chest.

The Nightmare twisted in the darkness, like a wolf stamping grass before lying down upon it. *Pity we had to go,* he said. *I was so enjoying the rousing conversation of beloved Nerium.*

I kept walking, kicking a stone with the toe of my boot until it was lost in the tall grass that grew along the ridge between the road and the river. *You'll see her again soon enough.*

And will you scurry off with your tail tucked beneath you once more?

You'd have me stay after that? I bit back.

Yes. Because running, dear one, is exactly what she wants from you.

It's easier this way—to avoid them. I heaved a breath. *To run. It's in my nature. Besides,* I added, my voice hollow, *my father wouldn't have abandoned me eleven years ago if he truly wished for my company. You know that—why bother taunting me?*

His laughter dripped like water down the walls of a cavern,

echoing, then fading into hollow silence. *Because that, my dear, is MY nature.*

I sat by the river, reveling in the smooth sound of rushing water. I picked at the yarrow, pinching the tiny yellow petals off one by one. I bought an apple and a wedge of sharp cheese from a peddler, and I stayed by the water until the light behind the mist was low in the sky. Some small hope told me Ione might leave my father's house early to follow me—that we might walk the forest road together—but the bell chimed seven times and she had not come.

I plaited my hair into a thick braid and brushed the dirt off my bottom, casting one last look up the road into town before clutching the crow's foot in my pocket and entering the wood.

Chapter Two

It began the night of the great storm. The wind blew the shutters of my casement open, sharp flashes of lightning casting grotesque shadows across my bedroom floor. The stairs creaked as my father climbed on tiptoe, my handmaid's cries still ripping through the corridors as she fled. When he came to my door, I was unmoving, delirious, my veins dark as tree roots. He pulled me from the narrow frame of my childhood bed and cast me into a carriage.

I awoke two days later in the wood, in the care of my aunt Opal.

When the fever broke, I woke every day at dawn to inspect my body for any new signs of magic. But the magic did not come. I slept each night praying it had all been a grave mistake and that soon my father would come to bring me home.

I felt their eyes on me, servants quick to scurry away, my uncle with a narrowed gaze, waiting. Even the horses shied away from me, somehow able to sense my infection—the sprouting persuasion of magic in my young blood.

In my fourth month in the wood, my uncle and six men rode through the gate, their horses slick with sweat, my uncle's sword bloodied. I cast my gangly body into the shadow of the stable and watched them, curious to see my uncle with a triumphant smile on his mouth. He called for Jedha, the Master-at-Arms, and they spoke in low, swift voices before turning in to the house.

I stayed in the shadows and trailed them through the hall into the mahogany library, the wooden doors left slightly ajar. I can't remember what they said to one another—how my uncle had gotten the Providence Card away from the highwaymen—only that they were consumed with excitement.

I waited for them to leave, my uncle fool enough not to lock the Card away, and I stole into the heart of the room.

Writ on the top of the Card were two words: *The Nightmare.* My mouth opened, my childish eyes round. I knew enough of *The Old Book of Alders* to know this particular Providence Card was one of only two of its kind, its magic formidable, fearsome. Use it, and one had the power to speak into the minds of others. Use it too long, and the Card would reveal one's darkest fears.

But it wasn't the Card's reputation that ensnared me—it was the monster. I stood over the desk, unable to tear my eyes away from the ghastly creature depicted on the Card's face. Its fur was coarse, traveling across its limbs and down its hunched spine to the top of its bristled tail. Its fingers were eerily long, hairless and gray, tipped by great, vicious claws. Its face was neither man nor beast, but something in between. I leaned closer to the Card, drawn by the creature's snarl, its teeth jagged beneath a curled lip.

Its eyes captured me. Yellow, bright as a torch, slit by long, catlike pupils. The creature stared up at me, unmoving, unblinking, and though it was made of ink and paper, I could not shake the feeling it was watching me as intently as I was watching it.

Trying to grasp what happened next was like mending a shattered mirror. Even if I could realign the pieces, cracks in my memory still remained. All I'm certain of was the feel of the burgundy velvet—the unbelievable softness along the ridges of the Nightmare Card as my finger slipped across it.

I remember the smell of salt and the white-hot pain that followed. I must have fallen or fainted, because it was dark outside when I awoke on the library floor. The hair on the back of my neck bristled, and when I sat up, I was somehow aware I was no longer alone in the library.

That's when I first heard it, the sound of those long, vicious claws tapping together.

Click. Click. Click.

I jumped to my feet, searching the library for an intruder. But I was alone. It wasn't until it happened again—*click, click, click*—that I realized the library was empty.

The intruder was in my mind.

"Hello?" I called, my voice breaking.

Its tone was male, a hiss and a purr—oil and bile—sinister and sweet, echoing through the darkness of my mind. *Hello.*

I screamed and fled the library. But there was no fleeing what I had done.

Suddenly it became bitterly clear: The infection had not spared me. I had magic. Strange, awful magic. All it had taken was a touch. Just a touch of my finger on velvet, and I had absorbed something from within my uncle's Nightmare Card. Just a single touch, and its power stalked the corners of my mind, trapped.

At first, I thought I had absorbed the Card itself—its magic. But despite all my efforts, I could not speak into the minds of others. I could speak to only the voice—the monster, the Nightmare. I pored over *The Old Book of Alders* until I knew it by heart, searching for answers. In his description of the Nightmare Card, the Shepherd King wrote of one's deepest fears brought to light—of hauntings and terror. I waited to be frightened, for dreams, for nightmares. But they did not come. I clenched my jaw to keep from screaming every time I entered a dark room, certain he would rip through the silence with a terrifying screech, but he remained quiet. He did not haunt me.

He said nothing at all until the day the Physicians came, when he saved my life.

After that, the noises of his comings and goings became familiar. Enigmatic, his secrets were vast. Stranger still, the Nightmare carried his own magic. To his eyes, Providence Cards were as bright as a torch, their colors unique to the velvet trim they bore. With him trapped in my mind, I, too, saw the Cards. And when I asked for his help, I grew stronger—I could run faster, longer, my senses were keener.

At times, he remained dormant, as if asleep. Others, he seemed to take over my thoughts entirely. When he spoke, his smooth, eerie voice called in rhythmic riddles, sometimes to quote *The Old Book of Alders,* sometimes merely to taunt me.

But no matter how often I asked, he would not tell me who he was or how he had come to exist in the Nightmare Card.

Eleven years, we've been together.

Eleven years, and I've never told a soul.

I did not often walk the forest road at night, and never alone. I cast my gaze over my shoulder, once more hoping Ione would come up behind me, that we might brave the darkness together, arm in arm.

But the only thing to stir at the edge of the wood was a white owl. I watched it soar from the thicket, startled by its quick descent. Night crept over the trees, and with it came animal noises—creatures emboldened by darkness. The Nightmare shifted in the back of my consciousness, sending shivers up my spine despite the tepid air.

I crossed my arms over my chest and quickened my step. Just a few more bends in the road and I would be able to see the torches from my uncle's gate, beckoning me home.

But I did not make it to the second bend before the highwaymen were upon me.

They came out of the mist like beasts of prey—two of them, garbed in long, dark cloaks and masks obscuring all but their eyes. The first caught me by my hood and slid his other hand over my mouth, smothering the scream that escaped my lips. The second drew a dagger with a pale ivory hilt off his belt and held the tip to my chest.

"Stay quiet and I will not use this," he said, his voice deep. "Understand?"

I said nothing, choking on fear. I'd walked these woods half my life. Not so much as a dog had given me pause—certainly not highwaymen, not this close to my uncle's estate. They were either brazen or desperate.

I reached into the darkness of my mind, grasping for the Nightmare. He slithered forward with a hiss, stirred by my fear, awake and present behind my eyes.

I nodded to the highwayman, careful not to stir his dagger.

He took a step back. "What's your name?"

Lie, the Nightmare whispered.

I drew a hitching breath, my hood still imprisoned in the first highwayman's clutch. "J-J-Jayne. Jayne Yarrow."

"Where are you going, Jayne?"

Tell him you have nothing of value.

So they might take their gain in flesh? I don't think so.

Rage began to boil behind my fear, the Nightmare's wrath a metallic taste on my tongue. "I—I work in the service of Sir Hawthorn," I managed, praying the weight of my uncle's name would frighten them.

But when the highwayman behind me gave a curt laugh, I knew I'd said the wrong thing.

"Then you know about his Cards," he said. "Tell us where he keeps them and we'll let you go."

My spine straightened and my fingers curled into fists. The punishment for stealing Providence Cards was a slow, grisly, and public death.

Which meant these were no ordinary cutpurse highwaymen.

"I'm just a maid," I lied. "I don't know anything."

"Sure you do," he said, pulling my hood until the clasp was pressed against my throat. "Tell us."

Let me out, the Nightmare said again, his voice slithering out from behind his jagged teeth.

Shut up and let me think, I snapped, my eyes still on the dagger.

"Hello?" said the highwayman at my back, tugging my hood again. "Can you hear me? Are you daft?"

"Wait," cautioned the one with the dagger. I could not see his face behind the mask, but his gaze held me pinned. When he stepped closer, I flinched, the scent of cedar smoke and cloves clinging to his cloak.

"Search her pockets," he said.

Trespassing fingers roved down my sides, across my waist, and down my skirt. I clenched my jaw and held my nose high. The Nightmare remained quiet, his claws tapping a sharp rhythm.

Click. Click. Click.

"Nothing," said the highwayman.

But the other was not convinced. Whatever he saw in my eyes—whatever he suspected—was enough to keep his dagger stilled just above my heart. "Check her sleeves," he said.

Help me, I shouted into my mind. *Now!*

The Nightmare laughed—a cruel, snakelike hiss.

White-hot heat cut through my arms. I hunched over, my veins burning, and muffled a cry as the Nightmare's strength coursed through my blood.

The man behind me took a step back. "What's wrong with her?"

The highwayman with the dagger watched me with wide eyes and lowered his blade. He lowered it only a moment—but a moment was all the time I needed.

My muscles burned with the Nightmare's strength. I struck the highwayman's chest with brutal force, knocking the dagger out of his hand and propelling him backward onto the road. His head slammed heavily onto soil just as the highwayman behind me reached for his sword.

But the Nightmare's reflexes were faster. Before the highwayman could free his blade from its sheath, I caught him by the wrist, my grip so tight my nails dug into his skin. "Don't come here again," I said, my voice not entirely my own.

Then, with the full force of the Nightmare's strength, I pushed him off the road into the mist.

Branches snapped as he struck the forest floor, a curse echoing through the moist summer air. I did not wait to see him get back up. I was already running—running full speed for my uncle's house.

Faster, I called over the drumming of my own heart.

My legs strained with effort, my steps so quick and sure my heels hardly touched the ground. When I reached the yellow torchlight, I threw myself against the brick wall near my uncle's gate and forced myself to take long, burning breaths.

I peered over my shoulder down the road, half expecting to see them chasing me. But the darkness was punctured merely by trees and mist.

The Nightmare and I were alone once more.

My arms continued to burn, even when my lungs grew steadier. I rolled up my sleeves, staring at the ink-black tributary of magic shooting down my veins, flowing from the crook of my elbow to my wrist. It looked just as it had that night eleven years ago when the fever took hold of me.

It looked the same every time I asked the Nightmare for his help.

I waited for the ink to burn off, grinding my teeth against the stinging warmth. *Do you think they realized I'm infected?*

They're Card thieves. Report you, and they report themselves.

A few moments later, the warmth was gone, its ghost twitching up and down my arms. I leaned up against the brick wall and heaved a rattling sigh. *Why does it burn every time?* I asked.

But the Nightmare had already begun to vanish into the dark chasm of my mind. *My magic moves,* he said. *My magic bites. My magic soothes. My magic frights. You are young and not so bold. I am unflinching—five hundred years old.*

Chapter Three

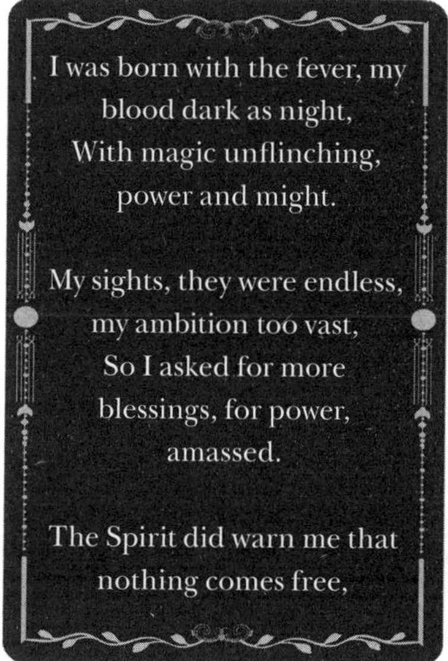

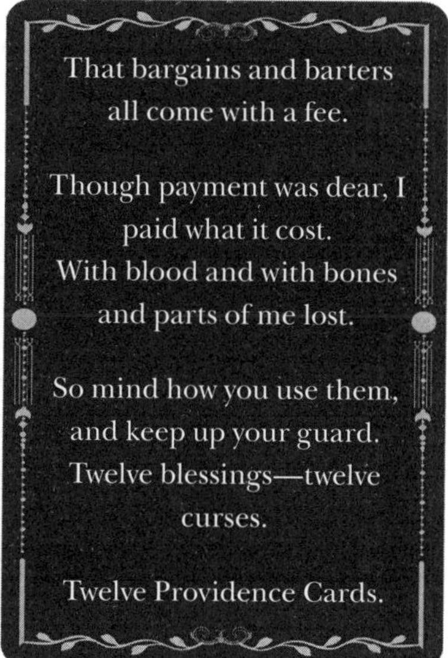

The messenger came while we were seated at the breakfast table. My younger cousins fought over hot biscuits while Ione and I drank our tea. When the steward entered the hall, Ione sprang from the table, her hazel eyes alight as she tore open the envelope.

"Yessssss," she sang through the gap in her teeth.

My aunt waved her butter knife in the air. Ione handed her the letter, the apples of her cheeks rounded, a skip in her step. My aunt perused the fine lettering several moments before my uncle, impatient at the other end of the table, demanded, "Well?"

"We've been invited to Stone for Equinox," she said, wrinkling her nose.

Ione let out a triumphant squeak, and my uncle's gray whiskers twisted, his lips curling in a grin. I folded my hands in my lap, already drafting an excuse not to attend the King's celebration.

"Don't look so pleased," my aunt said, handing the letter to her husband. "We're still behind from last year's tax, and King Rowan is after every penny he's owed." She wrung her hands in her skirt. "Talk in town is that this was the worst harvest the kingdom's seen in ages."

Across the table, my cousins fought over the last sausage, their iron cutlery weaponized into instruments of war. "Why was the harvest poor?" Lyn asked. "Because of the mist?"

"Who cares about the harvest," Ione said. "It's Equinox!" She turned to her father, rapturous. "Are we going, Father? Please say we'll go."

My uncle slathered his bread with strawberry jelly and grunted into his meal. "Yes, Ione," he said. "We're going."

Ione let free a jovial cry, punctuated by my aunt, who was coughing into her tea. "We are?"

My uncle took another bite of bread and pushed from the table. A moment later he returned, a deep burgundy light glowing from his pocket. He reached into his jacket, retrieving a Providence Card from its fold. His fingers traced the burgundy trim a moment, then he plunked it onto the table, shattering my morning calm.

My body went cold. I stared down at the Nightmare Card—the same one I had touched eleven years ago.

"There's your tax," my uncle said. "Worth more than we owe, and then some."

The only noise in the room was the groaning of chairs as my aunt and cousins leaned toward the table for a better look. "Is that...?" Ione whispered.

"The Nightmare Card," my aunt said. She looked back up at my uncle, the color in her cheeks gone. "Kings of Blunder have sought this Card longer than I've been alive, Tyrn. How on earth did you get it?"

"I pinched it off a highwayman on the forest road some years ago."

"And you didn't think to tell me?"

My uncle cast his wife a weary look. "I've been saving it." His eyes flickered to Ione. "For a rainy day."

My uncle sat, round and gray, as he always sat at the head of the table. But there was something strange about his eyes—something about his smile that I had not seen before. Something false.

Despite my aunt's questions, he gave no more detail of how he obtained the Nightmare Card—made no mention of the blood I had seen on his sword the day he had brought it home. I pressed my back into my chair and watched him, chilled by the thought that I knew far less about the man at the head of the table than I thought.

"What is that thing?" my cousin Aldrich said, leaning closer, his face contorting as he squinted at the creature on the Card.

"It's a monster," Lyn whispered, reaching out to touch it.

"Don't!" Aldrich cried, pulling his brother's hand back. "It's too old. You'll rip it."

My uncle snorted. "Hasn't your mother read you *The Old Book* enough times?" When my cousins stayed silent, my uncle reached for the Card, pinching it between his thumbs and forefingers. When he jerked his hands to rip it in half, I heard myself gasp.

But the Card did not tear.

My uncle set it back down on the table, the parchment aged

but without wrinkle. "Providence Cards cannot be destroyed," he said to his sons. "They are woven by old magic."

Lyn leaned forward and talked into his brother's face. Older by only one year, Lyn liked to play the tutor, Aldrich his reluctant pupil. "He means the Shepherd King's magic."

Aldrich swatted him away.

My aunt's voice rumbled, as if well used. "Magic gifted to him by the Spirit of the Wood, which he then used to create Providence Cards."

"*Gifted*," my uncle muttered. "Infected with it, more like."

The sound of the Nightmare's teeth echoed through my mind as he clenched and unclenched his jaw. *A heart of gold can still turn to rot. What he wrote, what he did, was all done for naught. His Cards are but weapons, his kingdom now cruel. Shepherd of folly, King of the fools.*

Ione traced the burgundy velvet at the edge of the Nightmare Card. I flinched, remembering the feel of that same velvet beneath my skin. "It must be worth a great deal to King Rowan," she said.

My uncle turned his gaze to his daughter. "It is, my girl," he said, his smile no longer false, but just as unnerving. "I'm counting on it."

My aunt's copy of *The Old Book of Alders*, the one she had shared with my mother, lay in a heap on the sitting room floor. I picked it up with both hands, its faded cover familiar to the touch. The book smelled of old leather, its binding feeble, cracked with use and time. On the inside cover was my aunt's inscription, written in the name she had once shared with my mother—the name she bore before her father had signed a marriage contract with Tyrn Hawthorn.

Opal Whitebeam. And next to it, scribed in my mother's swooping letters, was my mother's name. *Iris Whitebeam.*

I thumbed through the yellowing pages. Like my cousins, I, too, had been curious about Providence Cards as a child—about magic. My mother would let me crawl into her lap as she read to me from her copy of *The Old Book of Alders.* She had drawn pictures into the book's margins in green ink, swirling images of trees, maidens, monsters. When she read to me, her black hair would fall over her shoulder and I would twist the tips of it around my little finger, lost to the lull of the book's strange, eerie language.

One spring Equinox, my mother and I had come to visit with Aunt Opal. Curled up on a sheepskin rug like kittens, Ione and I had sat, wide-eyed, my mother and aunt answering our questions about the Shepherd King's strange book.

"Why did the Shepherd King make Providence Cards?" I'd asked. "How did he fashion them?"

My aunt had lowered her reading spectacles, eyeing me with a solemnity she rarely employed. "To answer that," she'd said, "we must first look to the Spirit of the Wood."

I'd shivered despite the crackling fire. The Shepherd King's description of the Spirit of the Wood was the sort of thing that made my childish imagination run wild with terror. An ageless deity, smelling of magic—of salt—that lurked, invisible, in the mist.

"Long ago," my aunt had said, "before Providence Cards, the Spirit of the Wood was our divinity. Folk of Blunder sought her out, combing the woods for the smell of salt. They asked her for blessings and gifts. They honored her woods and took the names of the trees as their own. This was old magic—old religion." Her brow had darkened. "For his reverence, the Spirit of the Wood granted the Shepherd King strange, powerful magic.

He wanted to share his magic with his kingdom, and so he made the twelve Providence Cards." Her voice had grown solemn. "But everything has a price. For each Card, the Shepherd King gave something up to the Spirit of the Wood."

"Like his soul?" Ione had asked, gnawing at her fingernails.

My aunt had nodded. "But it was the Spirit of the Wood, in the end, who would pay. With the Shepherd King's Providence Cards, people had magic at their fingertips. They did not have to go to the wood and beg her blessings. No longer venerated, the Spirit grew vengeful, treacherous." She'd paused, her lips pursed. "She created the mist, to lure people back to the wood."

I was young. But even then, I'd known to be wary of the mist. "Those who came upon it lost their way, and often their minds," my mother had said. "The mist spread, isolating us from neighboring kingdoms. Worse, children who tarried in it grew sick with fever, their veins darkening. Those who survived the fever often carried magical gifts like those the Spirit used to bestow, only more unruly—more dangerous." When her voice shook, she'd held a hand to her throat. "But these children degenerated over time. Some grew twisted in their bodies, others in their minds. Few survived to adulthood."

Ione and I had gone still, absorbed by the tale, too young to fully comprehend the dangers of the world we so innocently occupied. "To lift the mist," my aunt had said, "the Shepherd King went deep into the wood to barter once more with the Spirit. When he returned, he penned this," she'd said, tapping *The Old Book of Alders* on her lap. "He wrote about the dangers of magic, and how to safeguard oneself in the mist with a charm." My aunt had paused for effect. "On the final page, the Shepherd King wrote how to destroy the mist."

"Read it!" Ione and I had called in unison.

My aunt had cleared her throat, raising her spectacles to her eyes.

The twelve call for each other when the shadows grow long—
When the days are cut short and the Spirit is strong.

They call for the Deck and the Deck calls them back.
Unite us, they say, and we'll cast out the black.

At the King's namesake tree, with the black blood of salt,
All twelve shall, together, bring sickness to halt.

They'll lighten the mist from mountain to sea.
New beginnings—new ends…

But nothing comes free.

I'd squealed, the eerie rhythm like silk in my ears. Ione and I had peeked at one another, our lips curling as we basked in the delicious darkness that bled out of the Shepherd King's words.

"The Cards. The mist. The blood," my mother had said, her voice so gentle it came as a whisper. "They are all woven together, their balance delicate, like spider silk. Unite all twelve Providence Cards with the black blood of salt, and the infection will be healed. Blunder will be free of the mist."

"But the Shepherd King did not lift the mist, nor heal the infection," my aunt had said, her voice heavy. "The Spirit tricked him, telling him how to lift the mist only after he'd bartered his Twin Alders Card. Without his final Card, the Shepherd King could not unite the Deck. And so he never lifted the mist. No King ever has."

"No King ever will," my mother had mused. "Not until someone finds the Twin Alders Card and the Deck is completed. Until then…"

Ione and I had shared a somber glance. "The mist will continue to spread."

I found my aunt in her garden, where her husband rarely visited, singing to herself. She preferred it there, among the greenery—away from the noise of the house. Her wiry gold hair rolled down her back in wild curls. Dirt under her fingernails, crow's feet in the corners of her eyes, Opal Hawthorn was not as refined or delicate as the other ladies in Blunder. It made her and my uncle—a man of limited scruples, whose desire to be a great man of Blunder had him spending more money than he earned—a decidedly poor pairing.

I loved my aunt's wild beauty. I saw it in Ione. Some days, I could even see the shadow of my mother's face in their shared features.

I picked a mint leaf, crushing it between my molars. The garden birds, sensing my approach, quieted. My aunt turned and smiled, beckoning me to her collection of herbs. "I'm making a tincture," she said.

I looked at the mossy greenery she'd ground with a chalky substance in the bottom of her mortar. When I leaned in, the scent of feverfew met my nostrils. "What's that other bit?"

"Bark from a white willow," she replied. "For headaches."

I folded myself onto the grass next to her. "About Equinox, Aunt," I said. "I don't think I should go."

She snorted and leaned back into her work, the pestle scraping against herb and seed and stone. "Oh?"

Aldrich and Lyn flew through the garden, shouting and brandishing wooden swords. A moment later they were gone, crashing through the yard in a vicious campaign. When they'd vanished, I lowered my voice. "It's been a long time since I've gone to court. Besides," I muttered, "Nerium would hate it."

"All the more reason to go," she grumbled, her fingers tight around the pestle. "That young man will be happy to see you—the one who writes you letters. What's his name—Alyc?"

I groaned. Lord Laburnum's second son, the one with eyes the color of river rocks. The boy who'd sat next to me at the King's table and made me laugh when I was seventeen—the last time I'd attended Equinox.

The boy I'd been foolish enough, bored enough, to kiss. "Alyx. Alyx Laburnum."

My aunt faced me, an expectant smile lingering in the corners of her mouth. "And we no longer like Alyx, is that it?"

I waved my hand through the air, a dismissal. "Maybe I never liked him. Maybe he was just... there."

My aunt shook her head, her tongue clacking against her teeth. But the smile on her lips bloomed. "It won't always be so. Living like a hermit in your uncle's house is no sort of life for a young woman."

The old witch has a point.

I jumped, accidentally beheading a nearby flower.

My aunt did not notice. She pulled an envelope out of her apron. When she handed it to me, the dirt on her hand left a print.

But it did not matter. I knew the handwriting. It was from my father. And I knew what he would ask, just as he did every year when the King opened his castle for Equinox.

"He's trying, Elspeth," my aunt said, watching me.

I thumbed the letter, the oil on my skin smudging my father's scraggly penmanship. It wasn't just him and my stepmother and half sisters I wished to avoid. There was another reason I didn't like to go to court or Equinox or town.

Degeneration. That's what the Shepherd King called it in *The Old Book of Alders.* The sickness of mind or body that came with the infection. After the fever, the infection granted strange power, magical gifts. But everything had a price. For some, that price was obvious, draining one's life force in a slow, agonizing deterioration.

For others, like me, it was unknown, a weighted, invisible anvil that could drop at any time. And it felt reckless, being around strangers, knowing, at any moment, degeneration could ignite in my blood. I might do something horrible in front of the King and his Physicians and Destriers, and they would drag me away to the King's dungeons. Or perhaps I would grow sick and, no matter how I tried to hide it, waste away to nothingness.

Like my mother had.

I looked away from my aunt, my fingers tracing the purple petals of an iris. "I just think it would be easier for everyone if I stayed here."

My aunt sighed, her voice delicate as she reached to stroke my cheek. "I can never understand what it's been like for you," she said. "Know that you are loved, and that you always have a place here, with me. But do not let a fever eleven years past keep you from living your life, Elspeth. You're young. You still have so much ahead of you." She wrinkled her nose and lowered her gaze back to her work. "If not for your own enjoyment, go for mine. I would pay good money to watch Nerium Spindle squirm."

The night before we traveled to the King's castle for Equinox, I had a dream.

I had not dreamed since touching the Nightmare Card. Whatever his faults, the Nightmare did not disturb my wakeless hours.

I didn't know what he did when I slept, and he did not answer when I asked. I used to think he slept, too, but after so many years together, I realized he did not sleep at all. He simply disappeared into a part of my mind I could not reach. There, it was quiet, and when I slept, he roamed freely, unhindered by the current—the utter noisiness—of my thoughts.

It was as if, for once, I was trespassing on him.

In my dream, I was in an ancient room covered in vines. The old wooden ceiling had rotted, revealing beams of light beneath a canopy of green. Birds chirped, rustling above me, the summer day warm and pure despite the cold, weathered stone around me.

I could not recall how I'd gotten into the room. Like all dreams, it lacked a beginning and an end. In the center of the room stood a stone, wide and tall as a table. Seated upon the stone was a man decorated in gold armor that had long lost its sheen. He was aged, older than my father, grisly and stern. He bore the weight of his armor without wavering—his strength deeply rooted. On his hip rested an ancient, rusted sword with branches twisted into a crook carved into the hilt.

Lost in thought, his head resting upon his gauntlets, he did not see me.

I waited for him to look up, shuffling my feet on the leaf-strewn floor.

When he finally saw me, I gasped, recognizing the sharp quality of his unnatural, feline yellow eyes—the irises wide and the pupils narrow.

For a moment he was silent. I realized I'd surprised him, intruded on a moment—a place—the Nightmare had not intended to show me.

The room vanished, the noise of birds muffling to silence. The trees were gone, replaced by tall shelves overflowing with books and tomes and scrolls. A sturdy desk forged from cherrywood replaced the stone. I stood in my uncle's library, my breath hitching in my lungs.

The man and his armor had disappeared. In his place was a creature—more animal than man. Coarse black fur grew up the ridge of his back. He hunched over the desk, the long quality of his fingers making it impossible to tell where flesh ended and claw began. His tail, furred and long, whipped menacingly—like an angry cat's—and his ears, pointed, twitched at me.

I watched him, fascination and dread knotting in my stomach.

His yellow eyes narrowed. "You've come to spy?"

I stuttered, not knowing how to answer. He was angry, I could tell. Still, I had no hand in the making of my dreams. I inhaled, searching for courage. "Who was that man wearing armor?"

He drew a claw along the desk, scratching the wood. His lips, dark and thin, curled upward. "Someone long dead, I'm afraid."

I stood in the center of my uncle's sheepskin rug, the familiar texture cold beneath my bare feet. So strange, to hear a voice and almost never see the face behind it. I scrutinized his features, his dark mouth and short, jagged teeth. Creature, Nightmare, man—whatever he was, he was surely made for hauntings, frightening enough to scare the skin off any man.

As the edges of the library faded, I blurted, "He had yellow eyes."

The Nightmare clicked his tongue against his teeth and smiled. He sat, perched upon my uncle's desk, looking down on me with those same gold-yellow eyes.

"Would you like to hear the story?" he whispered.

His words echoed, the dream already beginning to fade. I nodded, the library around me eclipsing into darkness.

All that was left was the Nightmare's voice, silky and infinite.

"There once was a girl," he murmured, "clever and good, who tarried in shadow in the depths of the wood. There also was a King—a shepherd by his crook, who reigned over magic and wrote the old book. The two were together, so the two were the same:

"The girl, the King... and the monster they became."

Chapter Four

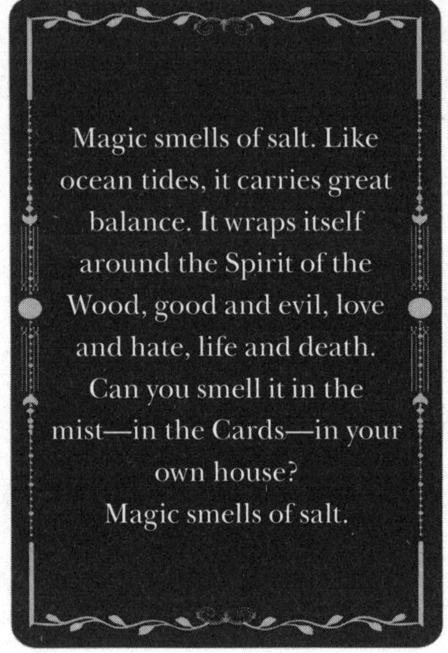

King Rowan dwelled in Stone, the castle just beyond the town, surrounded by treeless hills rich for farming. If the hills were beautiful, I did not know it. I could not see them. No one could.

The mist was too thick.

As if spun of sheep's wool, magical and smelling of salt, the mist blanketed all of Blunder in gray. It was heaviest in the woods. Every year it expanded, choking Blunder off from the outside world, slipping over our fields and farms. If the Deck of Providence Cards was not collected in my lifetime, even town—even roads and places of dwelling—would surely be caught in its snare.

And the Spirit of the Wood would roam freely.

But families of Blunder had learned long ago to keep out of the mist. They walked in droves down the road through great iron gates onto the King's lands, the promise of Equinox—a chance to dine at the King's table—spurring them on. Some came by carriage, but most traveled, by tradition, on foot. I held Ione's arm and kept my other hand on the clasp of my cloak.

Next to me, Ione filled my ears with excited chatter. "What do you think King Rowan will give Father for the Nightmare Card? More Cards? Gold? Land? An honored place in his court?"

The Shepherd King had made seventy-eight Providence Cards in descending order. There were twelve Black Horses, held exclusively by the King's elite guard—the Destriers. Eleven Golden Eggs. Ten Prophets. Nine White Eagles. Eight Maidens. Seven Chalices. Six Wells. Five Iron Gates. Four Scythes. Three Mirrors. Two Nightmares.

And one Twin Alders.

One of only two, the Nightmare Card was exceedingly rare. Which meant, despite the fact that Kings of Blunder had sought it for decades, my uncle had chosen to hold on to it in secret for eleven years.

I peered across my shoulder at my uncle where he walked in step with his sons. His expression was jovial, his mouth open in conversation. His beard had been trimmed, and his silk collar was finer than the ones he usually wore. "I suspect your father's had plenty of time to decide what he and the King will barter over for the Nightmare Card," I said, my voice grim.

The voice in my head slipped through my mind, like wind whistling through a window. *The Hawthorn tree carries few seeds. Its branches are weary, it's lost all its leaves. Be wary the man who bargains and thieves. He'll offer your soul to get what he needs.*

Ione tucked her yellow hair behind her ear. "Father asked, when he presents the Nightmare Card to the King, that I come with him."

My focus on my uncle broke. "What? Why?"

She scrunched her lips from side to side, something she always did when she hadn't decided what to say. "He wants to introduce me to Prince Hauth."

I snorted. "Sounds like a punishment, not a reward."

Ione had always been generous with her laughter—one of the many things I loved about her. She made me feel a great deal funnier than I was. But this time, she did not laugh. Her brow was creased, her hazel eyes distant.

Too slowly, I began to understand. "Wait, is Uncle trading the Nightmare Card…so that you and the High Prince may become acquainted?"

Ione shrugged, kicking a loose stone out ahead of her. "Would that be a horrible thing?"

I blinked. "How could it not be?" I lowered my voice and peered over my shoulder, remembering whose castle I was walking to. "The man's a brute. Both Princes are."

"How do you know?" Ione countered. "Have you ever met them?"

"They're Destriers," I bit back, more heat in my voice than I'd intended. "They're trained to be violent, horrid men."

"Not all of them. Your father was Captain not long ago."

The muscles along my jaw twitched.

"Besides," Ione continued, "perhaps Hauth will be a different kind of Rowan King than those who came before him."

The Nightmare growled at the name Rowan, his claws scraping through my mind. I shushed him. "How do you imagine?" I asked.

"He's so magnetic—attuned. A true leader. Perhaps, under

him, the Destriers will be a symbol of protection, not oppression. Perhaps he will be a King who does not hurt those who catch the infection, but lets them convalesce. A King of abundance, not fear. A better Rowan King."

I gritted my teeth. When I spoke, my voice was not gentle. "That Hauth Rowan does not exist, Ione. You've made him up in your mind."

My cousin's arm slipped out of my grip. "If everyone was as distrustful as you, Bess, Blunder would never change."

My laughter was hollow. "Better distrustful than delusional."

There was redness in Ione's cheeks—rarely displayed anger in her hazel eyes. "Having hope does not make me delusional, Elspeth," she said.

I opened my mouth to say something more, but Ione was stomping ahead, leaving me to walk alone, her words stinging me like wasps. I walked the rest of the way alone, already yearning for my time at the King's castle to be over.

We crossed the drawbridge just as the sky darkened. Aldrich and Lyn threw rocks into the moat and roared in delight until my aunt reined them by the ears and brought them into the castle with the rest of us.

I avoided Ione, moving with weary feet to meet my father and half sisters in a cluster of other Blunder families. Most faces I had not seen in years, but I knew them by the tree insignias sewn into their tunics and gowns. Spindle, Hawthorn, Juniper, Beech, Gorse, Ash, and so on. It was the history of our kingdom—an ancient homage to the Spirit of the Wood—to take the name of the trees.

Nya and Dimia, the spindle tree embroidered on their blue

silk dresses, stood by the hearth and waved at me. Nerium was with them. When she saw me, her eyes bulged, red around the edges.

My aunt had been right. It felt good to watch her squirm.

When my father approached, I tensed. He walked like an oak, stiff—a head taller than the men around us. His tunic was crimson, Spindle red. He glanced down at me through blue eyes, his emotions so guarded they might not have even existed. "I wasn't sure you'd come."

I reached for my charm—the crow's foot in my pocket—and stroked it absently, an anxious habit I was hardly aware of. "It's been three years since I've been to Stone," I said, my eyes lifting to the castle's vaulted ceiling. "It's colder than I remember."

My father paused. His eyes lowered to my face, only to shift away a moment later. "You look well."

I said nothing, watching his eyes, waiting for him to look at me again—knowing he would not. He ran his palm across his jaw, his calluses scratching against the wiry hairs of his untrimmed beard. "It won't be as jovial as past Equinoxes," he said. "It was not a good harvest."

I nodded. "The mist seems thicker every day."

My father peered over me at the mingling crowd. "The King is restless to obtain the last two Cards. And he's willing to pay handsomely for them."

I flinched, recalling my conversation with Ione.

The Nightmare crawled through my mind. *Desperate times,* he said.

No Card is worth a formal introduction to Hauth Rowan.

Says the girl who talks to the monster in her head. Not exactly Princess material, are we, my dear?

I ignored him.

"Tell the footman to send your trunk to the Spindle rooms.

You'll have your own chamber with us." He paused. "That is, unless you wish to stay with the Hawthorns."

I might have, had Ione and I not just had it out barely an hour ago. Besides, where I slept hardly mattered. The celebration of Equinox was not about sleep. "Thank you," I said.

My father caught the eye of someone in the crowd and hastily put his hand on my shoulder. "I'm pleased to see you, Elspeth."

A moment later he was gone, moving through the crowd to the great stairwell. I watched him go, casting one last glance out the door before the guards shut it—the final remnants of gray daylight disappearing behind night's ominous clouds.

I checked my reflection in a darkened window on my way to the great hall. I looked pale, my low cheekbones too sharp, my dark eyes too bottomless—infinite. I scrunched my face at the woman in the reflection and sighed, determined to keep conversations light and retire to bed early.

I was no more than three paces into the great hall when I realized a better plan would have been to hide out in my room indefinitely. Alyx Laburnum, brightly dressed in his yellow house color, lingered at the entrance to the great hall. His brown hair was combed impeccably to the side but for a few wild strands at the crown of his head, governed by an untamable cowlick. When his ash-brown eyes met mine, he smiled so wide I could see every tooth.

"Shit," I muttered.

The Nightmare groaned.

"Elspeth," Alyx said, hurrying toward me. "I thought I saw you earlier—but I feared I had dreamed you up from wishing too greatly."

Mercifully, Castle Laburnum was on the other side of Blunder from Hawthorn House. The chances of running into Alyx, even in town, were abysmal. Maybe that's why I'd tangled with him in a quiet part of the King's gardens when I was seventeen—I'd never have to face him again.

But only if I avoided Equinox.

I dodged an embrace, offering my hand instead. "Hello, Alyx."

His eyes traced my face. When his lips grazed my hand, I pulled back, my gut knotted by guilt and discomfort, and just the smallest hint of revulsion. I stepped past him into the great hall. "We should go in."

Alyx, light on his feet, was next to me in a breath. "I would consider it a great honor if you sat next to me, Miss Spindle."

"I'm supposed to sit with my father," I said without looking at him.

"Should I ask his permission for you to sit with me?"

The Nightmare swore under his breath. *Trees, how I hate him.*

He's thoughtful. Guilt stung me, wasplike. *And I've been awful to him.*

I see no problem with that.

The large, echoing hall was vibrant with color. The tables were long, set with gleaming silver platters and an endless line of candles. Behind the King's table, just out of scope of the candlelight, I counted eight Destriers, all of whom carried their Black Horse Cards in their pockets.

It took all my eleven years of practice to keep my expression blank. My palms grew hot with sweat. Nerium passed me in the crowd. I followed her, pushing away from Alyx, colors—the lights from Providence Cards stowed in pockets and satchels—shining all around me. Yellow—the Golden Egg. Turquoise—the Chalice. Piercing white—the White Eagle. Gray—the Prophet. Red—the Scythe. Black—the Black Horse.

The Nightmare shifted, slithering through my mind. *The color will not hurt you,* he murmured. *The Destriers, and that intolerable boy, on the other hand...*

I flung myself into the nearest unoccupied seat. "Another time," I said, casting Alyx a hasty glance over my shoulder.

Disappointment weakened his smile. He gave me a brief bow, then disappeared down the long table.

I clenched my jaw and rubbed my eyes with the heels of my palms. I did not realize others around me had stood to toast the King until a hand took me by the elbow and pulled me to my feet.

"To Equinox!" the crowd cried, the clinking of crystal echoing throughout the hall.

I raised my own goblet and met the toast of the boy next to me—the one who'd pulled me to my feet. I noticed a playful smattering of freckles across his nose beneath strange gray eyes.

"Thank you," I said.

The boy topped off his wine, then mine. "Are you well, miss?"

I took a deep swill from my goblet. When I looked back up, the boy was watching me. "Never better," I said.

He matched me with a strong gulp of wine. When he smiled, I caught myself wanting to smile back, the vibrancy in his unusual eyes contagious.

"I don't know you," I said.

He was taller than me, though unquestionably younger. When he said his name, he hunched his shoulders and leaned close, as if it were a secret. "I'm Emory," he said. "Emory Yew."

I choked on the wine lingering in the back of my throat. Across the table, my half sisters watched me with mirrored expressions of curiosity. They—like I—were no doubt wondering how I'd managed to be seated next to the King's youngest nephew.

"My name is Elspeth," I said through tight lips.

Emory took another sip of wine. "To what family do you belong?"

"Spindle."

"Elspeth Spindle," he said, his eyes drifting across the table, then back to me. "Elllspeth Spindle. Quite a mouthful."

Servants delivered the first course of summer soup, and a lull rushed across the room, Blunder's powerful families keen to eat at the King's table. But my appetite was gone. I stared at the dish and did not move to touch it, the wine beginning to swirl unpleasantly in my stomach.

"I agree," Emory Yew said, pushing his bowl away and taking another deep swill from his goblet. "Why waste the fine space of the stomach on soup?"

Someone at Emory's side elbowed him and the boy turned away, catching words that came in low, curt tones. I saw a tuft of auburn hair, illuminated by the blood-red beam of a Scythe Card.

I did not have to look long to know who it was. There were only four Scythe Cards in Blunder, and they belonged exclusively to the Rowan family. Prince Renelm Rowan, second heir to the throne, sat on Emory's other side, whispering something I could not hear into his cousin's ear.

Emory turned away from the Prince and drained his goblet, his lips twisted in a lopsided grin. "My apologies," he said. "I'm usually more agreeable. Equinox has a…strange effect on me. You were telling me about yourself."

Was I? I could no longer concentrate. Wine churned in my empty stomach. I felt dizzy, tired, the alcohol turning my thoughts. A wave of nausea moved through me, somehow made worse by the swell of clamor in the great hall. So burning was the urge to flee from the room, I found myself gripping the chair.

I forced myself to blink, the boy next to me almost forgotten. "I'm sorry," I said. "I'm not feeling like myself this evening."

"Are you unwell?"

"No. I just need—I just need some air."

Emory's chair scraped against the stone floor. When the King's nephew offered his arm, I pulled back.

"There is no need."

Emory smiled again, his lips and teeth stained purple. "Easy does it, Spindle. Even I can see you don't want to be here."

He reached for my arm. This time, I allowed him to pull me to a slow, hesitant stance.

Emory and I swam upstream against a sea of servants carrying the next course on silver trays. I followed him out of the great hall all the way to the grand staircase. There was no one around us—no Providence Cards, no Destriers. I gripped the railing at the bottom of the stairs and took deep, swelling breaths, my body slowly easing.

I didn't notice the flagon of wine Emory had stolen until he passed it to me. "Care for more?" he said.

I waved it away. Emory took a deep drink. Wine slid down his chin onto the green velvet of his finely embroidered collar. He wiped his mouth with his sleeve and smiled at me, a touch of absence in his gray eyes.

"You look terribly pale," he said, holding the flagon out to me once more.

When I waved it away a second time, my hand grazed his. "Thank you for your help," I said. "I can go the rest of the way on my own."

For a moment Emory said nothing, his eyes falling to where my fingers had touched the back of his hand. When he spoke, his voice was uneven. "I'll take you where you need to go. I know this castle better than the rats."

I moved up the stairwell. "I can find my way."

He caught me halfway up the stairs, closing the distance

between us, fast as a snake. His breath smelled of wine. "Spindle," he said, the word slipping between his teeth like a hiss. He reached for me, his hand closing around my arm.

I backed away until my spine pressed into the banister. The great room loomed below me. I looked over my shoulder, panic rising into my throat like bile. If I fell—if the boy were to push me over the rail—would the fall kill me?

Not kill, the Nightmare said. *Merely maim. Break.*

What's he doing? I cried.

I stared into Emory's face, trying to work out how to free myself from the strange, changeable boy. When I flinched, he cackled—curt rips of laughter echoing over the banister into the room below. "There's something odd about you, Spindle."

His grip tightened around my arm. He lowered his other hand to my wrist, his palm clammy as it rested against my bare skin. "I see you, Elspeth Spindle." His voice was near and far at once, as if underwater. "I see a pretty maiden with long black hair and charcoal eyes. I see a yellow gaze narrowed by hate. I see darkness and shadow." His lips twisted in an eerie smile. "And I see your fingers, long and pale, covered in blood."

I froze—trapped by dread and the boy's viselike grip on my arm. I tried to shake him off. When he did not let go, I raised my other hand, a hiss escaping my lips.

I slapped him, hard.

The mark from my hand darkened Emory's already flushed cheek. I moved to push away from him—to flee—but he held on to my arm, his grip so tight I cried out in pain.

But before I could call into the darkness for the Nightmare, I heard footsteps on the landing. A moment later, Emory released my arm, pushed with great force down the stairs by someone in a black cloak.

I reeled and ran up the stairwell, only to trip on my dress.

When I looked down the stairs, Emory was heaped in a pile on the bottom landing. A tall man leaned over him. I did not hear the words they exchanged—Emory's voice was broken by uncontrolled fits of laughter. But the low, even tones of the man were enough to still the boy.

The man pulled Emory off the ground and pointed him back in the direction from which we had come.

The boy trudged, suddenly lifeless, returning to the great hall. I rubbed my arm and watched him go, but Emory did not glance my way, as if he'd already forgotten me.

I was on my feet by the time the man approached.

"I'm sorry for my brother, miss," he said, lowering his eyes. "His behavior is inexcusable."

I stared at the tall, darkly cloaked man, my back stiffening.

"Elm—my cousin—told me Emory had been drinking. I came to be sure all was well."

At my silence, the man raised his gaze, observing me for the first time. Like his younger brother, his eyes were gray and stood out brilliantly against smooth copper skin. He watched me down a long, formidable nose, his eyes searching my face.

My breath faltered, a shiver crawling up my spine. Unmistakably handsome, he stood like one of the statues in his uncle's garden—cold and smooth as stone. He did not introduce himself. He did not have to. I knew who he was.

Ravyn Yew. The King's eldest nephew. My father's successor—Captain of the Destriers.

I withered under his stare but did not break our gaze, searching for courage I did not feel. "I didn't see you in the hall," I said. "That is—What I meant—" I huffed air out my nose. "I've never met you before."

"Nor I you," he replied. "What is your house?"

The Nightmare responded with a hiss. I stiffened, the

spindle tree embroidered on my sleeves betraying me. "Spindle," I said, taking a step backward. "My father is—"

"I know who your father is," Ravyn said, his eyes narrowing. "I also know Erik has only two daughters living at Spindle House. Why do you not live with your family, Miss Spindle?"

I tucked a loose hair behind my ear. "I don't see how that's any of your business."

If my cheek took him aback, the Captain of the Destriers did not show it. Still, I paled for my impudence, remembering with a pang just who I was talking to, and how dangerous he was. "Excuse me," I said. "I'm very tired."

"Of course." Ravyn climbed the steps, his black cloak smelling strongly of the world outside the castle walls—cedar and clove, smoke and damp wool. "I'll show you to your room."

He took a torch from the wall and led me down a long row of corridors. Upon the walls hung more of King Rowan's grand tapestries, homage to Providence Cards woven in rich colors. I ran my fingers across the gray Prophet tapestry, the familiar image of an old man shrouded in a long, hooded cloak coarse beneath my fingers.

Three doors beyond the tapestry, we stopped, the torch flickering between us.

"Sir Spindle's rooms," Ravyn said, his voice smooth.

I might have thanked him for whatever gallantry he'd displayed. But the wine had turned sour in my stomach, and the incident on the stairwell had left me drained. I fumbled with the latch, catching my sleeve on the knob.

"Here," he said, opening the door himself.

I flinched and stepped into the room, eager to close my eyes and forget the entire day. "Thank you."

He nodded, the torchlight casting severe shadows across his face. "I haven't introduced myself. I'm Ravyn Yew."

Even the sound of his name made my stomach tighten. "I know."

Steady in his features, Ravyn offered neither a smile nor a bow. He merely cast me one last glance and turned with his torch into the darkness of the corridor, his last words "Sleep well, Miss Spindle."

My bed ensnared me in moments. I closed my eyes and was lost to heaviness, casting away thoughts of the Yew brothers to the dark bliss of sleep.

Still, even as rest took me, I could not help but wonder just how Ravyn Yew had been warned of Emory's ill manners—had come to corral his brother—despite being nowhere near the great hall that evening.

Chapter Five

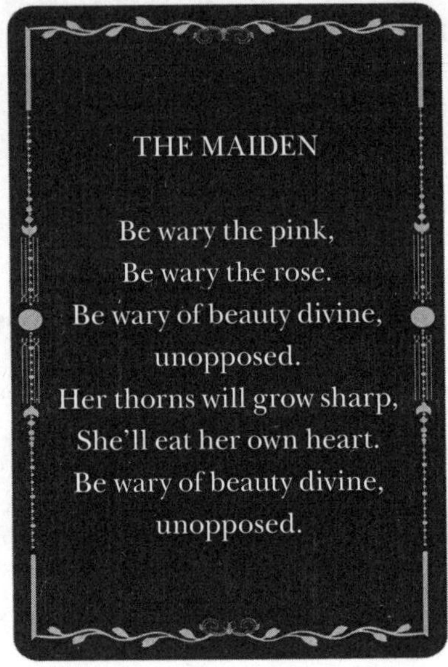

Daylight hit my eyelids. When I opened them, I muffled a scream, four eyes blazing onto me. Dimia and Nya sat on opposite sides of my bed, leering over me like vultures.

I sat up, my head heavy. "What time is it?"

"Almost midday," Nya said.

Dimia, with considerably less delicacy than her sister, leaned in so close I could see the spots on her chin. "We saw you leave the hall with Emory Yew."

I blinked at her. "Is there a question in there, Dimia?"

My door opened with a bang. I sat up in bed, my eyes narrowing when Nerium stepped into the room. "The sleeping princess finally wakes," she said with an unfeeling smile, raking her fingernails over the doorframe. When her eyes traveled to her daughters, pert, on either side of my bed, her smile evaporated. "What are you talking about?"

"Emory Yew," Dimia said. She fluttered her eyelids. "He's terribly handsome."

Nerium tittered. "He's not the sort of company a sophisticated young lady keeps." Her eyes turned to me. "Even you would do well to avoid him, Elspeth."

I pushed my way out of bed. "Your advice is always appreciated, Nerium." I moved to the wash table, splashing fresh water over my face. If it had been warm, that was many hours ago. The water was so cold it stung. "And if you must know, Emory Yew was a complete pig."

My half sisters' eyebrows raised in twin expressions of curious satisfaction. Even Nerium leaned in, thirsty for gossip. "There is something terribly off about that boy," Nya said, tucking a strand of golden hair behind her ear. "If he's not sequestered in his chambers for some new illness, he's drunk as a vagrant, saying the strangest things." She stepped next to me, her voice teeming with poorly masked excitement. "Did he say anything...odd to you?"

The Nightmare's laugh was oily, sticking to the corners of my thoughts.

I shuddered, cold from more than the water. *He mentioned yellow eyes. How could he possibly have known about your eyes? Do you think he—*

—knows there is a five-hundred-year-old monster stalking the dark corners of your mind?

That's impossible. I pulled at the hem of my nightdress. *Still... there was something so unnerving about him.*

I could see confusion begin to etch its way across my half sisters' faces—as it often did when the conversation in my head tarried too long. I ran a distracted hand through my hair and shrugged, offering a dispassion I did not feel. "He was drunk," I said. "He couldn't even make it up the stairs."

"Count your blessings," Nya said. "He's an absolute thorn. I can't remember a dinner at Spindle House when Emory didn't break something."

"That was ages ago," her mother corrected. "He's been living here at least two years."

I knit my brow. "The Yews sent Emory to live here, in Stone, with the King? Why?"

Nerium looked at me the same way she looked at her dog when it pissed on the carpet—endlessly annoyed. "So Prince Renelm can control that nasty little temper, of course."

I recalled the red light spilling from the seat next to Emory last night. Prince Renelm's Scythe Card. A Card reserved only for royalty. With it, the Prince had the power to control anyone he chose—in any way he chose.

Before I could hide my grimace, my father opened the chamber door from his room, startling all four of us. He cleared his throat. "Feeling better, Elspeth?"

It felt like a strangle, having all of them in my room at once. I was beginning to regret not taking a room with the Hawthorns. "Much better," I lied.

"You've missed the breakfast hour, but there will be a walk in the gardens after the men leave for the hunt."

I felt rocks in my stomach at the prospect of trudging through the garden with a herd of Blunder women. When my father closed the door, my half sisters hurried to their adjoining room, lost in the choosing of dresses.

I wore a gray dress made of fine linen—not too coarse, not too heavy. I wove matching gray ribbon in my hair and braided it in a crown around my head. It was the perfect ensemble for a warm day at the tail end of summer, its color so akin to the mist I almost felt invisible.

When we descended into the great hall, I cast my gaze over the banister to the room below. Dozens of women mingled, basking in each other's company, but I saw neither Ione nor my aunt.

My stepmother and half sisters abandoned me shortly, offering neither companionship nor introduction. Ahead, someone opened the outer doors and we went through the castle, shepherded by servants in purple garb out into the garden, the summer warmth floating in the mist like steam.

I ambled along the outside of the crowd. My slippers bore no fashionable heel, and I relished the silence of my step. I reached my hand over the greenery of the garden, my fingers trailing the delicate petals and stems of King Rowan's flowers.

I listened to the women nearby—the ebb and flow of conversation lulling me. Far ahead, the gray of two Prophet Cards shone through the crowd. Beyond it, I distinguished the enchanting pink light of a Maiden Card.

Be wary the pink, the Nightmare said as he sniffed the air. *Be wary the rose. Be wary of beauty divine, unopposed.*

I found myself missing the sound of Ione's voice in my ear. I began to search for her yellow hair in the crowd, anxious to mend the rift between us. Perhaps she was right, and I was too untrusting, too closed, too unfamiliar with the notion of hope. I admired the way she so readily embraced change—how keen she was to see the old, cruel ways of Blunder disappear. If the world were ever to change—if those infected were to be cared for, not hunted like animals—it would be by the hands and heart of someone like Ione.

But no matter how I combed the crowd, I could not find her.

I found my aunt instead. She was stopped on the side of the

path, admiring the splendor of the King's flowers. I put a hand on her back, and she embraced me heartily.

I lingered in her arms. She smelled of rosemary and warm soil, soft and earthy. I did not tell her about my fight with Ione. Instead, we walked arm in arm, speaking quietly as we moved with the tide of women.

"What can you tell me about Emory Yew, Aunt?"

She wiggled her brows at me. "A bit young for you, isn't he, dear?"

The Nightmare gave a sharp laugh.

"I didn't mean it like that." I lowered my voice, steering us to a quieter part of the path. "Do you think anyone—apart from myself—survived the fever as a child?" My stomach turned. "Without getting caught?"

Whatever she had expected me to ask, it was not that. The lines in her face grew taut, and when she spoke, her voice was small. "I don't know, Elspeth. I doubt it."

"Surely someone else—"

"The Destriers and Physicians bring every infected child here—to Stone. To the dungeon. And we know what happens in the dungeon."

I shuddered.

"It's law, I'm afraid."

"Yes, but I'm here," I whispered. "My father was the King's Destrier, and he did not turn me in when the fever struck. Surely there are other parents who have done the same."

"They have tried. But horrible as the infection was for you, Elspeth, it did not remain. You have no magic—no obvious tells for the Destriers to spot you by. Others are not so lucky."

I looked away. But before I could say anything else, someone came up behind us. When I turned, pink light clapped me over the eyes. I stumbled into my aunt, knocking us both into a tall hedge.

Ione, colored by the brilliant pink of a Maiden Card, stared down at me.

My aunt picked herself out of the hedge, brushing her skirt off. “Heavens, Elspeth.” She pulled me to my feet and began to pick leaves out of my hair, but I waved her off. All I could think about was the bright pink Card in my cousin’s pocket.

And the implications of the magic it held.

In the darkness, the Nightmare prowled, alert—aware. *Interesting,* he purred. *A gift from King Rowan in exchange for your uncle’s Nightmare Card?*

No, I managed, my mind turning over itself, panicked. *The Maiden Card is nowhere near as valuable as the Nightmare.*

Then perhaps the Maiden Card is merely part of a much larger sum.

My eyes traced Ione’s face. Her features were as they always were—her face unchanged by the beauty the Card promised. I felt a small relief. *She isn’t using it.*

Yet, the Nightmare replied.

Ione’s brow furled. “Elspeth?”

The crowd pushed around us. I could hear the titters of onlookers, Blunder’s women shooting me narrow glances as they passed.

I stared at my cousin, my eyes falling to the pink light in her pocket, then back to her face. “Where have you been?” I asked, my voice heavy. “I looked for you.”

The pink radiating off Ione’s Maiden Card almost made it impossible to distinguish her blush. Almost. “Nowhere,” she said. “Just wandering the castle.”

It was a poor lie. But that did not soften its blow. Ione was hiding something from me. When my cousin’s eyes met mine, I was certain she could see the hurt on my face.

But that only seemed to deepen the set of her brow. Whatever had happened between our argument yesterday and now, it was clear her anger with me was not yet spent.

"Come," my aunt said, "let's keep walking. We're blocking the path."

I said nothing. Then, spurred by my own anger, I reached out, snagging Ione's sleeve, and pulled her with me off the path.

"Bess, wha—"

"I want to talk, Ione," I said, marching us farther down the gravel path through the rose garden. I shot my aunt a backward glance. "We'll be back shortly."

I turned a corner, the two of us hidden behind the hedgerow. The air smelled of dying roses, so fragrant they could almost mask the scent of their own decay. Ione ripped her sleeve out of my grasp. Even bathed in the pink light of the Maiden Card, I could distinguish the red in her cheeks. "What's the matter with you, Bess?"

"Me, Ione? What about you? 'Wandering the castle'?"

"What of it?"

"It's a lie." I bit my lip. "You met with Prince Hauth, didn't you?"

She prickled. "I told you I would, didn't I?"

"You never told me there would be a Maiden Card involved."

Ione froze, her hazel eyes rounding, searching my face. "How do you know about the Maiden Card?"

I clenched my jaw. "Did *he* give it to you? Hauth Rowan?"

Ione brow furrowed. "I can't understand why you hate the Rowans so much, Elspeth. Hauth has five hundred years of legacy hoisted upon him. He needs support and understanding, not blind resentment." Her voice, so soft, had hardened. "Or can you only think of yourself?"

The Nightmare stalked the shadows of my mind, whispering. *The berry of rowans is red, always red. The earth at its trunk is dark with blood shed. No water, nor cloth, can lessen its spread. He'll ask for a maiden…*

Then turn her heart dead.

My stomach dropped, my anger with my cousin turning to desperation. I reached out for her hand, locking my eyes with hers. "I don't know what Uncle bargained for the Nightmare Card, but I beg of you, Ione, please do not use the Maiden." My throat tightened. "And if Hauth Rowan asks you to marry him, you must not say yes."

I saw the downturn of her lips, the flash of tears in her hazel eyes, the map of fine lines tiptoeing around her eyes. "You ask so much of me, Elspeth. And all of it for yourself."

I shook my head, vehement. "Can't you understand? You are *perfect*, Ione. Just as you are. The gap in your teeth—your voice, too loud in the mornings—the lines next to your eyes when you smile. The Maiden will steal those things from you." I clenched my jaw, fighting the rising lump in my throat. "The Rowans offer it as a gift. But they do it to control you, Ione. To distract you. To make you beholden to them. Please, do not let them."

Tears were falling from my cousin's eyes. But she didn't wipe them away. She let them fall down her cheeks and slip into the creases of her face. When she spoke, her voice cracked. "Do you love me, Elspeth?" she said.

Something in my chest snapped. "More than anything."

She took a rattling breath, then another. Then, slowly, as if bolstered by an invisible force, Ione's gaze grew stronger, harder. Still, her voice shook. "Then let me make my own choices."

She pulled her hand from mine, her steps so light I hardly heard them, then disappeared without a backward glance, leaving me alone, bereft, with the dying roses.

Utterly empty, I hardly noticed the thorns that snagged my palms as I stepped off the garden path. I walked deeper into the garden—walked until I ran. I did not care that I'd gone off the path into the mist. I ran until my heart threatened to burst. Then, at the base of an old poplar tree with sagging branches at the edge of the wood, I wept.

I sat by the tree and traced my finger through the damp soil where the foliage had begun to rot. In my other hand, I twisted my charm. I wiped my eyes on the back of my palm, tears stinging my skin where the thorns had cut it. *She's better than this wretched kingdom deserves. If she uses the Maiden too often, that will be gone. She'll be cold—heartless. She won't be Ione anymore.*

I took a twig from the foliage and snapped it several times until the shards were small enough to sit in my hand.

The Nightmare drummed his claws together. *The Maiden is not just a Card of vanity. Magic is not for vanity.*

It is if it's merely used to impress a Prince, I said, venom in my voice.

He snickered. *A deeply misunderstood Card, the Maiden.*

I stood and said nothing, shame and heartbreak washing over me.

In the end, the Nightmare continued, *it does not matter how and why the Cards are used. Nothing is free, nothing is safe. Magic always comes at a cost.*

Stop telling me that, I said, throwing broken pieces of twig on the ground. *For once, just shut up and leave me al—*

"Miss Spindle?"

I whirled, the depth of the voice behind me striking me like a blow to the stomach.

Ravyn Yew watched me with gray eyes, his head tilted to the side. He looked like his namesake, the raven: sharp, intelligent, striking.

But my gaze did not linger on the Captain's face. I was too caught up in the color—the light—radiating from his breast pocket. It was darker than the Maiden, but just as strong. Dread curled my chest and I choked on air. I had seen that hue of velvet before.

Burgundy—rich and blood red.

The second Nightmare Card.

Chapter Six

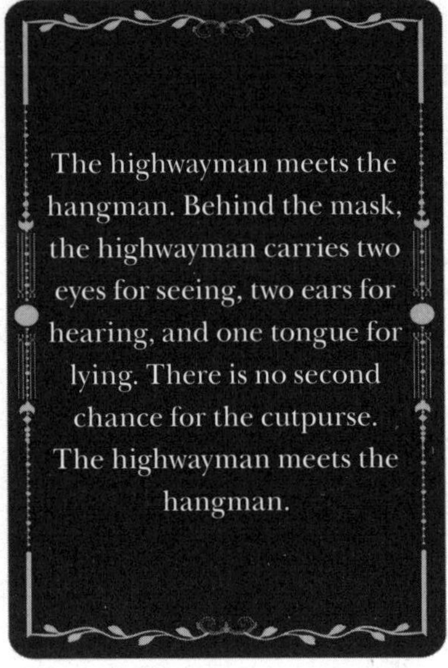
The highwayman meets the hangman. Behind the mask, the highwayman carries two eyes for seeing, two ears for hearing, and one tongue for lying. There is no second chance for the cutpurse. The highwayman meets the hangman.

Ravyn shifted his weight. When he moved, I noticed an array of knives sheathed across his belt.

"What did you do to your hands, Miss Spindle?" he asked.

When I managed to speak, it was through clenched teeth. "I was admiring the roses."

An invisible string pulled at the corner of Ravyn's lips. He approached. "May I?" he said, gesturing to my hands.

I was rooted, frozen. He took my left hand, turning it over to examine my palm. His skin was rough but his touch was gentle, his hand easily covering mine. He did not touch the cuts from the rose thorns but merely observed them.

He did the same with my other hand. When he'd finished,

his eyes moved to my face. "Forgive me, Miss Spindle. But I must ask you something."

I slipped my hand out of his grasp, my throat tightening. "Yes?"

"Why were you on the forest road, alone at nightfall, fifteen days past?"

The shock of seeing the Nightmare Card in his pocket disappeared, replaced by a cold, nauseous terror. The sound of insects and the beat of the owl's wings came back in vivid detail. I stared into Ravyn Yew's face, perhaps for the first honest time—and could not recognize it.

But the highwaymen had worn masks.

My eyes lowered to Ravyn's belt. There it was, plain as day. The ivory hilt—the dagger he'd pressed to my chest.

It's him, I gasped. *I assaulted the bloody Captain of the Destriers.*

The Nightmare's claws scraped through the darkness, the hair along his spine raising. *Let me out,* he hissed.

Across from me, Ravyn Yew was calm, his stance nonaggressive, his arms folded across his chest. He did not act like the same dangerous man I'd met on the forest road—but he was.

And I'd attacked him. I'd attacked a Destrier—a crime punishable by death.

He prowled the forest road for Cards, said the Nightmare. *A crime also punishable by death.*

A crime I and I alone was witness to. I took several steps back. "You must have me confused with someone else, Captain. I know better than to walk the forest road after dark."

Ravyn raised his dark brows. "Yours isn't a face I'd soon forget, Miss Spindle." When he asked the question a second time, there was an edge to his voice. "What were you doing on the forest road?"

I glanced again at the dagger on his belt, but he made no reach for it. He simply held me in his austere gaze, seemingly untouched by the panic that clutched my throat in a stranglehold.

I took another step back. *He's going to arrest me,* I said. *Or worse, kill me to keep his moonlighting secret.*

Around me, the mist was thick, the smell of salt lingering in the dense air. I could no longer hear the women in the garden. I could not even discern which direction the castle was. But I had my charm. I could keep the Spirit of the Wood at bay. I could hide long enough to make a plan.

But I could not say the same thing about going head-to-head with the Captain of the Destriers a second time.

"I'm terribly sorry, Captain," I said, stepping backward into the mist. "My family is waiting for me." *Help me escape,* I called into the darkness of my mind. *Now.*

I tore away from the Captain of the Destriers into the thick, impervious mist.

We were swallowed immediately, the Nightmare and I, the Captain and the wood disappearing behind us. My heart raced and my hands shook. But if I could lose myself in the mist, there was a chance I could lose Ravyn Yew as well.

He's coming, the Nightmare called.

I hiked up my skirt, veering left. I'd entered a field, the wheat harvested—the remaining crop left to decay among hardening soil. The stalks were slippery beneath my feet, but I did not trip.

He came through the mist like a bird of prey, his strong arms reaching out for me. I faltered, my footsteps tangled, but the Nightmare's reflexes were sure. Before Ravyn could catch me, I'd already scurried away, my heart a war drum in my chest.

"Stop!" his voice called through the mist. "I'm not going to hurt you—just wait a moment!"

Somewhere in the distance, I heard the bay of hounds. I swerved away, but my stumble had disoriented me, leaving me directionless. Still, I was faster than the Captain. I was going to get away—going to live. I just needed to—

The smell of salt hit my nose, as if someone had thrust icy seawater into my face. I felt it in my ears—my eyes—my nostrils, into the roof of my mouth. I coughed, gasping frantically for air, my mind and body suddenly gripped by something I could not fathom.

Wait, Elspeth Spindle, a deep voice called in my head. *I'm not going to hurt you.*

I screamed.

My foot caught on dirt clods and I fell, flattened by gravity and the sound of Ravyn Yew's voice in my head. I clasped my hands over my ears and screamed again, terror lashing me like the thorns in a bramble.

He was upon me with a flurry of burgundy color. He slid to the ground next to me, his hand quick to cover my mouth. "Hush!" he said, winded. "They'll hear us."

The dogs' baying grew louder. I could hear the thunderous beat of men on horseback, their booming laughter echoing eerily through the mist. It was the King and his men—returned from the hunt.

My fingers shook, the heat in my arms white-hot, the Nightmare's strength burning through me. I slapped Ravyn's hand away from my mouth and jerked to a stand, ready to flee back into the mist.

But the Captain of the Destriers caught me by the leg, and I fell again onto hard soil.

"Get off!" I cried. The Nightmare's strength flexed through my muscles. When Ravyn did not release my leg, I twisted, sending sharp kicks into his chest and face.

The sound of voices echoed through the mist, closer than before.

"Enough!" Ravyn seethed, his nose bleeding and jaw red. "Another sound and we're both dead."

I could almost hear what they were saying—the men on horseback, the growls of their dogs, the nervous whinnies of their horses. If I were to call out to them, they would surely hear me.

Be still, the Nightmare hissed, anticipating me. *The King is not a friend.*

My veins burned, the smell of salt lingering in my nose. My sleeve had been torn, and my hair, loosened by the tussle, fell from its braid down my back. I twisted the crow's foot in my pocket over and over.

Ravyn watched me, his eyes fixed on my arm. I looked down and sucked in a breath, trying to cover my bare skin with the tatters of my sleeve. But it was too late; he'd seen my veins—dark and twisted.

When he reached out to touch my arm, I jerked away.

"I'm not going to hurt you," he repeated. "You, on the other hand…" He wiped his bloody nostrils on his sleeve, wincing. "Fuck." He pinched the bridge of his nose. "That's twice you've handed me my ass and run off."

I doubted I was the first to take a shot at the Captain's prominent, beak-like nose. It was too easy a target. And I felt no remorse. I did not see a handsome young man with wild eyes and a bloody nose.

All I could see was a Destrier.

"You used a Nightmare Card on me," I hissed. "Get out of my head."

Ravyn pulled the burgundy light from his pocket and held the Card in his hand for me to see. His Nightmare was identical to my uncle's, the monster on its face just as fearsome. Ravyn shot me a narrow glance and tapped the Card three times with his pointer finger, then slid it back into his pocket. "There," he said. "I'm no longer using it."

He was too still—too stern to read. And I couldn't trust a man I could not predict. Ravyn's focus returned to my arm. When I looked down at my torn sleeve, we both watched my arm, pale but for the tributary of ink that coursed through my veins.

The infection's magic—black as night.

The Nightmare watched Ravyn Yew through my eyes, his voice slick and untrusting. *What creature is he,* he asked, *with mask made of stone? Captain? Highwayman? Or beast yet unknown?*

The echoes in the mist faded, the King and his men moving farther away.

At first, the Captain said nothing, his gray eyes lost in the darkness twisting down my arm. I waited, unmoving. When Ravyn finally spoke, his voice was controlled.

"This is why you ran?" he said.

No one talked about the infection. It lived like the dark dog of death, watching Blunder, waiting just beyond the tree line. Feared. Stoked by his Physicians and Destriers, King Rowan fed that fear. Neighbors turned against one another at any sign of fever. And with so much disquiet—so much fear—hate always followed.

I saw it in their eyes—heard in their voices. The people of Blunder hated those who caught the infection almost as much as the infection itself. It trapped them in perpetual surveillance—their eyes tired and anxious—their lips hewn by tight lines of apprehension.

But as I watched Ravyn Yew's face, his gray eyes tracing the darkness in my veins, there was no fear, no resentment in his gaze. Only concern. Concern and wonder.

I'd expected shackles—to be dragged off through the field and thrown in the dungeon. But the stillness of his body, next to mine, was enough to quiet those thoughts, if only for a moment.

Even the Nightmare waited in silence.

"Now what?" I said.

His eyes flickered, returning to my face. "What do you think happens next, Miss Spindle?"

As quickly as it had stilled, my apprehension returned. My shoulders stiffened. "I'm not going to the dungeon. Better you kill me than take me there."

"I'm not going to kill you," he said, raising himself to a stance. "I'm not even going to arrest you. But we need to get inside."

When he offered me his hand, I ignored it. I twisted the crow's foot in my pocket and stared at the Captain of the Destriers, wary of a trap. "What did you hear?" I said, studying his face.

Ravyn straightened his shirt and brushed the dirt from his knees. "Hear?"

"You used a Nightmare Card on me. What did you hear in my mind?"

He looked up. Perhaps the question had been too direct. I could tell by the furrow between his brows that he did not understand.

But that was the answer I needed. He had not discovered the creature in my mind.

"Nothing," he said. "Just a faint noise—a tapping, or a clicking. Why do you ask?"

The Nightmare's laugh echoed, wicked, his claws tapping their endless rhythm. *Click. Click. Click.*

"My mind is my own," I said coldly. "I didn't give you permission to enter it."

"I'd no time to ask," he countered. "Not with you plowing headfirst toward my uncle, half a dozen Destriers, and the entirety of the King's knighthood." He stepped through the mist, headed north. When I did not move to follow him, he turned, his gray eyes unreadable.

"I told you," I called after him. "I'm not going to the dungeon."

"Nor am I, Elspeth Spindle."

When I still didn't move, he crossed his arms over his chest and spoke sharply. "You are in no danger—you have my word. Your infection does not concern me. I merely wish to understand the gift you possess. And I have no intention of discussing it in an open field."

I unfurled myself from the ground slowly, my back arched like a cat's, never taking my eyes off the Captain. "I'll save you the trouble," I said. "I have no magic."

I wouldn't call the turn of his lips a smile. But it was perhaps the best he could do after the kicks I'd dealt his face. "You're a decent liar," he said, turning back to the mist. "You'll fit right in."

Beast yet unknown, then, the Nightmare murmured.

I clenched my jaw, hardly able to fathom that I, Elspeth Spindle, was willingly following the Captain of the Destriers into the King's castle. "I'll come," I said. "So long as we don't go through the garden." My thoughts flew to Ione. "I want to avoid the women and their Providence Cards."

"We'll take an eastern entrance." Then, as if he'd just heard me, Ravyn turned his head. "How do you know there are Providence Cards in the garden?"

Chapter Seven

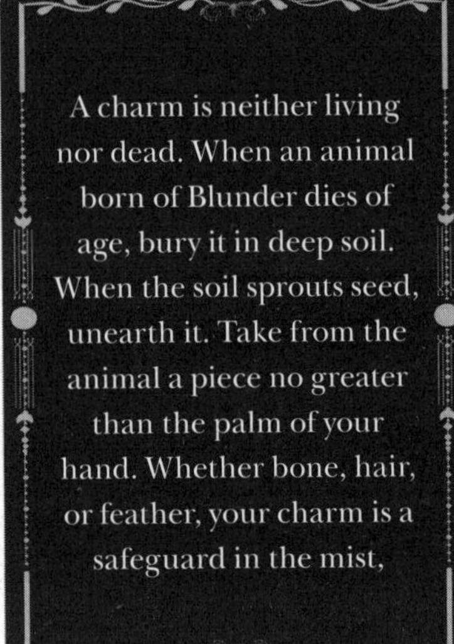

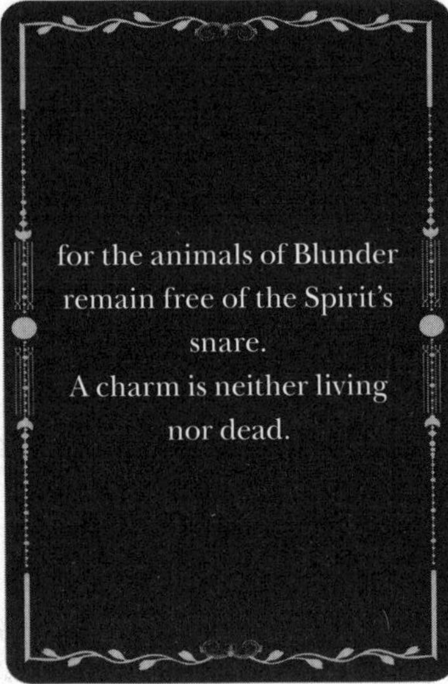

We found an old rope left by farmers that led us through the mist back to Stone. My legs jumped with phantom spasms—ready to run again at any sign of danger. But the Captain's path was steadfast.

Weeds and overgrown grass covered the walls on the east side of Stone. My hands shook as we came upon a rounded wooden door covered in cobwebs. Ravyn pulled a small brass key from his belt. I heard the click of the lock, and a moment later he ripped the door open, dust and vines displaced—the door hesitant to move.

Ravyn held it open for me, his gray eyes tight on my face. "After you," he said.

I hung back like an animal wary of a trap.

"Best we don't linger." He gestured inside. "You go first."

I peered into the dark corridor beyond. "Where does it lead?"

The Captain of the Destriers ran his hand over his brow, impatience cutting through his low voice. "Miss Spindle. You have nothing to fear from me."

Strange, coming from the man who might have pierced your heart on the forest road.

My breath hitched as I entered the shadowy corridor, my eyes slow to adjust to the dark.

"This way," Ravyn said, closing the door and leading me down twists and turns—a labyrinth of tall corridors and unmarked rooms.

We reached a stone stairway that descended into blackness. The Nightmare's voice pricked my ears. *In the cold and the dark, the stone does not age. The light cannot reach where the shadows doth rage. At the end of the stairs, by rope or by blade, they take the sick children, to burn in a cage.*

I shuddered. The King's dungeon and the rumors of what happened there had long since put their hooks in me. I glanced down the stairwell, the shadows, long and twisted, reaching for me with cruel, gnarled fingers.

I didn't realize I had stopped walking until Ravyn cleared his throat, halting a few paces ahead. He must have seen the terror on my face because, for a moment, the firmness around his eyes softened. He glanced down the stairwell. "I'll never take you there, Miss Spindle. You have my word."

With that he turned, leaving me no choice but to follow. He led me down another hall, past a long gallery of portraits—Rowan Kings of the past. We veered left, into an ill-lit servants' passage. There we took a short set of steps that dropped us at a door fashioned from wood so dark I couldn't tell its origin. Its only distinction was two stags carved into the wood just below the frame.

Ravyn fumbled for another key, his cloak so dark over his broad back it stole the dim light around us. Unlike the frosty shadow of the dungeon, I could feel the warmth radiating off him. I was suddenly very aware of how closely we stood—the shape of his shoulder blades—the calluses of his fingers as he searched for the correct key. His cloak smelled of mist and cloves.

It felt far too intimate, feeling his warmth. I tried to step back, but there was nowhere to go. Ravyn took another key—this one long and iron forged—and clicked it into place, releasing the lock on the stag door. When he glanced at me over his shoulder, I had the stark impression he knew I'd been watching him.

He pushed open the door, and I stepped inside.

A moment later I was pressed into the stone wall, the clamor of barking dogs in my ears. They snarled at me—two hounds with sharp white teeth, pulled from their bed of hay at the sound of intruders.

In the blackness, the Nightmare hissed, his claws flashing. But before the dogs could pounce, Ravyn pulled them back, jerking their collars and calling severe commands.

The hounds retreated back to their hay, their untrusting eyes never leaving me.

"They're not vicious," Ravyn said. "They hardly bark as often as they should, lazy things. I don't know what's gotten into them."

I peeled myself off the wall. "Animals don't like me," I murmured, my heart pounding as I took in my surroundings.

The room looked like an abandoned cellar. There were no

windows—no natural light. A small hearth nestled on the far wall illuminated the room. An old rounded table stood near the hearth, surrounded by chairs that did not match. A shelf with old tomes was positioned on the south wall, its contents perhaps older than the room itself.

Not the dungeon, then.

Don't be so sure, the Nightmare said. *There are many different kinds of cages.*

I ignored the bite in his words and moved to the table, wary of the dogs. "What now?" I asked.

The Captain ran his fingers through his dark hair, strain creasing his eyes. "Wait here. I'll be back in a moment."

He hurried out the door. I did not bother to listen for the click of the bolt—I knew he'd lock me in. I approached the shelf, looking for something—anything—I could turn into a weapon. The dogs watched me, growling their discontent, but did not stir from their beds.

Now we wait.

The Nightmare strummed his nails together, a sharp, ugly discord. *He knows you're infected. And he knows, to some extent, you are aware of the Providence Cards in the castle.*

I winced. I had not meant to say it, there in the mist, alone with the Captain of the Destriers. The moment I'd mentioned Providence Cards, Ravyn's ears had perked. I'd clasped my lips together, but it was too late.

I tapped my foot on the floor, an anxious, chaotic rhythm.

But the Nightmare was untouched by my disquiet, his voice almost lazy. *Suppose you simply told him you can see Providence Cards? Or rather, that I see them.*

I stopped fumbling with one of the dust-ridden tomes on the shelf. *Don't be stupid.*

He may surprise you.

He's already done that, I said, eyeing the door, listening for footsteps. *Not all surprises are good.*

The Nightmare laughed, as if he understood a joke I did not. *Mark my words. He's going to test your magic.* He tapped his claws. *Or, more accurately, test MY magic.*

I groaned into my sleeve, retreating to a wooden chair. The room was bare of weapons. Should danger arise, I would have to rely on the one in my mind.

Footsteps sounded once more on the stone steps, followed by the click of the key. The dogs perked their ears, and I braced myself.

Three people filed into the cellar. Ravyn Yew, a stranger, and a young woman. By the shape of her stern jaw and the short cut of her dark hair, her lean body fitted by a richly hemmed tunic rather than a stifling dress, I knew exactly who she was.

Jespyr Yew, Ravyn's younger sister, and the only female Destrier.

They stood in a crooked line before me, each with a fixed expression of caution. The man between the Yew siblings was older, his tunic plain and his beard untrimmed. I stared at him, unable to place him.

Then I noticed the small willow tree, woven in white thread, on the breast of his tunic.

I leapt from my chair. "You brought a Physician?" I cried. "Why not just run me through with your dagger?"

"Easy," Ravyn said, his voice smooth. "We just want to ask you questions. He's not going to report you. Isn't that right, Filick?"

"I am bound to obey the Captain," the older man said. He gave Ravyn a faint wink, then approached the table with caution, as if I were a wild, fretful horse. Taking the chair to my right, he lowered himself to a seat.

"My name is Filick Willow. What is yours?"

I cast Ravyn a hateful glance. My whole life, I'd managed to avoid Physicians. This time, there was nowhere to hide.

I lowered myself into my chair and straightened my back with a boldness I did not feel. "Elspeth Spindle," I said, my voice cold.

"How old are you, Elspeth?"

"Twenty."

He leaned in, observing me. "How old were you when you caught the infection?"

"Nine."

"I see. And what magical abilities did your infection grant you?"

I tried not to squirm as I weighed my options. If I lied and said I had no magic, they could hardly let me leave. I was still a witness to the Captain of the Destriers' moonlighting as a highwayman.

And what, my dear, was he looking for, dressed all in black, stalking the forest road?

A spark flickered through my mind. There was a way to lie and tell the truth at the same time.

That's how the best lies are told—with just a sliver of truth.

I took a deep breath, then another. Slowly, I eased the muscles in my face—the tension in my jaw, the furrow of my brow. By my third breath, my face was expressionless.

"My magic shows me Providence Cards," I said.

Filick's eyebrows shot so high they'd disappeared beneath his hairline. Jespyr's jaw dropped. Next to her, Ravyn leaned forward, shock momentarily cracking the stone control masking his face.

Filick returned his gaze to me. "What do you mean, 'shows you'?"

Not very bright, this Physician.

"Every Card has a color, like a magical signature," I said. "The color corresponds with the velvet on the Card's edge. A Black Horse is black. A Well is blue. A Maiden is pink, and so on."

"And you can see these colors?" Ravyn asked. "Even through the mist?"

I exhaled. "Yes."

Jespyr laughed—a quick, triumphant cackle. "Brilliant. This is just what we need to find the—"

"Wait a moment," Filick interrupted. "If Miss Spindle is telling the truth—and she has lived eleven years with this magic—then surely there have been repercussions." His brow hardened. "The infection's magic is degenerative. Nothing comes free."

I kept my face even. "I'm well aware magic has a cost, Physician." My voice quieted. "But I have yet to discover the extent of my debt. I know nothing of my degeneration."

There was a knock on the door. Three knocks, followed by a fourth and a fifth a moment later. Ravyn moved to the door. I did not notice the bright red light spilling into the keyhole, nor did I expect the vivacity of the Scythe Card's ruby-red color until it was already in the room.

Prince Renelm Rowan stepped into the cellar, mud still clumped onto his boots from the hunt. When his eyes found me, they were brilliant green. "Who the hell is this?"

"Elspeth Spindle," Jespyr said.

"Erik's daughter," Ravyn said, sharing a pointed look with his cousin.

The Prince surveyed me. He looked like a fox to me, with his wild auburn hair and bright, intelligent eyes. "I'm Renelm," he said, narrowing them. "But Elm will do."

I knew who he was. I'd always known. Renelm and his older brother, Hauth, were the kind of Princes ripped from the pages of a storybook. Handsome, clever, unmarried. Only, in the

Nightmare's storybook version, they weren't simply the kingdom's beloved Princes.

They were also its villains.

He snarled behind my eyes, watching Elm with curled claws. *The berry of rowans is red, always red. The earth at its trunk is dark with blood shed. Trust never the man who wields the Card red.* His voice seeped out of him, a poisonous fog filling my mind. *No peace will be known till the final Rowan is dead.*

I fought a shudder, my face muscles straining against the chill the Nightmare's words set upon me. For the Rowans, the Nightmare bore a bottomless, vengeful hatred. And I knew why. King Rowan, like his predecessors, used the ancient wisdom of *The Old Book of Alders* to instill fear—not wonder—of magic. He corrupted our ancient text. Defiled it so that it became a weapon to control Blunder by—just like the Scythe.

The red Card. There were only four of them in the entire kingdom. And the Rowans had always claimed them all. With it, they had the ultimate power of persuasion. Three taps of the Scythe, and you would do whatever a Rowan asked of you. If Elm asked me to hop on one leg off a cliff, I would gladly do so, not because the Scythe made my legs move—but because it made me *want* to jump.

I glared at the red light beaming from Elm's pocket, unsure if it was the Nightmare's animosity boiling in me, or my own.

Elm was taller and narrower than Ravyn. When I stood, I had to lift my chin to look him in the face. "Pleased to meet you, sire," I said through clenched teeth. "I'm Elspeth Spindle."

A coy smile danced along the edges of Elm's lips. "Spindle, is it?" he said. "Not Jayne Yarrow?"

I glanced at Ravyn, my stomach dropping. But the Captain's eyes were suddenly fixed on his boots, a hint of color along his neck and jaw.

I took a step back, the memory of the second highwayman—of fingers pulling tightly on my hood—the hostile notes of his voice—closing tightly around me. My rage swelled, trapped in a room with strange, dangerous men who had done their best to hurt me not three weeks ago.

I slammed back down into my chair and folded my arms over my chest. If I'd had more grit, I might have spat at the Prince's feet. "Quite the family you have," I said to Ravyn, shooting daggers. "One assault from the two of you was enough. Tell the Prince to take his Scythe and go, or I won't breathe another word."

Chapter Eight

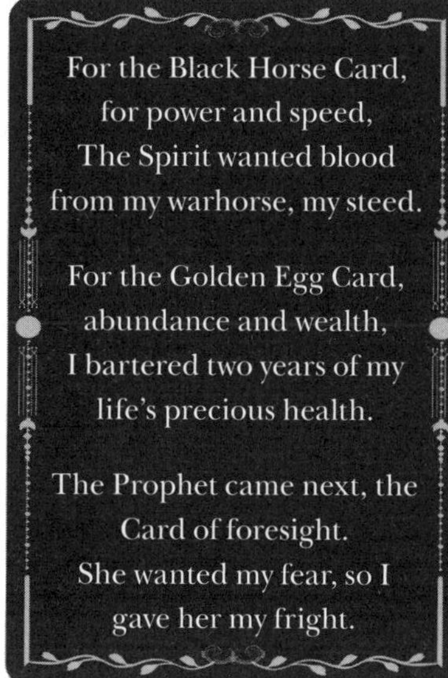

I put a hand into my pocket, tracing my charm. Filick, Elm, and Jespyr filed out of the cellar one by one. Ravyn followed them out of the room, exchanging words I could not make out.

Perhaps they were going to let him kill me after all.

The Nightmare stirred behind my eyes, watching the door.

Without windows, I had no idea what time it was. I slouched deeper into my chair, tired. Moments later, Ravyn stepped back inside. Only now, his pocket was bursting with light.

I sat up, my back stiffening and my eyes wide. There were Providence Cards in his pocket. The Nightmare had been right—he was going to test me.

Ravyn took a seat beside me at the table, his face a mask of austerity. His hand went so quickly into his pocket I didn't see it move. He slapped a White Eagle Card onto the table. I rubbed my eyes, more tired than I thought, because, for a split second, it seemed as if the light coming from the Cards in Ravyn's pocket had flickered out.

The White Eagle depicted a bird soaring above a wheat field, its eyes orange and its black talons sharp. *Courage,* it read on one side. On the other, the image inverted, it read *Fear.*

I stared at the Card, then back at Ravyn. "What's this for?"

"What do you see?" he asked. "What color?"

I crossed my arms. "Didn't I prove I could see the Scythe in your cousin's pocket a moment ago?"

"Many people are aware Elm carries his Scythe with him," Ravyn countered. "A lucky guess, perhaps."

"I wouldn't consider anything that's happened today lucky, Captain."

There it was again—the quirk at the corner of Ravyn's lips—that sliver of a smile. He cleared his throat and repeated, "What color?"

"White."

He reached into his other pocket, withdrawing a black silk cloth. "Tell me, Miss Spindle, can you see the colors with your eyes shut?"

My heartbeat quickened. "Yes."

"Good." He wrapped the cloth around his knuckles. "Would you object to a blindfold?"

I paused. Ravyn waited, his face unreadable as he watched me. When I nodded he stood, silk in hand. I tapped my fingernails on the table, my eyelids fluttering to a close.

Despite the way his rough fingers snagged the fabric, Ravyn's touch was soft. He tucked loose strands of my hair behind my ears. Then he wrapped the blindfold twice over my eyes before tying it in a true knot at the back of my head.

I saw nothing, the fabric smooth and opaque. I blinked against it and inhaled, knowing there was no blindfold in the world strong enough to mask the color of Providence Cards from the Nightmare behind my eyes.

I heard Ravyn move back to his seat. "Shall I continue?" he asked.

It wasn't my tiredness—the vibrant colors in his pocket flickered again. It wasn't until Ravyn snapped the next Card onto the table that I understood its color.

Black.

Even in the darkness of my blindfold, the black was distinct. Black like my eyes—black like magic. "The Black Horse."

Written like a fragmented tale of horror, *The Old Book of Alders* chronicled the Deck of Twelve Providence Cards, the magic they possessed, how to use them, and the consequences of overusing them.

The Black Horse made its beholder a master of combat. The Golden Egg granted great wealth. The Prophet offered glimpses of the future. The White Eagle bestowed courage. The Maiden bequeathed great beauty. The Chalice turned liquid into truth serum. The Well gave clear sight to recognize one's enemies. The Iron Gate offered blissful serenity, no matter the struggle. The Scythe gave its beholder the power to control others. The Mirror granted invisibility. The Nightmare allowed its user to speak into the minds of others. The Twin Alders had the power to commune with Blunder's ancient entity, the Spirit of the Wood.

But, just as there were two edges to every blade, there were two sides to every Providence Card. Magic came at a cost. If used too long, the Black Horse could make its holder weak. The Golden Egg led to all-consuming greed. The White Eagle's courage was replaced by fear. The Prophet's foresight made its user helpless to change the future. The Chalice's truth serum turned into poison. The Maiden's beauty chilled its user's heart. The Well's holder would be betrayed by a friend. The Iron Gate stole years from one's life. The Scythe caused great physical pain. The Mirror lifted the veil between worlds, exposing a world of ghosts. The Nightmare revealed one's deepest fears.

And the Twin Alders...No one knew what happened if you used the Twin Alders too long. There was no record of anyone having done so.

A moment later, the darkness of the Black Horse was gone, another Card hitting the table.

Pink. Piercing rose-blossom pink.

I squirmed in my chair. "The Maiden," I said. "I've seen a few of these floating around this Equinox."

"Have you?"

I exhaled. "Unfortunately."

"You sound disapproving."

A twinge of pain hit my stomach, Ione's face sharp in my mind. "It doesn't matter what I think."

The Captain's laugh rumbled in his chest. The pink hue of the Maiden disappeared, replaced by a smooth turquoise—the color of the sea. "The Chalice."

He drew another. A sharp, misty gray light floated about the room.

"The Prophet," I said.

The Prophet's gray light flickered a moment. "Tell me, Miss Spindle, do you keep any Cards yourself?"

I gnawed at my bottom lip. "No."

"But you live with your uncle. Surely he possesses Cards."

I shifted in my seat. "You seemed to think so when you ambushed me on the road."

I couldn't tell if Ravyn Yew felt remorse. There was a practiced calmness about him, his tone never straying far beyond moderate interest. Still, he was quick to change the subject. "How many people are aware of your infection?" he asked.

I bit my tongue and pulled the blindfold up over my eyes. Ravyn sat in his chair, watching me. I searched for hostility in his expression but found nothing beyond cautious curiosity.

"How do I know you won't arrest them for harboring me?" I asked.

"You don't, I suppose," he said. "But, as you see, I haven't even arrested you, a maiden strongly infected with magic." To my silence, he tilted his head, birdlike. "I'm merely trying to understand the extent of your situation."

I ground my molars together. "Why? Why haven't you arrested me?"

"Because you haven't done anything wrong." He paused. "And because your ability is extremely useful."

"Haven't done anything wrong?" I raised my brows. "I've broken the law—grievously."

But Ravyn merely shook his head. "Not everyone sees it that way."

"Your uncle does, and that's all that matters."

The Captain of the Destriers watched me, his gray eyes momentarily lowering to my mouth. "I'd like to continue, Miss Spindle." He gestured to the blindfold resting on my forehead. "If you don't mind."

I pulled the fabric back over my eyes with a lofty sigh. Gold light filled the room. "The Golden Egg." When the sound of the next Card hit wood, I blinked against the darkness of the blindfold, waiting. "Go on, then," I said.

"I've already placed the Card on the table," Ravyn replied smoothly.

"I see no Card."

"You see no color?"

The Nightmare stirred, his whisper tickling my ear. *There is no Card. He's playing a trick.*

"There is no color," I said. "There can't be a Card."

"I assure you there is."

I ripped the blindfold from my face, a small gasp escaping my lips as I stared at the image of ancient trees bound together by forest-green velvet. The Twin Alders Card.

The Nightmare and I realized the truth at the same moment. A laugh rippled in my throat. "There's no magic," I said. "Just paper and velvet. It's a fake."

Ravyn smiled, a shadow shifting along his striking nose. "Are you sure?"

"Positive, Captain."

When he pocketed the false Card, the others flickered and jostled. I caught a glance of the familiar burgundy light in the cluster of colors and narrowed my gaze. "There's a lot of talk about the two Nightmare Cards," I said, my tone sharp. "But no one seems to know that the King already has one. Or that his Captain uses it so freely."

Ravyn said nothing. When the silence between us grew too tense, I tapped my fingernails on the table. "So? Do I pass your test?"

The Captain leaned back in his chair, his gray eyes never leaving my face. "It certainly appears you can see Providence Cards. And that you've managed to hide your infection from Physicians and Destriers alike, despite being the daughter of one." He tilted his head again. "Who else knows about your ability to see the Cards?"

I tensed. "No one."

Ravyn raised his brows. "Another lie, Miss Spindle?"

"No!" I leaned forward, searching his face. "I swear it. My family merely thinks I caught the fever."

Ravyn said nothing, testing my fortitude with his silence. His jaw was firm, as if fashioned of stone.

The longer he was quiet, the angrier I became.

Whatever his motives, I said to the Nightmare, *he's still a Destrier. He's still a brute who hunts infected children and sends their families to the grave. One wrong move, and he'll surely do the same to me.*

Then be indispensable, the Nightmare purred, goading me. *Go on, make him an offer. See what he'll give.*

I stood so abruptly my chair fell backward.

The dogs in the corner yipped, and Ravyn's hand flew to his belt, his eyes alert. "What's the matter?"

"I know you want Providence Cards," I said, the words rushing out of my mouth. "I also know you don't want the King to find out. Otherwise, you would not have bothered disguising yourself on the forest road." I steadied my voice. "I'll help you find Cards. I won't tell anyone you and the Prince moonlight as highwaymen, and you, in turn, will keep my secret. But I need something else."

Ravyn crossed his arms over his chest, surveying me anew. "The decision regarding how to handle your magic does not rest solely with me, I'm afraid."

I stuck out my chin. Even reclined, calm in his seat, Ravyn Yew frightened me. Taking my silence in stride, the Captain asked, "What precisely do you want, Miss Spindle?"

My fingers shook. "I want you to leave my family alone. Do not punish them for hiding my infection."

He nodded slowly. "If that is your wish."

"And don't go back to my uncle's house," I added. "He carries no Card you have not already shown me today."

"I thought you didn't know anything about your uncle's Cards."

I blinked. "I wasn't about to tell a man with a knife to my chest how to steal from my own family."

"Brave of you." Ravyn shifted in his chair. "Anything else?"

He'll give anything to have your magic, the Nightmare cooed. *Ask for something extravagant.*

Like a magical procedure to remove the parasite from my head? I kept my face neutral and my eyes on the Captain of the Destriers. "One last thing."

"Yes?"

I put my hands on the table and leaned forward without breaking our gaze. "You must swear, Captain, no matter the circumstance, you will never use that Nightmare Card on me again."

Chapter Nine

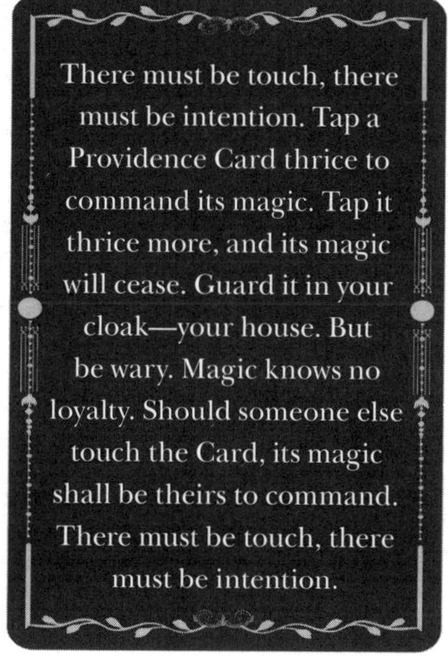

Ravyn saw me as far as the stairwell.

It was evening, Equinox night. Soon the second feast would begin, followed by court festivities—dancing, games, and all manner of debauchery fueled by the King's wine.

"I must speak to the others. I trust you can find your own way back to your rooms," Ravyn said, turning to leave. Then, as if he'd forgotten something, he looked back at me, his voice less strained. "I'll see you at dinner, Miss Spindle."

A threat or a promise? said the Nightmare.

I watched the Captain of the Destriers make his way across the hall, his steps hurried. *He doesn't trust me.*

You told him your mind is off-limits. If he didn't think you were hiding anything before, he certainly does now.

I AM hiding something, I said, fidgeting with the hem of my torn sleeve as I marched up the stairs. *You.*

The corridor was busy. Servants attended the rooms with trays of wine. Men loitered outside their doors in groups, laughing and smoking. I stayed clear of them, brushing up against the gray Prophet tapestry. So sudden was the ache to be back at Hawthorn House—away from everything and everyone—that I put a hand to my stomach.

When I opened the door to our rooms, Nya was in the parlor.

"For heaven's sake!" she shrieked. The attending maid's hands were white from cinching her into a very robust corset. "Close the door. Do you want everyone to see me in my undergarments?"

I ignored her and moved to my room, slamming the door. I sat on the bed, the last remnants of gray light fading to darkness. I'd been cooped up for hours in that cellar beneath the castle, most of the day lost to Ravyn Yew. He was a strange man, the Captain of the Destriers. I'd expected someone in his position to be a bit less quiet, more abrasive—more brutal.

I was happy to be wrong.

Still, there was darkness in Ravyn's quiet. I could see it in his expression—the cool control of his features. He, like me, had learned to still his face—to obscure his thoughts under a mask of control and austerity.

Which meant he, like me, had things to hide.

Why else would he and his cousin stalk the forest road when they had the mighty Destriers at their disposal? If the Nightmare was correct about anything, it was that whatever his motives, the Captain wanted my magic.

It intrigued him.

The Captain of the Destriers is dark and severe. Watching from yew trees, his gray eyes are clear. His wingspan is broad and his beak is quite sharp. Hide quick or he'll find you . . . and rip out your heart.

Dimia opened my door without knocking, her hair still wet from the washroom. When she saw me, her upper lip drew into a thin line. "Where have you been? You look a mess."

"I was in the garden."

"We were all in the garden," Nya said, following her twin into my room, her corset casting an airy quality to her voice. "You're the only one who came out with dirt on your dress and brambles in your hair."

"Hurry up," Nerium's voice called from the other room. "We're expected downstairs before the eighth chime."

I pulled a loose twig out of my hair. "Did you know Ione was given a Maiden Card?"

My half sisters jerked their heads toward me. "What do you mean she's been given one?" Nya said.

Dimia launched herself onto the bed, the mattress groaning. "Who gave it to her?"

"How much did it cost?"

"Does she look different?"

I moved to the washroom, peeling off my dirty dress. "All I know," I said, "is she had it this morning on the garden walk. Did she say anything to you about it?"

Dimia pouted. "No one tells me anything." Nya opened the washroom door, dragging my dark green gown. She held the dress up to me, examining it. "Fine enough make," she said. "Though the color is too dark for Equinox. Did Father give it to you?"

"No," I said, sliding the wet towel across my skin before snatching the gown. "Uncle."

She raised her brows. "He's far more generous than I imagined if he's fitting you with new dresses and spending half his fortune on a Maiden Card. Who knew living in the wood paid so well?"

"It doesn't," Nerium said, entering my room, making no effort to hide the fact that she'd been eavesdropping. "Which means he borrowed the money. Or traded something of great value."

The Nightmare's laughter startled me.

"Here," Nya said, handing me a fine-toothed comb. "Take this. Your hair's more tangled than a bird's nest."

There was a tall silver looking glass in the common area. When I'd dressed I stepped to it, blinking at the woman in the mirror—hardly recognizing myself in the vibrant green gown. Dimia sidled up next to me, plumping her cheeks in the mirror. "Alyx Laburnum asked me about you last night."

I clapped a hand to my face. "You didn't say anything, did you?"

Nya scowled, her mouth a tight line. "I can't understand why you snub him," she said. "He's amiable and thoughtful—far too good for you."

"That he is," I said without remorse.

Nerium came up behind us, wrangling her daughters, pinching their cheeks until they glowed red. "That's the chime." She shot me a brief up and down glance. "I trust you will find no reason to embarrass us this evening, Elspeth."

I could think of a fair few things that might embarrass my stepmother. Being chased through the mist by the Captain of the Destriers, for one.

And knocking him senseless, said the Nightmare.

My lip twitched, but I did not smile.

My father was waiting in the corridor with the other men to escort us, his tunic a deep crimson red. He offered Nerium his hand. The twins followed, their arms linked together, leaving me to trail behind, a shadow next to their brilliant Spindle red.

We stepped into the corridor and made our way to the great hall. I cast my gaze about for Ione and her pink light but saw few Cards. Color emanating from three sentinel Destriers, a Golden Egg, a Chalice, and a Scythe filled the room. But no Maiden Cards.

When the orator announced the name Spindle, my father and Nerium stepped forward first, followed by my half sisters, then, lastly, me. The crowd turned to watch us. Heat rose in my cheeks and I clenched my fingers into fists along my dress, determined not to feel like the afterthought they painted me.

Prince Elm Rowan stood at the foot of the grand stairwell, the red glow from his Scythe lighting our way.

The Prince's smile did not touch his eyes. "Erik," he said, extending a hand. "I'm sorry I missed you at the hunt. Welcome to Equinox."

"Highness." My father bowed deeply. "Thank you for having us."

"Always a pleasure to see you and your daughters."

Dimia giggled and Nya elbowed her, their swanlike necks bent low.

Elm blinked at them, his freckled nose wrinkling, as if he'd smelled something foul. His eyes shifted over them to me. "This must be your first wife's daughter."

My father looked back, as if only just remembering me. "Elspeth has not come to Equinox in years," he said, bidding me forward. "Elspeth, you remember Prince Renelm."

I bowed. When Elm extended his hand in greeting, our fingers met, cold and unfeeling. "Welcome back to Stone, Miss Spindle," he said, his green eyes cunning. "May I escort you to dinner?"

The Rowans are not to be trusted. They cling too desperately to their Scythes, hungry for power—for control, the Nightmare called in the din. *Be wary.*

I tensed, my eyes lowering to the red Card in Elm's pocket. But I took his arm anyway, the fabric along our sleeves sliding together. He was only two years older than me—the same age as Ione. His green eyes stood out against olive skin, and when his hair caught the light, thick and unkempt, it was the same color as the Equinox wreaths that hung above the arches of the great hall, bright with autumn hues.

He was undeniably handsome. But the red light from his Scythe cast strange shadows across his features. I looked away, unnerved.

We glided through the room with my father's second family behind us, the ocean of folk parting. Candles and torches had been lit and the great hall was aglow, illuminating the fine fabrics of Blunder's houses, namesake trees embroidered on the breasts of dresses and tunics alike.

I looked for Ione and the Hawthorns but did not see them, the crowd as thick as the mist.

A servant trotted by with a silver tray of brimming goblets. Elm took two and handed me one brusquely, spilling some wine on the floor near our feet. I took it with both hands, happy to no longer be touching him.

Elm drank deeply from the goblet, his green eyes tracing the room. "You must be very special," he said out the corner of his mouth, waving and nodding as members of his father's court passed us. "It's not often Ravyn lets anyone into his confidence."

"Confidence?"

"You were alone together for hours." A terse smile slithered across his mouth. "What's more, he's insisting you, or your magic, are somehow *useful*."

I stared at the King's second son, tightness creeping into my stomach. How easily he wore the mask of cordiality—of charm. But I could hear disapproval, doubt, in his voice. I smelled it on him like smoke.

I took a step back, distrusting the Prince as readily as he did me. But before I could walk away, a man—tall and handsome and broad—approached us, the crowd's eyes following him.

"Brother," High Prince Hauth Rowan said in greeting, his gaze shifting from Elm to me. "Who is this lovely creature?"

If my thoughts on Prince Elm were bleak, my opinion of Hauth was abysmal. The High Prince was a brute. Bathed in the red light of his Scythe Card, Hauth had no qualms forcing others to do his bidding, especially those who flouted Blunder's laws.

I'd heard he was fond of executing criminals with his Scythe, forcing them to do horrible things against their will. The High Prince would often call a great crowd at the edge of town. Then, with three taps of his Scythe Card, he sent the accused, without a charm, to die in the mist—lost to the salt and the ravenous hunger of the Spirit of the Wood.

It made my skin crawl just to stand next to him.

Hauth gazed down at me. He was wider than his brother—his muscles prominent beneath his gold tunic. His skin was olive and his eyes the same Rowan green, but where Elm's gaze was narrow and cunning, Hauth's stare was bold, aggressive. "You're Erik's eldest daughter?"

"Pleased to meet you, sire," I said, lowering my head.

"We haven't met before?"

Elm exhaled through his teeth. "Hence the introduction, brother."

Hauth reached forward, taking my hand and kissing it. "Better late than never."

Elm made a gagging sound. "That's enough of that," he said, steering me away from his brother before the High Prince could get another word in. I felt Hauth's eyes on my back but did not turn to face them, my skin crawling from his touch.

"I need another drink," Elm muttered, leaving me to stand alone without a second glance. "Don't go too far, Spindle."

I found my aunt lingering at a food tray.

She jumped when I touched her shoulder, then folded me in a deep hug. When she pulled back, she looked me up and down, her eyes wide. "You look lovely!"

I searched the crowd around her, recognizing the telltale bickering of my younger cousins as they sprinted across the room, crumbs flying from their open mouths. "Where is Ione?" I asked. "We...argued. I want things to feel right again."

The creases around my aunt's brow deepened. Tears glistened in her eyes, and she rubbed her nose. "Ione is somewhere with your father and the King. Oh, Elspeth." She raised a sleeve to her eye. "Your uncle is a stubborn man."

My stomach dropped. "What does the King want with her?"

When my aunt spoke, her voice hitched. "Your uncle has given away his Nightmare Card to the King and struck an accord—without consulting me."

The sound of crashing silver clamored nearby. My cousins raced past, laughing wickedly.

"Bless the trees!" my aunt cried. "Are none of my children right in the head?" She shook herself, then dashed through the crowd after her sons.

I stared after her, my insides twisting.

A bell chimed at the head of the table, and the room began to fill. I stayed where I was, my arms crossed over my chest. My dress hugged me tightly, and for a moment I held perfectly still, lulled by the soft material, lost in thought.

Someone tapped my shoulder. "You look beautiful, Elspeth."

I groaned, recognizing the voice. Alyx.

When I turned he was standing there in another bright yellow tunic, smile wide, eyes expectant. "I've just asked your father if you might sit with me and my parents," he said. "He gave his consent." He paused. "So long as you're agreeable, that is."

I know no one's going to ask me what I want, the Nightmare said, snide to his bones, *but just in case you were wondering, the answer is no. No, I am decidedly NOT agreeable.*

A surprise to no one, I muttered. "Look, Alyx, I'm—"

"My mother is anxious to meet you. I've told her so much about you..."

I didn't hear the rest. My gaze shifted over Alyx's shoulder, catching someone in the crowd. Ravyn Yew stood a few paces away, talking to two other Destriers, his hands clasped behind his back. He had changed his tunic since I'd last seen him. The belt of knives around his waist was gone, replaced by the gilded hilt of a long ceremonial blade. His tunic was dark blue with gold trim, and though I searched for the burgundy color of the Nightmare Card, no light emanated from his pockets. He was Cardless.

We'd only been apart an hour. Still, I couldn't help but feel every time I saw Ravyn Yew, I was looking at a different man.

Drawn by my gaze, Ravyn turned his head. His eyes captured mine, falling a moment to my dress before shifting to Alyx. For the briefest of moments, I thought I saw the corner of his lips curl.

Alyx was still talking when Ravyn approached. "And I—Oh, excuse me, Captain Yew," he said, bowing his head. "I didn't see you."

Ravyn returned his bow. "Enjoying Equinox, Laburnum?"

"Very much so. I was just inviting Miss Spindle to join my family and me for the feast."

Ravyn's eyes returned to me. There it was again—that nigh invisible smirk. "And how are *you* enjoying Equinox, Miss Spindle?" he asked me.

"As best I can," I said, my voice thinner than I liked. Then, for spite, "Though there are a few too many Destriers here for my liking."

Ravyn cocked a brow. "Do you have something against Destriers, Miss Spindle?"

"Not all of them." I searched his face. When I noted the bruise along his cheekbone where I'd kicked him earlier, a small smile of my own slid across my mouth. "But most."

Alyx's eyes darted between us. "Yes, well, we should take our seats, Elspeth, my parents—"

I put a hand on Alyx's arm. "You've been very sweet, Alyx. But I told the Yews I'd sit with them this evening. Isn't that right, Captain?"

Alyx stalled, midstep. Ravyn ran a hand over his jaw, hiding his expression. "Indeed."

Alyx pressed his hand over mine, trapping it against his arm. "I have your father's permission, Elspeth."

"But not mine," I said, more forceful this time. "Now, if you please—"

Alyx made like he was going to protest, his mouth open, brow knit. But an icy look from Ravyn was enough to smother whatever ire burned within him. He let go of my hand, shot me a look somewhere between anger and hurt, and hurried off into the crowd.

Ravyn watched him go, crossing his arms over his chest. "Not the winning moment he hoped for, poor Laburnum."

"Don't," I said, rubbing my hand, guilt tugging at me. "Alyx is too nice for his own good. He's gotten worse from me than he deserves."

"It's the nice ones you should look out for," Ravyn said.

I glanced up at him. "What about you, Captain? Are you too nice for your own good?"

He watched me, something I could not read flashing in his gray eyes. "No, Miss Spindle," he said. "I'm not nice at all."

The bell rang again, more eager in its chime. The crowd moved to the candlelit tables in the center of the room, hasty to claim their seats. I lingered, uncertain of my place.

"My family is over there," Ravyn said, gesturing to the table. "If you were earnest about sitting with me."

I glanced at him, my voice colder than I'd intended. "I suppose I don't have much choice in the matter."

He shrugged. "You could sit with Jespyr. She's easier to talk to. Or, if you prefer, Elm is right over there."

"I'd rather take my chances with Emory again," I bit back. "Or is he indisposed?"

A flinch crossed Ravyn's sharp face. A moment later it was gone, replaced by familiar, cool austerity. "My brother won't be in attendance this evening." He held his arm out to me. "Shall we?"

He led me silently to our seats, planting us near the head of the table where we stood with everyone else, waiting for King Rowan to arrive. My hand grew warm against the sleeve of Ravyn's tunic and I tensed, unsure when to let go.

Destriers lined the wall ahead of us, shadowed by their Black Horses.

"So many Destriers," I grumbled.

"That's the way things are in my uncle's home, I'm afraid."

"Your home, too, isn't it?"

"Duty requires I remain here, with the King," he said, his expression unwavering. "But it is not my home. My family's estate is in town. The Destriers often train there, as they once did at Spindle House."

I frowned. "The castle at the top of the hill?"

"The very same."

Castle Yew was old—the grounds historic. The wrought-iron gate and the dark, climbing ivy resided under the shadow of ancient yew trees—tall and foreboding. Beyond lay a statuary, a maze of stone and hedges, then the towering, ominous house. I had walked past the gate many times as a child, certain to my bones there was something to fear under those trees.

I'd never been inside.

The bell chimed a third time. We turned to face the head of the table. The shuffling of dresses and conversations quieted as the orator stood to give his announcements.

"Presenting His Royal Highness, King Quercus Rowan, Ruler of Blunder, Keeper of Laws, and Protector of Providence Cards."

We bowed as he entered. I recalled little of the King's features from my childhood. I had been allotted only brief glimpses of him over the years. Still, it was impossible to mistake the King for anything other than royalty. Garbed in gold robes trimmed with rich fur, a rowan tree embroidered across his chest, King Rowan stood tall and bold. His yellow hair—grayed with age—framed his sharply angled face, his broad nose crooked where it had been broken years ago.

He was not a charming, delicate ruler. Formidable—ruthless—fit his description more aptly, and though Blunder had been without war for hundreds of years, King Rowan had all the appearance of a great warrior stationed before his army, not a King at court.

"His Second Royalty," the orator continued, "Hauth Rowan, High Prince, Heir to Blunder, Destrier, and Keeper of Laws."

We bowed a second time. Though more handsome than his father, Hauth was still unmistakably a Rowan. Broad, strong, and brutal. Red and black lights emanated from the breast pocket of his silver tunic.

I moved to take my seat, but Ravyn shook his head, bidding me to wait.

"We've come together this Equinox to recognize our great kingdom," the High Prince called. "It has not been an easy harvest. The Spirit of the Wood's stranglehold on Blunder continues. Still, let us celebrate the triumphs we've achieved in family, in health, and, most importantly, in the trade and use of Providence Cards."

The great hall echoed with applause.

"Many of you have shared your wealth with my family," Hauth continued. "I thank you. But greater than wealth, there is duty. As High Prince of Blunder, it is my duty to share in my father's legacy—to follow his path, and the path laid out for all of us in *The Old Book of Alders*."

The Nightmare let out a hiss.

Hauth cast a brief glance at his father, and the King nodded. "Like Kings before him, it has been my father's mission to collect all twelve Providence Cards," Hauth said, his voice louder. "With them, we will lift the mist and banish the Spirit of the Wood, ridding Blunder of magical infection." He paused. "I am pleased to tell you that tonight, we are closer to achieving that goal."

Hauth turned to the side, gesturing forward someone I could not see.

Two lights warred for dominance. One burgundy, the other pink, carried by a strikingly beautiful woman with yellow hair. My heart plummeted into my stomach as Hauth's voice rattled over the din. "Tonight," he declared, "thanks to his generous contribution, my father has knighted Tyrn Hawthorn. We are proud to offer his daughter a place in our royal family."

Applause erupted around me, glass clinking and cheers sounding, the clamor enormous.

Next to me, Ravyn Yew exhaled, as if all the wind in his lungs had frozen. Across the table, Elm Rowan and Jespyr Yew had gone ghostly pale, their faces arrested in shock.

Hauth took the hand of the beautiful woman. She passed him the burgundy light, a smile on her full lips. Hauth, goaded by the crowd's uproar, held up the Providence Card trimmed by dark burgundy velvet. "I present to you," he called, "the elusive Nightmare Providence Card, and my future wife, Ione Hawthorn."

Chapter Ten

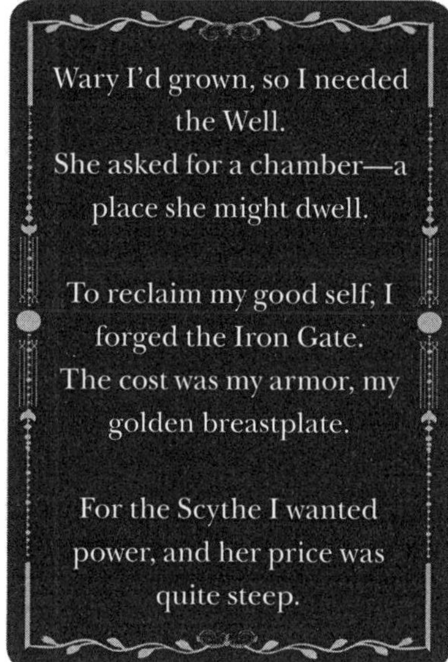

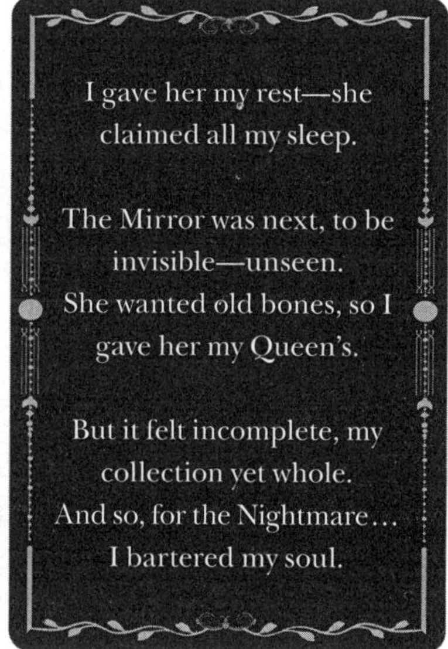

I couldn't rip my eyes away. I saw Ione clearly, despite the mar of color rising around her like a plume of pink smoke. She had tapped the Maiden Card three times, accessing its magic. Unlike this morning in the garden, she was unmistakably changed—the most beautiful woman I had ever seen.

The sight of her filled me with dread.

Tears pricked my eyes, her new beauty so great it had already begun to erode my memory of her previous self—the kind, soft features of my cousin's former face. Her lips were fuller, and when she smiled, the gap in her teeth was gone. Her hair, richly golden, was longer—shinier—and flowed, both weightless and heavy, like a waterfall down her back. Her lashes were long and her nose delicately narrowed. Her hazel eyes shone with a strange, ethereal vibrancy. When she peered down the table, I forced myself to look away.

It was still Ione, but also a stranger.

Chairs scraped the floor as Blunder's families took their seats. I remained standing, lost to the world.

Ravyn's arms were stiff as he pulled out my chair. When I still did not move, his broad hand grazed my back. "Please sit, Miss Spindle."

When the first course was served, excited chatter still sparking through the room, I did not touch it. I merely stared at my fork, the remnants of my previous life escaping like smoke up a flue.

"Your uncle had the other Nightmare Card?" Ravyn whispered in my ear.

A few traitorous tears escaped my eyes. "Yes."

"And you didn't think to mention it?"

I glanced up at the Captain of the Destriers, caught by something in his voice. His copper skin had lost its warmth, and when he spoke, I could see his jaw muscles clench, as if under great strain.

As if freed from a blindfold, my eyes opened. "You lied to me," I said, the heavy weight of dread filling my chest. "Why would the King want my uncle's Nightmare Card if his own Captain already possessed one?" My breath whooshed out of me. "Unless... he does not know."

"Quiet," Ravyn cautioned. He cast his eyes up the table to the King. Then, as if I'd pulled the words out of him, he lowered his voice. "I never lied. You merely assumed the King knew I had a Nightmare Card."

The Nightmare tapped his claws, laughter rolling off his back like snakeskin. *How wonderful,* he said. *Absolutely marvelous.*

Shut up and let me think.

Isn't it obvious? The Captain of the Destriers is a sneaking, contemptible traitor.

I had to sit on my hands to keep them from shaking.

Just answer the riddle, he called. *What has two eyes for seeing, two ears for hearing, and one tongue for lying?* When I didn't reply, he tittered. *A highwayman, darling girl.*

But Ravyn hasn't acted alone, I countered, my eyes shooting across the table to Elm.

Even more curious, the Nightmare purred. *Does the young Prince know his cousin is hiding such a valuable Providence Card from the King? Or is he a part of the scheme?*

Ravyn watched me, waiting. When I finally spoke, my voice was unsteady.

"Tell me what's going on," I said. "I'll not risk being branded a traitor as well as a magic carrier."

The Captain put his elbow on the table and rested his chin against the heel of his palm. He spoke through his fingers, his voice a muffled growl. "I'll tell you what you need to know. But I can't do it alone. We keep a council."

Be wary, the Nightmare said, stringing his words like spider silk in my ears. *The yew tree is cunning, its shadow unknown. It bends without breaking, its secrets its own. Look past twisting branches, dig deep to its bones. Is it Providence Cards he seeks—or is it the throne?*

I turned to Ravyn, emboldened. "You must tell me everything."

He raised a brow, glaring down his long nose at me. "There are things I have to do—"

"You want my magic?" I said, cutting off the Captain of the Destriers. "Call your council. I want the truth. Now."

We left the table separately. When I finally made my way out of the great hall and met Ravyn at the end of a servants' corridor, he did a poor job masking his impatience. "Did anyone see you?"

"I don't think so," I replied through tight lips. "My stepmother, perhaps."

I had to lift my skirt to keep up, thankful my cobbler had not heeled my shoes. Ravyn was swift in his step, maneuvering in and out of rooms I'd never seen before.

One of them—several flights above the great hall—was locked.

Ravyn reached into his pocket and withdrew a key. When the door opened, he hurried in, ushering me in with a jerk of his head.

"Where are we?" I fumbled in the dark, stubbing my toe on something flimsy—a book.

"My chamber. Close the door."

The room was dark but for the dying hearth, which glowed an amber red against the far wall. Ravyn crossed the room and swore. A book flew out from under his boot and crashed several feet away. He knelt beside the fire, coaxing it to life with his breath long enough to light a single candlestick.

The smell of dust and subtle hints of clove and cedar filled my nose as I cast my eyes across the chamber. It was no wonder he had tripped. Books were strewn across the floor, some stacked, others lying facedown, their pages splayed like the wings of a dead bird. So, too, were the Captain's clothes. Tunics—jerkins—cloaks all lay in heaps on the floor. Others were draped upon the backs of chairs and the frame of his wide, sparsely blanketed bed.

Had it been a smaller room, it would have felt cluttered, his belongings thrown in careless piles, leaving strange, ghoulish shadows across the wood floor. But the Captain's chamber was spacious—made larger still by a lack of decor, its only furnishings a bed, a few chairs, a small washing table in the corner—an aged looking glass propped precariously upon it—and a wardrobe.

It wasn't what I'd expected for someone so severe. Order, neatness, discipline—like my father. Those were qualities I attributed to the Captain of the Destriers. Either Ravyn Yew was in the middle of rearranging his chamber, or what was beginning to feel more apparent by the moment—

He was not the man I imagined him to be.

The rustling of keys pulled me from my thoughts. Across the room, Ravyn's candle flickered at the wardrobe. Behind it shone another light, a deep burgundy, so dark it was difficult to distinguish.

The second Nightmare Card. Ravyn's Nightmare Card.

I kept one hand on the door latch. "What are you doing?"

"You wanted me to call my council, yes? Did you expect I'd do so in front of my uncle's entire court?"

I heard the lock twist open. Ravyn swung open the wardrobe doors, revealing more burgundy light. He took the Nightmare Card and tapped it three times. I sucked in my breath and flinched. When nothing happened, the silence was deafening.

"How does it work?" I blurted. "The Nightmare Card."

"Best when I can concentrate."

"Yes, but what keeps you from hearing everyone in the castle? Does it take—"

Ravyn shot me a narrow look. "Concentration, Miss Spindle. Lots of concentration. So please, if you don't mind, be quiet."

I clenched my jaw, praying Ravyn would not break his word and trespass into my mind.

Be quiet. Be shrewd. He can't hear your thoughts lest he focus on you.

What makes you so certain? I demanded.

His laugh rumbled in the dark. *I know a few things about Providence Cards, my dear.*

I doubt that.

He said nothing, a weighted quiet. Even his silence felt like a game.

And, like most games I played with the Nightmare, I was bound to lose. *Do you actually know about the Cards?* I asked.

His laugh sounded again, crueler. Final.

I shook my head. *Unhelpful, as always. Now shut up, lest he hear all the noise coming out of my head.*

You're the one shouting, Elspeth.

My nostrils flared. *I'm merely trying to navigate this utter disaster without alerting the Captain of the Destriers to the fact that I've got a five-hundred-year-old MONSTER living in my head.*

I think you mean "traitor to lord and land," not "Captain." After all, dear one, there were only two Nightmare Cards ever forged. Long have the Rowans sought one, only for it to be here—hidden neatly in the King's castle—under his very nose.

I glanced at Ravyn, who stood so still he might have been another piece of furniture in the shadowy room. *We don't know why he's hidden his Nightmare Card from his uncle,* I said. *There could be a plausible reason.*

Plausible reasons are but a shadow at the gallows. The highwayman meets the hangman, one way or another.

Ravyn tapped the Nightmare Card three more times and shoved it into his pocket. He turned on his heel and marched toward me, so fast I jumped. "I've spoken to my family," he said. "We'll meet them in the cellar."

I opened my mouth as I pressed down on the door latch, wondering just how many members of Ravyn's family knew of his duplicity—his Nightmare Card. But before I could speak, the Captain was upon me, his hand pressing down on mine, stilling the latch between my fingers.

"What are you—"

"Quiet!" he urged, holding a single finger to my lips.

I froze, my ears perking to the sound of footfall.

"His temper has been foul of late," a man's voice called from the corridor. "Violent, uneven."

"That's expected," another voice said just outside Ravyn's door. "Without a Scythe, the boy can be difficult to control."

I could feel Ravyn's chest swell as he sucked in a breath, sharp lines of strain creeping across his face. I remained frozen, staring up at him, his finger still pressed against my lips. It was warm—the skin rough. I tried to keep my mouth from moving—to lessen the deep unease I felt to be trapped so near the Captain of the Destriers. But all I managed to do was hold my breath.

And even that did not last. Especially with my heart racing. I inhaled abruptly, my lips parting against the skin of his finger. Ravyn lowered his gaze to my mouth. His finger slipped off my lips, his eyes meeting mine for a fleeting glance before he looked back at the door. And though it was too dark to be certain, I thought I saw a flush slide up his neck.

The men in the hallway continued to speak. "I can strengthen his sedatives. Only, with the Captain of the Destriers so protective, I fear I will not be allowed to administer them."

"Do not bother the Captain with news of his brother," the other said. "If Emory gives you any more trouble, come to me. And whatever you do," he warned, "don't let the boy touch you. It will only unnerve you."

Their voices echoed in the hall, growing smaller. A moment later they were gone, my heartbeat the only remaining clamor.

I looked up at Ravyn, searching his face for answers I could not yet fathom. Emory. They'd been talking about Emory—his dangerous, inconstant nature.

"Who were they?" I whispered.

"Physicians," Ravyn said, deep lines in his brow. "Filick's cousin."

"Orithe Willow?" I managed.

"You know him?"

A narrow man with pale, milky eyes cut across my mind. "He came to my uncle's house, searching my family for any sign of the infection."

Ravyn tensed. "He never tested your blood?"

"No." I let out a small sound—as if fingers had encircled my throat and begun to squeeze. "My aunt hid me."

Ravyn looked down at me, some of the strain gone from his features. He slid his hand away from mine atop the latch, his warm, calloused thumb snagging over my knuckles. It was meant as a gesture of comfort—a quiet acknowledgment of my fear. And it was.

But that did not explain why we both looked away immediately afterward.

Ravyn moved to the open mahogany wardrobe in the far corner of the room. I heard the noise of fabric shifting as he pushed his clothes aside, revealing the wardrobe's firm wooden backboard.

I squinted. There was a Card in the wardrobe, I was certain. But I could not yet make out its color—only that it was dark.

Ravyn knocked on the backboard. Then again. On the fourth knock, I heard an echo of hollowness. Grunting, Ravyn pried something I could not see out of a hidden panel in his wardrobe.

It was only when the Card was free that I understood its color. Rich and royal purple, like an amethyst stone I'd once seen on Market Street. A second Card hidden away, nearly as rare as the Nightmare—and just as terrifying.

The Mirror.

The Nightmare clawed at the inside of my head, as if pressing against bars. I felt a smile stretch across his face, his tail flicking. *Even more delightful.*

Of all the Providence Cards chronicled in *The Old Book of Alders,* the Mirror had frightened me most as a girl. I backed into the door, afraid to even be close to the Mirror Card.

So much dread, the Nightmare said. *So much might. To see beyond the veil—what wicked delight.*

There's nothing delightful about being invisible, I said. *Or seeing the dead.*

He was quiet a moment. *Some would give anything to speak to loved ones passed.*

Ravyn shut the wardrobe and stepped toward the door, stopping only when our eyes met. "What's the matter?"

I stared at the Mirror Card in his hand. "Are you going to use that?"

"It's for you."

Air whooshed out my open mouth, and I shoved my hands deep into my pockets. "I can't," I said too quickly.

Ravyn cocked a brow. "Trust me, you want to avoid Orithe."

Now's your chance, the Nightmare said, his voice thick with mischief. *Tell him your real magic. Go on. Tell him why you refuse to touch Providence Cards.*

This isn't a game, I said. *If I tell him I absorb any Card I touch, he'll want to know the rest. He'll find out about YOU.*

Would that really be so horrible?

I ignored him, steeling myself. "I've no desire to use Providence Cards," I said to Ravyn.

The Captain's gray eyes tightened on my face. "Why is that, Miss Spindle?"

"Nothing comes for free," I said, forcing firmness into my

voice. "I don't take risks. Not even with Cards. Please, Captain. I cannot."

After a severe pause, his eyes lingering a moment too long on my face, Ravyn cleared his throat. "Very well. You won't mind if I do, will you?"

Hallway light flooded the dark room when I opened the door. I turned, waiting to follow Ravyn's lead, but he was suddenly gone—vanished.

Eyes wide, I yelped.

Faint laughter sounded from the space the Captain of the Destriers had stood.

"How—Are you still—"

"I'm right here," Ravyn said, making me jump.

I reached out, expecting nothing. But my fingers collided with the silk of his tunic, pressing into Ravyn's taut stomach muscles.

I retracted my hand immediately. "Right. Erm, sorry."

"Better if I'm not seen," he explained. "I'm supposed to be monitoring the crowd this evening. Can you see the Card?"

The purple light floated seemingly on its own accord—like an amethyst fairy on the wind. "Yes."

"Good. Now pick your jaw up off the floor and follow me."

"Providence Cards," I muttered as I followed the purple and burgundy lights through Stone. It had taken only three touches for the Mirror Card to work. And while my own ability to absorb Providence Cards made such close proximity to any Card churn my stomach with dread, I could not help but feel a thimbleful of fascination for the power they held.

But I did not feed that fascination. Better let it starve, knowing I would never touch another Providence Card as long as I lived.

The Nightmare's voice echoed through my mind. *Nothing is free,* he murmured. *Nothing is safe. Magic is love, but also, it's hate. It comes at a cost. You're found and you're lost. Magic is love, but also—*

Will you just stop? I snapped. *Just for a night—for one bloody night—can we give* The Old Book of Alders *a rest?*

But my frustration only seemed to please him, and for the next few minutes as I tarried after Ravyn Yew through the castle, it was to the sound of the Nightmare's laughter.

When we reached the bottom of the main stairwell, I heard the clamor of the great hall. The purple light bobbed in midair, then abruptly stopped.

I plowed into Ravyn, smashing my face against his shoulder blade. "What are you—"

"Elspeth," a voice called.

I knew the voice too well—the chill, haughty lilt of Nerium's voice.

My insides felt watery, every clack of her shoes a nail in my coffin. "Nerium," I said, rubbing my nose, aware I was seeing my stepmother through Ravyn's invisible body. "How are you enjoying Equinox?"

"Quite well," Nerium said, coming so close that Ravyn was forced to step out from between us, his Card now glowing at my side. My stepmother's voice grew eerily soft. "Until I saw you leave the King's table with Ravyn Yew."

"He was just escorting me—"

"Save it," she said, lowering her voice as Wayland Pine and his three daughters moved past us. "I don't care who you sully your reputation with, you little fool," she said. "So long as it's not the Captain of the Destriers. Have you even considered what might happen to us if he"—she looked around, her blue eyes narrowing—"found out what you really are?"

I let out a slow breath. "And what am I, Nerium?"

Her icy blue eyes narrowed. "The same thing your mother was. Strange, fevered." She whispered through her teeth. "Infected."

I had never heard her say the word before. She hadn't dared, not in front of my father. But the King's wine had emboldened her, uncaging the quiet loathing she carried for me, long held at bay.

Her hatred stung, but it did not startle me. If anything, I felt a small relief, the veil between us finally falling. But she had evoked my mother. And for that, she would not get away unscathed. Too long had I let her mistake my silence for weakness.

"It doesn't matter what my mother was—what I am. There will always be someone who cares for people like us, Nerium."

"Like who? Your father?" Her laugh was sharp, meant to injure. "But he sent you away, my dear. Your father sent you away. How can you be certain he cares for you at all?"

I bit my cheek, heat boiling up my neck into my face. "He keeps the rooms the way she made them, Nerium. That is why he refuses to let you remake Spindle House. He keeps them exactly as they were when she was alive. He orders irises for the parlor." I clenched my jaw to keep the angry tears at bay. "I can't say if he cares for me or not. But I am certain that, long after you and I are gone, when the house falls to ruin, only two things will remain at Spindle House. The spindle tree at the heart of the courtyard," I said, my gaze unflinching, "and the whitebeam tree my father planted next to it the day my mother died."

Glass formed over Nerium's eyes. Lips pursed, hands tightening to fists. For a moment I thought she might hit me. But she said nothing, freezing me out.

She turned, rejoining the festivities as quickly as she'd left. I watched her go and tried not to look at the purple light hovering nearby.

"Have you met my stepmother, Captain?" I whispered, the remnants of my anger distilled in a single tear that fell to my cheek. "Lovely woman."

The same calloused thumb that had slid over my knuckles in Ravyn's chamber caught the tear on my cheek—dragged it away. It was gone in a moment. His voice drifted past my ear. "Come."

The corridors below the stairs were poorly lit. Only the light from Ravyn's Cards kept me from tripping over myself. How he saw in the dark, I did not know. Perhaps he'd grown used to the path.

I recognized the way just before we got to the door with the stags, the same room we'd been in only hours ago. A moment later I jumped, startled by the sudden reappearance of the Captain of the Destriers at my side.

"You did well," he said, glancing down at me. "With your stepmother."

I ran a hand over my face. "We don't get along, she and I."

"Does she always talk to you that way?"

"If she talks to me at all. Though I imagine she might have chosen her words more carefully had she known we were not alone."

Ravyn slid his Mirror Card into his pocket, its violet light joining the Nightmare's burgundy. "I should warn you," he said, nodding to the door. "It's not going to be pleasant in there, either."

"What do you mean?"

"You said you wanted to know everything. It's a double-edged sword, Miss Spindle." He knocked three times on the door, then a fourth, then a fifth.

The door opened from the inside, the distinct growl of hounds meeting us at the threshold. I stepped in after Ravyn, my hands knotted in my skirt—my heart in my throat.

They sat at the rounded table, five of them: Jespyr Yew, Elm Rowan, Filick Willow, and two others I had not met but knew by the Yew insignia upon their clothes—Fenir and Morette Yew. Ravyn's parents.

A single chair was situated in the middle of the room, the light from the hearth casting long, ominous shadows across it.

Ravyn gestured to it, offering me a seat.

The Nightmare slithered to the forefront of my mind, acute—aware. *Let the inquest begin.*

Chapter Eleven

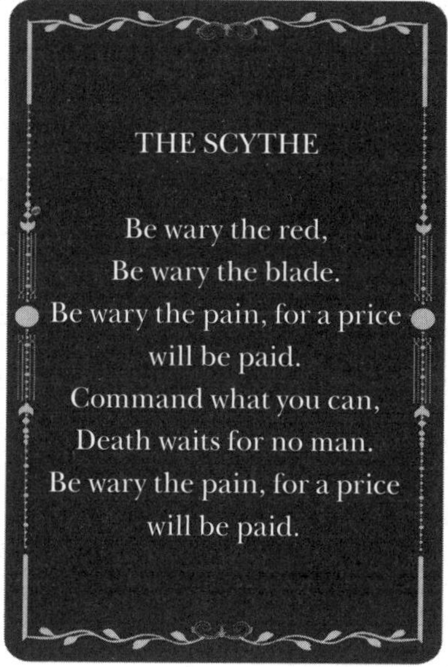

There were three other Providence Cards in the room besides Ravyn's. Elm's Scythe, a Chalice in Jespyr's tunic pocket, and the gray light of a Prophet emanating from Morette Yew. I gripped the edges of my chair, looking for softness in their faces.

But I was met with silence—their eyes masked by restraint.

The cellar door closed with a slam. I was getting used to the sound of the lock clicking behind me. When no one spoke, Ravyn cleared his throat. "This is Elspeth Spindle, Erik's first daughter, niece of Tyrn Hawthorn."

There were a few murmurs at my uncle's name. After a moment, Ravyn addressed me, his expression unreadable.

"These are my mother and father, Morette and Fenir Yew. Physician Willow, my cousin, and my sister, you already know."

The dim light in the room made it difficult to see much of a resemblance between Ravyn and his parents. Morette was the King's sister—her eyes were Rowan green. Fenir, like Jespyr, had rich brown eyes, much darker than Ravyn's and Emory's misty gray. The only similarity I could make out was a long, distinguished nose on Fenir Yew's stern face, same as Ravyn's.

"I understand, Miss Spindle," Fenir said, his voice deep, "that you wish to know the truth about us. About why we are seeking Providence Cards."

I nodded, my muscles tense.

"Before we unravel the truth, we must first see if you are deserving of it," Fenir continued. "Are you willing to submit to our forum—that this council might test your trustworthiness?"

Ravyn moved behind me. I glared at him over my shoulder. "Submit?"

He crossed his arms over his chest. "It's what you wanted, isn't it? Our trust?"

"I wanted answers."

"And I wanted a night of drunken debauchery," called Elm from the table, the Scythe slipping in and out of his long, narrow fingers. "Yet I'm back in this broom closet for the second time today. So, if it's not too much trouble, Miss Spindle, have a bloody seat so we might get on with it."

Ravyn shot his cousin a nasty glance and put a hand to his brow. He looked tired. Tired and deeply annoyed. "This is how you get your answers, Miss Spindle," he said. "Nothing comes free."

Nothing comes free, the Nightmare murmured in accord.

I sighed. I was going for irritation, but the crack in my voice betrayed the disquiet lingering deep in my chest. "All right, then," I said. "I submit to your forum."

Elm and Jespyr stood from their seats and approached me. Ravyn joined them at my side. "This is simple enough, Miss Spindle," he said. "We each present a Providence Card. Choose one, and we'll proceed."

Elm, Jespyr, and Ravyn pulled the Cards from their pockets: the Scythe, the Chalice, and the Nightmare. Red or turquoise or burgundy. Control, truth serum, or the violation of my mind. The Mirror, Ravyn kept in his cloak.

My stomach knotted instantly.

"They're to gauge your honesty," Jespyr explained.

To keep you from lying, more like, the Nightmare said.

To my silence, Jespyr softened her voice. "It's a test we all must take, I'm afraid."

The Nightmare sat in the darkness, his mind bleeding into mine. *Choose the Scythe, child. Trust me.*

I glanced at Elm. Even at a slouch, the Prince was easily the tallest of the three. His auburn hair fell over his brow, unruly. When he caught me watching him, he winked, his lips twisting, a fox-like sneer. A challenge.

Anger spiked my blood. "The Scythe," I said, crossing my arms across my chest.

The Prince's smile widened.

Jespyr shrugged, returning to Filick and her parents at the table. Elm continued to flip the Scythe Card, twirling it between his thumb and forefinger as he moved to the hearth, resting his elbow upon the mantel.

Ravyn did not sit. He pocketed his Nightmare Card and moved to the wall opposite me. The dogs followed him, yawning, before folding themselves at his feet. I could only see half the Captain's face, the other half lost to shadow. But I could not mistake the directness of his gaze. Two eyes the color of storm clouds, aimed at me.

My heart raced.

Elm tapped the red Card three times. "Have you ever been in the grip of a Scythe before, Spindle?"

"No."

"It's less abrasive than you might imagine. I cannot make you tell me the truth—not like the Chalice. I can only affect your emotions, your willingness to tell me everything I need to know."

"Sounds horrible."

The Prince smiled. But there was no humor behind his green eyes. "Some think the Scythe forces the mind to turn against itself—to feel emotions not its own. But the truth is, the Card doesn't force anything. You'll feel a little strange—your eyes may glaze over. But in the end, you'll *want* to do everything I ask of you. A tad less frightening, no?"

"I'm not frightened," I said through my teeth.

Warmth crept over me—a lightness of being. Gone was my fear, my strain. Suddenly the room felt less dark. The dogs, curled at Ravyn's feet, seemed an adorable picture. When I glanced at the others, I felt joy, my frown transforming to a smile as laughter lines creased my face.

Darling, the Nightmare said. *You can't make it so easy for him to control you.*

I couldn't help it. I was happy—euphoric. My laughter filled the room like bread rising from a tin. I brushed tears from my eyes and put my hand over my mouth, trying to control the giggles bubbling inside me. I eyed Ravyn, wishing for a sign of his elusive half smile. He watched me from the shadows, his mouth a tight line. And it made me happy all the more, knowing his eyes were fixed on me. Doubled over, hands on my stomach, I let go of a lifetime of strain and laughed, not a care in the world.

My joy siphoned away, replaced by hopelessness and the sudden, violent urge to hurt myself.

I slapped myself across the cheek. Hard.

The Nightmare hissed, anger flaring across my mind. I looked up at Elm, my eyes wide.

But the urge to hurt myself raged on, insatiable, fed only when I slapped myself again. I cried out, my cheek tender, abruptly aware I was not in control of my own emotions, powerless to stop them.

At the table, my audience shifted.

"Elm," Morette Yew warned.

"I need to be certain she's under my hand before we begin," the Prince said, his handsome face calm. "Otherwise, there will be holes in the influence."

When I slapped myself a third time, Ravyn pushed away from the wall so abruptly the dogs leapt up with a snarl. "Enough," he said, ice in his voice.

"All right, all right," Elm said, winking at me. "Sorry. I had to make sure there was a tether."

My cheek was half-numb, half-aflame. "You couldn't have made me spin around the room?" I hissed through my teeth.

"Anyone might spin. Not everyone is willing to hit themselves."

I should have chosen the Chalice. At least Jespyr's not a raging asshole.

Easy now, the Nightmare said. *Let him think he's in control.*

He IS in control.

Elm leaned on the mantel once more and inspected his fingernails, as if he'd already grown bored. "She's all yours," he said to his uncle.

Fenir Yew folded his hands on the table. "Why don't you start by telling us about yourself, Miss Spindle."

I tried to ignore the pain in my cheek. Gone was the impulse to hurt myself. In its place, I felt an urgent desire to be truthful—earnest. I shot Elm a narrow glance, the Scythe spurring me to reply. "I was born twenty years ago in Spindle House in Blunder," I said. "But I only lived there until I was nine."

"When you caught the infection and moved to Hawthorn House?"

I nodded.

"Your father was the Captain of the Destriers," Fenir said, his brow low. "Why did he not report your fever?"

I had anticipated the question. "He felt I was a danger to his second wife and their children, so he sent me away." My voice hardened. "But he did not wish to see me die."

Elm continued to pick at his nails. "Who knew Erik Spindle had a heart?"

Fenir ignored his nephew. "Why did he place you with the Hawthorns?"

"My mother and my aunt were very close." I paused. "Though I suspect the fact that Hawthorn House is in the wood, out of sight, greatly appealed to my father. He offered my uncle coin."

Jespyr leaned forward. I did not miss the surprise in her voice. "Erik paid them to take you in?"

It sounded so pitiful, said aloud like that. I had little stomach for pity. "He paid my uncle," I bit back. "My aunt had no price."

"Fond of coin, old Tyrn," Elm muttered.

Fenir watched me, weighing my words on a scale I could not yet fathom. "You've lived with the Hawthorns for many years. You must know how your uncle came by his Nightmare Card."

My stomach coiled. "I don't. That is—I was a child. I only recall that when he returned with it, his sword was bloodied."

Fenir blinked. "A child? How long has Tyrn had the Card?"

I grimaced. "Eleven years."

A collective gasp filled the cellar. "That Card is worth a

fortune," Jespyr cried. "Why on earth would Tyrn Hawthorn hold on to it so long?"

"He was waiting for the right price," Morette Yew said, her long, dark hair falling over her shoulder. "And now, with his daughter betrothed to Hauth, Tyrn's bloodline will inherit the throne."

My stomach dropped. So cold—so calculating. And I realized, though I had spent the majority of my life in his house, I hardly knew my uncle.

Deep and rough as gravel, Ravyn spoke from the shadows. "I have a few questions."

Elm straightened at the hearth. Gone was the look of boredom, his face lifted by a fox-like smile. His green eyes shifted between me and the Captain of the Destriers. Whatever he anticipated, it seemed to promise a good time.

Ravyn stepped out of shadow and stood before me, eyes fixed on my face. I fought the urge to squirm in my seat. "Do you trust us, Miss Spindle?" he asked.

The Scythe's influence warred within me. All I wanted to do was answer with the earnest truth. But what Ravyn Yew and his cousin did not know was that I had great practice being at war with my own mind. Eleven years' practice.

I gripped the seat of my chair tighter, sweat pooling in my palms. "I don't know what I believe yet," I said.

"What about Ravyn?" Elm called from the hearth. "You seem to trust him."

I looked at the Captain of the Destriers, his gray eyes full of me. He stood with his hands clasped behind his back, his feet shoulder width apart. He looked every bit the soldier—stoic and severe.

But Ravyn Yew was more than a soldier. He was the shadow on the forest road. The keeper of keys and secrets, invisible but for his purple and burgundy lights. A man with many masks.

A traitor, said the Nightmare.

A highwayman, I replied.

No sooner had our eyes met—a flash of gray—did I think back to standing against the door in Ravyn's chamber, his body towering over me, his finger pressed against my lips.

I looked away. Fast. "How can I trust him?" I said to Elm. "I've only just met him."

Elm's smile held no hospitality. "Do you think he's handsome?"

The Prince was toying with me, like a cat its prey. I bit down, determined not to answer, but the Scythe's influence—the desire to reply—was overwhelming.

My head began to pound. Sweat came in beads along my brow and the nape of my neck. When I spoke, my voice sounded strangled. "Yes." Then, out of spite, "For a Destrier."

Elm cackled. Ravyn shot him a narrow glance. Still, I did not miss the way the Captain's lips pulled at the corner; the elusive half smile, tugged by an invisible string.

"Tell us more about your magic," Filick Willow said from the table. "Is it contained merely to seeing Providence Cards by color? Or do you possess other gifts?"

Tread lightly, the Nightmare warned. *Feel the Scythe's influence?*

I could. I had hardly known an urge so vital as the one imploring me to tell the council everything they wanted to know about me. I felt trapped in the crumbling shelter of my thoughts, as if the Scythe were knocking against a weight-bearing pillar, the stone ceiling of my mind cracking.

When I hesitated, Ravyn's brow perked. "Forgive me, Miss Spindle, but you do not have the appearance of someone trained in combat. It might have been luck, knocking Elm off his feet," he said, shooting his cousin a wry grin, "but not me. Do you have other magic?"

I wanted to be honest. Rather, Elm Rowan and his Scythe

wanted me to be honest. I looked at the others, many of whom had leaned forward in their chairs, eyes sharp, waiting for my answer. My palms were slick with icy sweat. One wrong word, and they'd realize it wasn't my magic they needed…but the monster's in my head.

Help me, I called into the void.

The Nightmare slithered across our shared darkness, churning against the current of Elm's influence. *It will be easier with me here, my dear. After all, the Scythe has no sway on me.*

I blinked. *What? Why didn't you say before?*

You did not ask.

Magic. I felt it like salt water up my nostrils. The Nightmare stirred, loosening the rope Elm Rowan had tied across my mind. The Scythe's magic lessened, the desire to be honest—malleable—obedient—fading, washed away by a wave of salt.

I gasped, as if coming up for air, my mind suddenly calm, the last remnants of the Scythe's control fading like ripples on still water. When I spoke, my voice was ironclad. "No," I said to Ravyn. "I have no other magic. I can only see Providence Cards."

The Captain's eyes narrowed as he cocked his head to the side. I held his gaze, forcing my features to remain still. If he suspected I'd beaten the Scythe's control, he did not say so. Still, I did not miss the sharp edge of doubt that crept into the corners of his eyes. "Who trained you in combat?" he asked.

"No one," I said. "I taught myself how to survive."

"And you never told anyone about your magic?"

I glared up at him. "As I told you, Captain, no one else knows. Not my father or stepmother or half sisters—not my uncle, aunt, or cousins." I faced the others, my temper flaring. "I avoid town, Destriers, and Physicians. I keep to the wood, which, until lately," I said, shooting Ravyn a cold glance, "was the safest place for me to be." I crossed my arms across my chest. "Until today, my life has been one of caution, not one of magic and risk."

A weighted silence filled the room, broken by Morette Yew's austere voice. "Then let us proceed." She opened her hands to the table. "Does anyone have anything new to ask Miss Spindle?"

No one spoke. After a severe pause, Morette's gaze returned to me. Deeper than I expected, I could almost hear the iron in her voice—the sheer resolve. "Do you swear what we tell you does not leave this room, Elspeth Spindle?" she said. "Do you give your word?"

I reached in the darkness, but the Nightmare did not speak. He, like the others, was waiting for my answer.

The Scythe no longer controlled me. I was free to lie at will.

But I didn't. "Yes," I said. "I swear."

Ravyn approached, kneeling beside my chair. He rested his arms on his bent knee. Had he not been clad in all black, severe as a crow, I might have thought him a knight kneeling before a maiden, slipped from the pages of a book. "We need you to help us collect the Deck of Cards, Miss Spindle," he said.

Suddenly I was a little girl, sitting next to Ione as my aunt read to us from *The Old Book of Alders.* The silky rhythm of the ancient text swept over me, the poem on the final page and the sound of my mother's voice ingrained into my very soul.

What was it she had once said? *The Cards. The mist. The blood. They are all woven together, their balance delicate, like spider silk. Unite all twelve Providence Cards with the black blood of salt, and the infection will be healed. Blunder will be free of the mist.*

I stared at the faces around me. "King Rowan, and all the Rowan Kings before him, have wanted to collect the Deck." I gripped the lip of my chair so tightly my knuckles ached. "But you're not working with King Rowan. Otherwise, you would have already given him your Nightmare Card. You're collecting the Deck on your own account…" My eyes flew to the table. "Is there going to be a rebellion? Are you going to depose the King?"

Fenir's voice was sharp. "Nothing of the sort. Rebellion would destroy Blunder."

Then why not work alongside the King to collect the Deck? the Nightmare said, coiling through my mind. *They're hiding something.*

I waited, the room so quiet it might have been a tomb. "With the Deck of Cards," Fenir said, "the King will lift the mist, regaining ownership of Blunder from the Spirit of the Wood." He took his wife's hand, his face drawn. "And he will be able to cure the infection."

I waited, my breath fast.

"But as *The Old Book of Alders* so loves to remind us," Elm said from the hearth, twirling the Scythe, "nothing comes for free. Now that my father has the Nightmare Card, he needs only two things to unite the Deck: the lost Twin Alders Card and blood. Infected blood." He looked toward the flames, his shoulders tight. "And he's going to kill Emory to get it."

The strange boy—his erratic, fitful nature. Infected. Which meant Emory Yew was not a resident in the King's castle as a token of hospitality.

He was a captive.

And they were going to commit treason to save him.

Even the Nightmare was stunned into silence.

I looked away, ashamed of the cruel thoughts I'd had about Emory. The boy was sick—addled by magic. And his uncle was going to sacrifice him for it.

How easily it could have been me.

"There is more to tell," Fenir said, breaking the doleful silence, "but not here. The hour is late, and we are still within the King's walls. If you agree to help us, we will take you to Castle Yew."

This time, Jespyr spoke. There was a rasp in her voice, warm, like cracking kindling. "All we need is the Well, the Iron Gate, and the Twin Alders," she said. "After that, our Deck is complete." She laced her fingers together. "Finding the Twin Alders won't be easy. But with your ability to see Cards, we have an advantage the King does not. Help us, Elspeth, and we can cure Emory's infection." Her brown eyes searched my face. "Help us, and you can cure your own."

Her plea tugged at me. I looked down at Ravyn to speak—to argue—I was not sure. But I couldn't find the words. He looked suddenly quite young, kneeling next to me. Only then did I recall that, despite the gravity of his station, the Captain of the Destriers was not much older than I was.

Still, I was wary of joining him. He had not become Captain of the most dangerous men in Blunder because of a handsome face. "Whose infected blood will you use to unite the Deck, if not Emory's?" I asked, twisting my hands in my skirt.

"Someone close to the King," Ravyn said, his shoulders tight. "Someone who has committed great wrongs."

I stilled my features and reached into my mind.

If the Deck is united, will I truly be cured?

Who says you need a cure?

Be serious!

His laugh echoed in the cavernous dark. *I know what I know. My secrets are deep. But long have I kept them, and long will they keep.*

I shut my eyes and sighed. Just as I could not fathom Blunder without the mist, I could not fathom finding the Twin Alders, a Card that had been lost for centuries. Worse, the notion of sacrificing someone, deserving or not, and spilling their infected blood to unite the Deck of Cards made my stomach twist. Perhaps that was why the final page of *The Old Book of Alders* had always seemed like a fairy tale to me—dark, strange. Impossible.

I felt it in their eyes, their shoulders, the air we shared—tense, yet somehow hopeful. They were desperate for my help, for my magic.

I slid my hands up my arms, knowing what waited under my sleeves. I had felt it in my veins the moment I'd asked the Nightmare for help—the moment I'd broken the Scythe's influence. It was always there, just like the creature in my mind, waiting.

Blackness. Dark as ink. Magic.

Magic strong enough to find a Card that had been lost five hundred years.

"I'll do it," I said, my heart drumming in my chest. "For the cure, I'll help you find the Twin Alders."

Chapter Twelve

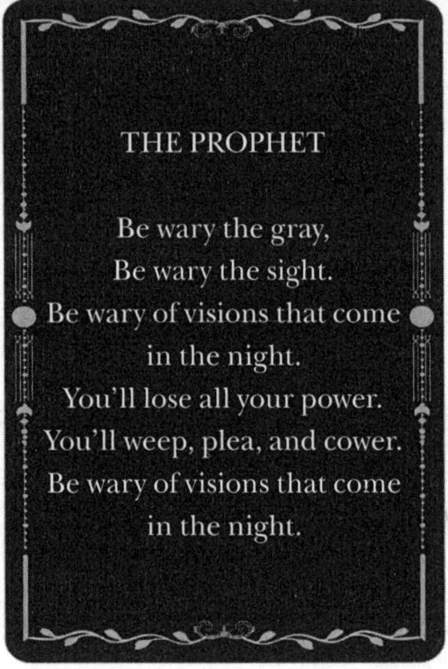

I waited outside the cellar on the stone steps with my head in my hands. It had been only an hour since I'd met the council, but the hour had felt like a lifetime. Above me, I heard the gong strike eleven. The feast was over—the celebration had moved outside for dancing and wine.

Inside the cellar, they discussed my fate.

I spun my charm between my fingers. Behind the cellar door, I could discern Lady Yew's tone from the others. Someone coughed. I rubbed my eyes. *Why didn't you tell me?*

Tell you what?

That the Scythe doesn't work on you.

A vile scraping sound echoed through my mind. The

Nightmare was picking at his teeth. *None of them work on me, dear one.*

I gaped. *Something you casually forgot to mention? For ELEVEN years?*

But I have mentioned it, my clueless little companion. His claws grated against his teeth. *I cannot, however, be held responsible for your feeble comprehension.*

I wanted to reach into the darkness and smack him across his monstrous face. *You really know how to make a girl feel special.*

He laughed. *You'll understand soon enough. The truth always outs.*

Had I not been bone-tired, I might have argued—pressed him for more—hungry for the secrets he guarded like a greedy dragon. There was still so much I did not know about him.

But he had chosen his moment well—dropped a bread-crumb at the top of a mountain. If I wanted to know more, I would have to work for it.

And I was far too tired for that.

Laughter from Equinox rolled down the stairs. I yawned, my eyelids drooping as I frowned at the cellar door. *What's taking them so long?*

The Nightmare's tail made a whooshing sound. *Find out.*

How am I supposed to do that?

Best stick to the old ways.

Which are?

Pressing a bloody ear to the door, I should think.

The wood was thick, their voices difficult to distinguish. I slipped to the door, praying the dogs on the other side would not betray me. I held my breath and cupped my ear, sliding it against the crease between the wood and stone framework.

"The Hawthorns will need a reason to let her go to Castle Yew," someone said. "As will Erik."

"I don't trust her," another voice said. Elm. "Her manners are too practiced, her words too careful."

"Of course they are," Jespyr said. "She wouldn't have evaded Destriers and Physicians this long if she wasn't cautious."

"She's supposed to be here," another voice said. Filick. "Morette saw it. Elspeth is going to help us find the Deck. What's there to argue about?"

"Aunt Morette saw a shadowy figure on the forest road," Elm countered. "Forgive me, Aunt, I do not doubt you or your Prophet Card. But your description was vague. Ravyn and I could have stumbled upon anyone that night."

Fenir spoke. "Yet you happened to find a woman with the ability to see Cards when we've only three left to claim?"

"The Prophet showed me a hooded figure with a shadow," Morette Yew's voice called above the clamor, stern and sure. "The shadow remained, even when the light faded. The figure walked to the wood, and behind it trailed Providence Cards, one by one—followed by a thirteenth I have never seen before. Behind the figure I saw my Emory, alive and well. That was what I saw. That was why I bade you watch the forest road."

They were silent for several moments. My heart hammered in my chest, the small piece of the puzzle slow to place itself into an image I could not yet comprehend.

They'd been waiting for me on the forest road, Ravyn and Elm, though they had not yet known it. And I—I was embedded in a prophecy of magnitude so great it had led me to the Yews, one of Blunder's oldest families...and into the depths of treason.

I bit my lip and pressed my ear tighter to the door, praying for more.

Fenir broke the silence. "There's no direction to move but forward," he said. "We'll bring Elspeth into our household and learn more about her magic. When we move to find the Cards, she will accompany us to retrieve them."

Someone scoffed. Elm. "We don't have time to play guardian to a timid girl."

"Timid?" Jespyr chuckled. "That's not what you said when you came limping back from the forest road."

Ravyn's voice cut through the room. "Whatever she is, it isn't timid. We'd be fools to underestimate her."

"Spindle House is close by," Filick said. "Why not put her with her own family?"

"No," Ravyn said, hasty.

"If she's going to be privy to our plans, she needs to be kept close to us," Fenir said. "We can't have the Spindles or anyone else delving into our business."

"Which again raises the question—what are we going to tell her family? They'll need a reason to send her our way."

A strained silence followed. It was hard, keeping my breath quiet. Harder still to be kept out of the room like a petulant child while they discussed my fate.

"I've got an idea," Jespyr said, her voice slow, gentle, as if to soothe an angry animal. "But you're not going to like it."

"Because everything up until this point has been so enjoyable."

"I didn't mean *you*, Elm," Jespyr said. "I meant Ravyn."

I pressed so hard against the gap in the door my head began to ache.

Ravyn's voice was a growl. "What, Jes?"

"Just don't say no right away."

"Jespyr."

She paused. "What if we tell Erik Spindle and the Hawthorns that we've invited Elspeth to stay at Castle Yew...so that you might court her?"

I skipped a breath, my fatigue suddenly gone. I felt wide awake, my pulse quickening, an unwelcome flush sliding across my neck and into my face.

Behind the door, Elm barked a laugh.

But there was no laughter in Ravyn's voice. "No. Absolutely not."

"It's a good idea! You've already been seen together today—no one will suspect the real reason we've asked her to stay with us at Castle Yew." To the biting silence that followed, Jespyr heaved a sigh. "You don't actually have to woo her, merely give the impression of wooing her. Just, I don't know, smile at her once in a while. You remember how to smile, don't you?"

They all began to speak at once, their voices a chaotic buzz. "We needn't elaborate much," Fenir said. "There will be gossip, of course. Ravyn's never taken time to properly court anyone before."

"Trees," Ravyn muttered, his voice dripping irritation.

There was excitement in Morette's voice. "It could work. If anyone asks, I can tell them I invited Miss Spindle on Ravyn's behalf," Morette said. Her tone turned scolding. "He needn't pretend to initiate the courtship if the prospect is so loathsome to him."

"I suppose I don't have much of a say in this," Ravyn said on a harsh exhale.

"No," Jespyr said, sounding far too delighted. "None whatsoever."

Fenir cleared his throat. "What exactly do you object to, Ravyn? She's clever, striking."

I wondered the same thing. The Captain's adamant refusal to court me—not even court me, *pretend* to court me—felt like a dozen wasp stings, leaving me wounded, hot with anger.

"Make no mistake, she's beautiful. Only, I—" Ravyn's voice cut out. Then, as if the words were bitter in his mouth, "If the ruse will help..." He heaved a sigh. "I'll try. Though I doubt I'll play a convincing suitor."

I huffed hot air out my nostrils. "Don't do me any favors," I said into the din. As if I would ever deign to court someone like him. I had enough struggles of my own without adding the chore of coaxing a smile out of Ravyn Yew to my list.

Somewhere in the darkness, a wicked purr echoed. *What's the old adage, my dear? Something about ladies and protesting far too much?*

I hissed him into silence. But just as I was convincing myself that playing at courtship with Ravyn Yew was the last thing in the world I wanted, they'd come to the opposite conclusion on the other side of the door.

"Then it is settled," Morette called firmly. "She'll remain at Castle Yew under the assumption of an arranged courtship with Ravyn. I'll ask her father and the Hawthorns tonight. They won't deny her an extended stay if I assure them I will be there to chaperone."

There was a rustling, a noise of agreement. "We should bring her there tonight."

Elm's snicker was becoming easy to recognize. "Shouldn't the Captain be seen at the celebration with his new leading lady?"

I couldn't make out Ravyn's reply. But it sounded undeniably threatening.

"Let's take an hour to show our faces at Equinox," Fenir said. "Then we'll return to Castle Yew." A pause. "Care to fill her in, Ravyn?"

Footsteps shuffled.

"Don't forget to smile!" Jespyr called as the handle turned.

I jerked away from the door, unsteady on my heels. I fell backward with a thud. When Ravyn Yew opened the cellar door, I looked up at him from a heap on the floor, cheeks red, guilty as sin.

He perked a brow, glaring down at me. "Didn't your aunt ever tell you not to listen at doors, Miss Spindle?"

I shot to a defiant stand, dusting off the backside of my dress. "I wasn't listening."

The Nightmare laughed. *We're going to have to work on your lying.*

Ravyn shut the door behind him. "How much did you hear?"

I moved to the step above him, where we stood almost eye to eye. Almost. "Enough."

He gazed down his nose at me. "And is the plan to your satisfaction?"

The sting I felt in my chest returned. I narrowed my eyes. "If the ruse will help, I'll try."

He did not appear keen to have his own words used against him. Ravyn stared back at me, his gray eyes severe as they traced my face, landing momentarily on my mouth before flickering away. "What about Laburnum?"

"What about him?"

Ravyn tilted his head. "He's in love with you."

I winced and shook my hands, as if to fling what he'd said off me. "We're not attached. A"—I struggled to say the word—"*courtship* would bear no weight. I've promised him nothing."

Ravyn said nothing, watching me. He lowered himself to a seat, rubbing his eyes. For a moment he seemed spent, tired to the bone. It was the first time I considered that someone else's day had been as grueling as mine.

Eyes red from rubbing them, Ravyn looked up at me. "I assume being under the Scythe is not a pleasant sensation. Are you all right?"

I kicked my foot against the stone floor. "Your cousin is a complete—"

"Ass. I know. But it was either the Scythe or the Chalice, considering the Nightmare is off the table."

I did not miss the edge in his voice. My lips sealed in a tight line as the Captain of the Destriers watched me. When I offered no explanation, he continued. "Finding the Cards will be dangerous, Miss Spindle. You realize that."

I tried to shrug, but there was no hiding the apprehension pooling in my stomach.

"Fortunately, we've been toeing this line of lawlessness for some time now. We know how to keep you safe."

"And if I'm caught? If your uncle finds out I'm infected?"

He rose to his feet. "Then you're back in the situation I found you in this morning. The difference is, you've gained some considerable allies."

I stared at the King's nephew, searching for something I could not find. Fear—apprehension—anything I might relate to my own disquiet. But Ravyn Yew was still, smooth as glass, untouched by the horrendous risk he'd thrust upon me.

My voice faltered. "And if I should like to leave?"

He held my gaze. "You're not a prisoner."

There are many different kinds of cages, the Nightmare said.

I tried to ignore him. "I'm free to go—back to my aunt's house—should I wish to?"

"Of course," Ravyn said. "Only, I thought you wanted to find a cure."

"I do."

"Then help us. Help us, so we might help you."

I reached into the darkness, my mind snagging the gristly hair along the Nightmare's spine. *I won't get out of this unscathed without your help.*

He twisted, his ears perked. *You're giving me a free hand?*

I gritted my teeth. *I'm asking you to keep me alive, Nightmare. If only long enough so that I can finally get rid of you.*

His laughter twisted through my mind like a ghost combing a corridor, near and far at the same time.

I looked up at Ravyn. For eleven years, the infection had

been a leash around my throat. I had cowed under that leash, the hope for a cure beyond the scope of my imagination.

But as I gazed into the Captain's gray eyes—a man who, by law, should see me dragged to the dungeon—the leash around my throat loosened. He had opened a door—taken a key from his belt and unlocked a part of Blunder I had not allowed myself to believe in. I was a child again, wrapped up in *The Old Book of Alders*. There was magic in the world. Terrible, wonderful magic. Magic great enough to undo magic. A cure for the infection.

And a way to get the Nightmare out of my head.

"When do we start?" I asked.

The Captain of the Destriers took a step up. We stood toe to toe, his shadow swallowing me whole. "I'd say we've already begun."

With that, he strode up the steps two at a time, the Cards in his pocket casting eerie light along the dark stone walls. When I didn't follow, he turned and said, "An hour, Miss Spindle. Just so we're seen. After that, we can be free of this wretched castle."

The drinking and dancing had moved into the gardens. The clamor of dozens of families echoed across the castle grounds, cloistered by mist that rested just beyond the hedges.

Ravyn led us through the great hall, back up the main stairwell.

"The celebration is that way," I said gesturing to the wide gilded door that led out into the gardens.

"I want you to see why we've gone down this path, Miss Spindle," Ravyn said. "Why we're risking everything to get the last three Cards." He glanced over his shoulder at me. "Emory," he said. "We're going to see Emory."

Dread coiled with curiosity in my stomach. It seemed too dark and cruel that the King would sacrifice his own nephew—even if the outcome could forever change Blunder for good.

A King's reign is wrought with burden, the Nightmare whispered, his voice uncharacteristically heavy. *Weighty decisions ripple through centuries. Still, decisions must be made.*

"Why Emory?" I asked. "I know the infection is rare...but surely there is someone else..."

"Blood must be spilled," Ravyn said, his voice far away. "Could there ever be an easy choice?"

We were already a flight higher than the rooms I shared with my father, stepmother, and half sisters. So steep my knees ached, Stone felt like one long, endless staircase. I heaved my dress and tried to keep from panting. Anything to avoid another scrutinous look down Ravyn Yew's narrow nose. When we reached the fourth floor, I rested a hand on the banister, pretending to admire a Golden Egg tapestry as I sucked in lungful after lungful of air.

If Ravyn noticed my breathlessness, he was decent enough not to mention it. "This is the royal wing," he said. "Emory's kept comfortable. As comfortable as he can be." When I said nothing, he lowered his voice. "But he's dying."

My gaze jerked to his face, my breathlessness forgotten.

Ravyn continued. "That's why the King has chosen Emory's blood to unite the Deck. He thinks he's saving my brother from a long, painful degeneration. A mercy killing." He ground his boots into the carpet beneath our feet. "My uncle could have sent him to the Physicians—killed him outright as soon as he learned of Emory's infection. But he didn't. He bent the rules—let Emory live." He ran a hand over his brow. "And I've repaid him with lies."

I felt the sudden urge to reach out and touch his arm. But

the gesture seemed far too intimate. "You wouldn't have to lie if the King withdrew his Physicians and let people like Emory and me walk free," I said.

"I've tried to work it out a hundred ways. But the King will brook no argument. Emory has been conspicuous with his magic—too many people have guessed at his infection." He gritted his teeth. "My uncle is bound to his Rowan lineage. Everyone infected by magic must die." Ravyn ran his hand over his face. "And so we have no choice. If we want to save Emory, we must collect the Deck ourselves. By winter Solstice."

"Why Solstice?"

"Emory's magic flares at the shift of seasons. And *The Old Book of Alders* states the Cards should be joined at the darkest part of the year." He took a deep breath. "Emory may not survive another turn of the year. I may be a liar and a traitor," he said, "but at least I can say there is nothing I would not do to save my brother."

We walked on through a brightly lit corridor. The rug beneath my feet was a heavy wool, richly embroidered and dyed a crimson red.

Two guards stood beneath the torches on either side of a tall, narrow door. They were armed with swords and a long, ominous cord of rope. When they saw Ravyn, they shrank back into shadow.

Ravyn ignored them and opened the door. By its groan, I could tell it was heavy—fortified. I filed into the chamber behind the Captain of the Destriers, my eyes wide as I took in my surroundings.

The candles in the room were not lit. They'd been blown out by the strong wind that caught just below the window. Ravyn sealed the shutters as I stepped to the old oak table in the center of the room, my eyes wide.

The hearth was lit. The smell of wine and the must from the hundreds of books atop mahogany shelves filled my nose. Across from the table along the far wall was a large bed, covered with blankets and more books.

But for its warmth and rich furnishings, the room was still—lifeless. Empty.

Emory Yew, the King's captive, was gone.

Chapter Thirteen

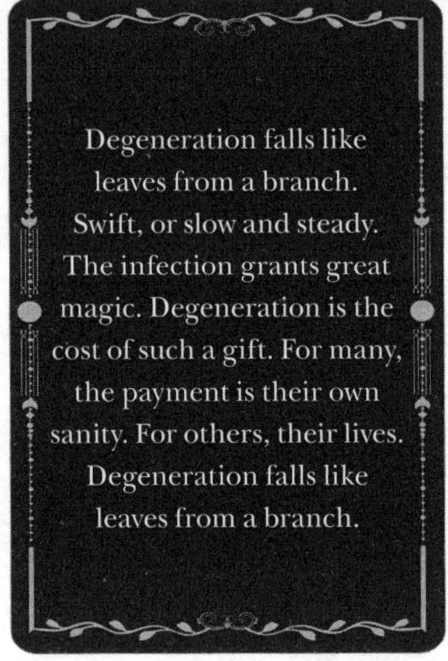

We ran back down the corridor—down the winding stairs—all the way down to the doorway into the gardens. Ravyn tapped his Nightmare Card, his jaw strained.

"My parents and sister are going to search the castle," he said, skidding to a halt just before the garden door and the clamor beyond. "You can wait here for them, if you like."

I struggled to catch my breath. "What happens if we can't find him?"

"We will," Ravyn said. "When he's clever enough to fool the guards, Emory wanders. But I'd rather it was my family that found him, not a Physician or a Destrier."

I looked out into the gardens, the crowd dense. "You'll need another pair of eyes out there," I said. "I'll go with you."

Music spilled through the open doors. The King's guests were loud, the veil of propriety thinned, laughter echoing against the castle's stone walls. Servants bustled to keep wine goblets full. A dance began, torchlight casting a soft glow across the garden as the couples swayed in the humid evening air.

But before Ravyn and I could join the crowd, just as the gong struck midnight, a booming voice called from behind, echoing through the cavernous hall.

When I turned, the hall dimmed, enveloped in darkness. Three Destriers, armed with Black Horses, marched through the castle toward us. Ahead of them, bathed in the red light of his Scythe, broad and fierce, strode His Royal Highness, Ruler of Blunder, Keeper of Laws, Protector of Providence Cards.

King Quercus Rowan.

Ravyn slid his Nightmare Card into his pocket. "Uncle," he said coolly.

"Enjoying the feast?" the King asked, stopping in front of us.

"Very much."

"You look winded." Just like his sons, the King boasted green, intelligent eyes. "What's the matter?"

"Nothing, sire," Ravyn said, his face expressionless, as if carved of stone. "I was escorting Miss Spindle to the gardens."

When the King's eyes moved to me, my ears filled with the sound of my own heartbeat.

"Miss Spindle," he said. "Of course. Erik's daughter. I have not seen you at court."

It took all my might to smile. The Nightmare, provoked by my fear, stirred, his claws sharp. I stepped forward and bowed, my knees unsteady. "I don't often leave the quiet of home, Your Majesty."

I could feel the King's eyes tighten on my face. "A pity," he said. His gaze drifted over me to Ravyn. "It seems you've already made an impression."

Ravyn stood still as a statue, jaw hewn shut.

"I look forward to seeing you more, Miss Spindle," the King said. He shot Ravyn a pointed glance. A moment later Ravyn and I were enveloped in a heavy cloud of darkness, the King and his Destriers disappearing into the garden.

I watched them go, careful not to look Ravyn in the eye. "We should find your brother before the King finds out he's escaped his room."

I felt it again, Ravyn Yew's hesitance—his discomfort when the King noted us together. Was it the lie that bothered him, pretending to court me?

Or was it me he could not stand?

Drunk off the King's wine, dizzy with dance, the King's guests moved without restraint along the garden path. Ravyn muttered under his breath as we squeezed through the masses. "I fucking hate Equinox."

The crowd shifted, knocking into us. I caught a glimpse of two White Eagles, the Cards of courage. They flickered like snow on the wind, white and clean, in the less crowded side of the gardens, near the rowan tree grove.

Bouncing between the white lights stood a boy, his hair dark and his movements erratic—as if lost to the world all around him.

Emory.

"There!" I said, pointing. "I see him."

Ravyn pushed through the crowd in a flurry of black, leaving me behind. I tried to watch him, but a group of drunken men jostled me off the path.

One of the men laughed, patting my head as if I were an animal underfoot. When I swiped his hand away, the crowd shifted. The men pushed into me again, this time with enough force to knock me to the ground.

I hit the garden path hard, wind shooting out of my lungs. A moment later a hand reached for me, hooking beneath my shoulder. I moved to slap it away but froze, recognizing the man that raised me to my feet.

Elm Rowan looked down at me through rich green irises. When I was on my feet, he wrapped a firm arm around me, shielding me from the crowd. "All right there, Spindle?"

"Go away," I said, the feeling of slapping myself so fresh my cheek still stung.

"I think you mean 'thank you,'" the Prince said, pulling me through the crowd, up the path.

"Let go." I twisted in his arm, the Nightmare hissing behind my lashes.

"And let you get trampled?" Elm said. "Our aspirations will have ended before they'd begun."

The crowd surged again. I pressed into Elm, the shrieks of drunken laughter all around us.

"By the bloody trees," said the Prince, his fingers glowing red as he pulled the Scythe from his pocket and tapped it three times. For a brief moment, his eyes glazed over and he was lost—deep within himself, consumed by magic.

I watched him, dread and fascination knotting in my stomach.

The crowd's eyes turned to us. Still, they moved, commanded by the red Card, men and women blowing like ash on the wind, parting ways until there was a distinct path through the mayhem. Then, only once there was a clear path to the rowan grove did Elm tap the Scythe thrice more, releasing the crowd from his control.

I stepped hesitantly down the new makeshift path.

He just made fifty people as docile as paper.

The Nightmare clicked his tongue against his teeth. *He couldn't control you, could he?*

The path diverted, woven through manicured box shrubs. Elm led us, pressing the heels of his palms into his brow. "Well?" he said, slipping the Scythe into his tunic pocket.

"He's over there," I said. Emory Yew and the lights from the White Eagle Cards returned to view.

Emory's cackle ripped through the grove. He swayed, jostled like a willow reed between two men with White Eagles. The men were taller than him—older and broader and a great deal angrier. I could not hear their words, but by their stance—the strain in their thick shoulders—I could tell they were not exchanging pleasantries with the King's youngest nephew.

A moment later Emory was on the ground, blood seeping out his nostrils from the hit he'd taken.

"Here we go again," Elm said, hastening down the garden path.

Emory lay on the grass, his words coming out in bursts of laughter. Elm and I were still too far to discern his words, but whatever Emory said, it was enough to make one of the men yank him off the ground by the collar.

But before the man could strike again, he was reeling backward, a black sleeve wrapped around his throat.

The Captain of the Destriers had arrived.

Dark greenery rushed past my periphery. The path twisted, leading Elm and me to a row of hedges. When I peered over the hedge, I saw Ravyn, the deep tones of his Nightmare and Mirror Cards standing in contrast to the men and their White Eagles.

The second man stepped forward. "That little runt picked my pocket!"

Ravyn let go of the first man's throat. "He's a foolish boy," he said. "Leave. Now."

"Not until I get my coin back!"

Spurred by the courage his White Eagle granted, the first man swung at Ravyn with brute strength, his fist balled like a mace. Ravyn dodged him, twisting through shadow. He stepped between Emory and the men, pushing his brother away from the tumult.

Emory retreated to a nearby tree, his lips twisted in laughter. He climbed onto a low branch and dangled, eyes wide and glassy.

I pushed into the hedge, but Elm put his hand on my shoulder to stop me.

"You're not going to help him?" I demanded.

The Prince leaned against the greenery and yawned. "It's been a long day. Let Ravyn have a little fun."

The Nightmare watched the brawl behind my eyes, his tail flickering. The men moved in unison in an attempt to catch Ravyn off guard. Ravyn merely turned, vicious in his accuracy, and sent one them sprawling across the ground with a swift jab to the jaw.

The man landed in a slump beneath the rowan tree. Emory howled from his perch, his smile so wide I could see his teeth. "Apologies for the sticky fingers," he called as he dropped gold coins, one by one, onto the man's chest. "It's a family trait, I'm afraid."

I stared at the boy, transfixed. I had sensed it on the stairs. There was something strange about Emory Yew. Now I understood what it really was. The infection—it was eating at him, ripping away his sanity.

He's degenerating, the Nightmare said. *Little by little. Magic always comes at a cost.*

I twisted the crow's foot in my pocket. "What magic did Emory's infection grant him?"

Elm's gaze shifted to his young cousin. "He can read people," he said. "As if all their secrets had been transcribed onto the pages of a book. All it takes is a single touch."

Coldness crept up my spine. *I see a yellow gaze narrowed by hate,* the boy had said to me. *I see darkness and shadow. And I see your fingers, long and pale, covered in blood.*

Elm, unaware of my distress, continued. "But the infection has taken its toll. In the last two years, he's grown weaker, changeable, and violent. Sometimes he can't even remember his own family. Every Solstice and Equinox, he seems to worsen."

Ravyn and the second man continued to tussle. Ravyn parried his jab, answering with a brutal backhand. Elm watched them, cracking his knuckles one at a time.

"Emory told me about you last night," he said. "He said there was a woman in the castle with black eyes and dark magic." His smile did not touch his eyes. "The poor boy was too excited. He's never met anyone else infected before. Anyone besides his brother, that is."

It felt as if a hundred bees had flooded my lungs, their wings fluttering in a torrid panic. I struggled to breathe, heat climbing out of my chest and wrapping around my throat.

Ravyn Yew. Infected.

Did you know? I gasped at the Nightmare.

He purred, gratification dripping like hot wax off his voice. *I had my suspicions.*

And you didn't think to tell me?

You've had the man in your gaze all day. Surely you saw more than a handsome face.

Elm watched me, tracing the shock on my face. This time, his smile was full. "He didn't tell you?"

I blinked, my tongue caught in a snare. "He—He's—"

"Infected," Elm said. "Yes. Terribly so."

What creature is he, with mask made of stone? the Nightmare said once more. *Captain? Highwayman? Or beast yet unknown?*

The Nightmare and I peered over the box shrub, the tussle now at its climax. Both Ravyn's opponents were on their feet, their White Eagles beaming from their pockets. Emory crowed at them from his perch in the tree. When the first man moved to strike, Ravyn took a hit to the stomach and slapped him away as if he were no more than a dog.

The second man—the one who'd struck Emory—lashed out. Ravyn countered, catching him at the elbow. A moment later the man let out a brutal cry and fell to the ground, his arm twisted unnaturally behind him.

I watched the Captain of the Destriers, alone and victorious, lean over the men. I could not hear the words he spoke. Still, I did not miss the way the men cowered, neither able—nor willing—to get back up.

Ravyn held out an open palm to them and waited.

The Nightmare leaned forward, honing my eyes. We watched both men, bruised and bloody, place their White Eagle Cards onto Ravyn's open palm.

The moment the Cards touched the Captain's hand, the white color disappeared.

Chapter Fourteen

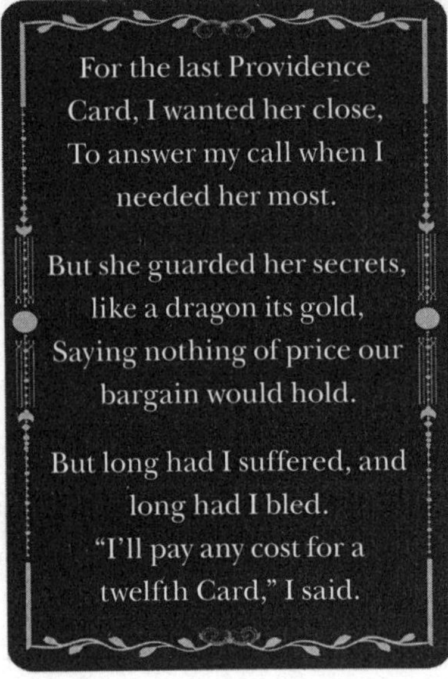

The salt stung my nose and
her spite filled the air.
I woke in the chamber, the
Twin Alders Card there.

And so, my dear kingdom,
my Blunder, my land,
The Cards fall to you, paid
by my hand.

For her price, it was final,
our bartering done.
I created twelve Cards...

But I cannot use one.

My feet moved without me, confusion, anger, and utter bewilderment warring for dominance between my head and chest. When I approached, Ravyn's lips curved in half a smile that disappeared the moment he saw my face.

"What's the matter?" he said.

"I know what you are," I said, pointing an accusatory finger in the Captain's face.

Ravyn's spine straightened. I discerned neither anger nor fear in his expression, only intelligent silence. He stepped closer, lessening the space between us. When he spoke, his voice was low. "Do you?"

"Who's the pretty lady?" Emory asked, peeling a twig off the rowan tree and plucking its leaves one by one. "Methinks she is a tree spirit. Nay—a King! Nay." His smile twisted. "A villain."

"Emory!" Ravyn snapped, eyeing his brother over his shoulder. "You've had your fun. Now shut up."

"I said she was pretty, didn't I?" Emory twirled the twig wildly through his fingers. A moment later he swore, having poked himself in the eye.

"Now, now," Elm said, coming up from behind the hedge, his Scythe alight in his hand. "We've had a lot to drink tonight, haven't we, my boy?"

Emory swatted his cousin with the twig. "Away with you and your Card, Rrrrrenelm. I'm not a baby in need of swaddling."

When Elm glanced at Ravyn and me—our backs straight and our mouths drawn—his lips curled into a guilty grin. "You two have a few things to discuss. I'll manage the brute."

"Brute?" Emory began to climb the rowan tree again. "I am Emory Tydus Yew—son of warriors—ancestor of great men—harbinger of all that is to c—"

He fell out of the tree with a thud, and the garden roared with Elm's laughter.

"Come with me," Ravyn said without looking at me, the muscles along his jaw tight.

I followed him back up the path with stomping steps, the words coming out all at once. "First your Nightmare Card, then this. I'm growing tired of your lies by omission, *Captain*."

Ravyn said nothing. The sound of Equinox—of laughter and music—grew louder. But before we could reenter the crowd, Ravyn stepped off the path into the shadow of a sycamore tree.

I had no choice but to follow him.

"What I can't seem to fathom," I said, knocking branches aside until we were face-to-face, "is how you've lived your life so publicly. You're the Captain of the bloody Destriers. I thought you, of all people, would be irreproachable." I paused, heat in my words. "But you're not, are you? You're infected."

"Keep your damn voice down," he said, looming over me.

Somewhere in the back of my head, alarm bells were ringing. I'd spent most of my life cautious not to invite attention, let alone wrath, from a Destrier. But loud as they were, the bells were drowned out by an even louder din—

Anger.

"Well?" I said through my teeth. "Are you or are you not infected?"

Ravyn looked away. He was quiet a long time, his lips a fine line beneath the shadow of his nose. Finally, he spoke. "I am."

"Does the King know?"

"Yes." He shifted his weight, crossing his arms over his chest. "You'd be surprised by the counsel my uncle keeps."

"And you're—what? His magical pet? You trade service for a normal life while the rest of us cursed with the infection are forced to tiptoe through life, execution waiting around every corner?"

Ravyn flinched, his gray eyes narrowing.

But I kept going, my blood up. "In the cellar, the light from your Cards flickered. I didn't understand until just now." My eyes fell to his hand. "The White Eagles. As soon as you touched them, their light extinguished." I searched his face, seeing him for the first true time. "What is your magic?"

Ravyn did not answer with words. Instead, he held his right hand out between us. Slowly, he unfurled his fingers. There, nestled in the palm of his hand, devoid of light and color, were the two White Eagles.

He gave me a fleeting glance. Then he turned his palm over and let the Cards fall.

The moment the White Eagles left Ravyn's skin, their color returned. I winced, blinded by light. The Cards fluttered to the ground, falling like two white beacons. They landed between our feet, their color and light as strong as any Providence Card.

I stared at them, my breath quickening.

The Nightmare understood before I did. He clawed to the forefront of my mind, his eyes fixed on Ravyn as if he, too, were seeing the Captain for the first time. *Twelve Black Horse Cards, yet thirteen Destriers,* he murmured. *Have you ever seen him with a Black Horse? No, because he cannot use it.* He gave a sudden laugh, startling me. *Don't you see? He cannot use Providence Cards. Or at least, not all of them.*

My gaze shot up to Ravyn, the white light from the Cards casting new shadows across his face. "You can't use them?"

The Captain was statue still. "No. But neither can they be used against me. Such is the nature of my magic. Cards like the Chalice—the Scythe—have no effect on me."

My thoughts spun, leaves in a windstorm. "But I saw the Cards in your pocket. When you blindfolded me, I saw their lights. And I've seen you use the Mirror and the Nightmare."

He bent at the waist, retrieving the White Eagles from the ground and slipping them into his pocket. "Cards lose their magic the moment they touch my skin. The Mirror and the Nightmare—and perhaps the Twin Alders—are the only Cards I can still use."

I still did not understand. "Why only those?"

Discernable frustration touched the edges of Ravyn Yew's face. He opened his mouth to reply, but the sound of giggling outside the sycamore tree silenced him.

I turned around. I could only see in fragments through the leaf-strewn branches. Courtiers walked the garden path, oblivious of us, their voices loud and uninhibited as they wandered into the gardens.

Ravyn waited for them to pass. He leaned closer, his voice in my ear. "This is neither the time nor the place to discuss it, Miss Spindle."

With that he pushed past me, out from the shelter of the tree and back onto the path.

His aim was to silence me—to extinguish talk of his infection, perhaps. But there were too many questions, too many unspoken truths. I balled my hands into fists and followed him to the center of the gardens where the celebration still raged.

Defiant, I caught him by his tunic and yanked. He stopped in his tracks, turning on me like a great bird of prey. But before he could speak—unleash all that frustration chiseled across his face—someone called my name.

"Elspeth!"

I looked over Ravyn's shoulder, recognizing Dimia's too-loud, bubbly voice. She stood in a group of girls several paces away. When she caught my eye she waved, spilling wine from her goblet. She lifted her skirt and bounded toward us. Behind her came a reluctant Nya, her blue eyes, normally narrow and shrewd, glassed over.

Ravyn rolled his eyes and swore under his breath. "Take my hand."

My eyes flew to his face. A face that, in that moment, I wanted to tear my fingers across. "What?"

"We're meant to be courting," he said, stepping closer, his voice a growl. He offered his hand. "Or have you forgotten?"

My half sisters were a pace away. There was no time to think. I slipped my hand into Ravyn's upturned palm, my throat constricting as he turned my hand over and laced his fingers with mine. His skin was rough, calluses tugging at the soft skin between my fingers.

We turned to face my half sisters. "Nya, Dimia," I said, breath in my voice. "Enjoying yourselves?"

The girls were holding half-empty tumblers, ribbons loose

in their hair, cheeks splotchy red. But the twins were merely drunk—not blind. Their gazes flew from Ravyn and me to our hands, woven together. Dimia's eyes bulged, a banshee squeal slipping between her lips.

Nya did nothing but stare, mouth agape—fishlike.

"It seems you are enjoying Equinox, too, Elspeth," Dimia said, sending a bawdy elbow into her twin's side.

Nya blinked, her gaze darting between me and Ravyn. "But—Are you—"

"About to dance, actually," Ravyn said, cutting her off. "A pleasure to see you both," he said with no pleasure at all, pulling me away from my half sisters and deeper into the crowd.

The dance had already begun, the lutes and cymbals striking a steady rhythm. Ravyn and I slipped into the circle of dancers, his hand still entwined with mine. I did not miss the way more than one set of eyes followed us, whispers trailing our steps.

I clenched my jaw, my anger returning as the Captain and I paired off. He did not want to dance to appease my sisters, and he certainly had no interest in enjoying the frivolity of Equinox.

The only reason he held my hand—stood opposite me in front of half of Blunder—was to keep me from asking any more questions of him.

Whispers echoed all around us, their static rhythm in competition with the instruments. "Is this really necessary?" I said as we turned to the music, my dress moving at the hips as we turned in half circles, one direction, then the other.

Ravyn looked down his nose at me. I felt his hand press against the small of my back. "Trust me," he said. "Pretending is half the work."

I met his gaze. "But I don't trust you, Captain. How could I trust a man who hasn't been forthright with me?"

The dance slowed, the final notes near. Ravyn's hand slid

from the small of my back up my spine, slower than it should have. When he leaned in, his jaw scraped against my ear. "I'd call an admission of treason exceptionally forthright for one day, Miss Spindle," he whispered.

The song ended in a triumphant flurry, followed by the crash of drunken applause. Ravyn's hand slipped off my back. When our fingers fell apart, he ran a stiff hand over his forehead and through his black hair. His gray eyes traced the flush in my cheeks, the furrow in my brow, the line of my lips.

But he said nothing.

The air was stifling, stoked by the crowd and Ravyn Yew's silence. I lowered my brow and glared up at him for a final moment, then stalked back to the castle.

I found Emory and Elm seated near the great hall, no doubt on their way to Emory's chambers. They'd stopped to take a drinking break.

When Elm saw me, he cracked a grin, holding up his goblet in a mock toast. "To the lord and lady of the dance. Looks like you two made up."

I ignored his gaze and rubbed my neck, as if to erase the flush that had settled into my skin. My eyes turned to Emory, who had slipped out of his chair. When the boy saw me, his gray eyes widened.

"The Nightmare," he said, quoting *The Old Book of Alders*, swinging his finger at me as if he were conducting an invisible orchestra. "Be wary the dark. Be wary the fright. Be wary the voice that comes in the night."

"Enough, Emory," Elm groaned.

When Emory's smile deepened, the hairs along my neck stood on end. I was suddenly certain that when he'd touched my hand on the stairwell, Emory Yew and his strange, dark magic had truly seen every last one of my secrets.

"It twists and it calls, through shadowy halls. Be wary the voice that comes in the night."

Before I could say anything—before I could even shiver—Emory heaved, hunching his back, and coughed blood on the stone floor.

Shame, the Nightmare said. *I was just beginning to like him.*

PART II

The Mist

Chapter Fifteen

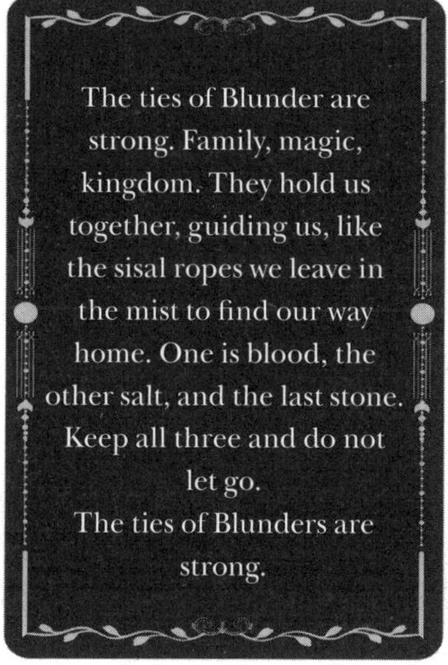

The ties of Blunder are strong. Family, magic, kingdom. They hold us together, guiding us, like the sisal ropes we leave in the mist to find our way home. One is blood, the other salt, and the last stone. Keep all three and do not let go.
The ties of Blunders are strong.

The horses did not slow to an easy pace until we were a mile away from Stone, just beyond the first hill. Only then did the eerie echo of Equinox disappear beneath the clamor of the Yew carriage.

It had not been an easy farewell. My aunt had clung to me, fresh tears in her eyes, though I'd promised we would be together again soon. My uncle had pulled her away, muttering something about it being a miracle the Yews even knew I existed, let alone wanted to facilitate a courtship with their eldest son. They left to retrieve Ione, but I did not linger to say goodbye. I could not lie to my cousin, not about the Yews, not about the horrid taste her betrothal to Hauth Rowan left in my mouth.

And I could not face her new appearance under the light of the Maiden Card, so changed from the Ione I'd grown up with.

The Yews had fared no better. Emory had spit up more blood and sobbed, inconsolable, when he finally remembered why he could not come with us. Elm volunteered to stay and comfort him, the Scythe the best tool in their arsenal to help get the boy the rest he desperately needed.

I sat in silence, the country road from Stone to town bumpy, the hour somewhere between midnight and dawn. I felt drained—tired and alone, the jostling of the carriage making it impossible to rest. When I reached into the darkness, I felt for the Nightmare—searching for something familiar.

He was there, curled up like a cat in the corner of my mind, quiet.

Across from me, Jespyr put her head on her mother's shoulder and closed her eyes. Fenir sat on her other side, gazing into the blackness outside the carriage window.

I bore the misfortune, orchestrated no doubt by his sister, of sharing a bench with Ravyn. We sat in frosty silence, pressed as far away from one another as the carriage width would allow. I did not look at him. I had not looked at him since we'd left the King's gardens.

But that did nothing to erase the anger I felt, unbidden and unexplained, toward the Captain of the Destriers and his heavily warded secrets. Neither could it erase the memory of his fingers laced with mine—the way the tepid garden air caught in my throat when he pulled me close.

I heaved a rattled sigh to dispel the unwelcome fluttering in my chest. Morette looked up at me, mistaking my restlessness for concern. "Our home is old and strange," she told me, her voice warm. "But Castle Yew is safe. You'll be comfortable there."

No one spoke the rest of the way. By the time the wheels struck cobblestone, I was pinching myself to stay awake.

The carriage jerked to a halt.

I stared into the blackness. A wrought-iron fence surrounded a castle at the top of the hill. Behind it stood a statuary, the statues and hedge maze shadowed under the ominous height of ancient yew trees.

Fenir pulled a skeleton key from his belt, unlocking the gate, holding the iron open just long enough for the carriage to slip inside the grounds.

Angels and gargoyles stared down at me from their places in the statuary. I shuddered, recalling how often my aunt had told me Castle Yew was haunted.

We quit the carriage. When we got to the tall, fortified door, Fenir banged three times with an open palm on the ancient oak.

His steward greeted us, opening the door wide and beckoning us inside. "I was expecting you sooner," he said, shadows dancing across his face in the dimly lit castle.

"We had trouble with Emory," Morette said, her voice heavy.

The steward turned to me. He was a round man, no taller than I, stout, with heavy gray eyebrows that hovered over wide, focused eyes. When he smiled, his mustache twitched. "Welcome to Castle Yew, milady. My name is Jon Thistle."

I tried to return the smile, but it came out a yawn. "Elspeth."

"You must be exhausted," Thistle said. "Allow me show you to your room."

The castle door closed with a slam. "I'll take her," Ravyn said. He reached for a nearby candlestick and lit the wicks, waiting a moment for the flame to catch, shadows flickering across his features—brow and nose and jaw sharp in the dim light. Eyes narrowed and cold.

He moved through the hall, past the slumbering hearth to the long, winding stairwell, once again leaving me no choice but to follow him.

I trailed him with heavy steps, shooting daggers into his back. I wanted to shout, to break the glass of his control. But I could not find the words. The day had stolen them. And the night had buried them.

Weariness was king, and I his servant.

Ravyn took me down a dark corridor with jumping lanterns and strange, unnerving portraits to the last door in a long row. The Nightmare sniffed the air, tapping his teeth together as I took in my surroundings. His pupils flared, easing the darkness of the castle.

We stopped in the middle of a long hall of rooms. Ravyn opened a door, the hinge creaking its welcome. I stepped into the room, gray moonlight seeping through the window. I turned to close the door, but the Captain remained at the threshold, his brow strained.

My voice was sharp. "Anything else?"

He ran a hand over his jaw and shook his head. "It was not my intention to be unfeeling, Miss Spindle," he said, a bite to his words. "I've had to pretend for so long, hidden parts of myself—my magic—so deep, I've forgotten how to talk about them." His eyes met mine, searching me for something I could not name. "Can you understand that?"

I could. Better than most. Hadn't I hidden my ability to absorb Providence Cards from Ravyn from the very start? Hadn't I lied to his family and told them I could see Providence Cards when, in truth, the five-hundred-year-old monster in my head was doing that for me? I carried my own lies by omission, kept my own secrets. Dark, dangerous secrets.

Which perhaps was why Ravyn Yew enraged me so deeply. It

was easier to hate him for being secretive and dishonest than admitting I hated myself for the same reasons.

But I could not tell him that. I could hardly say it to myself.

I stepped forward, forcing Ravyn out of the room, feigning a civility I did not feel. "Your house seems very private—fixed at the edge of town, so close to the woods. Far from wagging tongues."

Brow furrowed, Ravyn's eyes dragged across my face, as if I were a book written in a language he could not decipher. "And?"

It felt good, watching him struggle to read me. He'd wounded my pride. And now, my pride called for blood. "It relieves the burden of a pretend courtship—which, as I understand, is abhorrent to you." My smile did not touch my eyes. "Here, away from the gossip, we needn't pretend to be anything we're not."

Ravyn's eyes did not leave my face. If my words had stung him, his stonelike features bore no tell. He leaned forward. "And what are we, Miss Spindle?"

The intensity of his gaze sent me back a step. "Nothing," I said. Then, for spite, "Isn't that what you wanted?"

Something flared in Ravyn's gray eyes. Not anger—but just as strong. For a moment, strain broke across his fixed expression. His fingers flexed along the candlestick, his shoulders rigid—his body tense, and honed entirely on me.

But he said nothing—offered no explanation, no denial.

His silence held an edge. It cut at my insides, a bitter sting. In my attempt to wound him, I had only injured myself. "That's what I thought," I snapped, slamming the door in the Captain of the Destriers' face.

The dream was a ghost, and when I woke, it slipped away, vanished on chill air that had settled into my room during the night. I wrapped myself in blankets and tried to go back to sleep, but there was no peace to claim, and I lay there fretting, cold and worrisome, afraid of what the day might bring. Afraid, yet filled with anticipation.

I'd slept in my Equinox dress. When I sat up, there were lines in my arms were the fabric had dug into my skin.

The room was dark, the curtains drawn. But a rhythm inside me told me it was long past daybreak. I sat up and looked around, bleary-eyed. "A little help," I said aloud.

He didn't answer at first. *Can't you do it yourself?*

"And deny you the pleasure of gloating over my helplessness?"

The Nightmare snorted. Then, as if snapping a switch in the back of my head, my pupils widened like a cat's, revealing the shape of the room—the contours in the furniture—the dimmest hints of light slipping out from beneath the curtains.

I had not taken much note of the room last night, collapsing onto the bed and resigning to sleep the moment I'd slammed the door in Ravyn Yew's face. My chamber was small but ornate, the furnishings elegant—the bed frame engraved with a delicate, swirling design. The chair in the corner was upholstered with a green-and-gold brocade. An eagle was carved into the mahogany mantel, its beak parted and its talons curled. The drapes were a rich crimson, and the carpet had been woven into an elaborate landscape, depicting a gilded knight atop a black horse.

I stared at the carpet, still half-lost to sleep, tracing the man on the horse. I could not see his face—the visor of his helmet was shut. It was his armor that caught me.

Even woven in wool, it was bright, gold, beautiful.

A knock on my door ripped me from my thoughts. Before

I could answer, the door pushed open, heavy boots clomping toward me. "Elspeth—Oh shit, sorry—I thought you'd be awake."

Jespyr.

I cleared my throat. "I'm awake."

She paused. "And you're just sitting here? In the dark?"

Not exactly. "I was just getting up."

Jespyr stepped into the room, dragging something behind her. When she drew the curtains, gray morning light flooding the room, she dropped the heavy object near the foot of the bed.

My trunk, filled with all the clothes I'd brought with me to Equinox.

"Thank you." I winced against the morning light and hung my legs over the side of the bed. I gestured to the carpet. "Jespyr, who is that?"

Her eyes traced the man in armor. "Supposedly, he's the Shepherd King. We've plenty of his likeness in this castle, collected by centuries of Yews."

I frowned, searching the wool. It felt like a forgotten dream, looking at the man with gilded armor. A reflection in water too murky to make out.

The Nightmare paced behind my eyes, guarding himself with a heavy, resolute silence.

"I've got something else for you," Jespyr said, saying nothing to the fact I was still in yesterday's clothes. She pulled an envelope out of her tunic pocket. "It arrived this morning."

By its hurried scribbles, ink splattered across the parchment where she'd flung the quill, I'd recognized the handwriting immediately.

The letter was from my aunt.

I tore through the envelope, suddenly painfully homesick.

Darling Elspeth,

I'm happy, though a touch surprised, that you have found friendship with Ravyn Yew. He seems a strange, severe man. But the Yews are regarded well, and his mother, Morette, is a good woman. I pray you feel at home in their company, and that it is a warm and welcome change.

With you at Castle Yew and Ione and your uncle to remain at the King's court, Hawthorn House will feel quite lonely. I find myself wishing I could set the clocks back—that we had decided not to attend Equinox and everything had remained the same. But those are just the ramblings of an old woman, set in her ways. If anyone deserves a change of scenery, Elspeth, it's you.

Be safe, my love. And, if you will, humor an old woman—be careful in Castle Yew. There is old magic there.

She signed with a familiar Blunder motto.

Be wary. Be clever. Be good.
Opal

I played with the frayed ends of the parchment, my heart heavy.

She's worried.

We all have our woes, the Nightmare yawned.

It's good I came here, I said. *It was the right thing to do. Helping them find the Cards… helping Emory, helping myself, after so many years of hiding away with the Hawthorns… it was the right thing to do.*

Are you trying to convince me or yourself?

The bed shifted, Jespyr landing with a plop at the foot. "Is it bad news?"

I shook my head. "A letter from my aunt. She must have written it after we left Stone last night."

"Keeps a tight leash on you, does she?"

I shook my head again. "I don't spend much time away from her. She worries." Then, after a pause, "Everything's changing. Ione's engaged to a Prince. I'm here, plotting with your family." I wrinkled my nose. "I'm worried about Ione—about my aunt—about getting caught. About everything."

Flecks of gold in Jespyr's brown eyes shone in the morning light, her irises full of fire, so different from the silver moonlight that shone in Ravyn's and Emory's gray eyes. Her dark hair was wavy, save a few wild curls that framed her face. It was cut shorter than the fashion and tied behind her neck by a strip of leather. Her tunic, a deep green with white trim, rested loosely along her lean frame.

When she smiled at me, unrestrained, I could not help but smile back.

"I worry, too." She leaned back. "I worry about Emory. I worry about Elm and Ravyn and myself, that the King or Hauth or the other Destriers will discover our double lives. That we'll be caught. I worry all the time."

"How do you manage it?"

She shrugged, crossing a dirty boot over her knee. "I tell myself I am stronger than my doubts—that I'm good. Even if it doesn't always feel that way." She opened her mouth to say something else, but she seemed to catch her tongue. Her eyes widened and she stared at me, her gaze caught on my face.

I squirmed. "Jespyr?"

"Sorry," she said, blinking. "The light in here is playing tricks on me. For a moment your eyes almost looked yellow."

It took all my years of practice to keep my expression steady. I blinked, a nervous giggle rising in my throat. "How strange."

But Jespyr didn't seem to notice my discomfort. "But I've forgotten my purpose. Elspeth, I came to fetch you."

"Oh?"

"Sylvia Pine and her daughters are traveling home early from Equinox. My mother spoke to Sylvia last night and invited them to stop for tea on their way back from Stone." She stood, her steps light—excited. "You and I will join them."

Trees, the Nightmare muttered, scraping his claws. *Now we must play at tea with Blunder's bottom-feeders? You said joining these fools would be dangerous. You said nothing of torture.*

I made a face. "Are you close with the Pines?"

"Not at all." Jespyr brushed a curl from her eyes. "Sylvia is an odious woman. Her daughters are more tolerable, if we manage to find something worth discussing." She gestured to herself—her tunic and leggings, her muddy boots. "I don't have much in common with them."

"I don't see what help I'll be. I'm—erm—not much of a talker."

The Nightmare snorted in my ear.

"Ah, but this time," Jespyr said, "we'll have something to talk about." To my blank expression, she laughed. "I keep forgetting you have no idea what's going on."

I crossed my arms over my chest. "And whose fault is that?"

She gave a wry smile. "Right. Sorry." She cleared her throat. "My mother invited Sylvia Pine because we believe it is very likely her husband, Wayland, owns an Iron Gate Card. Sylvia may be a tight-lipped crone, but her daughters, bless their simple hearts, are delightful chatterboxes."

My brow perked. "And if they tell us where their father keeps his Iron Gate?"

She smiled that contagious smile. "Then we're one step closer to stealing it."

Chapter Sixteen

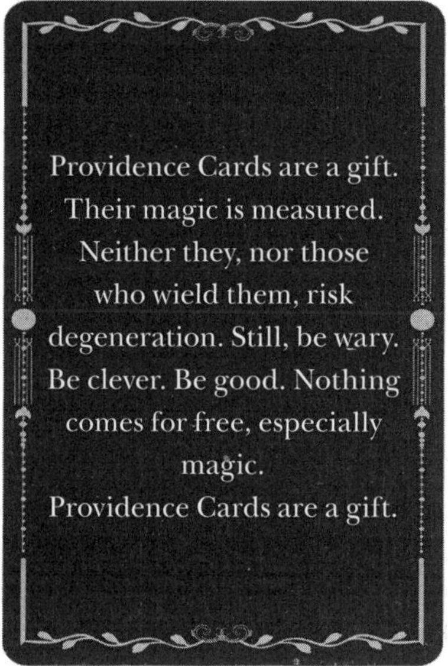

Morette, Jespyr, and I waited in the parlor, seated strategically one chair apart around a spacious oval table. I wore a dark gray dress paired with a white shawl my aunt had knit, a Hawthorn tree embroidered in its center. I wrapped the shawl around my neck and chest, reveling in its warmth, needing the comfort.

Across from me, Jespyr tugged at her frilled collar. Her mother had insisted, since wearing a dress was out of the question, that she don something more formal than her usual attire, which Morette had deemed with an upturned nose "woolens unfit for a stable boy."

Morette's eyes flared when she glanced at her daughter. "Are you drinking?"

Jespyr shoved a hip flask under the table. "No."

"It's not even midday!"

"Think of it as medicine." When her mother shot her a look cold as murder, Jespyr threw up her hands. "You can't expect me to endure Sylvia Pine without a single drop of alcohol."

"We won't be enduring her long if she thinks my daughter is a drunkard."

Jespyr tossed me the flask. I caught it, its contents swishing in the small leather encasement. I smelled wine. "Have some," Jespyr said. "Trust me, it'll help."

I glanced down at the flask, Morette's eyes boring into me from the other side of the table.

Go on, then, the Nightmare said. *Anything to put me out of my misery.*

Shut it, grumpy.

I undid the stopper and pressed the lid to my lips. The wine was warm, rich—too strong for so early in the day—but a pleasant burn nonetheless. "Will anyone else be joining us?"

Jespyr eyed me from across the table. "Like who?" Her lips curled, mischievous as a goblin. "Like Ravyn?"

I tossed the flask back, hard. Jespyr caught it with one hand, doing a poor job of tucking her smile away. "He rode back to Stone early this morning. No rest for the Captain."

The sound of the carriage wheels rumbled. All three of our heads turned to the parlor door. Outside, hooves clattered against stone. The wheels stopped and the horses whickered, only to be drowned out by the sound of high-pitched chittering, several voices competing for air.

The Pine women had arrived.

"Remember," Morette said in a low voice. "Concealment is key. Don't make it obvious you are interested in the Iron Gate. Just get them to *talk*."

Their steward opened the parlor door with a bang, so abrasive the silver tea set vibrated. He wasn't a delicate man, Jon Thistle. "Lady Sylvia Pine and her daughters, milady."

"Thank you, Jon," Morette said. Her brows raised. A nod, a smile, a soft gesture to the table. The performance had begun. "Please have a seat, Sylvia. Farrah, Gerta, Maylene, please make yourselves comfortable."

We were flanked by the Pine women. I was seated between Lady Pine and her middle daughter, Gerta. Jespyr sat between the eldest Pine girl, Farrah, and the youngest, Maylene, who was no older than my half sisters.

In the brief moment when the chairs had stopped scraping, before anyone spoke, the silence in the room felt so oppressive I felt it might strangle me. I shot Jespyr a frantic look, but she—fearsome Jespyr Yew, Blunder's only female Destrier—looked as uncomfortable as I felt, gnawing on her fingernail, eyes like a trapped animal's.

Jon bustled around us, pouring the tea. For such an unfinished-looking man, he did not spill a single drop. Morette cleared her throat. "Did you ladies enjoy Equinox?"

Lady Pine opened her pursed lips to answer, but her voice was drowned out by her daughters, who talked over one another like yowling cats, each boasting an Equinox story greater than the next.

I was pinned by Gerta, who leaned close to me and told me, with painstaking embellishments, the exact detailing of her three Equinox dresses. I wouldn't have minded so much—there are worse things to discuss than clothing—if the Nightmare hadn't been gnashing his teeth the entire time.

Death by a thousand cuts, he groaned. *Ask her where the bloody Iron Gate is and be done with it.*

And invite a world of suspicion once it's stolen? Just because they talk too much doesn't make them idiots.

That's precisely what it makes them.

I rested my cheek on my hand, checking that my face was still calm—neutral.

"Speaking of beautiful frocks," Gerta said, taking a long sip of tea, "your cousin Ione looked beyond stunning when they announced her engagement." Her brow wrinkled, straw-yellow hair falling over her eyes. She swept it away. "I don't remember her looking quite so becoming—and I saw her at court nigh last year."

A rock dropped in my stomach. I didn't want to talk about much, but I especially didn't want to talk about Ione.

Is this why they wanted my help—to use my relationship with Ione to stir talk of Cards? I glanced at Morette. *Seems a bit unfeeling.*

A family trait, perhaps.

I turned back to Gerta, picking up my teacup, my voice even. "Ione is luckier than most. She was given a Maiden upon their betrothal."

Gerta's face bloomed, her eyes wide, her lips curling up, the gossip so sweet it was as if I'd handed her the key to the city. "She's got a Maiden Card?"

"Indeed." I reached to the platter of sweetbread in the center of the table, though my stomach was in knots and I couldn't take a bite. "It was part of the arrangement my uncle made. He gifted the King his Nightmare Card. The rest you saw at Equinox."

Gerta nodded. She glanced around the room. "And you, Elspeth? You've done well enough for yourself as well—invited to stay in a castle most of us have never seen the inside of." She took a sip of tea. "Has your father done the same and offered the Captain of the Destriers a Card as your dowry?"

I coughed. Across the table, Jespyr glanced at me. Heat climbed, unwelcome, into my cheeks. "I'm not betrothed to anyone," I managed. "Especially not Ravyn Yew."

Gerta gave me a knowing smile. "Of course not."

Noise from around the table buzzed, but I tried to ignore the others' voices. The Nightmare scratched his claws idly across my mind. *Keep going*, he said, his voice slick with oil.

I took a deep breath. "Then again," I said to Gerta, "my father was given a Card as my mother's dowry. I suppose someday it will be mine." I smiled, praying I looked welcoming and not too eager. "Does your father have Cards set aside for your dowry?"

Gerta took a bite of bread, covering her mouth with her hand when she spoke. "In theory." She rolled her eyes. "Though I suspect Papa is too fond of them to let them go. He's always carrying them with him, wherever he goes—like a boy with his toys."

My heart quickened. But Gerta's face remained soft, her tone conversational, her eyes easy at the corners. She showed no sign of knowing she'd revealed too much. I shot Jespyr a tight look. Her brown eyes caught mine, her brow perked.

We were close.

"Who could blame him?" I said, ripples forming in my tea from my shaking hand. I put the cup down. "Are they very rare, his Cards?"

"Not enough for him to make such a fuss over," Gerta said, forlorn. "Just a measly Prophet." She took a sip of tea. I held my breath. "That and an Iron Gate. Pity, isn't it? I would so love a Maiden, like Ione."

I smiled. Only this time, it wasn't pretend. "Pity."

We waved at the Pine carriage as it passed through the statuary, stilling our hands only when it disappeared into evening shadow, made darker by the looming yew trees above the drive.

"Come," Morette said, her stern mouth bent by a grin. "Fenir will want to know at once."

Castle Yew was dark, old, rich, and oddly delicate. Its ceilings were vaulted, so high I had to crane my neck to see them. Along every way there hung tapestries, some depicting maidens and landscapes and woodland creatures, others Providence Cards.

And some, always with his visor shut, the same knight with gilded armor from the carpet in my room.

I smelled leather and wood and cloves, warm, rich, old. I fought the urge to walk the corridors on tiptoe, my echo so unusual against the castle walls it might have been a specter tucked away behind tapestries, lingering along the long corridors.

The Nightmare's wakefulness was stirred by the strange, aged stone. I could feel the flutter of his consciousness—his curiosity. I followed Morette and Jespyr up a second winding staircase. I ran my hand along the stonework, smelling the cherrywood banisters, watching the fading sunlight cast itself on thousands of tiny dust particles.

The staircase led us to a balcony, laden with books, and a wide entryway. The doors, wood and engraved with designs I did not understand, looked extremely heavy. They stood ajar. Morette did not bother to knock, her shoulders flexing as she pushed them open.

Evening light poured into the wide room from a row of arched windows. Ceiling-to-floor shelves filled with candles, plants—alive or dried—and books covered all four walls, save in front of the windows. A partition, painted with the yew tree insignia, kept me from seeing much of the bed.

Fenir Yew sat at the long chestnut table in the center of the room, poring over scattered parchment. When he looked up and saw us, his brown eyes widened. "Well?"

Jespyr vaulted toward the table. She took a chair and spun

it on a single leg until it faced the table backward. She sat with a plop, folding her arms over the back of the chair. "Wayland Pine has an Iron Gate. On his person. Right now."

Fenir's eyes shot to Morette. "Truly?"

She nodded. "He's still at Stone, enjoying Equinox. He's set to travel home tomorrow."

It was strange, watching Fenir Yew smile. I wouldn't have guessed a face that severe could boast one. But it suited him. For a moment, I saw Emory in his face.

"We'll have to let Ravyn and Elm know at once."

"Should they act before Pine leaves Stone?"

Fenir shook his head. "Too many opportunities to get caught. Better out in the open, where they can be properly disguised." He turned to his daughter. "You must go tell them."

Jespyr ran a hand over her brow. "No rest for the Captain, nor his sister, it seems." She pushed out of her chair with a sigh. When she passed me, she put a hand on my shoulder. "Good work today. Rest up. You're going to need it."

She slipped out of the room. I watched her, a question stirring my thoughts. I took the chair she'd abandoned, pulling myself to the table. "These men whose Cards you take," I said to Fenir, "men like Pine. Do you hurt them?"

Fenir raised his brows. "You take us for brute thugs, Miss Spindle?"

I raised my brows back at him. "Two of your children are Destriers, are they not?"

Morette cleared her throat. "That's where you come in, Miss Spindle. With your keen eyes, we should be able to locate and retrieve the Card as hastily as possible. Violence is something we avoid."

I shifted in my chair, Ravyn's ivory-hilted dagger flashing across my mind.

"My steward will join us in a moment." Fenir walked to a far shelf and pulled free an old, sooty tome. "But while we wait, there is something I'd like you to see, Miss Spindle."

The tome's leather cover was embroidered with two alder trees, tall and narrow, which stood next to each other in perfect unison. One tree was sewn with black fabric, the other—grayed with age—with white. It was older than my aunt's copy, its binding more frayed.

I recognized it immediately.

Fenir placed the volume upon the table. "Have you studied *The Old Book of Alders*, Miss Spindle?"

I wanted to laugh. Had he asked it of me, I could have recited the text from cover to cover. "A bit."

Fenir opened the cover and coughed, turning the aged parchment until he'd reached the last page. He read it aloud.

The twelve call for each other when the shadows grow long—
When the days are cut short and the Spirit is strong.

They call for the Deck and the Deck calls them back.
Unite us, they say, and we'll cast out the black.

At the King's namesake tree, with the black blood of salt,
All twelve shall, together, bring sickness to halt.

They'll lighten the mist from mountain to sea.
New beginnings—new ends...

But nothing comes free.

"The Cards, the mist, the blood," I said under my breath.

Morette joined us at the table. "Kings of Blunder have long tried to do what the Shepherd King instructed. But none could bring the Deck of Twelve together. None could find the Twin Alders."

I tapped my fingers on the table. "Does King Rowan know where to find it?"

"No," Fenir answered. "He consults with the kingdom's best cartographers. They gather over an old map of Blunder. Over the years, the map has been colored in with all the places the King's men have searched. Still, no Twin Alders. There is no record of it being traded, no history of its use. The only two documents that even speak of it are *The Old Book of Alders* and the history of Brutus Rowan, the first Rowan King."

The Nightmare hissed through his teeth at the Rowan King's name. It took all of me not to react. "And what does Brutus say about the Twin Alders?" I asked.

"The same thing everyone else says," Morette replied. "That the Shepherd King took it into the mist one day and returned without it."

I frowned. "Surely the Shepherd King has his own history—his own documents."

Fenir's voice was grave. "Most of what we know of the Shepherd King we take from lore. His histories were destroyed, and none of his children survived to claim the throne. Brutus Rowan, his Captain of the Guard, became the next King of Blunder."

The Nightmare's tail twitched, stirring the darkness in my mind.

I paused. "Suppose we manage to find the Twin Alders." I looked up at the Yews. "Whose blood do you intend to use to unite the Deck?"

Fenir leaned forward. "You may have met him. He's head of the King's Physicians."

The tall, narrow man with eerily pale eyes. "Orithe Willow?" I cried. "He's infected?"

Fenir picked up *The Old Book of Alders*, gingerly placing it back onto his shelf. "Like yourself," he said, "Orithe caught the infection as a child. But the King kept him alive for one reason. Orithe's magic allows him to spot the infection in others. Surely you've seen the apparatus he wears around his hand?"

I had. It was a metal claw, with long, angry spikes reaching out from each of his pale fingers. I felt the blood drain from my face. "Orithe uses that—that device—to see the infection in others?"

Fenir's voice was grave. "He claims he can see the infection in their blood." His brow lowered in a deep frown. "He hunts and bleeds anyone he suspects has caught the fever. That is why the King appointed him head of the Physicians."

I placed my fingers along my temples to soothe my spinning head. "Spare Emory's blood, spill Orithe's," I murmured. *A man responsible for the deaths of dozens of infected children. Two birds . . .*

One stone, said the Nightmare.

Fenir's steward opened the door. Jon Thistle regarded me with a nod, then placed a leather pouch teeming with brilliant colors onto the table ahead of Fenir.

Light filled the room as Fenir opened the pouch. "Our collection, Miss Spindle," he said.

I surveyed the Cards through a squint. "They're not all here."

"No," Morette said. "The Destriers keep their Black Horses close. And Elm, as you know by now, is reticent to go anywhere without the Scythe. The Mirror and the Nightmare are often with Ravyn."

I searched the colors, blinked, then searched again.

Gray, the Prophet.

Pink, the Maiden.

Turquoise, the Chalice.

Yellow, the Golden Egg.

White, the White Eagle.

"Three Cards are missing," Fenir said. "The Well, the Iron Gate, and the Twin Alders."

I stared at the pile, the unity of colors strange and beautiful, like a stained glass window. "Do you have a plan for finding the Well?"

"The Well will be tricky to claim," Jon Thistle said, rubbing his beard. "Given the nature of the Card, men keen to have it are usually wary to begin with."

The Yews were quiet, their brows knit.

I chewed my lip, clicking my fingernails against the table. The Nightmare slithered behind my eyes, waiting for me to speak. When I did not, his voice filled my mind like steam off a kettle. *Go on,* he said. *Tell them.*

My eyes fell back to the collage of color radiating off the Providence Cards. The Cards. The mist. The blood.

I raised my gaze to the Yews. "I know someone who owns a Well Card," I said. "He lives just down the street."

Chapter Seventeen

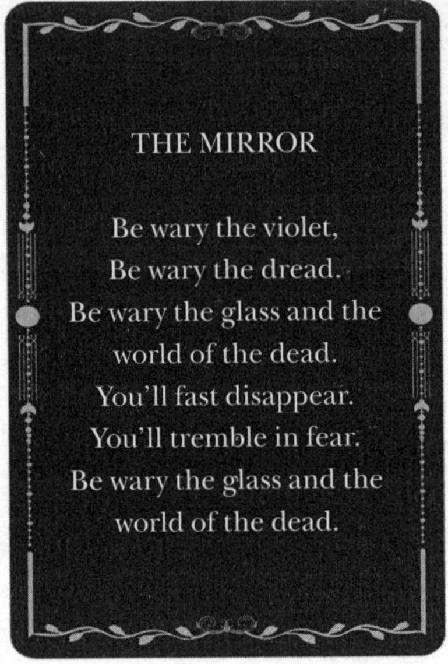

Ravyn returned to Castle Yew the next morning.

I heard the clatter of hooves. I slammed shut the tome I was reading and slunk out of the library in a cloud of dust, navigating the back passages and hallways of the castle until I found a small wooden door that led straight from the castle into the wild gardens beyond.

Ducking beneath an old willow tree, I let out a long breath and threw myself onto the lowest of the branches, the bite of morning frost stinging my fingers and cheeks.

The Nightmare hummed, his words slippery. *The Captain of the Destriers is dark and severe. Perched atop yew trees, his gray eyes are clear. Be wary his magic, be wary his fate. The Yews and the Rowans do not ready friends make.*

Be quiet, I said, slapping the branch above my head, morning dew falling onto my brow. *I don't want to talk about it.*

But I didn't need to talk about it. Ever since the night I was attacked on the forest road, the line between talking and thinking had begun to blur. The more I asked for his help, the more potent the Nightmare's presence in my head became. I understood his emotions—his interests and revulsions—without words, sometimes so strongly I mistook them for my own. I felt his wakefulness, his focus. I saw more clearly—heard more soundly—with his senses.

But I did not fully know his mind. There were still secrets between us.

Mourning doves cooed, the noises of dawn lively in the garden. I snapped thin reeds off the willow tree and wove them into a simple crown and placed it on my head. Charm in hand, I slid from my seat out into the mist, searching the garden for wild carrot blooms.

As far as I could tell, Castle Yew housed no gardeners. As orderly as he kept the castle, Jon Thistle's attentions did not extend beyond the statuary. The gardens were wild. I liked that about them. Unlike the manicured hedges and blooms at Stone, Castle Yew's eclectic assortment of herbs, weeds, and blooms looked as if they might rise up and take the castle by storm—wild and strong and free.

The cobbled path had been absorbed by plant life. I slipped over mossy stonework and trod deeper into the greenery in search of flowers.

But it was the wrong time of year for blossoms. Soon the wild soul of the garden would grow tired and retreat deep into itself, the looming chill of winter drawing closer each night. I had to look deep within the bramble for blooms, only the most protected plants still willing to share their flowers with me. Crouched on my knees, I spotted a cluster of purple phlox and added several flowers to the weave of my willow crown.

A sharp pain stung my hand. I whirled, unaware I'd rested it on a rose bramble, its buds harvested by hungry deer. Only one flower remained. Red as blood, so fresh I could almost feel its smell, the rose stood alone among the thorns, as if waiting.

I did not pluck it. I'd had my fair share of punishment going after roses without gloves or shears. Still, I found myself running a finger up the stock of the stem, testing its fortitude, the sharpness of its thorns pressed precariously into my flesh.

"Those thorns are vicious," a deep, familiar voice called.

I spun, my heart in my throat.

Ravyn stood a few paces away, his boots, cloak, and hair made darker by the morning rain. In his pocket beamed familiar burgundy and purple hues, brighter than any flower in the garden. On his belt rested the ivory hilt of his dagger, and when he drew it, my muscles tensed, the memory of the blade's tip at my heart still vivid.

But the blade did not touch me. Stepping to my side, Ravyn took the rose by the base and lifted it from the bramble of thorns, freeing it with a single cut. He held it for a moment and said nothing, the silence between us loud enough to drown out even the most enthusiastic morning birds.

When he finally spoke, his voice was rough, as if unused. "Are you well?"

My voice hitched, still shaken by his sudden arrival. "Yes."

"My family is seeing to your needs?"

"I haven't starved, if that's what you mean." I pulled out my charm and twisted it between my fingers. "They've been kind. I'm embarrassed to think I was afraid to walk by your gates as a girl." I looked out into the garden. "It's very beautiful."

"Why were you afraid?"

I shrugged. "My aunt told me the castle is haunted."

The corner of Ravyn's mouth tugged. "I wouldn't be so quick to refute her." His eyes roved my face, flickering to the flower crown atop my head. Neither of us spoke, a day apart enough time to make strangers out of us once more.

If we'd ever been anything else.

He took a step forward, holding the blood-red rose in his hand out to me. "May I?"

I looked at the rose, then back at his face. Trees, that face. Austerity and beauty. An imperfect, breathtaking statue. "I thought we weren't pretending," I murmured.

He stripped the rose's thorns with his blade. "It's just a flower. Flowers don't play games." He offered it again, once more asking my permission. "May I?"

This time, I nodded. He stepped to me and placed the rose atop my head, weaving its stem into the willow crown with strong, deft fingers. When he pulled back, his hand grazed the hair along my cheek.

I kept still. I could smell the wet wool of his cloak—smoke and cloves. "How did you know I was here?"

"You weren't in your room." He gestured around the garden. "If I was trying to avoid someone, this is where I would go."

I opened my mouth, but nothing came out. There was no point lying.

He offered a small smile. "Would you like a tour?"

I looked around, the garden soft in the mist. "I didn't realize there was an allotted design."

"Quite the opposite," Ravyn said. "Which makes it the most interesting part of the estate. Only don't tell Thistle. He'll take enormous offense."

The corners of my lips twitched.

"You won't need that," Ravyn said as I pocketed the crow's foot. "You haven't needed it for eleven years."

I stared at him. "But the mist—The Spirit of the Wood—"

"Does not catch people like us," he said.

"But the book says—"

"You and I already carry strange magic. We're the very things the book warns against, Miss Spindle." He smiled, gesturing away from the house into the garden. "We needn't be afraid of a little salt in the air."

Ravyn didn't know the names of the plants or the flowers. The trees, of course, he knew. I followed him at a distance, listening to his voice as I took in the garden. Weeds clung to the hem of my skirt, and untrimmed branches reached for my hair as we trod deeper into the thicket, the brambles unaccustomed to visitors—the path almost hidden.

"Where does this lead?" I asked, untangling my hair from a low-hanging branch.

"The ruins," Ravyn answered. "The original castle. Or what's left of it."

Piqued, the Nightmare's interest spurred my steps, and I followed the Captain of the Destriers through a particularly dense thicket to a meadow beyond. My eyes widened as I took in the landscape—the dewy grass, the enormous trees, and the graveyard of stonework: the last remains of a crumbled castle, nestled in the mist.

The stones stood, strangely balanced, in the meadow.

I trod on tiptoe among the crumbling limestone pillars laid out across the grass, afraid even my footsteps might topple them. "I didn't realize there was another castle here," I murmured.

Ravyn nodded. "It's old—older than Stone. No one knows exactly when it was forged. Or when the fire felled it." He pointed to the east beyond the ruins, a rusted iron fence poking through the mist. "Only one room remains."

The Nightmare clawed through my mind and inhaled deeply, the salt in the air strong. I leaned against one of the pillars but jerked away a moment later—afraid I'd knock it down with my weight.

Ravyn watched me. "It's all right," he said. "They've been here hundreds of years. They won't fall."

The sandstone was rough under my palm. I slid my hand along the pillar's perimeter, surveying the ruins with wide eyes. "What's that?" I asked, gesturing to a stone chamber nestled beneath the shadow of a tall, ancient yew tree.

"The last room left standing."

The stone chamber—enveloped by moss and vines—stood tall at the edge of the mist. How strange it looked, alone in the ruins, unmarked but for one dark window situated on its southernmost wall.

The Nightmare's tail whipped through my mind, the chamber fixed in our shared vision. *Go in*, he said.

Go in where? My eyes caught on the ivy-laden room. *There?*

Yes.

Why?

I want to see it.

There is no door. Only—

A window. His voice swarmed in my ears, near and far at once, slick with oil. *That's all she ever required.*

Who?

The Spirit of the Wood.

The hair at my spine prickled. *You've been here before?*

He laughed. But there was no joy in it. It was an empty laugh, ominous—like falling down a well. Like being eaten by darkness. It stole something from me, leaving me terrified of the place—the doorless chamber—he so desperately wanted me to take him.

My muscles strained, every part of my body begging to heed him—to go to the chamber. I clenched my jaw and turned away from the dark window at the lip of the tree line, denying the Nightmare his request.

A monstrous hiss echoed through my mind.

Ravyn kept talking, oblivious of my struggle. "The rumors are folklore, mostly," he said. He retrieved the purple Card from his pocket and twirled it absently in his hand. "If this place is truly haunted and ghosts linger here, they are not keen to show themselves. At least not to me."

I watched him, forcing my focus away from the Nightmare and the chamber, shifting to the light of the Mirror Card in Ravyn's hand. "What does it feel like," I said, my eyes tracing the amethyst velvet embroidered along the Card's edges, "being invisible?"

Ravyn twirled the Mirror between his fingers, flipping the Card between each digit so quickly it blurred.

Show-off, the Nightmare muttered.

The air around us shifted, and suddenly Ravyn was absorbed into the landscape—into nothingness. Disappeared. "It feels cold," his voice called through the air. "But not unbearably so."

"Can you see any... spirits?"

"Not yet," he said, his invisible steps treading a distinct path in the grass. "I'd have to remain invisible longer. I try not to use it too often."

The purple light moved closer. I turned, watching the light. A moment later, Ravyn reappeared, close to me, a mischievous grin on his mouth.

"You're the only one I can't sneak up on," he said.

My heart quickened, seeing his stern mouth turned by a smile. I stepped away, tarrying through the overgrown meadow, my mind laden with questions. "And the Nightmare Card?" I said. "You use that Card often enough."

He did not deny it.

"What of its ill effects?" I paused. I'd never spoken to anyone who had used a Nightmare Card before. And though I was certain the monster in my head was so much more than the Card I had absorbed, there was still so much I did not know. "Do you see a creature—hear a voice?"

Ravyn did not answer right away. "Every Card user experiences the negative effects differently."

"You're not very clear with your answers, Captain."

His gray eyes flashed to my face. "When I use the Nightmare Card too long, I don't see a creature. But I hear him. Does that answer satisfy you, Miss Spindle?"

Not by half. "What does he say to you?"

"It's hard to explain," he said, running a hand over his jaw. "Most of the time, he doesn't say anything. But when he does... it's like he knows everything I've ever thought—ever feared. He taunts me, telling me I'm going to fail—that my efforts are meaningless." His gray eyes met mine. "But it's just a voice, not a creature at all."

"How do you know?"

"Because when he speaks—relaying my worst fears over and over in my mind—it's not a stranger's voice," he said quietly. "It's mine."

Ravyn had returned to Castle Yew to steal the Iron Gate Card. Rather, to retrieve me, so that I might point out the Iron Gate

Card to him and his fellow—I wasn't sure what to call them. Thieves. Traitors. Highwaymen.

After Jespyr had relayed what we had learned at tea with the Pine women, Ravyn and Elm had set to mapping Wayland Pine's travel arrangements. He and a few fellow travelers would caravan from Stone to their separate estates, of which House Pine was the last. We would intercept Pine's carriage on the forest road. If we departed Castle Yew just after midday, we would have enough time to get to the Black Forest before nightfall. There, at the edge of the road, just beyond the tree line, we would wait for Wayland Pine.

And steal his Iron Gate.

Ravyn and I left the ruins through the mist, the same brambles hungry for my hair. I tripped on my skirt and would have fallen had there not been a firm boxwood to catch me. Winded, my dress wet and muddy at the hem, I stomped out of the thicket like an ogress, wild and weary.

Ravyn, having the good sense not to laugh, waited as I plucked brambles from my hair.

"Tell me, Miss Spindle," he said, watching me. "Have you ever used a blade before?"

I swore, a vengeful bramble taking some of my hairs with it. "Do garden shears count?"

This time, he did laugh. "Decidedly not."

We rounded the castle. Servants brushed past, offering Ravyn stooping bows. I could hear the clatter of hooves on stone and the yip of hounds in the distance, the soft quiet of the garden lost as we stepped out of the mist toward the cluster of outbuildings on the west side of the estate.

"Your father said there would be no violence. Am I expected to fight, Captain?"

"No," he said over his shoulder. "But I imagine you'd like something to protect yourself with just the same."

The path led us to the yard—the dirt arena situated in the heart of three outbuildings. On the yard's left stood the armory, and on its right, the stables. They sat nestled beneath the shadow of the castle, the hour not yet midday.

We came to the armory. Swords, knives, quivers, and arrows littered the walls, the shelves equipped with every tool and weapon a man-at-arms might wield. Jerkins, armor, and chainmail lay in crates along the floor, and in the center of the room stood a long oak slab held up by two barrels. Around the slab stood four men and a woman dressed in blackened leather. At the opening of the door, they turned to me with expectant eyes.

I surveyed them, my breath quick and shallow. Jespyr and Prince Renelm stood together, Jespyr equipped with a bow and quiver filled with goose-fletched arrows, Elm with his signature red glow. Next to them, two men I did not recognize looked up from a whetstone, appraising me with shifting eyes.

The last of the lot was Jon Thistle, who greeted me with a broad smile. "Pleased to see you, milady. Welcome to our fine collection of ruddy outlaws."

I heard Ravyn fasten the door behind us, torches and hearth the only sources of light in the armory. I took a step back, surveying the room a second time.

"That's Wik Ivy and his brother Petyr," Ravyn said in my ear. "Thistle you know, and of course my sister and cousin."

To my silence, the Captain of the Destriers smiled. "Come now, Miss Spindle. Surely you've seen a party of highwaymen before."

Chapter Eighteen

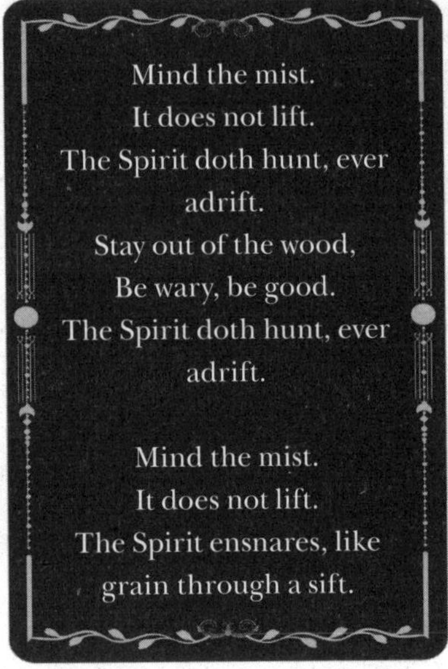

We'd been in the armory only a short while before Thistle, kind as he was, made it abundantly clear I was no use to them in a dress.

Elm snickered, his green eyes roving my body, resting on the flower crown in my hair. "But she's made such an effort to look pretty today."

Jespyr elbowed her cousin. "Shut it. We've enough to do without your tripe."

Two servants arrived, carrying a bundle—tunic, jerkin, cloak, leggings, and boots. Wool, linen, and leather, all black. One by one the others filed out, leaving Ravyn and me alone.

I frowned at my gray dress, its hem muddied by the tromp

through the garden. "I wasn't aware I'd dressed improperly," I said, suddenly deeply conscious of my appearance.

"We can't exactly wear our family seals, can we?" Ravyn said. He paused, gently extracting the flower crown from my hair. "I'll have your clothes sent back to your room. Join us when you're ready."

If he looked back at me as he slipped through the armory doors, I did not know it. I was trying with all my might not to look back at him.

Five minutes later I was leaning against the door, willing myself to open it.

The Nightmare shot hot air out his nostrils. *By the trees— They're just leggings, Elspeth.*

I felt exposed, naked without my wool skirt. I plaited a long knotted braid in my hair that started at the crown of my head and traveled like a rope down my back.

The Yew girl wears a tunic and pants. Why not you?

Jespyr's entirely more fearsome than I am. I glanced down at my legs. *I look like a bloody stable boy.*

How you look is—and perhaps always has been—utterly irrelevant.

I groaned, wishing him gone. Still, he was right. This wasn't about me. This was about Cards, mist, and blood. What did it matter if I was dressed in clothes suspiciously similar to those of a boy Emory's age? If I was going to take up with highwaymen, I had to look the part.

After a final rattling breath, I pushed my way through the armory door.

They waited, clustered at the entrance of the yard. When they saw me, one of the Ivy brothers whistled, only to be silenced by Jespyr's sharp elbow.

I didn't know where to look. "Well?" I stepped forward, my hands knotted in my sleeves. "Am I better suited for the task?"

I didn't miss the way Ravyn's eyes jumped up and down my body. "Much better," he said, a flush inching up his neck into his cheeks. He handed me two finely sewn gloves. "You'll need these."

I stared at them. "Riding gloves?"

"Did you think we'd be walking?" said Elm.

"We get to the Black Forest on horseback," Jespyr explained. "The rest of the way we travel on foot, out of sight in the mist. When Pine's carriage passes, we halt it. You tell us where to find his Iron Gate, and we're in and out in less than five minutes."

I surveyed the group. For a party without the intention of violence, they were curiously well armed. "Then what?"

"Then we'll come back," Elm said. "And you can tell us all about the Well Card in your father's house."

Ravyn, Elm, and I remained in the stable while the others retreated for final supplies. "You'll be needing a horse," Ravyn said, retrieving a brown mare from one of the stalls. When I paled and stepped away, he raised his brows. "Don't tell me you've never ridden a horse before?"

Elm's scoff filled the stable. "Good god, what were you doing all these years in the forest?"

I glanced at him through narrowed eyes. "Animals don't like me much."

The Prince took a seat atop a nearby bench. "If that doesn't tell you something," he said under his breath.

Ravyn ignored his cousin, holding out the reins to me. "Horses are skittish," he said. "You need to be calm—assured. Once she feels safe, she'll trust you." When I didn't reach for the reins, he leaned against the horse. "Do you want me to help you?"

It felt like a challenge. And how I wanted to deny him—to

see the impress on his face when I took the reins and mounted the beast without him. But I couldn't. I didn't know a damn thing about horses. "If it's not too much trouble, Captain."

His stone expression eased, the corner of his lips tugging. He'd won the challenge. He took my hand and pulled me next to him. "Put your hand here," he said, holding my gaze as he stripped away my glove. He placed my palm on the horse's flank just below the saddle. "Feel her breath, her energy."

The mare's eyes widened, her nostrils flaring as my hand roved across her side. My fingers moved across her broad back and the coarse mane along her neck. *Calm,* I told myself. *Calm, assured.*

It cannot be, the Nightmare purred. *She knows you're not alone. She knows she's not safe.*

The horse stirred and took a step away, raising her head and swishing her tail.

"Easy, girl," Ravyn said, patting her firmly. When she'd recovered, his gaze returned to me. "Shall I help you up?"

Trees, I was tired of giving him the satisfaction. "Fine," I said.

But in the end, the victory was mine. When Ravyn stepped to me, he hesitated, the flush from before returning to his jawline. Our eyes met a moment. Then, as if he was proving something to himself, he reached for me. His hands, broad and firm, met me at the dip of my waist, resting a moment on my hips. They were warm, his hands. And I caught myself wondering what the calluses along his palms would feel like against my bare skin.

He inhaled sharply, lifting me with ease and placing me on saddle. I sat there a moment, unsure what to do with my legs. It felt crass, swinging a leg over to ride astraddle, but instinct told me if I didn't, I would incur more scathing ridicule from Elm, who remained on the bench, his Princely face fixed in an expression somewhere between humor and revulsion.

But the moment I swung my leg over, my thighs flexing

around the saddle, I felt I'd made a terrible mistake. The smell of hay and sweat wafted off the mare, her skin flinching beneath my touch. I sat like a rock in the saddle, clinging for dear life to the horse's mane. "Where do I hold?"

"Try the reins," Elm called.

Ravyn put his hand on my ankle. "Take a breath, Miss Spindle. She's nervous because you're nervous."

"Or because she doesn't know what you are," Elm offered.

Trust me, she knows exactly what you are, the Nightmare cackled. *Watch this.*

His hiss radiated through me—an animal noise that seized my muscles—an invisible calling to the horse beneath me.

The mare reared, struck by a sudden panic that sent her screaming from the stable.

I didn't recall falling. Only that it hurt like hell.

When I came to, the horse was gone, and the low, silky laughter of the Nightmare echoed through my skull. Ravyn and Elm knelt at my sides, their eyes wide as they stared down at me.

"Trees." Ravyn tucked his hand behind my neck, cradling the top of my spine. "Can you hear me?"

I tried to sit up. Dizziness struck me, and I heaved a long, aching breath, wind rushing back into my lungs. "I—told—you," I wheezed. "Animals don't—like me."

Ravyn and Elm exchanged a glance. A small, mischievous smile crossed the Prince's lips. "Well," he said. "That was unexpected."

I coughed, pushing to an upright position. "Don't look so pleased."

Ravyn's hand slid from the back of my neck to my shoulder. "Anything feel broken?"

Only my pride, I fumed into the darkness. *What the hell was that?*

Just a bit of fun.

I could have died!

Don't be dramatic, the Nightmare said. *People fall off horses every day.*

That doesn't make it a particularly pleasant experience.

At least now you realize what you're getting yourself into—who you really are.

"Miss Spindle?"

I snapped back to Ravyn. "Nothing's broken," I said.

"She's fine," Elm yelled, footsteps rushing toward us.

Jespyr and Thistle skidded to a halt nearby. "You'll have a few bruises, no mistake," Thistle said.

I blushed red to my roots. "Did everyone see?"

"No," Elm said. "Just the servants, the fletcher, the groomsmen, the blacksmith—"

"Enough," Ravyn growled. "We've got to get going."

"We can't go now," Jespyr said, gesturing at me. "She'll fall to her death."

Elm yawned. "She'll be fine. Strap her to the beast and be done with it."

Nausea hit my stomach anew. "Strap me?"

"No one's going to strap you in," Thistle said. "What about a carriage?"

Elm shook his head. "They'll hear us a mile out."

They debated transportation. I said nothing, keeping my eyes straight ahead as I inched my fingers up and down my ribs, wincing.

There would surely be bruises.

"I still think we should use a carriage," Jespyr said. "If we stash it a mile into the wood, they won't hear it."

"And if they see fit to chase us?" Elm bit back. "Last time I checked, you couldn't outrun a warhorse, cousin."

Jespyr pulled her Black Horse Card from her pocket. "Is that a wager?"

"Both of you, shut up," Ravyn said. "Collect your charms and go to your horses. Thistle, find the Ivys. We leave in five minutes."

They scuttled away, a few final scowls darting between Jespyr and Elm.

Ravyn turned to me, his voice low. "Are you all right? Truly?"

I coughed, then winced. "I'll survive."

"May I?"

There he was again, asking to touch me. I nodded, and when his hand traced up and down my rib cage, I almost forgot the pain, too worried he'd feel the rapid beat of my heart.

"You'll be all right," he said, pulling his hand away, almost too fast. "I'm sorry, Miss Spindle. We've no choice but to go on horseback. Your best option is to ride with our most skilled horseman—so that he might thwart any of the animal's unease."

I eyed him narrowly. "And who, pray tell, is your most skilled horseman?"

Elm's riding was much the same as his overall demeanor. Pitiless and abrasive.

By the time we entered the Black Forest, I felt so battered and winded I might have fallen off the horse a dozen times more. When we dismounted, the Prince let out a wheezing breath.

"Trees!" he coughed. "Grip tight enough? It felt like I was wearing a corset."

"Everyone all right?" Jespyr called up ahead.

"Marvelous," Elm said through his teeth. "Best ride of my life."

"I wasn't asking about you."

"Who else is there?"

Ravyn dismounted in a gust of black. "Your bickering isn't impressing anyone," he called. "Get your charms. Best we keep quiet from here on out."

The Black Forest was a dense collection of poplar trees and bramble. The horses were nervous to leave the path, but we coaxed them with sugar and stepped, apprehensive, into the mist.

It felt strange, not needing my crow's foot. For the others, the need for a charm was more dire. I could smell the salt in the air. The Spirit of the Wood lingered in the mist, invisible, watching, held at bay by only our magic and our charms.

The Ivy brothers carried identical hawk feathers. Jespyr tossed a small femur bone between her palms. Thistle twirled a dog's canine tooth on a leather string. Elm wound a tight braid of horsehair around his knuckles.

I followed behind Ravyn, his burgundy and purple lights purposeful as they moved through the mist. Next came Jespyr, fitted with a Black Horse. Thistle and the Ivys were Cardless. Elm—who had left the conspicuous Scythe behind, fitted with a second Black Horse—took the rear.

Thistle passed bread and cheese up the line, and we ate as we walked, like travelers in one of my aunt's old books. At twilight the crickets sang, waking owls and other creatures of the night.

The mist grew heavier, so dense it swallowed the fading daylight, casting us into darkness.

Rock or bramble, hill or dell, it did not matter—Ravyn moved on sure steps. His boots were silent, his pace unflagging. Only once did he stop, holding up a hand to halt the group, his eyes trained on the mist.

I slipped on crumbling poplar leaves, the Nightmare's vision the only thing keeping me from blindness. "How can you tell where we're going?"

He shrugged. "Practice."

Up ahead came the distant rustle of leaves. A moment later, a doe and her fawn ambled across our path. Ravyn watched them, his shoulders easy, his face untroubled. Only when they'd cleared the path did he signal us forward.

The temperature in the wood dropped. I shivered and rubbed my twinging nose, the air dense all around us. "The salt is strong," I said.

"It's the Spirit of the Wood," Ravyn replied.

My aunt had told me many stories about the Spirit of the Wood. She'd said the Spirit could take the form of animals, but never an exact replication. There was always something *other* about the animals the Spirit pretended to be. Their bones were too long—their teeth too jagged.

Their eyes too knowing.

My gaze darted across the mist. But the doe and her fawn were gone. "Do you think," I whispered to Ravyn's back, "if we manage to collect the Deck—to lift the mist—that the Spirit will remain in Blunder?"

The Captain pondered this. "*The Old Book* says magic sways, like salt water on a tide. I believe the Spirit is the moon, commanding the tide. She pulls us in, but also sets us free. She is neither good nor evil. She is magic—balance. Eternal."

The Nightmare whispered behind my eyes, his claws sharp. *But the Spirit was neglected, no matter her plea. The Rowans erased her, as they once did to me. But she keeps her own time, and I keep a long score. The tide that comes next will blot out the shore.*

I shivered. But it had nothing to do with the cold.

"So, no," Ravyn continued. "I don't think the Spirit of the Wood will disappear with the mist. But perhaps she will no longer be a danger. Perhaps she will rest."

A few moments later, he stopped. "Tether the horses here," he called to the others. "I can see the road twenty paces beyond."

I moved aside, clear of the horses. When Ravyn joined me, he held a knife.

"It's no garden shear," he said, offering me the blade. When I hesitated, he smiled. "You won't need it. But it's a poor disguise without a weapon."

I looped the hilt of the knife through my belt. "Now what?" I said, a slight tremor touching the edge of my voice.

"We wait."

Apprehension built like soil tossed upon a new grave.

An hour later I was fighting to keep still. The others milled quietly, scattered in the mist among trees and rocks and shrubs. Only Ravyn remained unmoving, his eyes forward on the road ahead.

When a twig snapped beneath my foot, he broke his stillness, casting me a sharp glance.

"Sorry," I whispered.

Reaching into his pocket, Ravyn extracted a dark, silky fabric—the cloth he'd blindfolded me with on Equinox.

I bit my lip. "What's that for?"

Ravyn pulled a second cloth from his pocket and secured it to his face just below the eyes, obscuring his nose, mouth, and jaw.

A mask.

So vividly returned the memory of that night along the forest road, the men in masks—the violence and fear—that I recoiled, tripping on bramble.

Ravyn must have understood because a moment later, he took off the mask. "I'm sorry," he said, stepping to my side, his voice no more than a whisper. "Miss Spindle?"

I ran my hand over my face and did not look at him. "I never thought I'd be dressed as a highwayman," I managed. "With the same men who attacked me, no less."

Ravyn sucked in a breath. "Had I known who you were—"

"You would have—what? Been a bit nicer?" My nostrils flared. "I was alone on the road. You were awful, the both of you."

He did not deny it. After a long, uneasy pause, he sighed. "I came back to the road—alone—the next night. I kept to the forest for three days, hoping to catch a glimpse of you, to speak to you if I could." He looked off into the distance. "The Prophet Card leaves holes in our understanding. Yes, my mother predicted where you'd be—your connection to the Cards. But the rest was conjecture. We had no idea what we were stepping into. Had I known you carried magic—" He paused again, his brow furrowed. "There are so few of us, Miss Spindle. You are more special than you know. And it pains me to think I might have hurt you. I'm—sorry." He paused. "Trees, I'm sorry."

I listened to the wind through the wood, the lull blending with Ravyn Yew's voice. He seemed different dressed as a highwayman—changed. Gone was the austere, controlled persona he displayed as Captain of the Destriers. Here, in the wood, he was just a man in a black cloak seeking repentance.

I extended my hand. "You're forgiven. On one condition."

The invisible string tugged the corner of his mouth. "What's that?"

When our hands touched, heat moved into my cheeks. "Call me Elspeth," I said. "We're about to commit treason together, after all."

The elusive half smile, cautious though it was, overtook Ravyn's mouth. When he shook my hand, his calloused skin caught along my palm.

A shrill whistle ripped through the trees, echoed by another, then another.

The signal.

Ravyn froze, his hand still in mine, the noise of approaching horsemen rumbling in the distance. “Best put that mask on, Elspeth,” he said. “It’s time.”

Chapter Nineteen

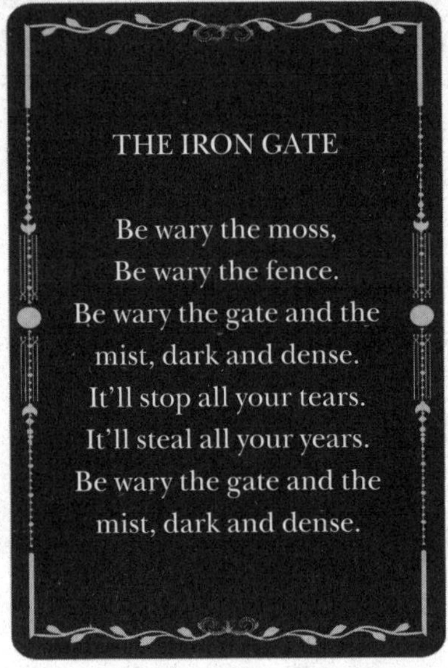

It took only a moment to realize something was wrong. The tumult was too loud, the sound of their horses too many. Had I not known they were coming, I might have mistaken their clamor for thunder.

I peered through the mist and watched two carriages round the corner, their lanterns casting ghostlike shadows across the road. The flames blended with another light, a deep mossy green, its source somewhere within the first carriage. A light only I could see.

The Iron Gate.

But before I could point it out to Ravyn, the clamor heightened, four more lights coming into view, only these lights were no flicker of flame, nor were they bright like the Iron Gate. They were dark, so deep I felt as if I were falling into them.

Four Black Horses, their riders atop warhorses that flanked the carriage. Four Black Horses and one brilliant red beacon.

A Scythe Card. Hauth Rowan.

I tugged Ravyn's sleeve, the Nightmare crawling behind my eyes. "The Prince is there, with a Black Horse and a Scythe. You didn't say anything about fighting Destriers!"

Ravyn's jaw muscles flexed. From the size of his eyes—the stillness of his shoulders—I could tell he was as surprised as I was. A moment later he reached into his pocket and tapped his Nightmare Card three times, communicating silently with the others. His brows drew firmly together.

The horses on the road whickered, their ears perked.

Ravyn turned to me. "Do you see the Iron Gate?"

I blinked at him, my mouth agape. "You're not still thinking of attacking?"

Ravyn's gaze darted between me and the road. "We need that Card."

"But the Destriers—"

Ravyn's voice was steady. But when he looked at me, I saw a wildness in his eyes I had not seen before. "We'll handle the Destriers," he said. "If we rush Hauth, he won't have enough focus to wield the Scythe. The quicker we retrieve the Iron Gate, the quicker we will be free of danger. Do you still wish to help us, Elspeth?"

The Nightmare said nothing. Still, I felt the weight of him as he sat, crouched, waiting.

I took a deep breath, my lungs tight. "The Iron Gate is in the first carriage."

Beyond, the riders grew louder, closer. Even through the mist, I could see the dust of their fervor, their horses slick with sweat. Crows stirred in their wake and took to the sky, cawing their distress as the horsemen thundered on.

Ravyn reached into his pocket once more, retrieving the Mirror Card. "Sure you won't use this?"

I shook my head vehemently.

"Suit yourself." He tapped it three times, disappearing. "You and I will go last," said the air where he previously stood. "Lead me to the Iron Gate. Once we're close, run back here and hide in the mist. Understand?"

I didn't have time to answer. Without warning, several goose-fletched arrows tethered with rope shot across the road, blocking the path a mere pace ahead of the carriages. Jespyr and Elm's Black Horses shone dark and menacing in the distance as they and the Ivys continued to shoot arrows, obstructing the road—forcing the carriages and Destriers to come to a screeching halt.

The horses brayed. One reared, throwing its rider, who plummeted to the ground. I could not see Ravyn, but I felt him next to me. A moment later he grabbed my hand and we ran full speed through the trees toward the fray.

My breath came in hurried, desperate gasps. All I could see was the road ahead—just beyond the tree line—and the men scattered there, the green light centered within their midst.

"Take up arms!" one of the Destriers shouted.

"We're under attack!" another cried.

But they'd no time to regroup—the highwaymen had come.

The sharp ring of steel on steel rattled me, the clash of swords loud in my ears. Ravyn pulled me forward onto the road, his grip on my hand never wavering. Ahead of us, men spilled out of the carriages and Destriers fell from their horses in a flurry, weapons drawn.

I saw Elm up the road. A moment later the Ivys joined the fray, met by Hauth and two other men. They clashed together—might against might—swords and fists wielded with bone-breaking strength. But Ravyn pulled me deeper into the struggle, and I quickly lost sight of them.

The green light from the Iron Gate was no longer in the first carriage. It had moved on to the road, hovering in Wayland Pine's cloak. The light spun about, Wayland bobbing through the tumult, stationing himself between Destriers and another man-at-arms. "It's in Pine's cloak!" I called in Ravyn's direction. "Right side."

Ravyn squeezed my hand, yanking me down as arrows pierced the air. "Go," he said, my hand suddenly cold as he released it. "Go now!"

I did not wait to be told a third time.

I turned my heel and ran—ran with all my might. Dirt kicked up beneath my feet and I slipped, narrowly avoiding the wild slash of a Destrier's blade.

Get up, the Nightmare snarled, so awake I could feel his claws in my head. *Get up, Elspeth!*

The Destrier turned, his sword engaged by Jon Thistle. I launched myself off the ground, the tree line and the mist a mere fifteen paces away. I ran, my eyes cast backward for a final glance at the glow of the Iron Gate...

And careened straight into my father.

He seemed taller, the blood-red spindle tree sewn into his sapphire cloak. He held a dagger in one hand, and in the other, he brandished my grandfather's sword with great strength, employed in a violent struggle with Elm. To me, he offered little notice, repaying my bump with a sharp elbow to the cheek that sent me hurtling to the ground.

I tasted blood and blinked, my vision spinning. Only then did I notice the familiar shape engraved in the door of the second carriage.

A spindle tree.

You've bit your tongue, that's all, the Nightmare called above the bedlam. *Get up.*

The clang of steel grew closer, as if on top of me. Keeping to my hands and knees, I crawled, dust clinging to the tears in my eyes. When I reached the edge of the road, I flung myself into a pile of foliage beneath a tall poplar tree.

Wiping the dirt from my eyes, I peered back at the mayhem—searching for my father. He stood, still in combat with Elm. Only now, Elm's sword had been knocked to the ground. Dread crawled up my spine as I watched the Prince struggle, trapped between the carriage and my father's looming blade. Three strikes he dodged, every last bit of the Prince's focus spent avoiding my father's next blow.

He's going to get hurt, I said, panic clutching my throat.

He's not your bloody concern!

I was on the ground once more, scrounging for something—anything. My fingers closed around a dense, cold rock. When I stood, Elm was off his feet, knocked to the ground.

My father loomed above him, sword in hand, the clinching blow a breath away.

I stepped back onto the road and closed my eyes, turning to the blackness of my mind. When I spoke, the Nightmare's voice melded with mine in loud, determined dissonance.

"Do. Not. Miss."

The rock slammed into the back of my father's head, knocking him off balance, denying his sword the kill. Elm, fast to his feet, tore from the fray, disappearing beneath the shadow of his Black Horse.

My father whirled on me, a violence in his eyes I had never seen before.

Now what? the Nightmare hissed.

I backed away, my limbs suddenly frozen. I pulled the knife from my belt and held it shakily between my father and me. *Help me,* I called to the Nightmare, my legs weak with panic.

My father scowled. He pivoted, shifting his dagger back behind him. "Fucking highwaymen," he said, preparing to throw it. At me.

And I knew he would not miss. I'd come all this way, only to be killed by the man who, eleven years ago, had risked everything to keep me alive.

Help me help me help me HELP! I cried, shutting my eyes, the vicious sound of the singing blade buzzing through my body.

Salt filled my nose. I felt as if I'd fallen beneath a sheet of ice. I gasped, desperate for air I could not taste. Pain ripped up my arms—the dark magic of the infection and the Nightmare's strength swimming through my veins. When I opened my eyes, the world was bright and vivid behind the Nightmare's gaze. My father stood before me, fearsome, a small touch of surprise etched into his dark scowl...

...and his dagger tightly fisted in my hand.

The Nightmare was faster than he'd ever been. My eyes, my arms, my mind, danced with violent intent. In only a few swift steps, I closed the distance between myself and my father. Before he could level his sword, I slammed my foot into his diaphragm, knocking him off his feet.

He fell to the ground in a heap. I stood over him, a wicked smile twisting my lips as I balanced the tip of his dagger to his throat. "Be wary the blue," I said, my voice melding with the Nightmare's oily tone. "Be wary the stone. Be wary of shadows the water hath shown. Your enemies wait. The wolves stalk the gate. Be wary of shadows the water hath shown."

Fear shattered my father's austerity. He stared up at me, his blue eyes glassy and wide. When he saw my eyes above my mask, I knew he did not recognize me.

He'd never seen me with yellow eyes before.

But before my father could speak—his mouth agape and his face ghost white—a spooked horse rushed by, knocking me to the ground.

I dropped his dagger and my head struck stone, the world suddenly buckling, as if turned on its head.

Hands reached for me. I swiped at them but could not push them away. My vision dizzied, the heat in my veins so great it burned me.

A moment later I was wrenched off the ground and placed on my feet.

Her face was obscured by her mask. But I knew her eyes, her voice. When Jespyr offered her hand, I took it, the bedlam around us as loud as war drums.

Jespyr and I dashed headfirst into the mist.

I was immediately lost. Still, I ran. Jespyr's breath came in steady huffs, and she might have kept going—

Had a Destrier not come out of the mist and knocked her full force onto the ground.

She fell with a slam onto the forest floor, taking me down with her. I smothered a scream, the Nightmare flooding my mind. *Hush, child,* he warned. *They will hear you.*

Jespyr was on her feet in a moment, blocking me with her body, squared off with the Destrier. When he lunged she parried, matching his strength, Black Horse against Black Horse. Their swords collided, a piercing knell that echoed through the mist. Jespyr's elbow collided with the Destrier's jaw and he faltered, stepping back, slashing wildly.

The edge of his sword tore through her black tunic, cutting into her shoulder.

She hissed but did not falter. Pivoting with speed so immense I could hardly measure it, Jespyr came up beside the Destrier, dodging the second slash of his blade. He swore, pulling a wickedly curved dagger from his belt.

But before his dagger could find its mark, Jespyr slammed the pommel of her hilt into the side of the Destrier's head. He teetered a moment, eyes wide and unfocused, before crashing to the ground at my feet. He lay still, eyes shut.

I stared down at him. "Is he...?"

Jespyr knelt beside him, her shoulder bleeding where he'd cut it. She put two fingers to the Destrier's neck, just under his jaw. "Unconscious," she murmured. She glanced up at me, pausing on my eyes. "Are you all right?"

I felt as if I'd been carved out of wood—stiff, splintering. "I'm fine," I said through gritted teeth. "Where are the others?"

"I don't know." She reached into her breast pocket. "I got turned around." Her face grew drawn—her hand more urgent. She unturned her pockets, then her cloak, searching for something. "Shit," she breathed.

"What?"

"It's not here," she cried. "My charm. I must have dropped it when he knocked into me."

Somewhere behind us, a branch snapped.

"What was that?" Jespyr said, her eyes wide.

"We shouldn't linger," I managed, my neck strained as I looked around. "The other Destriers can't be far."

But Jespyr merely shook her head, her eyes glassy with fear. "I—I..." She coughed, as if she'd swallowed too much water. "Can you smell it?" she said. "Can you smell the salt?"

I stared at her, my breath turning cold. "Jespyr?"

Fingers shaking, she rubbed her eyes. "I—I—I—can't—see." Her eyelids fluttered wildly. "No, no, no!" she choked.

What's happening to her? I said, a chill crawling up my spine.

Don't you know? Can't you smell it?

Salt filled my nose. Magic. Dark, uncontrolled magic. The Spirit of the Wood, come to exact balance.

Come to steal Jespyr into the mist.

I dove into my jerkin, my fingers trembling. But my pockets were empty. I'd left my charm neatly folded in my dress back at Castle Yew.

A fox screamed in the distance, making us jump.

"Jespyr, we've got to get out of the mist."

"Can't," she managed. "The road—n-not safe." She turned west, called by something I could not hear. "We've got to go deeper into the wood."

"No," I said. "You're confused. We've got to get—"

She did not hear me. She was lost, her brown eyes glazed over. A moment later she was running, diving deeper into the trees, swallowed by the mist.

I forced my tired limbs after her, my heartbeat so loud it shook me. I reached my hands out ahead of me, the path so dark it swaddled my eyes, but I was hollowed out from the Nightmare's strength and didn't dare ask for it again. Tree limbs snagged my hair, and the soil beneath my feet was tangled in roots, every step a snare.

Ahead, an animal scream ripped through the trees. The Nightmare laughed, his voice trickling through my mind. *The Spirit has no forgiveness, no pardon to lend. She calls out our names, neither kin, foe, nor friend. She watches the mist like a shepherd its sheep...*

The animal screamed again, only this time, I discerned two words in the frantic notes of its wail.

"Help me!"

It was not an animal screaming. It was Jespyr.

And pays those she snares with the great, final sleep.

Her cries echoed in the mist, fearful and wretched. I rushed toward the din and found Jespyr tangled in vines beneath an old poplar tree, her ankle twisted in roots.

Her eyes were unfocused, lost on something far away. "Limbs of the land, come to bring me home," she laughed through clenched teeth. "Don't be afraid, Elspeth. The roots and the animals of the wood are servants to the Spirit, just like you and I."

Nausea rolled through my stomach as I stared down at her unnaturally turned ankle. I took my knife and freed her of vines. "Jespyr," I said. "Does your brother have a charm?"

She didn't seem to hear me. "I tarry—I tarry in darkness, never in light."

"Jespyr!"

She blinked, her hands digging into the dirt around her. "Yes," she managed. "Ravyn—charm. Hurry."

I tore through the wood, my eyes wide, frantic to catch a glimpse of the Captain of the Destriers' telltale burgundy and purple lights.

But I was immediately lost, swallowed by mist.

I searched the darkness for any hint of color, my arms stretched out against vicious brambles that snagged at my face and hair. Animals scurried in my wake and I hurried my step, certain something horrible would befall Jespyr if I did not find her a charm.

I stumbled down a ravine, branches cutting at the cloth still covering my face.

Where is he? I cried. *Which way do I go?*

Wait, the Nightmare cautioned. *Listen.*

I perked an ear to the wind. At first, all I heard was the beat of my own heart. But then—footsteps. Something was coming my way. Something, or someone.

I peered out from behind a boxwood, searching for color.

Another animal scream sliced through the wood, and I muffled a cry. I wanted to call out, but the Nightmare hushed me and I remained quiet, waiting.

More footsteps sounded, branches snapping under heavy footfall. Beyond the boxwood, difficult to discern in the dark, I saw Black Horses and a Scythe. They came from the other side of the ravine, slow, wary, swords drawn. Destriers, three of them, approaching a fourth Black Horse that lay motionless upon the ground.

Lost, I'd run back the very direction we'd fled.

Don't move, the Nightmare said.

My hands shook. I placed one over my mouth and the other on the hilt of the knife Ravyn had given me. They could not see me from behind the boxwood; the mist was too thick. But they were close enough to hear me.

I held my breath.

The men picked up their fallen Destrier, draping his arms over their shoulders. One of them swore as a screech owl tore through the trees, and the others retreated behind him. Whatever their resolve, they did not intend to be long off the road. Only one of them hesitated, searching the mist a mere stone's throw from my boxwood.

His face was illuminated by the menacing black and red lights of his Cards. The High Prince of Blunder, Ione's betrothed.

Hauth Rowan.

He stepped closer, ears perked in my direction. "Who's there?"

He was the hunter, and I the prey. A single cold tear slid down my cheek. But when I peered around my shoulder, the High Prince was gone.

I blinked, testing my eyes. He hadn't used a Mirror Card—I'd have seen the purple color. After a tense moment's silence,

I slid out from behind the brush. My hands shook and the boxwood trembled.

But Hauth Rowan, along with the other Destriers, had disappeared.

I let out a shaky sigh and turned back to the ravine. If I could find my way back to the horses, I could find the others. More importantly, I could find Ravyn and his spare charm.

Jespyr was running out of time.

But before I could take a step, something shifted behind me, dark and unearthly fast. I turned, the hair on the back of my neck bristling.

He darted out of the mist with brutal speed and caught my wrist. I tried to flee, but he twisted me back, his Black Horse and Scythe casting sinister color across my vision.

"Who are you?" Hauth said, shaking me.

He twisted my arm. I felt a strange, unnatural snap, and suddenly my wrist was swimming in vicious agony. I cried out, the pain visceral as it tore up my arm.

The Nightmare's hiss became a roar. He flooded my mind with a sudden, venomous fury. *Prince of brutes,* he snarled.

Hauth shook my wrist, squinting, as if trying to peer through my mask. "Who are you? What are you doing here?"

I didn't answer. I didn't have the chance to. I struck the High Prince, my hand a blur in the mist. The sound of ripping fabric caught the air. My eyes widened as I looked down, my hand slick with blood.

And it wasn't mine.

Hauth's screams filled the wood. "Who are you?" he shouted again, stepping away from me, ferocious lacerations clawed across his shoulder all the way up to his jaw.

I did not answer. I was already running—full force—into the wood, his blood still on my fingers.

What did you do? I cried, too afraid to look back.

The Nightmare's voice was like hot iron. *The berry of rowans is red, always red. The earth at its trunk is dark with blood shed. But a Prince is a man, and a man may be bled. He came for the girl...*

And got the monster instead.

Hauth's cries echoed in the wood, guttural as the fox's screams. I tore through the trees, my muscles strained, desperate to get away. I didn't know if I was going north or south, only that I had to put as much distance between the High Prince and myself as I could.

Tears stung my eyes, and my wrist, hot and swelling, sang in pain. When I heard leaves rustling behind me, I veered right, slashing through a daphne shrub. Weeds caught my legs and I fell hard, unable to brace myself.

I groaned, my vision blurring.

Get up, the Nightmare called. *Get up, Elspeth.*

I rolled, listening to the wood. Footsteps sounded through the mist, but this time when I looked up, I saw the faintest hints of color in the distance—burgundy, violet, and mossy green. The Nightmare, the Mirror, and the Iron Gate.

Ravyn.

He must have heard me coming, because when I came crashing through the mist, he was gone—vanished with three taps of the Mirror Card.

I ran into him with a bang, my lungs swelling with relief. I heard him exhale, and suddenly the shroud of magic was lifted. The Captain of the Destriers reappeared in front of me. "Elspeth." His eyes widened above his mask as he took me in. "What—"

"Shhh!" I said, pulling him behind a tree and covering his mouth with my hand. "The High Prince is behind me."

Ravyn's breath caught in his throat. He reached down to

his belt and pulled a dagger. My fingers slid off his mouth. But before they could fall, he caught them, lacing our fingers together. A screech owl called nearby and I jumped, my face cold with tears I hadn't realized I'd shed.

Ravyn watched me, listening to the mist. When stillness crept over us, I peered around the tree, looking for any sign of Hauth Rowan's black and red lights.

But there was nothing. The High Prince was gone—retreated back to the road to lick his wounds.

"I can't see his Cards anymore," I whispered.

Ravyn slid his knife back into its sheath. "Pine and his party fled in their carriage the moment we retreated. The second carriage followed, but the Destriers remained, so we scattered. I doubt they'll stray too far into the mist."

"I saw them heading back to the road."

"Did Hauth see you?"

I nodded. "I think he broke my wrist."

The Captain's eyes flashed. He reached for my injured arm, but I flinched away. "We don't have time. Jespyr—she's lost her charm." My boots dug into the dirt as I pulled him away from the tree. "We have to go back. Now."

We found Jon Thistle and ran deeper into the wood, wary of Destriers. But the black and red lights were nowhere in sight. I was afraid I wouldn't be able to recognize the path, but my frantic flight from Hauth was easy to follow, and from there, we found the ravine that led us back to Jespyr.

She hadn't gotten far, her ankle too weak to support her. Ravyn kneeled over his sister and pulled a charm wrapped in linen from his pocket. He placed it in Jespyr's rigid fingers and pressed his forehead to hers, whispering something I could not hear.

I watched, my heart racing. After a time, life reentered

Jespyr's glassy eyes and she stopped fidgeting, no longer straining to crawl deeper into the mist.

She winced and sat up. "What the hell happened?"

"You dropped your charm," Ravyn said, brushing his sister's hair out of her eyes. "You hurt your ankle. But everything's all right, Jes. You're safe."

I exhaled, relief melding with nauseous pain. Behind us, the trees rustled and the noise of bickering echoed through the wood. The Ivys had returned.

"All right, boys?" Thistle called.

Petyr's profanity filled the air. "Royce Linden broke my goddamn nose."

"It's your own fault for not bashing him," Wik hollered.

"Captain said not to kill 'em, didn't he?"

"Did anyone see your face?" Thistle demanded. "Did anyone recognize you?"

"Course not."

"You sure?"

"Don't I look bloody sure, Jon?"

The crunch of leaves sounded. Someone was running toward us, a dark, bottomless shadow cutting through the trees. I grabbed at Thistle's arm, to warn him, but before I could speak, a head of tousled auburn hair shot through the darkness.

Elm.

"Oi!" Petyr called. "Took you long enough."

The Prince was in no easy mood. "Said the dimwit who thought he could take on a Destrier without a Black Horse. You'd be bleeding out on the road if I hadn't stepped in to save your flat-footed ass." His green eyes shot to Ravyn, then Jespyr, still seated on the forest floor. "What's wrong?"

"Dropped her charm," Thistle said. "Strong as salt, that one. She'll be right in a minute."

Elm's gaze returned to Ravyn. "You better have gotten that damn Card."

"He's got it." Wik laughed. "Look at that smug face."

"Let's see it, then," Petyr demanded.

Ravyn pulled the green light from his pocket, the light flickering to nothing as he twirled it between his bare fingers, the corners of his lips curled by a devilish arrogance. Something tightened deep in my stomach, watching him gloat.

The party passed the Iron Gate among themselves, voices shedding strain, breaths of relief filling the air like smoke. They returned the Card to Ravyn, who placed it back in his pocket, the green light, free of his touch, vibrant once more.

Tension slowly eased, laughter perforating our small corner of the wood. I moved a few paces away, suddenly aware of just how sore my body was. I found a log and lowered myself onto it with an unceremonious thud.

Elm approached me, his eyes tight on my face. "Still alive, then?"

I managed to nod before another wave of pain hit my wrist. My skin felt hot, swollen, and angry.

"Did he recognize you?" Elm asked.

"Who?" Ravyn called, watching us.

"Her father."

Thistle's eyebrows disappeared beneath his hairline. "Erik Spindle was there?"

"In the second carriage," Elm said, wiping blood from his nostrils. "The bastard caught me off guard—practically ran me through."

"What happened?" Jespyr said, wincing as she stood, leaning on Petyr for support.

"I'm still in one piece, aren't I?" Elm glanced at me, his brows drawn together. "She fought him off."

The others quieted, their eyes falling on me. I cradled my arm and kept my eyes low as I let out a long, tired breath. "He didn't recognize me."

"You're sure? Because if he did, we're royally f—"

"Do you really think he'd try to kill his own daughter?"

Ravyn approached, kneeling at my side. He took my injured wrist and made a crude wrap with his cloth mask, supporting the joint until I could no longer move it. I clenched my teeth but did not look away, a few stray tears falling down my cheeks.

Elm watched us. "Who did that?" he said.

Ravyn's voice was cold. "Hauth," he said, tying off the makeshift bandage, his eyes raising to my face. "You never said how you got away from him."

I stiffened, the Nightmare's wicked laugh resonating in the din. When I spoke, the low notes of my voice were slick, as if dipped in oil. "Perhaps it was he who got away from me."

Chapter Twenty

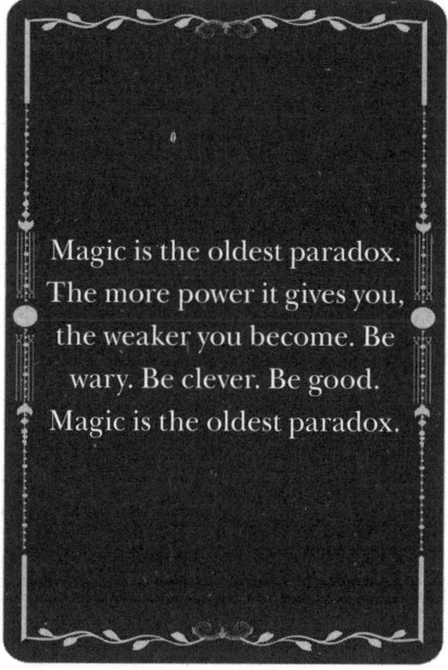

The others rode ahead, triumph spurring them on. Only Elm lingered, waiting by his horse.

I gritted my teeth, dreading another jostling journey with the Prince, my wrist stiff and aching. But before I got close, Ravyn stepped between his cousin and me.

"I'll spare you a rider," he said to Elm. "Go on with the others."

Elm raised a brow, his green eyes shifting between Ravyn and me. "You sure?"

"Very."

"Suits me," he said. "I'm bruised enough without a pair of arms belted around my ribs." The Prince mounted and spurred his horse without a backward glance, disappearing behind the shadow of his Black Horse.

I leaned against a nearby tree, hollowed out. "What was in the wrapping?" I asked.

"What wrapping?"

"The charm you handed Jespyr."

Ravyn fastened his saddle. "The head of a viper. I keep it covered, lest I injure myself on the fangs."

I raised my brows. "I didn't think you carried a charm."

"I do." He gave me a fleeting smile. "Just not for the same reason as everyone else."

I shuddered and looked away. "I suppose venom is a happier death than torture in the King's dungeon." Then, after a pause, "You have only two Cards left. You must be pleased."

"I am," Ravyn said, adjusting the saddle atop his black palfrey. "Though it was harder to procure than I initially imagined."

"Steal," I corrected. "Harder to steal."

He turned and leaned against his horse. "Call it what you will. We would have never succeeded against the Destriers if we didn't know exactly where Pine held his Iron Gate." His voice softened. "We couldn't have done it without you."

I gave a mock sweeping bow. "I risk my neck for a chance at your gratitude, Captain."

Ravyn exhaled, half sigh, half something else. But he said nothing, as if I hadn't just thrown his thanks back in his face. Instead, he crossed his arms over his chest, a shadow from his distinct nose cast across his face. "You frightened me earlier."

"What do you mean?"

"The way you came running out of the trees...I didn't think it was you." Ravyn paused, watching me. "It's hard to explain."

"Try," I said.

He shrugged. "You'll think me odd."

"A bit late for that, isn't it?"

The corners of his lips curled. "It's just that, sometimes when I look at you, I feel like I know you—understand you. And other times..." His brow furrowed. "Your eyes flash a strange yellow color. I feel a stillness about you I do not recognize. A darkness."

When I remained silent, cold to my bones, the Captain's voice remained gentle. "The truth is," Ravyn said, patting his horse, "there is darkness in all of us. We don't need *The Old Book of Alders* to tell us that. You and I carry the infection and, with it, strange, brilliant magic. But there's always a price. Nothing comes for free."

We rode in silence, our pace slow. I dozed despite my aching wrist, sleep heavy on my brow. Above the road, the moon shone through the mist. The forest, filled to the brim with animal noises, echoed around us, owls and crickets and wildcats undeterred by our trespass.

Ravyn and I did not speak—not about magic, not about my strange yellow eyes, not about my father or Hauth. Silent and calm, peace settled behind my eyelids, and I leaned into Ravyn's broad back, too tired to hold myself straight, the faint beat of his heart hardly discernible through his jerkin.

I cast my thoughts inward, searching for the Nightmare, who, since the mayhem in the wood, had remained still. Strange, how quiet he felt when I was with Ravyn. Almost as if he was gone altogether.

Almost.

I felt him there in the darkness. When I nudged him, he stirred but did not speak, stretching his claws like a yawning cat before retiring deeper still into blackness.

I slept until the familiar clack of cobblestones met my ears. The moon, no longer high in the sky, rested behind the eastern tower. I sat up with a jolt, light rain misted across my lashes.

We'd returned to Castle Yew.

"What time is it?"

"Some hours before dawn," Ravyn said, his voice reverberating in his chest.

Ravyn guided us to the castle's iron gates. He dismounted, pulling a skeleton key from the saddle. I heard the click of the bolt and yawned, wanting nothing more than my comfortable bed and a long, dreamless sleep.

Ravyn led the horse to the castle door. When I slipped from the saddle, he caught me at the waist and lowered me onto the cobblestones, his fingers flexing just above the curve of my hips. They lingered there, even when my feet were firmly on the ground.

I looked up, desperate for sleep, wide awake.

"There will be more eyes on us than just my family in the coming days," he said, his voice low, a rumbling whisper. "Do you still wish to pretend?"

He didn't say the word—*courting*. My lungs twisted, like the wings of a caged, frantic bird. I knew what I wanted to say, but something in my chest, small, delicate, resisted the *yes* haunting the tip of my tongue. "Do you?"

I felt resistance in his pause, he, too, lost to the world of things unsaid. "Of all the things I pretend at," he said, his thumb drawing small, gentle circles along my waist, "courting you has proven the easiest."

His elusiveness infuriated me. But as soon as it came, the fury was gone, leaving behind hot embers that burned low in my stomach. When I slipped away from him, my entire body was warm.

I made my way to the castle door. "How flattering."

He paused a beat. "What's your answer?" he called after me.

I turned. It felt good, provoking him. Better than it should. "Infuriating, isn't it, Captain? Answers given only in halves?"

"Ravyn," he said, his eyes tracing my face, flashing a moment to my mouth. "If we're going to be convincing, you should call me Ravyn."

A smile tugged at my lips. "Good night, then, Ravyn."

He responded with a slow, satisfied grin. "I'll take that as your answer, Elspeth."

I tiptoed through the dark castle to my chamber and waited for Filick, my eyelids heavy. When I sat on my bed, something soft gave beneath my hand. The flower crown I'd made that morning had been placed atop my pillow. When I turned it over, a rose petal fell into my hand, red as blood.

I stood in the ancient room covered in vines. The old wooden ceiling had rotted, revealing beams of light beneath a canopy of orange and yellow. Birds chirped, rustling playfully. Only this time, it was not summer. The air had cooled, the autumn day crisp and pure.

Seated upon the dark stone in the center of the room rested the same knight I'd seen in my last dream. His gold armor that had long lost its sheen glistened dully in the autumn light. On his hip rested the same ancient sword with strange twisting branches carved into the hilt.

Clouded by thought, he did not see me.

I waited for him to look up, once again shuffling my feet on the leaf-strewn floor.

When he finally saw me, his gaze widened. "Elspeth Spindle," he said, his eyes—so strange and yellow—ensnaring me. "Let me out."

The room burst into flames.

I woke with a start, gasping for air. I looked around, but

the fire was gone. I was alone in my chamber in Castle Yew, no fire—no flames licking the sides of my face. Bright morning light shone through my window and I blinked, unsure how long I'd slept.

Filick Willow had wrapped my wrist the night before. But as I rolled off the bed onto my feet, white-hot pain seared my arm. I hissed—my left wrist so sore beneath the linen binding that the hand was entirely useless. It took me a full ten minutes to strip away yesterday's clothes, the black fabric tattered and dusty.

My maid had left a basin of water at my night table. I crept to it, my entire body full of aches. I surveyed myself in my small looking glass and cringed. My back was covered in ugly purple marks from being thrown from the horse. A dark bruise had budded beneath my eye from the blow my father had dealt me. I touched it and flinched, the skin angry and sore.

Even my eyes were swollen. I rubbed them, hoping to bring a little life back into my face. But when I pulled my hands away and gazed back into the mirror, my heart froze in my chest. I jolted back from the glass, choked by the scream that rose in my throat.

A creature—neither man nor animal, fur bristled along his tall, pointed ears—stared back at me, his yellow eyes wide.

But when I looked again, he was gone. The face in the mirror was mine once more. Only now, my features were contorted in fear, and my dark eyes—wide with terror—had gone glassy.

My aunt had told me once that my strange charcoal eyes were special, beautiful even—a dark window to the soul beneath. But as I glanced back into the looking glass, the reflection of my black eyes flickering to that bright, eerie yellow, I had to wonder…whose soul was it?

The Nightmare's? Or mine?

I fumbled down the stairs, my thighs stiff from holding me so long on a horse. I kept my gaze lowered to my feet, careful not to catch my reflection in any of the castle's decorative suits of armor. I hardly noticed the sound of footsteps on the stairwell until Ravyn, clad in his usual black, called my name from the flight above.

His voice stopped me in my tracks. I waited for him on the landing. When he caught up with me, his gray eyes searched my face.

"No worse for wear, then?" he asked, his gaze shifting to the bruise on my cheek. "How's your wrist?"

"Swollen."

"May I?" he asked.

I nodded, his hands warm against mine. When Ravyn looked down at my injured hand, a strand of black hair fell from behind his ear over his brow. I resisted the urge to push it back into place. Gingerly, he loosened the white cloth Filick had tied around my wrist the night before. I grimaced as he pulled it away, the skin hot and swollen, mottled by purple bruises.

Ravyn's fingers traced the damaged joint. He retied the wrapping. "It's not as frightening as it looks," he said. "But you're not easily frightened, are you, Miss Spindle?"

"Elspeth," I reminded him.

His nose wrinkled, the corners of his mouth lifting. My chest constricted, watching him smile. "Some things frighten me," I said. "The King. Physicians. Destriers."

Ravyn tilted his head. "All Destriers?"

"I don't know if I qualify you as a Destrier anymore."

"What else would I be?"

My lips curled. "A highwayman."

His smile widened. But before he could reply, the parlor door at the bottom of the stairs opened. Out came Morette Yew and, behind her, the most beautiful woman I had ever seen. When she saw me, her lips parted.

"There you are, cousin," Ione called, her hazel eyes darting between Ravyn and me. "Finally awake."

We sat in the parlor by the fire. Ravyn and his mother sat in high-backed chairs. Opposite, Ione and I shared a long blanketed bench. I watched my cousin over my shoulder, lost in the ethereal shine of her skin, her hair, her eyes, unsure if I was more spellbound or horrified by her new beauty.

But there was no brilliant pink light. She pulled her beauty from the Maiden Card, but for a reason I could not work out, she did not carry it on her person, a horrid risk hardly anyone practiced.

Providence Card magic was not limited by distance—a Card could be tapped and left elsewhere. But, without the Maiden a touch away, Ione could not release its magic at whim. Nor could she release herself from its negative effects when they inevitably sank in.

And for the Maiden, the negative effect was one that felt like an utter betrayal to the Ione Hawthorn I had always known.

Heartlessness.

When she caught me watching her, Ione raised her brow. "What is it, Bess? Surely you still recognize me?"

I hardly did. Even her voice was different. "You look… lovely."

"Being engaged suits me," she said, her eyes lingering on the bruise on my cheek. “It’s a shame your new life hasn’t done the same for you.”

And there it is, the Nightmare said, his voice so sudden I jumped. *A pinch of beauty, a whit of wit, and just a touch of unabashed coldheartedness.*

“Miss Hawthorn is traveling from Stone to her home and was kind enough to pay us a visit,” Morette said, her voice warm, hospitable. But, like the rest of the Yews, I was beginning to understand when she was pretending.

She was as surprised to see Ione at Castle Yew as I was.

Ione smiled, the gap in her teeth erased by the Maiden. “And how kind you are, letting me barge in on you. I haven’t been to Castle Yew since childhood.”

Despite the ache in my stomach for how much I’d missed her, I could not shake the feeling that something vital had altered between us, our disagreement at Stone and the Maiden Card’s magic making strangers of us.

But Ione said nothing of our argument. She talked about Stone and the conclusion of Equinox, of court and of the King. She spoke of wedding arrangements but little of Hauth, and nothing of why she had dropped in on Castle Yew.

Across from us, Morette played the part of hostess well, nodding and making small sounds to mirror Ione’s inflections. Her son, however, looked as if he were being led by the collar to the executioner. Ravyn slouched in his chair, watching Ione speak, his mouth a fine line, nothing behind his eyes. He rested his chin against the claw of his hand, his dark hair falling over his brow.

He looked like a petulant boy, forced to endure niceties, brooding in all black. Painfully, unfairly handsome.

He must have felt me watching him, because when he raised his gaze to mine, light returned to his eyes, the elusive half smile tugging at his mouth.

Last night filled my mind. The beat of Ravyn's heart against my ear as I leaned into his back, his warmth soaking into me. The feel of his hands on my waist.

There was a pause in the conversation. All eyes turned to me. I blinked, unfocused. "Sorry, what?"

"I asked what happened," Ione said, her voice uncharacteristically even. Her eyes fell to my bandages. "To your arm."

"I fell off a horse," I replied, a touch too quickly.

Ione put a hand to her mouth, as if to guard against laughter. But none came. "Of course you did." She twirled a strand of her yellow hair. "I hope they haven't been overexerting you, Bess," she said, an arch to her perfect brow as her gaze jumped to Ravyn. "Men of Blunder can be so obtuse when it comes to women."

Ravyn, too composed to appear uncomfortable, buried his hands in his pockets and stared Ione down. "You would know better than most, Miss Hawthorn. My cousin Hauth is a renowned brute, after all."

As if summoned, another Rowan—a brute in his own right—rambled by the open doorway. When he caught a glimpse of Ravyn, Elm stuck his head of tousled auburn hair into the parlor.

"Well?" he said. "They're here, *Captain.* I hope you've had time to wipe the stars out of your eyes—"

"Renelm," Morette said, eyeing Elm threateningly. "We have a visitor."

Elm turned, noticing Ione for the first time. He stared at my cousin, his green eyes wide, then, immediately, narrow. His lips drew into a tight line. "What are you doing here, Hawthorn?"

I turned to my cousin, expecting her embarrassment—a flush in her cheeks. It's how the old Ione would have reacted to such a blunt question from a Prince. But this Ione was different.

The Maiden had remade her. And not just skin-deep. She stared back at Elm, ire matched with ire, defiant. Somehow, it made her even more beautiful.

"I came to speak to your brother," she said, her voice forged of stone. "As I understand, he and the Destriers come to train today."

My eyes shot to Ravyn. But he remained still, his gray eyes unreadable.

"I thought you'd come to see me, Ione," I said, forcing my expression into a dull neutrality. Hauth Rowan—the man who had tried to twist my arm off—here. Now.

She gave half a shrug, folding her hands in her lap. "Two birds, one stone. Besides, I haven't been to Castle Yew since I was a girl—back when I was certain it was haunted."

Elm cast me a sidelong glance. "Who says it isn't haunted?"

Chapter Twenty-One

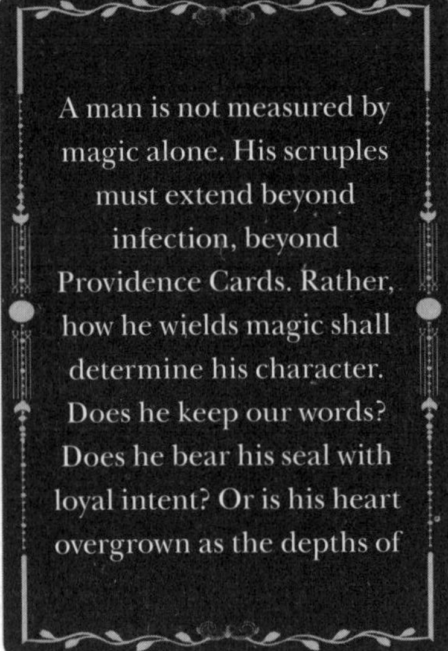

Ione looped her arm in mine as we stepped into the midday light, trailing behind Ravyn and Elm on our way to the yard. "Did you hear?" she said. "A group of highwaymen attacked Hauth on the road last night."

I tried not to squirm. "How would I have heard that, Ione?"

"I assumed your new suitor told you."

There it was again—the edge in her lullaby-soft voice. "What's the matter, Ione?"

She bit the inside of her cheek and did not look at me. "Nothing. I was simply surprised when Father told me Morette Yew had made a match between you and her son, and that you'd been invited here to court him." A low laugh rumbled in her chest. "I hardly believed it."

"No more than I was surprised to hear you were betrothed to Hauth Rowan."

"Dark horses, the pair of us," she said, the midday light casting a glow along the apples of her cheeks. "Be careful, Elspeth. Don't let yourself be swayed by a handsome face. There is so much you don't know about the world. About powerful men. I worry for you. Truly, I do."

But she didn't sound worried. She sounded cold.

I slipped my arm out of her grasp. "You needn't bother," I said. "I can handle myself."

Darkness plumed ahead. We stepped through the broad gate into the yard. There, ten men-at-arms waited, their Black Horses darkening the sky, their tunics bearing no insignia.

Destriers.

My cousin pressed a finger into her bottom lip. "Speaking of powerful men, Hauth was furious when the highwaymen got away last night." A smile I was unfamiliar with crossed her lips. Almost wicked. "He was injured quite grotesquely by the cutpurses, you know."

My eyes shot to the High Prince. "How terrible."

Hauth Rowan stood with the other Destriers, his Scythe and Black Horse Cards in his pocket. Four lines of scabbing red flesh trailed down his neck, disappearing just below the collar of his tunic. It looked as if a giant cat had swiped at him, the claw marks distinct.

But it hadn't been a cat. Not by a long shot.

I stared at the High Prince's neck. *Did I... did I really do that?*

The Nightmare's laughter filled my head, echoing eerily in the cavernous black. *If you have to ask, you're not ready to know.*

Ravyn and Elm waited at the lip of the yard. Ione and I came up next to them. Ravyn said nothing, keeping his eyes on the Destriers. But he lowered his hand to his side, his knuckles dragging against mine, answering my unspoken question. "I called them," he said.

I looked up. "Oh?"

"We train here when we're away from Stone. Clearly, we're in need of training. It seems four of my men, including the High Prince, defied my orders and, instead of returning to town, prolonged their stay at Stone. They were ambushed in the Black Forest." His lips curled. "Hauth is rather... unnerved."

"As he should be," Elm said, picking dirt from beneath his fingernails. "Looks like something took a piece out of him in the wood last night."

Hauth crossed the yard to us. With him came Royce Linden, a broad, muscular Destrier with cropped brown hair and a stern brow bone. I'd seen them together many times, Hauth and Linden, alike in their severity and loud, crude voices.

Hauth's green eyes jumped between Ravyn and Elm. "Where's Jespyr?"

Ravyn tilted his head, smooth as stone. "Sick in bed," he said. "I gave her the morning off."

"Get her up," Hauth demanded. "We need everyone here."

Ravyn did not move. "We're fine as we are."

Ione peered over my shoulder, drawn by the tension between the Captain of the Destriers and her future husband. When her gaze landed on Hauth, I thought I caught a glimpse of something in her narrowed hazel eyes—something more than coldness.

Something that looked a great deal like hatred.

But a moment later, it was gone, her eyes the shape of waning moons, eclipsed by her dark, full lashes.

Hauth barely glanced at her, his eyes lowering to me.

"Darling," Ione said, her voice swelling like music. "You remember my cousin Elspeth. She's visiting the Yews."

My heart drummed in my ears. I slid my swollen wrist into my cloak and fixed my face with a vague, demure expression. I had worn a mask. Still, there was keenness behind the Prince's green eyes—sharp, violent, intelligent.

When Hauth spoke, his voice was distant, cold—so different from his Equinox charm. "We met at Stone." He glanced at Ravyn. "I've heard she's the reason you've been so difficult to find of late."

Ravyn's composure was unflinching. "I don't owe you a reason, cousin."

The muscles beneath Hauth's scabs flexed. "You heard what's happened?"

"That four Destriers and a handful of men couldn't withstand a pack of ruddy highwaymen?" Elm winked. "I wouldn't broadcast that too loudly, brother. Doesn't exactly look Princely."

"It was an ambush," Hauth snapped. "Wayland Pine and Erik Spindle were traveling from Stone. We happened upon them on our way to town. It was them the highwaymen were after. Three men were injured and Pine's Iron Gate stolen." He ran a hand up the cuts on his jaw. "One of them did this to me," he said.

Hauth's jaw was lined with stubble, the skin too raw to shave. I traced the injury, the memory of him catching my arm, my scream, the Nightmare's fury flashing across my mind.

He had felt my wrist—heard the cry of my voice. Strange, that he did not tell them it was a woman who had attacked him.

The Nightmare's laugh was like a match struck in the dark, nearly making me jump. *Pride,* he said. *A fool's pride at that.*

Ravyn and Elm stared at Hauth's injury. "Get a look at who did it?" Elm said.

"I caught him in the wood," Hauth said. "The rest were gone, but he was lost, stupid bastard." He puffed his chest. "I broke his wrist."

The air turned hot in my lungs, the Nightmare's hate melding with mine.

Next to me, Ravyn and Elm had gone still. The only one who moved was Ione. Her head turned a fraction, her hazel eyes leaving her betrothed, falling to my sleeve, just above my broken wrist.

I did nothing. I didn't even breathe. "Did you arrest him?" Ravyn asked, his voice laden with frost.

"No," Hauth said. "He must have had blades in his gloves because the next minute he was slashing my face."

Elm toyed with his Scythe Card, flipping it between his fingers. "I'm surprised you let someone get the best of you. And ruin your pretty facc, at that."

Ione covered her mouth, but not before I caught the edge of a smile dancing along her lips. Elm noticed, too, and his own smiled widened.

Hauth's neck reddened. He rolled his shoulders and stretched his arms. "I'll have my fun when we catch them and string them up in the square. The highwayman meets the hangman. If they meet him in pieces, so be it."

The Destriers muttered their agreement. Ravyn watched them, his face unreadable but for a flex of muscle along his jaw. For the first time, I considered Ravyn Yew more than disliked pretending to uphold the King's laws as Captain of the Destriers.

He loathed it.

"Let's begin the training," Ravyn said, brushing past Hauth into the yard. "How about you and I demonstrate how best to thwart a highwayman, cousin?" he called. "Unless you're worried I'll mark up more of that pretty face."

Hauth hesitated. "Linden will demonstrate."

Linden's nostrils flared. "I'm not sparring him." He lowered his voice. "Infected bastard."

Elm's hand closed in a fist around his Scythe. "What did you say?"

Linden stepped back, his eyes lowering to the red Card in Elm's hand. "Nothing."

Hot air shot out Elm's nose. He crossed his arms over his chest, his gaze turning to his brother. "You're not scared to spar him, are you?"

Corralled once more by his own pride, Hauth gritted his teeth, shot his younger brother a murderous glance, and tromped into the yard after Ravyn.

The Destriers circled their Captain and the High Prince. I stood between Elm and Ione, my wrist burning and my muscles tight. Members of the Yew household gathered, drawn by the King's men and the promise of violence.

"Remember," Ravyn called to the Destriers, "a highwayman does not bear the law in mind. He—or she—may even carry the infection. You cannot be too careful." He eyed me briefly over his cousin's shoulder. "Highwaymen can be far more formidable than the mask shows."

"Get on with it," Elm called.

Hauth's Black Horse darkened the yard. He tapped it three times, then placed it back in his pocket. The Scythe he did not touch. Ravyn's mouth twisted into a knowing grin. "Focus on his hands," he called. "A highwayman may have a knife at your throat with one hand, but you can be sure he's picking your pocket with the other."

He slapped Hauth's hand. Elm snickered under his breath. Before Hauth could skirt away, Ravyn landed another slap across his face, splitting one of his scabs.

"Use your Black Horse well," Hauth instructed the Destriers, wiping the blood from his scabs onto his sleeve. "Speed and accuracy are your greatest attack."

The High Prince moved with unearthly quickness, jolting across the yard, striking Ravyn in the stomach with his fist.

"I thought most Providence Cards could not be used against Ravyn," I whispered to Elm.

"Hauth can still use the Black Horse to enhance his own speed," Elm said under his breath. "But see how he doesn't touch his Scythe? He knows it won't work on Ravyn."

"Highwaymen are most lethal in packs, like wolves," Ravyn called to the Destriers. "Separate them and they're nothing more than rabid dogs that stalk the forest road." He closed his eyes, and this time, when Hauth moved with unearthly speed, he reached out and caught his cousin's cloak, slamming the High Prince onto cold dirt.

Hauth rolled before Ravyn's boot could collide with his shoulder. A moment later he was on his feet, a snarl on his lips.

"What did he look like?" Ravyn asked, thwarting a brutal jab. "The man who tore up your face."

"Couldn't tell, could I?" Hauth said, blocking Ravyn's slap. "He wore a mask."

"Anonymity," Ravyn called to the Destriers, landing hits along Hauth's ear. "Anonymity is the highwayman's greatest advantage. Tear it away, and you've already killed him."

"Or her," Ione whispered, her voice so quiet I might have imagined it.

Hauth took a dagger from his belt. Ravyn narrowed his eyes and bent his knees, moving in rotation with the High Prince's steps. He stepped on light feet, as if walking on glass, and when Hauth slashed his dagger, Ravyn dodged it.

They moved about the yard in a river of steps, dodges, and clashes.

"Stop playing around," Elm heckled from the sideline. "We came to see a proper thrashing."

Hauth spat blood and toppled over in a failed attempt to clip Ravyn's legs. Next to me, neither Ione nor Elm bothered to hide their smiles as they watched the Captain of the Destriers make a spectacle of the High Prince.

When Hauth missed another jab, he swore, the veins in his neck bulging.

"You broke a wrist," Ravyn said to his cousin. "You should at least be able to make me bleed."

Hauth launched the dagger through the air, clipping Ravyn's jerkin just shy of the collar. I flinched, searching Ravyn's tunic for blood. But the Captain of the Destriers pivoted, his foot loud as it landed on Hauth's ribs and sent the heir to the throne back into the dirt.

Then Ravyn stomped, full force, on the High Prince's hand.

A sickening snap echoed through the yard, followed by Hauth's brutal scream. I flinched and looked away. Elm leaned in with wide eyes. The Nightmare hissed with gratification.

Ione merely laughed.

It took three Destriers to peel Ravyn away from the High Prince. "Get off me," Ravyn barked, pushing his way out of the yard, his smooth control cracked by anger. "Training concluded."

I watched the Destriers escort the High Prince out of the yard. Hauth swore mercilessly, cradling his bloody hand as he and the Destriers disappeared into the castle under a plume of darkness.

"He'll live," Ione said, her voice flat. She turned her heel and sauntered out of the yard, her long yellow hair catching the fading light.

My heartbeat did not slow until the yard was quiet once more. Only Elm and I remained. "What just happened?"

The Prince shrugged, his green eyes lingering on Ione's shape in the distance. "Hauth broke your wrist, Ravyn mangled his hand. Balance."

I searched for Ione, but I heard the low rumbles of Hauth's voice coming from her room and quickly steered myself in the opposite direction. Her gaze along my arm in the yard had shaken me. And though she had no way of knowing what had happened in the wood last night, wariness dogged me. There was so much I did not understand about this new version of Ione.

And it frightened me, not trusting the person, nigh a fortnight ago, I had known bcst in thc world.

Ravyn and Jespyr and Elm took dinner with the other Destriers. It was just me and Fenir and Morette seated at the long, crooked tree of a dinner table. When they decided to turn in early, I did not complain.

I walked the long corridor back to my room, humming one of the Nightmare's tunes to myself. *The Cards. The mist. The blood,* he called in the dark. *You're getting closer. Can you smell the salt?*

Footsteps sounded up ahead, followed by low voices. I would have gone into my room, anxious not to be caught eavesdropping, if I hadn't heard one of the voices say my name.

Elm's words were half whispered, half hissed. "We have no idea what happened in the wood," he said. "Spindle—her abilities—"

"Are incredible. She saved your life. I think she's earned a reprieve from your usual hostility, don't you?"

"I'm not saying I'm not grateful to live another day at the

edge of a sword, Ravyn. Only that we should be careful. Hauth looked like he'd been attacked by an animal, not a woman. There is too much we don't know about her." Elm paused a moment. "Your Nightmare Card could help with that."

I felt myself go cold.

Ravyn's voice was rough. "No. I'm not going to do that."

"You don't have a problem using it on the rest of us. Why not her?"

"The rest of you have consented. She hasn't."

"And you don't think maybe that's because she has something to hide?"

"She's had things to hide most of her life." Ravyn's voice cut. "Can't you see that?"

"Not as well as you, it seems."

"What does that mean?"

"Nothing," Elm said. "But we can't afford to make mistakes, not when we're this close. Breaking Hauth's hand—enjoyable as that was for me—was reckless."

Ravyn was quiet a moment. "I know."

"You shouldn't let your guard down, Ravyn. Especially not for her."

"Duly noted," the Captain said, frost in the low notes of his voice. "Good night, cousin."

Footsteps sounded. I fumbled at my latch, making far too much noise. I'd hardly stepped into my room and shut the door behind me when three sharp knocks rattled against the wood.

The Nightmare sighed. *You do make it hard for yourself, my dear.*

"Who is it?" I called, my voice pitching, too high and breathless.

"Ravyn."

When I pulled the door open, the knot in my stomach constricted, the Captain of the Destriers startlingly handsome in a deep green tunic. He leaned against the doorframe, his calloused fingers drumming a static rhythm on the old wood. He regarded me, tilting his head like an inquisitive bird of prey.

"I thought you'd still be at dinner."

"None of us were very hungry. I just got back."

"Yes. I heard you."

He didn't ask if I'd been listening to his conversation. No doubt he already knew. He heaved a heavy breath. "I'm sorry about today," he said. "I'm sure it wasn't easy, seeing Hauth after last night."

The Nightmare's claws clicked across my mind.

"It wasn't about you," Ravyn said, "when I broke his hand. I mean, it *was* about you—but it's more than that."

"Oh?"

"We've a remarkably hostile relationship, my cousin and I."

I snorted. "I've noticed."

"Hauth hates the infection. More than most. And he hates that his father made me Captain." Ravyn bit his lip, his posture stiffening. "He's the one who told the King about my infection. Ten years later, he did the same when Emory caught the fever."

I could almost feel the strain in his shoulders. I wanted to reach out and touch his hand—tell him I understood, better than perhaps anyone. But I didn't.

"But that isn't why I came to see you," Ravyn said.

"No?"

"There's something I meant to show you yesterday, only there wasn't the time," he said. "But if you're tired, it can wait."

I was tired. But something stirred in my stomach—something without a name that, if ignored, would gnaw at me all night. I leaned up against the opposite side of the doorframe, my brows perked. "What is it?"

The corner of Ravyn's lips lifted. "You'll see."

Chapter Twenty-Two

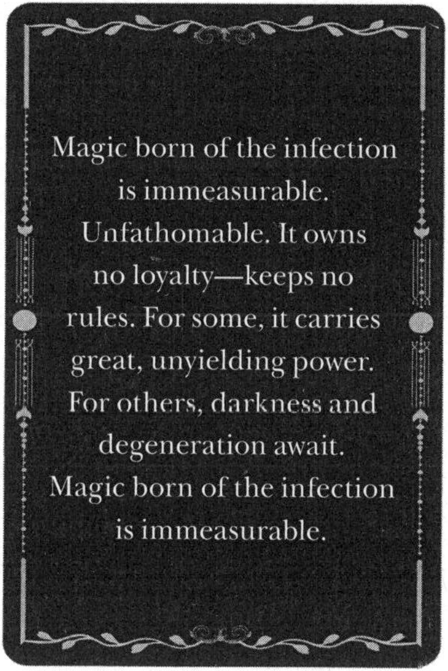

We did not take the main stairwell out of the castle but rather the winding servants' passage, our steps hasty until we reached the small wooden door to the gardens. Outside, the full moon cast eerie shadows through the mist, the garden wraithlike as it caught the autumn breeze.

I followed Ravyn down the same path we'd trudged the day before, careful of my step. When a screech owl sounded above my head, I jumped, moving closer to Ravyn as he led us through the bramble, the path wrought with shadow.

The ruins of the ancient castle looked even stranger by night. They sat, nestled by mist, absorbing moonlight.

At the edge of the cemetery stood the stone chamber, its

window dark and ominous.

The Nightmare's gaze alleviated the darkness around us. *Go inside,* he murmured.

"We're going there?" I whispered, Ravyn's steps sure as he led us past the looming yew tree.

"Yes."

The chamber had no door, only the one window. Ravyn swung himself over the lip of the window, his movements graceful, practiced, as if done a hundred times before. A moment later he was inside.

He leaned over the sill and held out a hand to me.

I hesitated. There was something magical inside the chamber—I could sense it, the sudden pang of salt in my nose distinct. Roused from the depths of my mind, the Nightmare sprang forward, so abrupt I nearly lost my footing.

Go inside, he urged.

I took Ravyn's hand and he guided me over the stone windowsill. My feet hit soil, and for the half second it took for my eyes to adjust, everything was perfectly black.

The chamber was a square. Moonlight flickered from above, the wood ceiling atop the chamber rotted out—fractured. I could see the shadow of branches above, the yew tree watching us through the broken wood ceiling.

In the center of the room, there was a tall, broad slab of stone. My breath caught in my throat and I looked around, this time in earnest.

I recognized the room: the ivy-laden walls...the fractured wooden ceiling...the stone in the center of the room.

All that was missing was the armored knight perched upon it.

This is the place, I gasped. *The room from my dreams.*

Yes, the Nightmare called, his voice shifting like a ghost on the wind.

What is it? Who was the man seated atop the stone?

A place of time—a man of fault. Both fueled by rage—both buried in salt.

Ravyn and I approached the stone in the center of the room. "When I was a boy," Ravyn explained, "I liked to play here."

I shivered. "Rather terrifying place to play, isn't it?"

His eyes found mine. "Perhaps."

I poked through my mind, demanding an explanation—a reason why he'd shown me this place in my dreams. But the Nightmare stayed silent, waiting, watching.

"Why are we here?" I asked.

Ravyn withdrew his hand from his cloak. "I'll show you."

He placed his palm upright in the center of the stone slab, moonlight dancing along his skin. I didn't see the small silver blade—drawn from his belt in a sudden, fluid motion. I didn't see much at all. He was too quick.

Before I could even blink, Ravyn's hand was covered in blood.

"What are you doing?" I cried.

He pocketed the knife, a cut slashed across the flesh below his thumb. Blood dripped down the lines of his palm to the stone beneath. "Don't worry," he said, his voice shockingly even for someone who'd just wounded himself. "Watch."

Breath caught in my chest as Ravyn turned his palm onto the stone, the world and the Nightmare behind my eyes suddenly still. Then, out of the depths of the stone—bright and true—emerged several unmistakable beams of light.

Providence Cards, hidden in the depths of the ancient stone, unlocked by blood.

Ravyn's blood. Infected blood.

Magical blood.

The center of the stone, once dark and impenetrable,

became clear as water. I could see through it, like looking through a door. Deep within its depth sat the Providence Cards, stacked, hidden, and waiting.

I fought the words. "How—how did you…?"

Ravyn smiled, reaching into the hollowed-out center of the stone and grasping the stack of Providence Cards.

Their colors vanished—snuffed out by Ravyn's touch. I watched, fascinated, as he laid them out across the stone, color and brightness returning one by one as he let them go.

Prophet, Maiden, Chalice, Golden Egg, White Eagle, and the newly acquired Iron Gate.

"Your collection," I said, my eyes lost in the colors. "Your father showed them to me."

"And this is where we hide them," Ravyn said, patting the stone.

"How on earth did you discover this hiding place?"

He shrugged. "Playing as a boy. I'd cut my shoulder on the window and stumbled in, blood on my hand. When I touched the stone…well, you saw."

"But why is it here?" I asked, the smell of salt lingering in the room. "What is this place?"

"I don't know. It's old—as old as the ruins outside." He reached into his pocket, retrieving the burgundy and purple lights—the Nightmare, the Mirror. "I found these inside the center of the stone."

I prodded the darkness, the Nightmare. When he spoke, his words dripped like rainwater. *An offering, bartered with blood. That's how the Spirit bargains—always with blood. So the Shepherd King built her this chamber at the edge of the woods, this altar. And here, they bartered.*

How do you know so much about it?

He did not answer. I ran my hand over the stone, its surface cold and rough beneath my palm.

Ravyn wiped away his blood on the sleeve of his tunic. "Others have tried to open the stone to no avail. Should something happen to me, you are the only one here who can open it. Only infected blood will unveil the chasm."

I looked up at him. "Is something going to happen to you?"

His smile did not touch his eyes. "Not if I can help it."

He collected the Cards once more, each surrendering its color at the touch of his hand. As he reached for the White Eagle, I grasped his sleeve and held it. I stared at the Cards in his hand—all devoid of color, save the Nightmare and the Mirror. "Why can you use only these two?"

Ravyn did not speak at first, his eyes intent on my face. Perhaps, like other things between us, he wished this secret to remain unspoken. But I held his gaze, waiting, emboldened by the stillness around us.

"I was thirteen—older than most—when I caught the fever," he said, breaking the silence. "But I saw no sign of magic, no new abilities. I avoided Physicians. I thought I had escaped the consequences of the infection. A year later, I was training to be a Destrier." His tone darkened. "But when I was offered a Black Horse, the Card would not yield to me. I couldn't get it to work, no matter how hard I tried." He paused. "Hauth told Orithe Willow, who cut me with his claw and confirmed my infection to the King."

I had never heard him speak so much at once. His voice bore the depths of dark water, smooth, unwavering. It lulled me. I traced the Captain of the Destriers' face with my eyes, lost in his past—starved for his story.

Ravyn continued. "But like his pet Orithe, the King saw value in my infection. Without the Black Horse, I became a better fighter than the other Destriers. The Chalice did not work for me—but neither did it work against me. No one could see me in the Well Card. The Scythe cannot control me." He paused. "That is why he made me Captain."

He ran his hand through his hair. "Every year, I lose the ability to use another Card. Only the Mirror, Nightmare, and, I assume, the Twin Alders remain." To my wide eyes, he gave a shrug. "Magic comes at a cost. If we do not collect the Deck and heal my infection, I will not be able to use Providence Cards at all." He looked at me, his face shadowed. His eyes found mine. "I rarely talk about it, save with Elm."

My brow twisted, the words slow to come. "But he's... he's—"

"A Rowan."

"Aren't you afraid he'll tell his father?"

Ravyn smiled. "If you knew him, you'd realize how impossible that is. Elm is loyal—to a fault."

I thought of Ione. Or, my stomach dropping, how Ione used to be. "And he's loyal to you, not his own father and brother?"

Ravyn paused. "Elm was a clever child. But he hated training, preferring his books. The King took displeasure in his mildness and thought him weak, leaving his upbringing to the Queen. When she died, Elm was...mistreated at Stone." He struggled with the words. "Hauth brutalized him. So one day I just...brought him home. My parents became his parents, my siblings his siblings. He's wary, untrusting, but he'd die before he'd betray us."

There was something new, something fierce and raw, about the Captain of the Destriers. Perhaps, like me, the salt in the air had set him on edge—woken him. Gone was the unyielding expression, the unflinching austerity. In its place, deeply rooted intent.

Ravyn turned back to the Cards atop the stone. He stacked them, the colors disappearing as soon as they touched his skin.

Then he reached into the stone, setting them down to rest. When his hand retracted, their colors returned.

He pulled the same knife as before from his belt and brought it to his hand.

"Wait," I said, catching his arm. "Let me."

His brow furrowed. "No, Elspeth."

"I mean it," I said. When he did not budge, I stuck out my jaw. "If I'm to know how to do it properly, you must let me actually do it."

Ravyn's grip on the blade did not let. He said nothing, something at war behind his gray eyes. Still, he did not give me the knife.

"Fine," I said, turning away from him.

He caught me by my good wrist and pulled me back. He brought my hand close to his chest. Above it, he held his knife like a violin bow, its wicked edge a whisper from my palm. "It doesn't take much blood," he said, his voice a growl. "Just a small amount. An offering."

A barter, whispered the Nightmare. *Nothing comes free.*

Ravyn's skin was rough, like the cover of a long-forgotten book. But it was warm. My breath swelled as I waited for the pain of the blade, my eyes never leaving his.

He slid his knife along the heel of my palm. I gasped, watching a trail of red beads escape the nigh-invisible cut Ravyn had just dealt. He pinched my flesh, pulling more blood to the surface. "Just a small cut," he murmured. "Nothing too deep. No need to scar these beautiful hands."

If there was pain, I hardly felt it. Something else was stirring in me. Not quite pain; an *ache.*

Ravyn guided my hand to the stone, pressing it against the textured, ancient stone. When he pulled it back, droplets of blood remained. A moment later the Cards were gone, sealed back in the stone, the chamber dark once more.

Gone, too, was my blood, my barter, lost to the strange magic of the stone.

"Nothing comes free," I whispered.

Ravyn pulled my hand back to him, only a few beads of red remaining. He pressed two calloused fingers into the cut, stopping the bleed. A strand of hair fell over his brow, his eyes lowered to my palm.

I pushed the hair out of his face with my other hand, my fingers shaky as they brushed over his forehead.

Ravyn looked up, his gaze lingering on my mouth before climbing to my eyes. His fingers slid to my wrist, languid in their journey. "I can feel your pulse. Your heart is racing," he said.

I was suddenly thankful for the cover of nightfall—the darkly shadowed chamber. Had it been daylight, the intense heat in my cheeks would have been unmistakable.

I felt tethered—wrapped in an invisible string that tied me to the Captain of the Destriers. I was painfully aware of how closely we stood—the warmth of his broad body—the curve of my breasts above my neckline as I took quick, unsteady breaths—the feel of his calloused hand on mine. "I don't know why," I said.

His lips curled into the ghost of a smile. "Don't you?"

I kept still, waiting for something I didn't have the courage to name. With his free hand, Ravyn cupped the side of my face, his thumb lingering perilously close to my mouth.

Breath hitched in my lungs and my lips parted, anticipation melding with a lightness I did not understand. Ravyn let out an abrupt exhale—his thumb brushing across the flesh of my bottom lip, snagging it.

When he leaned closer, I closed my eyes, his mouth a whisper from mine. His voice caught at the edges. "Is this you pretending, Elspeth?" he said, the tip of his nose grazing mine. "Because if it is…" His breath stirred my eyelashes. "You're very good at it."

His words moved something in me. The same calling from before—the same ache. I wanted him to run his hand over my mouth again—to feel the texture of his rough, hardened skin. My body was screaming, a mindless, impatient call for touch.

His touch.

"No better than you, Captain."

Ravyn's throat hitched, his eyelids lowering. He placed my hand firmly on his chest, across the Yew insignia, just above his heart. His chest thumped—his heartbeat ragged, as if he'd just been running. When I looked up, he was watching me, his eyes softer than before. "Does this feel pretend?" he said, his mouth close now, so close his lips tugged at mine.

It felt…raw. Honest. Something I was deeply unfamiliar with. It had taken Ravyn Yew, Captain of the Destriers, my supposed natural enemy, to make me realize what I truly, deeply wanted.

To stop pretending.

Our lips collided, there, among the salt. Ravyn growled into my mouth and I pressed my entire self into him, wanting—needing—to feel him against my body. His hand slid over my jaw to the nape of my neck, his fingers twisting in my hair, his mouth opening to mine. Our tongues touched, hot and unfamiliar, tentative at first, then greedy.

He drew me out of my Nightmare-infested mind into *myself*. The kiss deepened. I cupped Ravyn's jaw in my hand, my fingers digging into the stubble that grew there. I didn't think about being soft with him. I was so tired of pretending not to want this.

The hardening of his body told me he felt the same. Ravyn hooked his arm around the small of my back, pressing me against him. He brushed his mouth across my cheek, his teeth nipping my earlobe before lowering to my neck. Shivers danced up my spine. His fingers curled in my hair, pulling it just enough so that my head tilted back, my neck bared to him. He kissed me below my ear, under my jaw, down my throat.

Had I kept my eyes shut, I might have surrendered entirely to Ravyn's touch. But I opened them a sliver, and when I did, something over Ravyn's shoulder caught my gaze. A shadow shifting across the dark chamber. When I followed it, my eyes returned to the stone in the center of the room—the one that, only moments ago, Ravyn had opened and I had closed, with blood.

Only now, perched atop it, his gold armor dimly glistening, sat the man from my dreams.

He watched me as I stood with the Captain of the Destriers. When he spoke, I recognized the silky quality of his voice. "Elspeth Spindle," he said, his eyes—so strange and yellow—ensnaring me. "Let me out."

I ripped away from Ravyn, fighting to suppress a scream. But when I looked back at the stone, the knight was gone. The only thing left was the smell of salt, invisible as it lingered all around us.

Ravyn's eyes were wide, wild. His black hair untidy, his hands—hands that, a moment ago, had been tangled in my hair, my body—dropping to his sides. Even in the darkness, I could trace the flush up his neck. He opened his mouth to speak, but I was already turning away, afraid to stay another second in the strange, magical chamber.

"I'm sorry," I said as I moved to the window. "I have to go."

"Elspeth," he called after me.

But I did not turn back, and graciously, he did not pursue me. I ran into the meadow, released from the salt—the magic. I exhaled short, hot breaths that did nothing to soothe me, and did not stop running until I'd reached the small wooden door at the base of the castle.

What's happening to me? I cried, my fingers balled into fists. *Am I losing my mind?*

The Nightmare slithered through my thoughts, like a serpent over grass. *I know what I know,* he murmured.

I shouted into the chasm of my mind. *Enough, Nightmare! Tell me the truth. Who is that man? Why do I keep seeing him?*

He is a vestige of the past, haunting the chamber he built for the Spirit of the Wood, nothing more than a memory of a man who once was. His voice grew harder. *A man I once was.*

I slammed my chamber door shut and flung myself into the room. But my foot caught on the carpet. I swore, kicking the ancient wool.

My eyes froze. There he was, woven into the carpet of my room, his gilded armor bright atop his black horse. The knight from the chamber. Only now, as I scanned the wool, I noticed a distant object, woven into the green at the edge of the carpet, nestled at the edge of the woods, just before the tree line.

A doorless chamber with one dark window.

My youth came slamming into me. I saw myself as a little girl, poring over my aunt's copy of *The Old Book of Alders,* fixed on the Nightmare Card's page. So certain had I been that the creature in my mind was an embodiment of the Card itself—the monster on its cover matching him entirely—that I had failed to understand what was written just a few pages prior.

But it felt incomplete, my collection yet whole. And so, for the Nightmare, I bartered my soul.

I put a hand to my mouth, fingers shaking. My voice came out hollow. "But that would mean I absorbed your soul when

I touched the Nightmare Card. Which makes you...the Shepherd King."

A growl, a sneer—oil, bile. His voice called, louder than it had ever been, as if he was closer. Stronger. *Finally, my darling Elspeth, we understand one another.*

Chapter Twenty-Three

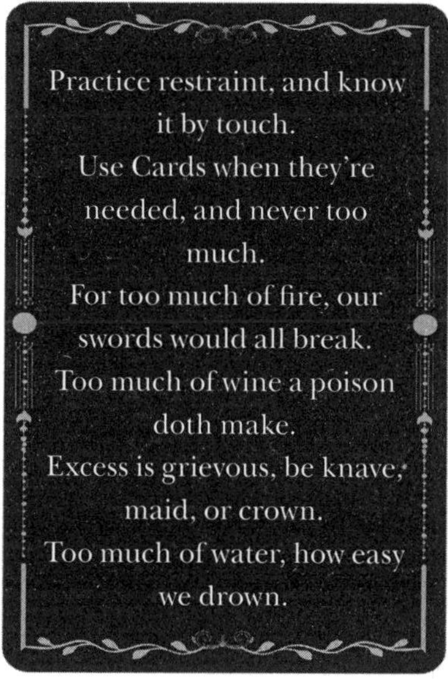

"Miss? Miss Spindle?"

I woke with a start, my wrist stiff and painful, violent shivers ripping up and down my spine.

Mourning doves called above my head. I sat up in a daze, startled to see the cool morning sky, my bedroom ceiling and walls vanished. My skin hurt, pricked by gooseflesh. I was in my nightgown, dirty and damp from the flattened grass beneath me. I looked around, recognizing tall yew trees, the bramble of unkempt foliage growing, unbidden, around me.

In the distance stood the stone chamber I'd left only hours ago, surrounded by mist.

Filick Willow stared down at me, his hood damp and his eyes

wide. “Are you all right, Miss Spindle?” he asked.

I pulled myself up, my body stiff with cold. Still wary of Physicians, even one in the Captain of the Destriers’ pocket, I took a step back.

I could not recall drifting off to sleep, nor taking an impromptu walk back to the meadow. Probing the darkness in my head, I found the Nightmare curled up, quiet in his respite, perfectly content not to offer up an explanation.

“I—I must have walked in my sleep,” I said.

Filick unfastened his cloak and handed it to me. “Come, I’ll make you a cup of tea. You’re cold as death.”

I did not stop shivering until I’d sat by Filick’s hearth a full ten minutes. He called for tea and I drank it in three gulps, hardly noticing when the water singed my tongue. Filick sat next to me, unwrapping my swollen wrist.

“Does that happen often?” he asked after I’d regained a whit of color. “Walking in your sleep?”

I shook my head. “No.”

“Had you ever been to the ruins before?”

“Yes.” I shivered. “What is that chamber? The one with the magic stone?”

Filick took a sip of tea. “Ravyn showed you, then?”

Memory of last night flooded my senses. I faced the fire, a blush rushing into my cheeks.

If the Physician saw, he made no mention of it. “I can’t say for certain. Castle Yew is old, full of artifacts,” he said. “There is strange, ancient magic in that chamber. I walk there often, in the mornings.”

I eyed him with a healthy dose of distrust. “You seem to place a lot of value in old magic,” I said. “For a Physician.”

Filick smiled, retrieving fresh linen from his shelves. “We Willows have been Physicians for hundreds of years. Ages ago,” he said, "we knew the mist was full of salt—full of magic. But we did not fear it. We venerated the Spirit of the Wood and the gifts she gave. Those who suffered the fever and the degeneration that followed were treated—not hunted."

"What changed?" I asked.

He wrapped the linen around my wrist. "There are no surviving records. But stories remain—a chain of events." He rewrapped my wrist with the dexterity of someone long acquainted with injuries. "To her own detriment, the Spirit of the Wood granted the Shepherd King magic so great, he created the Providence Cards. He shared them with his kingdom, and people stopped going to the woods to ask the Spirit for magical gifts. Instead, they vied for the Cards, greedy for magic that would not degenerate."

I nodded. My aunt had told me this story. "And so, the Spirit created the mist, to draw people back to her. By force."

"Precisely." Filick's brow furrowed. "When the mist locked Blunder away from the rest of the world, the Shepherd King went to bargain with the Spirit. When he returned, he wrote *The Old Book of Alders*, that the people of Blunder might ward themselves with charms. But all bargains bear a price."

"The Twin Alders."

"The Twin Alders." Filick shook his head. "A fool's bargain."

"Why do you say that?"

"The Spirit is cunning, 'neither kin, foe, nor friend.'" Filick leaned back in his chair. "It takes the entire Deck to lift the mist, no? So then why would a King, who sought to save his kingdom from the mist, give up the Twin Alders, the only Card of its kind?"

A latch in my mind lifted. "The Spirit tricked him," I whispered, recalling what my aunt had told me years ago. "He didn't know he needed the Twin Alders to lift the mist until he'd already bargained it away."

Filick nodded. "It's a common theory among those of us who like to look into the past. And, to the Shepherd King's credit, it wasn't an entirely empty bargain. We got *The Old Book of Alders* and learned to be wary of magic, to carry charms in the mist." He took a long drink of tea. "You ask what changed, Miss Spindle? Brutus Rowan, the first Rowan King. That's what changed. He took *The Old Book of Alders* and made it doctrine, twisting the words until they'd become weapons against anyone infected."

Closer—I was getting closer to knowing—understanding—something that, for years, had lived in the dark corners of my mind, obscured but ever present. I leaned forward. "Why should Brutus Rowan hate the infection?"

Filick tapped his finger on his cup. "Perhaps he feared old magic—magic he could not control." His brow darkened, his eyes distant. "Or perhaps in a kingdom where balance is the only constant, he simply sought to cheat the scales. He stole the throne from an infected King. And now his lineage strives to kill anyone with enough magic to take it back."

A chill crept over me. "Is that what happened? Rowan stole the throne from the Shepherd King?"

Filick's eyes found me again, his furrow easing. "Of course, this is all just theory, Miss Spindle. A story."

But it wasn't. Not for me. "What happened to the Shepherd King?"

"He died. How, I cannot say."

Darkness overtook my eyes. For a moment, I lost vision, the sound of the Nightmare's laugh, hollow and cruel, blotting out all noise.

A moment later it was gone, my vision returned. Filick must have seen the disquiet behind my eyes because when he patted my hand, my new bandage perfectly knotted, his voice was soft.

"It's easy to get lost in the past in a strange, old castle like this. Have no worry, Miss Spindle. A wrong done five hundred years ago has no bearing on today. You and Ravyn will find the Twin Alders Card and unite the Deck. Of that, I am certain."

He was trying to reassure me. And while I was sure Filick Willow was one of the cleverest men in Blunder, there was one thing he was terribly, terribly wrong about.

What happened five hundred years ago mattered. Far more than I had ever realized.

I pushed out of my chair. "Thank you. I'm sorry if I disturbed your morning walk."

"Not at all," he said, escorting me to the door.

I might have gone back to my chamber—hurried through the castle, my hem still soaked with morning dew. But I lingered at the Physician's threshold.

"There is something I still don't understand," I said.

"What's that?"

"Degeneration." I searched for the words. "Ravyn's degeneration does not allow him to use Cards. Emory's is slowly killing him, body and mind." I paused. "But I... I can't seem to understand what mine is."

Pity washed over Filick's aged face. "No two infections are the same, Miss Spindle. Emory's degeneration is widespread, while Ravyn's doesn't seem to affect his health at all. What is certain for the Yew brothers may just be a whisper of truth for you." He shook his head. "I wish I could offer more comfort. But I simply do not know."

Lost for words, I gave the Physician a simple nod and stepped into the corridor.

I waited until I'd turned the corner before barking into the blackness. *Sleepwalking?* I demanded. *Really?*

He stretched lazily across my mind. *What of it?*

You can't do that—not here, not anywhere—but especially not here!

Who says I did anything?

Don't play me for a fool, Nightmare! My voice was blade sharp. *Or should I call you Shepherd King instead?*

He slithered through the darkness, his voice ricocheting in the din, as if there were many voices, not his alone. *Call me what you will, Elspeth. It changes nothing.*

I gritted my teeth, eleven years of his games—his secrets—boiling in me. All I felt was rage, the desire to banish him from my mind so violent I might have struck the wall had it not been made of stone. *If it's your soul I absorbed when I touched my uncle's Nightmare Card,* I said, *then I absorbed a King. But you—you are not a King. You're a monster.*

He laughed at me again. *I am both.* There was a pause. *Don't you remember the story, Elspeth? Our story?*

My stomach dropped. The story. Whispers, near and far, always as I was drifting off to sleep. The haunting lullaby of the maiden, the King.

The monster.

I leaned into the wall, my legs suddenly unsteady. I pressed the heel of my palm to my brow. But that only made the darkness behind my eyes more oppressive. *Why, now, am I seeing your memories?*

You don't need me, or that Physician, to tell you why. You have your own theory regarding that.

I shook my head. *Well?* I demanded. *Is it true?*

You tell me.

I'm ASKING you.

But you already know. Deep down, you've always known.

I felt cold again, a profound, unbidden frost emanating from the center of my chest. *You're becoming stronger,* I whispered, my voice hardly audible in the dark din. *That's why I'm seeing your memories. I may not be getting weaker like Emory, but I'm . . . fading.* A lump rose in my throat. *That's my degeneration, isn't it?*

He said nothing, his jagged teeth clicking as he clamped and unclamped his jaw. *Click. Click. Click.*

It's my payment, I said, filled with biting clarity. *Every time I ask for your help, you grow stronger. And I'm—I'm losing control.*

I told you, child, he said, *nothing is free. Nothing is safe. Magic always comes at a cost.*

Yes, but I didn't realize that meant you were taking control of my body—my mind!

I'm not TAKING anything, Elspeth Spindle. He hissed, claws flashing, suddenly vicious. *I cannot TAKE. I am capable only of what I am willfully given.* He slinked into the darkness, hasty to be away from me. *Remember that, when you finally have the courage to admit it. In the end, I took nothing you had not already given me.*

I was not sorry to feel him go. I felt cold again, afraid and hollow.

But that hollowness soon gave way to a scorching anger. I would not succumb to my own annihilation, victim to degeneration or the Nightmare. I would free myself—cure myself—and go back to the life I'd abandoned eleven years ago.

Only two more Providence Cards stood in my way.

I hurried through the galley on my way to my room, but stopped when I heard the clamor below.

Dozens of voices melded together in loud discord from Castle Yew's great hall. I heard the clank of steel—armor and swords and chainmail. The Destriers milled below, their Black Horses glowing ominously from their cloaks. Some were eating, others examining their weapons. Hauth Rowan stood among the fray, his broad back covered in a black cloak. He spoke to the others in a curt voice, his demeanor characteristically dominant.

The corner of my lips curled when I saw his wounded left hand wrapped heavily in linen.

"Like what you see?"

I jumped so violently I nearly flew off the banister.

Elm watched me, a small, satisfied grin on his face. "Sorry," he said. "I thought you'd heard me."

"Well, I didn't." When the Prince eyed me up and down, I cringed, still draped in Filick Willow's cloak, the hem of my nightdress soaked by morning dew. "I got lost," I lied.

"Still can't find your way around?"

"Something like that."

The Prince rolled his eyes and pointed a sharp finger back behind us. "That corridor will take you back up through the galley and into the guest hall. Your room should be somewhere along that corridor. Or should I call Ravyn to take you? I'm sure he'd be delighted—"

"No," I said quickly. "I'll find it."

"Hurry," Elm said, moving down the stairwell. "We're heading out soon."

"Heading out where?" I called.

But he was already halfway gone.

"*Elm,*" I hissed. "What's going on?"

"Market Day," he called without stopping. "Wear your colors. That is, if your father ever condescended to give you any."

Chapter Twenty-Four

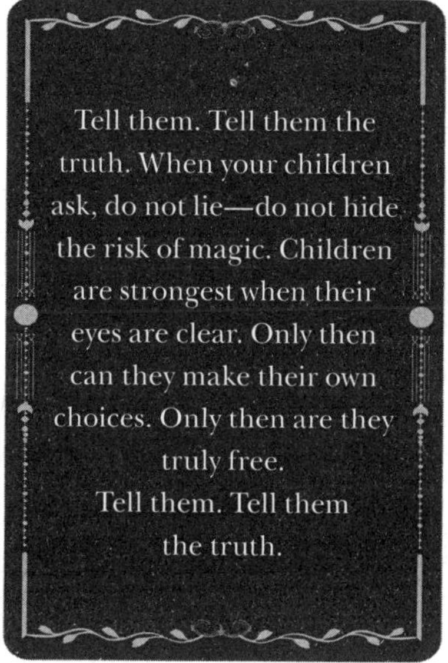

I stared at myself in the foggy looking glass, trying to recall my mother's face. Her dress was long and richly made, deep crimson—like heart blood. Across its breast was embroidered a tangle of golden branches that wove together into a long, delicate spindle tree.

I'd inherited the dress, along with a few other trinkets, at her death. I'd brought it to Equinox but had left too early to wear it. The style was older, but I did not begrudge the gown its draping sleeves. They would help hide my bandaged, aching wrist.

When my maid reached for my wooden comb, I stopped her, pointing to the flower crown on my nightstand. "The rose will do," I said, plaiting my hair into a long, plain braid and fastening the rose just above the nape of my neck.

Out of habit, I placed my charm in my skirt pocket. I smiled into the looking glass, searching for energy I did not feel.

The woman reflected in the glass matched my smile, her feline yellow eyes flashing.

Jespyr waited at the foot of the stairs, her injured foot stuffed into a thick black boot. She wore her black Destrier tunic, her brow covered in an intricate felt mask of the same color—a Market Day tradition. When she glanced my way, her brows rose above her mask. "You look lovely," she said. "I've never seen you in your house color before."

As always, Jespyr's smile was contagious. "I didn't bring a mask," I said. "I almost never go to Market Day."

"Thistle will find you one," she said, offering me her arm. "Shall we?"

We stepped through the ancient doorway into morning sunlight. My mask was a deep green but for the gold trim painted along the edges of the eyes. It tied in a silk ribbon behind my head, covering my face from my brow bone to just below the apples of my cheeks.

I saw Ione up ahead in a cream-colored mask, her gold dress hemmed in Hawthorn white. Fenir and Morette Yew stood together in matching green, their yew trees embroidered ornately up the spine of their cloaks. Hauth, who wore no mask—his Princely face on display—had abandoned his black Destrier's cloak for a rich tunic, the gold branches of several prominent trees woven into a strange, complex pattern along his chest, shadowed by the Rowan insignia.

He stood with Ione near Elm and Ravyn, who, with matching masks, remained adorned in Destrier black.

They stopped speaking as Jespyr and I approached, their eyes turning to me.

Warmth moved across my chest, swimming up my neck into my cheeks. When no one spoke, Jespyr let out a snort. "Clearly they've never seen a woman before."

I tried not to look at Ravyn, the memory of last night encasing me, the feel of his hand in my hair—his mouth on mine—still a shadow on my skin. I felt his eyes tracing me. When I finally raised my gaze, I caught the tail of a smile roving across his mouth, his eyes lingering on the rose in my hair.

But before Ravyn could greet me, Hauth stepped in his way.

The High Prince's voice was smooth—charming once more. "Miss Spindle," he said, offering me his uninjured hand.

I took it hesitantly, bowing. "Your Highness."

"You must forgive my brutish manners. Yesterday was a trying day."

The High Prince did not let go of my hand, his gaze tight on my face. "You're very striking, even under that mask," he said. He pulled me closer. "I wonder," he said, shooting Ravyn a pointed look over his shoulder, "what it is you see in my cousin."

I could tell by the sly tones of Hauth's voice that I held little interest for him—I was merely a toy to steal from his cousin. Still, my gaze turned to the Captain of the Destriers. I noted the shadow of the beard and the flex of muscle beneath it along Ravyn's jaw. The sharp contours along the ridge of his distinct nose. The way his hair, neither long nor short, framed his stern brow. His gray eyes—stark beneath his black mask—so sharp they cut at me.

It was all of those things—and none of them at once. Something else drew me to the Captain of the Destriers. Something I had, caught up in our game of pretend, overlooked. Something ancient—born of salt. We were the same, he and I. Gifted with ancient, terrible magic. Woven in secret, hidden in half-truths. We were the darkness in Blunder, the reminder that magic—wild and unfettered—prevailed, no matter how desperately the Rowans tried to stamp it out. We were the thing to be feared.

We were the balance.

But I could not say that in front of Hauth Rowan. Instead, I offered Ravyn a rare, unconstrained smile. "He's very...tall."

Ravyn's eyes flared. He caught my smile and matched it with his own, stepping forward. When he squared off with the High Prince, I noticed Hauth straighten, his spine rigid, chin held high.

But it was to no avail. Ravyn was taller than him. And, given the condescending turn of his mouth, it wasn't the only thing Ravyn felt superior to his cousin over. He offered me his hand and I took it, grateful to be free of Hauth's touch. "If you're done peacocking," Ravyn said to his cousin, lacing his fingers in mine, "Market Day awaits. Best put a glove over that mangled hand before your subjects see it, Prince."

Hauth's nostrils flared. Not reticent to be outdone, he caught my other wrist—my injured wrist. "You'll save me a turn on the square, won't you, Miss Spindle?"

So acute I saw stars, pain shot through my wrist up into my arm. It took all my effort not to cry out in pain. And while my bandage was obscured by my sleeve, there was no hiding the strain on my face.

Hauth's expression shifted from bravado to surprise, his green eyes wide, lowering to my sleeve. "Something wrong with your arm, Miss Spindle?"

Next to me, Ravyn froze. But before he could speak, someone shifted in my periphery, a flurry of gold, long yellow hair catching the light.

Ione.

“Careful, darling,” she said, stepping between me and Hauth, forcing him to drop my arm. Her voice was pitched higher than normal—sickly sweet. “Elspeth and I went riding yesterday morning. She fell off a horse, poor dear.” Her hazel eyes turned to me, narrow, keen—opposite of the sweetness in her voice. “Isn’t that right, Bess?”

For a moment I thought I caught a glimpse of the old Ione—the one who would block me from my stepmother’s frigid glares. Shield maiden, Ione Hawthorn, ever my protector. I nodded, my wrist still throbbing. “Indeed.”

Hauth’s gaze skipped from me to Ione. When it landed on his betrothed, something cold slid into his green eyes.

But I had no time to work out what it meant, or why Ione had lied to him for me. Elm and Jespyr swooped upon us. Jespyr slid her arm into Ravyn’s, and Elm did the same to mine, pulling both of us away from Hauth and Ione. “You know what they say,” Elm said. “Don’t mix horses and drink. Now, if we’re done with pleasantries, let’s go. It’s practically midday, and on the subject of drink, I’m behind on my daily quotient.”

He pulled me through the statuary toward the gate. I felt Hauth and Ione watching me, but I did not turn. I couldn’t let them see all the fear welling in my eyes. Ravyn shot me a fleeting glance, but his sister kept him at a steady pace ahead of us, her head close to his in conversation.

“Do you think Hauth recognized my injury?” I whispered to Elm.

Elm ran a hand through his tangled hair, leading me out the gate onto the cobbled street. “My brother’s not half as clever as he thinks he is,” he said. “By the trees, Spindle, wipe all that apprehension off your face.”

But I wasn’t convinced. There was something about Hauth

Rowan that deeply unnerved me. Just like in the wood, I could not shake the feeling he was hunting me. With every look—every touch—he was seeking me out for the kill.

The street sloped, busier the closer we got to the square on Market Street. We were close to Spindle House. I could see the red flag at the gate. A guard stood sentry, one I'd never met before.

I slowed my pace, an idea sharp in my mind. But when I tried to step beyond the crowd to the gate, Elm held me back.

"Keep walking," he said.

"I was just going to—"

"I know what you were doing," he snapped. "Now's not the time."

"Why not?" I demanded, pulling out of his grasp. "My father won't be home. We can look for his Well Card."

Elm glanced up the street, but Ravyn and Jespyr were too far ahead to call out to. He groaned, muttering under his breath. "Don't leave me with this nitwit."

I tugged his sleeve, forcing him to face me. "It's a good idea," I said.

He looked at me like I was a bug he'd like to squash. "And you think—what? That Erik's left his Well Card out on the table for us to nab? It's not the time," he said again.

"You're a Prince—you can do as you wish! You carry one of the strongest Cards in the Deck." I crossed my hands over my chest. "Or are you too afraid to do anything without Ravyn there to help you?"

Elm's eyes flared, his brow twisting in disdain, and I knew I'd hit a nerve. "No more than you, Spindle," he said, his voice dangerously low.

"I'm trying to keep things moving and not waste time with pageantry."

"It's *pageantry* that keeps us looking like everyone else," the

Prince said, his hand tight on my arm as he led me away from my father's house. "Let's go."

The Nightmare sat like a caged cat behind the bars of my head—fidgeting, awake, and aware. When we stepped onto Market Street, the long, winding spine of Blunder, Providence Cards emanating colorfully from a few pockets, he clawed through my mind, his oily voice tight in my ears.

Beware. There are more than Destriers here in the King's service.

I couldn't see Ravyn. When Jespyr joined us again, cheerful smile intact, Elm rolled his eyes and mumbled something about needing a drink. I watched him and his red light disappear into the crowd, happy to see him go.

Around us, Blunder's families stood in their house colors, some old and worn, some freshly tailored. They weaved in and out of tents and merchant stalls, their voices culminating in a plume of noise that clamored against cobblestone and brick from every direction.

A pair of girls in lilac dresses brushed past me, giggling as they devoured slices of lemon sweetbread. I felt an ache in my chest, remembering how, before the infection, Ione and I would wander the cobbled streets on Market Day. We would run between merchant stalls and sit by the fountain with crisp autumn apples, Ione clothed in Hawthorn white and I in deep Spindle red.

It felt a lifetime ago.

Next to me, Jespyr paid five coppers for a new pair of sheepskin gloves. "I love Market Day," she said. "It gives people a chance to step out of their routines—to have a little fun. Life isn't always about sword fighting and Card stealing, you know."

I glanced back up the street, the crimson flag at the Spindle House gate still visible. I wanted to tell her that I was running out of time, that the Nightmare in my head was growing stronger by the moment. But I didn't.

I turned away from Jespyr and ambled through the cobblestone streets. Clamor from the crowd engulfed me—color and noise. I let it toss me back and forth, aimless, my mother's dress a sail upon a directionless sea.

No one bothered me. I kept walking, wondering what it would feel like if the Nightmare took over my mind completely. Would it hurt, or would it be gentle, like slipping into the wood unnoticed—disappearing into the mist? Perhaps I'd leave my dress behind as a final farewell to the world and steal into the trees like a ghost, absorbed by darkness and moss.

I felt a hand on my shoulder, and when I turned, Ravyn was there, his head cocked familiarly to the side.

"I thought I was alone," I said.

"Here?" he said, gesturing to the mass of people around us.

When I did not reply, the Captain stepped closer, his broad shoulders shielding me from the sway of the crowd. My chest tightened in the confines of my dress, the desire to reach out and touch him just as strong as it had been the night before.

When he offered me his hand, I took it. His fingers flexed around mine, and when I looked up at him, there was strain I had not seen before—tiredness and determination. How handsome he was, beyond the smooth mask of stone. I saw myself reflected in his expression, the brutal world of the infection embedded on our brows alike—all the fear, all the isolation. I saw the world through his gray eyes—felt the weight of his responsibilities and treacheries—as if they were stones sewn into the fabric of my dress.

I leaned into him. "I want to help."

His fingers found my jaw, his thumb pressing just above my chin. "You are helping, Elspeth. More than you know."

"Not parading around like this," I said, gesturing to the crowd. "I felt less disguised dressed as a highwayman than I do in family colors."

"It's easier, being a highwayman. Cards, the infection—they don't matter. Family—duty—everything is obscured by the black mask. Things are simpler."

I sighed. "But things are never simple for people like us, are they?"

Ravyn's eyes traveled to the rose in my hair. He didn't say anything, silence tugging between us like invisible wire, painful, taut.

Behind my eyes, the Nightmare's voice was coy. *You're running out of time, dear one,* he said, slithering past my ears. *Tell him how you feel. If you don't say it aloud, can it ever be real?*

I flinched. Ravyn watched me, his eyes tight on my face. I tried to turn away, but his thumb atop my chin would not let me. "What is it?" he said.

Guilt settled over me like a thick fog. No matter how deeply I yearned to stop pretending, secrets remained. Mine, and the monster's. And I had no idea how to include Ravyn in them. "About last night..." I said. "When I ran off."

He inhaled. "Perhaps it's good you did."

The rejection stung. I tried to pull away. "Oh?"

Again, Ravyn's hand held me in place. His eyes lowered to my mouth, twin furrows drawn between his brows. "When my sister suggested I court you at Equinox, I resisted."

I frowned up at him. "Adamantly, as I recall."

He traced the curve of my chin. "I resisted, Elspeth, because I was already imagining how I might press my finger against your wet lips again, like I had in my room." He took in a breath, his mouth dropping to my ear. "And that was nothing to the wicked things I was imagining after we argued in the garden."

I let out an abrupt breath, warmth twisting deep in my stomach.

"I resisted," Ravyn said, "because I haven't stopped thinking about you since that first night on the forest road. And I realized at Equinox that the closer I let myself get to you, the less I'd want to be the King's Captain—the less I'd want to pretend. And it's dangerous for me, for my family, to stop pretending." He pressed his lips to the shell of my ear, a low, scraping whisper. "It's not safe to draw too close to me. I'm a liar, Elspeth. A traitor. And someday, there will be a reckoning." He pulled back, his gray eyes tight with strain. "The highwayman meets the hangman. Always."

His voice startled me. It shattered the stone I'd so long envisioned around him—the visage of the severe, untouchable Captain of the Destriers crumbling. This was him, letting me in—showing me the true Ravyn Yew.

A man just as terrified of the future as I was.

I stood on my toes and pressed my forehead against his, my voice so quiet my lips hardly moved. "Then be a liar, Ravyn. Betray. Upturn the kingdom that would see you and me and Emory killed. The King keeps you close so he can control you. But you are the only one who can withstand his Scythe Card."

I pulled back and looked him in the eyes. "It is not they who bring the reckoning, Ravyn. It is you. It is us."

His chest rose and fell, his gaze locked with mine. For a moment I thought he might be angry, my words too direct—too hot-blooded. I was still learning to decipher emotions behind his well-guarded eyes.

But he wrapped his arms around me, pulling me against his chest in a hug so deep it blotted out Market Day entirely. He held me, resting his cheek against the crown of my head, his heart drumming against my ear. I inhaled him, leather and smoke and cedar, settling into his arms like a rabbit in its warm, safe den.

I had not fit into anyone's arms like that since childhood. And even then, no one had ever held me so tightly—as if they needed me in their arms as much as I needed to be held. As if nothing else mattered but to hold one another.

As if we had all the time in the world.

A familiar voice ripped me from my comfort. "There she is," it called, too loud, too bubbly. "With the Captain, like I told you."

Ravyn exhaled into my hair. When he pulled away from me, all four of them stood before us, their eyes wide, curiosity and shock and disbelief all trapped behind icy blue irises.

My father, my stepmother, my half sisters.

My father, former Captain of the Destriers, clasped hands with his replacement, their palms bearing matching calluses from years of swordplay. He and Ravyn stood a head above my half sisters, Nerium, and me, shoulders broad. When their hands fell apart, my father's eyes jumped to me.

He blinked, deep lines etching into his furrow. I squirmed beneath his gaze, our struggle on the forest road—the Nightmare's strength, the look of fear in my father's eyes—twisting my thoughts. But when I summoned enough courage to meet his gaze, I realized my father was not looking at me at all.

He was looking at my mother's dress.

His shoulders slumped a moment. The muscles in his jaw flexed, as if he were forcing all his teeth together. And his eyes, brilliant blue, had gone glassy. At last, his gaze met mine. "Hello, Elspeth," he said. "You look like your mother in that dress."

Nerium shot me an icy look but swiftly corrected it to a reticent smile when she noticed the Captain of the Destriers staring daggers at her. I shifted next to Ravyn, our fingers grazing.

My half sisters glanced at one another, speaking a silent language only they knew. I did not miss the way they looked at Ravyn, their eyes wide and upturned, their pink lips slack.

Dimia turned to me, dragging Nya with her. When the twins linked their arms in mine, begging for a turn around the square, I did not have a ready excuse. I shot Ravyn a glance over my shoulder, but the twins were rapid in their steps, their voices in my ears so alike they harmonized.

They marched me down Market Street, Blunder's bustling crowd moving around us like a herd of colorful sheep. I felt anger without truly knowing why, steeling myself against the questions I knew were coming. And though they were young, ruled mostly by fancy, I held my half sisters at great length.

They were still Nerium's daughters.

Dimia stopped us near the fountain. "Elspeth," she said, her voice quick, loud. "You are courting Ravyn Yew."

I looked away. "And?"

Nya blinked at me. She was not as soft as Dimia. She crossed her thin arms over her chest, her words sharp. "He's Captain of the Destriers. He could have his men at our door in moments if he found out you had the fever as a girl."

She sounded too much like her mother. I gave Nya an icy glare. "He isn't going to do that."

"Why wouldn't he?"

A familiar red light danced along my periphery.

Dimia picked at her fingernails, her eyes bright, voice dreamy. "Perhaps because he likes her far too much to arrest her." She put a hand to her heart. "How romantic."

This is insufferable, the Nightmare muttered.

Beyond, the red light grew closer. "Not every story is a fairy tale, Dimia," I said.

Nya's eyes narrowed. "Then explain why he was embracing you."

But I was already slipping away. When my half sisters shouted after me, I merely waved, trailing the tall man in black and the red light emanating from his pocket.

I reached Elm in several leaping steps. When I clung to his arm, he jumped, spilling half his goblet of wine onto the street.

The Prince looked down at me with wide green eyes. I found myself almost smiling. "I've a favor to ask," I said, glancing back. "You'll need your Card."

A moment later, Nya and Dimia were giggling like maniacs, their blue eyes wide as they let out long, singsong giggles. "Such a beautiful day!" Nya gleamed, her smile so wide I could count every tooth.

"Let's go find the wine cart," Dimia twittered, offering Elm and me a swooping wave before skipping with her twin out of the square, the red ribbons of their masks flickering in the mid-day light.

I laughed, watching them go. "Silly little things."

Destriers passed us, nodding to Elm before dispersing throughout the square. The Prince tapped his Scythe Card, releasing my half sisters from its compulsion, and drained the remnants of his goblet. "Terribly annoying, your clan."

"Can't choose family, can we?"

He chuckled, hoisting a new goblet off a nearby merchant's table. "Sadly, no."

I didn't push it—didn't ask what had tipped the King's youngest son over the edge into lawlessness and treason—what had made him betray his own father. There was an unevenness to the Prince's temperament that made me nervous, and I did not think he would react kindly to the violation of his privacy.

"Wine?" he said, retrieving a second goblet.

"It's a bit early, isn't it?"

"You intend to endure Market Day sober?" He looked up and down the stalls, his voice low. "You don't see any...you know... Chalice Cards, do you?"

I cast my eyes about for the telltale turquoise color. "No. Why?"

"Can't be too cautious," he said, taking a deep swill. "Truth serum is the last thing I need these days."

The wine was sweeter than I'd imagined. I sipped it slowly, my eyes on the shifting crowd. "What happens now?"

"A few families will be gifted some worthless trinkets from one of my father's merchants. My brother and a few knights will drone on about the Card trade and the decline of crime—maybe parade Ravyn and the Destriers around for good show. Same old, same old."

I tapped my finger on my goblet. "We could be in my father's house right now, doing something of actual use."

"Hauth and the Destriers would notice our absence. Besides," Elm said, taking another deep swill, "you seem to be having a lovely time reconnecting with your sisters."

I rolled my eyes. "Half sisters."

"What did they want?"

"Nothing," I said. Then after a pause, "They think Ravyn's going to find out what I am and arrest me."

Elm smiled into his goblet. "He might not arrest you," he said, "but he'll eventually find out what you are. The truth always outs."

Something in his voice caught me. "What do you mean?"

Elm turned to me, his green eyes narrowing. "It's different for Ravyn," he said. "He's not skeptical of your infection, your magic. When he looks at you, he feels he knows you—wants to help you. You make him remember why he's done everything he's done, and why he must continue on doing it."

The Prince took small, purposeful sips from his goblet, savoring the wine. "But when I look at you, Spindle, I see something else," he said. "I see someone secretive, guarded. I see someone who hasn't been forthright with us."

To the color draining rapidly from my face, he merely smiled.

"A woman who's spent most of her life hiding in her uncle's house, quiet and secluded, can stand in combat against trained men-at-arms? Can catch knives midair and maim my brother without the aid of a Black Horse?"

He brushed the hair from my forehead, tucking it behind my ear. "And your eyes," Elm said. "Black as ink. Only, when the light is just right, I can see yellow in them. The same yellow I saw two nights ago in the wood, when you knocked your father to the ground."

I felt as if I'd swallowed my tongue.

In the darkness behind my eyes, the Nightmare slithered, his claws scraping against bone. *Let me out.*

Absolutely not.

He's already seen my eyes. Why not let me speak to him?

They're my eyes, I stammered. *Mine, not yours! They should be black, not yellow.*

Should they? he purred. *You said so yourself. I'm getting stronger.*

When I remained silent, the Nightmare swaddled my mind in darkness. *What's yours is mine when the shadows draw near. You asked for my help—and now I am here. With your eyes I do see, with your ears I do hear. There's no going back—this is payment, my dear.*

I felt sick, the wine turning to bile in my stomach. *What do I tell him?*

"Elspeth?"

Tell him the truth.

I can't do that.

"Elspeth."

I jerked away from the voice in my head and set my goblet down, forcing my shaking hands into my sleeves.

Elm watched me fixedly, some of the levity drained from his features. "You still there?" he asked.

But I had no time to respond. I'd barely a moment to brace myself before I was knocked aside by three Destriers pushing into the center of the square, their weapons drawn.

"Make way!" one called, his voice ripping through the crowd. "Make way!"

Elm was upon them in a moment, all hint of intoxication faded from his voice. "What the hell is going on?" he demanded.

"An infected child, sire," a Destrier answered, out of breath. "He's been collected by Physician Orithe, and his parents arrested. High Prince Hauth wants an example made of them."

Suddenly the square was filled with the dark color of Black Horses. Five more Destriers stepped forward, a man and a woman—bloodied—carried between them. The crowd opened up, engulfing them.

Shouts echoed, and I was pushed with the rest of the onlookers to the edge of the square, Hauth Rowan and the Destriers were busy at work tying the prisoners by their hands. A hush fell over the crowd, all joy and camaraderie evaporated, replaced with sickening silence. I wrapped my arms across my chest, retreating into my mind, searching for courage.

But I felt only darkness.

Chapter Twenty-Five

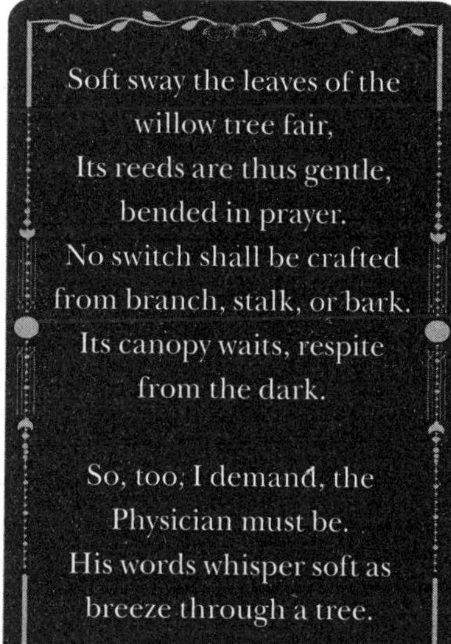

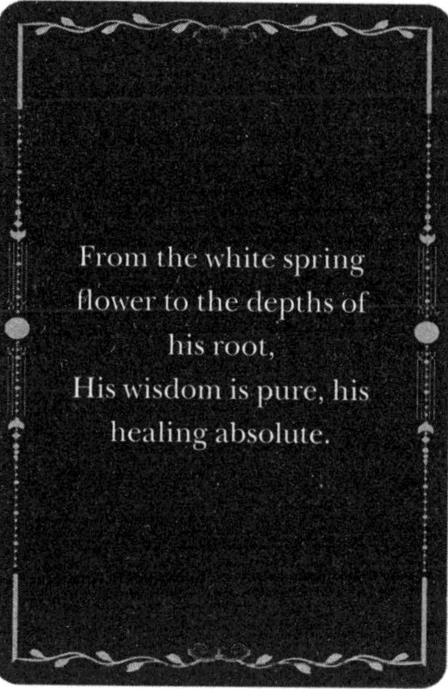

When the first lash fell, a cumulative scream shot through the crowd. The man, stripped of his tunic, moaned wordlessly, blood falling down his back and pooling into the stones at his feet. The woman, tied separately, watched with the rest of us, her eyes wide and glassy.

Oppressive as smoke, the veil of death fell over the square. It strung itself through the crowd, crawling through my nostrils down into my throat, choking me. Tears pricked my eyes, and when the Destrier cracked his whip again, the sound ripped through me, so visceral I doubled over.

Elm put his hand on my elbow and did not stir, as if cast of stone. Only when Hauth addressed the crowd did his face shift, his green eyes narrowing and his mouth drawing into a tight line at the sight of his brother.

The red and black lights of Hauth's Cards surrounded him like a venomous cloud. "This man and woman betrayed your trust." The whip lashed again. The woman cried silently, defeat stamped onto her brow.

"They did not report the infection," Hauth continued. "They kept their child hidden, allowing the infection to fester, putting all of Blunder at risk." The whip ripped again, and I jumped, a long, helpless wail echoing across the square. "And now, they pay the ultimate price."

I craned my neck, searching the crowd. "Where is the child?" I whispered, my voice breaking.

Elm shook his head. His green eyes had gone cold.

Around me, Blunder's citizens were frozen to the cobblestones. Their faces were drawn, colorless. Some had tears in their eyes. Others hardly seemed to blink. Some bore heavy brows, their expressions twisted. There were no cries of triumph—no support for the High Prince and the Destriers. They did not claim this violence.

But they were too afraid to stop it.

When the Destrier with the whip moved back, Hauth stepped in front of the prisoners, pulling the Scythe from his pocket.

He tapped it three times. "Give me your charms," he commanded.

The prisoners dug at their clothes, their eyes dull and unfocused. Hauth waited with his palm extended, like a tax collector awaiting his coin. The woman pulled a rabbit foot from her shift. The man, his hands bloody, an owl feather.

They handed them to Hauth, who crushed them beneath his boot. "The infection is a blight," he called, his words cutting through the cavernous silence. "It is poison that seeps through the mist, fashioned by the Spirit of the Wood. Those who fail to report it commit treason." He turned to the prisoners. "By the authority of the King, I, Hauth Rowan, High Prince of Blunder, sentence you to death."

The sudden sharpness of the Destriers' shouts hit my ears, painful after all that terrible silence. "Go!" they called, flanking the crowd. "To the gates!"

Pushed in every direction, Elm and I were carried with the tide, bodies pressed all around us. The Prince clung to me, his fingers tight on my arm as we jostled about. I heard the moans of the prisoners behind us but did not turn, forced forward by Destriers on horseback and the sway of the crowd.

We flocked out of the square back onto Market Street. I whipped my head around for any sign of Ravyn or Jespyr, but the crowd was too vast, onlookers joining us by the minute.

The shadow of Black Horses surrounded us.

The Destriers led us to the edge of town. We moved through the tall fortified gates, then followed the road some fifty paces. There was nothing, just road and a wide, open field. Hauth stood at the edge of it, joined by Linden, two other Destriers, and the bloodied prisoners.

Behind them, not fifty paces, the mist loomed, waiting.

The crowd came to a crashing halt. I was pressed up against several others. I heard the boom of Destrier voices, the whicker of their warhorses. "Make room!"

Half of Blunder poured onto the road. We looked grotesque in our house colors, our clothes too bright—too alive—for what we were about to witness. I was wedged tighter into Elm's side as the crowd split, making room for the Destriers, Hauth, and the prisoners.

A carriage rolled through the gates, its horses snorting steam. It came to an abrupt halt near Hauth and the prisoners.

Out of it spilled two men clad in white, between them a boy no older than twelve.

I clenched my jaw, something inside me boiling over, the Nightmare's hiss blistering through my mind.

Like his parents, the boy was tied at the wrists. I expected tears—wails of despair—but the boy was silent, his shoulders high, his hands balled into fists. His shirt was torn at the neck, his hair strung with sweat. Whatever had happened, he had put up a fight.

I leaned close to Elm. "What will they do to him?"

Don't you know? the Nightmare whispered.

Elm's voice was lifeless. "He'll be made to watch his parents disappear in the mist. Then he'll be taken to Stone. If my father deems his magic without use..."

I blinked away tears of rage. "He'll be murdered."

Elm did not answer. His eyes were back on the carriage. I turned just in time to see a third Physician step onto the road. He was taller than the others, his frame leaner—his eyes unnaturally pale.

Orithe Willow, head of the King's Physicians.

Elm jolted beside me. "Hauth shouldn't be doing this, not in front of everyone." His head whirled. "Where the hell is Ravyn?"

Up ahead, the Physicians and the boy between them joined Hauth. Orithe folded the length of his white sleeve back several inches, revealing a clawlike contraption with long, angry spikes reaching out from each of his pale fingers—a device made for only one purpose.

Blood.

When the Physician flexed his fingers, the metal spikes made a grating clang, an ominous knell that cut through the crowd. The boy tried to move toward his parents, but Orithe extended a spike to his throat, forcing him to remain still.

A single drop of blood fell from the boy's neck. Not a fatal wound, but enough for Orithe Willow to sentence him to death.

Orithe's voice boomed in the naked silence. "This child carries the infection. His magic is unsanctioned—dangerous. Let his death, and the death of those who harbored him, be a warning," he called, his pale eyes wide. "There is no hiding the infection. Whether today, tomorrow, or years ahead, we will discover every fever—every degeneration—every unsanctioned magic."

Hauth raised his Scythe over his head. "Card magic is the only true magic. Everything else is sickness." He tapped the Card three times, turning once more to the prisoners. "We of Blunder surrender you who have broken our laws to the mist." A cruel smile curled his lips. "Be wary. Be clever. Be good."

The prisoners turned toward the mist, their movements jagged, their legs shaking. For a second it seemed as if they would not step off the road.

But there was no fighting the red Card.

The woman stepped forward with a bloodcurdling scream and took slow, rigid steps into the field. Her husband followed a pace behind, casting his gaze backward, shouting something I could not hear to his son.

Their feet dragged through dead grass. In a minute, they would be swallowed entirely by mist.

The sound of the Nightmare's hiss—the tap of his claws—juddered in my ears, hollowing out my fear until all that was left was rage. *When the shadows grow long, when our names turn to dust, what we loved, what we hated, will spoil to rust. All will be forgotten, save one truth, unshaken...*

What did we do when the children were taken?

My heart raced, my cheeks burning with tears. "We need to do something, Elm."

The Prince's green eyes were locked on the prisoners, who

drew closer and closer to the mist. I felt a tremor in his arm, the muscles of his jaw rigid. "We can't risk Orithe seeing you," he said.

"I can handle myself." I looked down at my red dress, marked by the spindle tree. "Give me your cloak."

The Prince's shoulders stiffened. "Why?"

I tugged at his sleeve until it slipped off his shoulder. "Trade me masks."

The Prince cursed beneath his breath and shrugged out of his cloak. When I put it on, my red dress disappearing behind the clasps, the wool was so dense it swallowed the light. So, too, was his mask. My fingers shook as I fastened it behind my head.

Elm turned, searching the crowd once again. I knew who he was looking for. But there was no time. I wrapped my hand around his arm, searching his green eyes. "You don't need Ravyn," I said in a low, urgent voice. "That boy is innocent, just like Emory. You are the strongest magic user I have ever seen. You have a Scythe." My voice hardened. "You must do something."

Hauth and the Destriers faced the mist, watching the prisoners, talking in low voices. Hauth tilted his head back in a sharp, ugly laugh.

The sound of his brother's laugh snapped something in Elm. His green eyes narrowed, prey to predator. He reached into his pocket, retrieving his red Card, muttering something under his breath I could not make out—prayer or curse.

An audible gasp ripped through the crowd. The Physicians turned to the mist with wide eyes; the Destriers' backs stiffened. Laughter died on Hauth Rowan's mouth.

The prisoners had stopped walking. They stood, frozen midstep, as if cast into stone, caught in the battle of the Princes—Rowan against Rowan.

Scythe against Scythe.

Elm slipped away from me. “Stay out of sight,” he said, eyes ahead. “Don’t do anything stupid.” He twirled the Scythe between his fingers and stepped through the crowd like an actor at encore, all of Blunder his stage.

When Hauth saw his brother, the green in his eyes was eclipsed by red. His neck bulged, his uninjured hand locked in a fist. “What—”

Elm sucked his teeth. “Too far, brother. Even for you, this is too far.”

The Physicians cowered, offering Elm a wide berth. I pushed through the tightly knit crowd, the Nightmare spurring my steps. I kept my eyes on the boy, who still stood at the tip of Orithe’s brutal claw.

Red versus red, the Princes faced off in front of their kingdom. Elm stood a head above his brother, lean and sly, his unruffled demeanor stark in contrast to Hauth’s, who burned with anger enough for the both of them. “It is within my right to sentence criminals,” Hauth barked. “Withdraw your Scythe. *Now.*”

Elm shot his brother a smile. A challenge. “I don’t think I will.”

Linden stood at Hauth’s shoulder, hand on his hilt. He lunged for Elm. But before he could land a blow, Elm’s green eyes shot to him, focus honed. He held out a hand between himself and Linden, fingers splayed, muttering words I could not hear.

Linden stopped midstep, then, with a bloodcurdling shriek, fell to the ground at Elm’s feet. Elm looked down at him, lips curling, a drop of blood slipping from his nostrils.

The Scythe was taking its toll on him.

The Nightmare laughed, pitiless. *Be wary the red, be wary the blade. Be wary the pain, for a price will be paid. Command what you can, death waits for no man. Be wary the pain, for a price will be paid.*

Hauth glared down at Linden, then back at the prisoners. They were still frozen, mere paces from the mist. I slunk closer to the Physicians—the boy. I had no plan, only the beat of blood in my ears as the Nightmare's clicking claws drove me forward.

Hauth opened his mouth, his entire body cued for violence. But before he could speak, a ripple moved through the crowd, the flurry of color parted by two figures, both dressed in all black, hands on the hilts of their swords.

Ravyn and Jespyr Yew.

And it was all the distraction Hauth needed. He slammed his elbow into his brother's face, knocking Elm back a step, shattering his focus.

A cry ripped through the boy's parents, their feet moving once again, propelling them toward the mist. The boy tugged against the Physicians, a desperate cry escaping his lips. I put a hand to my mouth, my eyes burning as I watched the boy's father slip beyond sight, consumed by the blanket of gray, his mother disappearing into the mist a moment after him.

But their voices remained, wordless cries growing more and more frantic as the salt in the air twisted their minds.

Someone was shouting commands—Ravyn. Destriers dropped from their horses, most of them joining Ravyn and Jespyr, a few rallying behind Hauth. I heard the ring of steel. But I did not turn to face it. My gaze was on the boy caught between the men in white robes. I was close now—so close I could see the sweat on his brow, melding with his tears.

I felt an enormous push. The crowd erupted in pandemonium. No longer commanded to bear witness, men and women ran in every direction, desperate to get away from the Destriers and their infighting. A woman knocked into me, colliding with my broken wrist. I saw stars, the pain white-hot. But my legs kept going. I ran, crying out for the monster I so desperately needed.

Help me!

My veins burned. The Nightmare sprang forward, shrouding my mind in darkness. My steps quickened and my eyes locked on Orithe Willow, who turned as if summoned.

We collided at full tilt. He was larger than me—broader, heavier. But he was not stronger than the Nightmare. His head hit the ground with a thud, his eyes wide, his mouth slack. He swiped at me with his grotesque claw, but the steel fingers did not find me—I was already slipping away.

A hand pulled at me from behind—a second Physician. I sent an elbow into his diaphragm, and he fell onto dead grass with a violent cough, knocking the boy down with him. The third Physician did not approach, his eyes widened, hands shaking. He turned on his heel and ran, joining the crowd's torrid mayhem.

The boy lay at the lip of the road. He tried to get up, but before he could find his feet, metal flashed through the air.

The boy screamed, Orithe Willow's claw catching the hem of his tunic, holding him in place. I don't remember leaping forward. Darkness clouded my eyes, and the next moment, I was standing over Orithe, the heel of my shoe sure as it collided with the Physician's jaw, knocking him back to the ground.

The boy's tunic ripped free. He stumbled a few steps. When his gaze rose to me, his spine straightened.

"Come with me," I panted, reaching for him.

The boy's eyes narrowed, straining to see my face beneath my mask. A moment later his gaze shifted over my shoulder. When I looked back, I saw the third Physician. He'd brought a Destrier with him, his Black Horse a flurry of darkness, his eyes fixed on me.

Linden.

"Fuck," I said just as the boy took my hand. I did not look back—not for Orithe or Ravyn. There was no time. Before Linden could reach us, the boy and I darted headfirst into the mist.

Heat ripped up and down my arms, the Nightmare's presence all around me, like a second skin. I took a deep breath and coughed, the salt in the air thick. I dug frantically in my skirt pocket, my fingers snagging on the charm I no longer needed, and doubled our pace.

Linden entered the mist behind us, the dense air contorting the sound of his approach, his steps near and far at once.

We hurried through a meadow, the grass dampening the hem of my dress. When the ground sloped, my feet caught me up, but I did not fall, faster and surer than I had ever been. Behind me the boy was panting, every ounce of his strength summoned to keep my pace.

The salt in the air clung to me, stinging my eyes. My vision blurred with tears. When I rubbed them away, the world around me disappeared. The sky was suddenly black, daylight smothered into nothingness. I was no longer in the meadow between town and the wood, but somewhere else. Somewhere full of long, flickering shadows, a strange orange light reflected on my golden armor.

I whipped my head around. Flames licked the sky behind me, the walls of an enormous castle engulfed in an inferno. The boy was still behind me, only now he wasn't alone. More children hurried behind us, their frightened faces illuminated by the flames.

Words formed on my tongue, but I did not speak them. All I knew was a deep, debilitating fear and an impulse to continue on—to save the children from the fire and the danger that awaited us if we did not flee. That's when I noticed it—waiting at the edge of the flames, resting beneath the shadow of an ancient yew tree.

A chamber at the edge of the meadow, its one dark window, black and infinite, beckoning me forward.

"Miss!"

I tripped on the hem of my dress and fell onto the grass. I coughed, choking on air. When I looked up, the sky was gray once again, hidden beneath the green tops of the wood. Gone was the chamber—the fire—the smoke in the air. All that was left was the boy, wide-eyed as he looked down at me. "I can hear them, miss."

I clawed inside my mind for the Nightmare. But his jaw was sealed, his pointed ears perking, listening. *There,* he said. *Do you hear it?*

I did. Shouting—a man and a woman's voice, deep within the mist. But they were not alone. The tread of heavy footfall sounded from whence we'd come—the clang of metal—the sinister darkness of a Black Horse Providence Card.

He's close, the Nightmare warned. *You cannot outrun him. Not with the boy.*

I scurried to my feet, pressing my charm into the boy's hand. "Take this charm for your parents," I said. "They'll have to share it, but it should wake them."

The boy blinked down at the crow's foot. "But you won't have one."

"I don't need it," I said. "The Spirit does not harm people like us." I checked my mask was secure, Linden's steps drawing near. "Go," I said, releasing the boy.

His footfalls sounded like bird wings as he fled through the trees. I did not watch him go. My back was hunched, my ears perked to the sound of the Destrier. The Nightmare's hiss ran up my spine, stunning me, the world around me blurring.

Linden came out of the mist, his sword aimed directly at my neck.

I dodged him. When I stood straight, my fingers curled, my

eyes narrowing. My legs sprang forward, my steps powerful as I closed the distance between myself and the King's soldier. I saw the fear in his eyes—confusion and panic. But I did not care. I was lost to the magic—the Nightmare's wrath enveloping me.

I struck him in the jaw, then the ribs. He fell to the ground, his sword reckless as he slashed at me. But he might as well have been slashing at a ghost. The Nightmare moved like lightning, twisting my body. My foot collided with the Destrier's shoulder, pinning him to the ground and knocking his sword free.

I leaned over him, my hand poised like a claw. Salt prickled my nose and my arms burned. For a moment, my mind clouded. I forgot where I was, why I'd come. All I could see was darkness.

Bloodcurdling screams brought me back. *Stop!* I cried, but it was too late. Linden lay on the ground, his hands held up to his neck, blood oozing through his fingers.

I jerked away, trapped by a bitter rage. My thoughts hammered against the Nightmare's wrath, confusion and dread leaching into my mind. *What did you do?* I cried.

The Nightmare did not answer. But he did not have to.

A scream caught in my throat. I tore from the wood, my feet unsteady, the dark shadow of the Destrier's Black Horse growing smaller and smaller as I pelted through the mist.

I did not see the second Destrier until I'd already crashed into him.

I shouted and pushed against the chest of his black tunic, but he caught me along the arms. He said my name, but I hardly heard him, my mind caught in a riptide, the Nightmare's presence so strong it stupefied me.

The Destrier pulled me to him. When I looked up, I saw gray eyes behind his mask.

Ravyn Yew's chest heaved against mine. When he spoke, his voice was ragged. "Elspeth—Elspeth, can you hear me?"

I gasped, my breath coming in rapid, violent swells. Tears fell down my cheeks, the salt in my eyes and the magic in my veins white-hot.

"Breathe," Ravyn said, reaching for my face. "You're safe now. Just breathe."

I blinked, the flames of the Nightmare's wrath still licking my mind. My voice hitched, my breath shallow and uneven. "The boy—the Destrier—my magic. I...I don't know what happened."

Ravyn leaned into me, his forehead resting against mine, his breath on my face. "Your eyes are yellow."

I snapped my eyelids shut. *Please go away,* I begged the Nightmare, knowing all too well there was nowhere for him to go. I heard the echo of his laugh, his steps slow—his claws painful—as he stalked through my thoughts into darkness.

I let out a breath, and Ravyn reached for me. But no sooner had his fingers touched mine than the Captain recoiled, his gaze frozen on my hands.

When I looked down, my hands were curled like claws. My fingers, long and pale, were covered in blood.

Chapter Twenty-Six

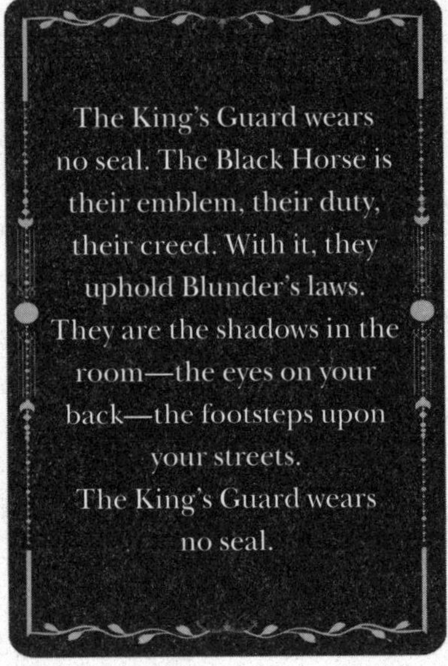

Ravyn took my hands and ran them against his tunic, the black wool absorbing the blood on my fingers. When he released me, I hid my arms in my sleeves, balling my hands into fists to keep them from shaking.

Ravyn's voice was cool—his eyes unreadable, his spine straight. Gone was the highwayman. In his place stood the Captain of the Destriers, cold and austere once more. "Who was it?" he said, keeping his voice low.

I hardly knew. All I had truly known was rage—a rage I had never felt before, so strong it, even now, was hesitant to release me. "Another Destrier," I managed, nodding back toward the wood. "Linden."

The muscles in Ravyn's jaw flexed. "Dead?"

My stomach curled. "Hurt."

"And the boy?"

"Somewhere in the wood."

He gave a curt nod, his ears perked to the wind. "More Destriers are coming," he said. "Stay here."

A moment later he was gone, disappearing into the mist. I could still hear him, his voice sharp as a knife as the sound of heavy footfall echoed through the grayness, the shadow of two Black Horses darkening the mist.

I held still, listening.

"Wicker," Ravyn called. "Get Gorse and Beech and gather the Physicians. See to anyone hurt in the mayhem." His voice hardened. "Larch. Head west, into the wood."

My stomach twisted, knowing what awaited west of us, crumpled and bleeding beneath the trees.

What did you do? I cried into the darkness.

He retracted his claws, his voice slow, idle. *We did it together. Just as we always do.*

I didn't want that!

You asked for my help. And I delivered it.

I shook my head. *You're a monster.*

Ravyn appeared again in a gust of black, his eyes trained on my face. "Elspeth?"

I wiped old tears from my cheeks and flinched. The pain in my broken wrist teemed with a new vengeance. I felt dizzy, unable to balance the events of the past hour—Hauth and his condemnation of the boy's parents—Orithe's brutal claw—Elm and his Scythe—the strange vision as I fled through the mist—the look of terror in Linden's eyes as the Nightmare's wrath overpowered my body.

"What happened, Elspeth?" he said.

I closed my eyes and took a deep breath. "I couldn't let Orithe take that boy back to Stone."

Ravyn's eyes flashed to my mask—my cloak. "Were you recognized?"

"I don't think so. It all happened so fast. Elm—his Scythe—" I paused, my mind segmented, broken between the Nightmare's thoughts and my own. I looked at the Captain of the Destriers. "I freed the boy and took him into the mist. I gave him my charm so he might save his parents. But the Destrier followed us. I…I didn't intend to…"

Ravyn waited. "What of the yellow that flickers through your eyes?" he asked.

"I can't tell you," I said, more forceful than before. "You won't want anything to do with me if I do."

Ravyn exhaled. "Then your estimation of me is lower than I imagined." He reached into his pocket, tapping the burgundy light three times.

"What are you doing?"

"Telling Jespyr to take Orithe to Linden." The Nightmare Card in the Captain's pocket cast strange shadows across his face. After a moment, his eyes closed in concentration, and he tapped the Card thrice more. "Let's go."

We hurried back up the hill and through the meadow, our silence strained. Voices sounded in the mist—two more Black Horses moving in the distance. Ravyn's shoulders tensed, but he did not slow our pace, merely putting a finger to his lips to signal my silence.

I did not reach into the darkness for the Nightmare. Still, he was there, looming like a shadow across every corner of my mind.

By the time Ravyn and I crept out of the mist and back onto the main road, the pandemonium had ceased. The crowd had gone, hurried back through Blunder's gates, the frivolity of Market Day long dead.

"Take off your mask," Ravyn said. His eyes flickered across my cloak—Elm's cloak. "That too. You're just a maiden who got caught in the mist, yes?"

I nodded. But the lie erased nothing. The blood was off my hands, but the feel of it remained. A dark, menacing stain.

We were met by a sea of black and red—Destriers and Hauth Rowan clustered at the edge of the mist. The High Prince's voice ripped down the road, brutal and loud.

Elm stood apart from the others, hands in his pockets, his green eyes bleary. His shoulders were hunched, his cheeks colorless. A thin sheen of sweat glistened on his brow. I moved to his side, searching his face.

"Still alive, then," he said without looking at me.

I slipped him his cloak. "And you?"

"Fit as a fiddle." He raised his sleeve to his face, wiping his nose. When he pulled it away, his cuff was dark with blood. "The boy?"

"Escaped, for now. Linden caught me up. We fought." I clenched my jaw, afraid I might be sick. "I may have killed him."

Elm looked at me, his eyes slow to focus. "Shouldn't you know?"

The Destriers parted for Ravyn, their heads lowered to their Captain. Ravyn paid them no attention, his gaze fixed on Hauth. "What the fuck do you think you're doing?" he said, so severe I flinched. "You called for a public execution on Market Day?" His voice dripped venom. "Without my leave?"

The High Prince turned, his broad jaw set and his cheeks aflame. "I have the right to execute any person guilty of harboring an infected—"

Ravyn closed the distance between himself and his cousin, his anger unrivaled. "It is your right to uphold the King's law," he said. "But not without my leave." His voice lowered, menace in the low, scraping tones. "Don't think me deaf to the dissent you sow behind my back, cousin. If it's command you want"—he spread his arms wide, an invitation—"take it."

Hauth's nostrils flared. Next to me, a smile slipped across Elm's tired face. Both he and Ravyn, and perhaps the rest of the Destriers, knew Hauth would not take his chances against someone immune to the Scythe.

Given the flash of rage in his green eyes, Hauth knew it, too.

Ravyn whirled on his men. "Would you follow a man so unwilling to take a simple challenge?"

The Destriers said nothing, motionless, as if carved of wood.

Ravyn sneered. "Your Prince is just that—a Prince. And you are not his brutes. You do not disrupt Blunder's peace, nor force its citizens to witness cruelty. You are as shadows—silent and swift. Most essentially, you are keepers of our words. Wary. Clever. Good. Is that understood?"

The Destriers clasped the hilts of their swords, their eyes trained on Ravyn. "Yes, Captain," they called in accordance.

Only Hauth remained silent.

Ravyn turned to him. "I did not hear you, cousin."

Hauth's green eyes narrowed. "Nor I you, *Captain.* After all, when the child was discovered and the Destriers summoned, we had no commands to obey—you were nowhere to be found." He glared over Ravyn's shoulder, his eyes finding mine. "Even now, your attention seems concentrated elsewhere."

Ravyn shifted, blocking me from Hauth's view. For a moment I was certain he would lash out—break his cousin's other hand. But he did not. He merely glared at Hauth, leaching ice. The High Prince glared back until the red in his face moved behind his eyes. Then, weaponless against Ravyn's unyielding silence, hands balled into fists, Hauth lowered his gaze.

Ravyn turned. “Stay alert,” he commanded the Destriers. “Do not let anyone who does not carry a Black Horse or a Physician’s seal through the gates without inspection. Keep to patrols. If the boy is found or another infection reported, find me at Castle Yew.”

“And if the boy is not found?” a Destrier called.

Ravyn pushed from the group without a backward glance. “Then let the Spirit have him,” he snapped.

I followed him up the road, Elm trailing behind us. The sky had darkened, the shadows of the gate long as we crossed into town. No one said a word, the only sound among us the thump of our heels upon cobbled streets.

Then, as if reading my thoughts, Ravyn spoke. “Jespyr will search for the boy and his parents,” he said, pulling the Nightmare Card from his pocket and tapping it three times. “We have a place for children like him, if we’re lucky enough to find them first.”

I stared at the back of his cloak. “You’ve saved infected children before?”

“That’s the entire point of collecting the Deck,” Elm muttered behind me. “Or did you imagine we were committing treason for a laugh?”

Ravyn stopped in his tracks, so sudden I had to pivot to avoid him.

Elm, not so swift, crashed into Ravyn’s back. “Trees—What’s the matter?”

Ravyn’s eyes were closed. A moment later he tapped his Nightmare Card thrice more. “I just spoke with my father.” He opened his eyes, his gaze locked on Elm. “We need to get back to Castle Yew. Now.”

Without another word, the Captain of the Destriers ran up the street. Elm and I shared a bewildered glance. A moment later we were running, weaving through the remnant crowds of Market Day as we fought to keep Ravyn's lightning pace.

We ran until we met Fenir Yew at the square. He'd summoned a carriage.

"Hurry," he said as I climbed in. "Thistle says he snuck in the gate after we left this morning, which means he escaped last night. If Orithe hears, he won't be gentle with him."

"He won't hear," Ravyn said as he slammed the door shut. "He'll be busy for hours."

Ravyn pulled himself next to the coachman and cracked the reins. The horses spurred and the carriage lurched forward, dark curtains drawn over the windows.

Next to me, Elm drew long, ragged breaths. More blood had pooled under his nostrils. He wiped it away, a lifeless fatigue lingering in his shoulders—behind his green eyes—the payment for the red Card's magic steep.

"Is someone going to tell me what's happened?" he demanded. "Who snuck into the gate? Why are we returning to the castle?"

Fenir's voice was grave. "Emory," he said. "Emory has run away from Stone."

Chapter Twenty-Seven

The rain began long before we reached the gates. It pelted the roof of the carriage, forcing us to slow our pace, the sky dark despite the afternoon hour.

When the carriage rolled to a stop at Castle Yew's threshold, Ravyn leapt down from its perch and ripped open the door. I tried to search his gray eyes but he turned away, his steps anxious as he led us into the castle.

Thistle met us at the door. "He's in the library," he said. "Poor boy is cold to his bones."

I followed Elm and the Yews, our steps thunderous as we ran up the stairwell.

The library doors were open. I felt the warmth of the hearth the moment we stepped into the room, its flames tall and newly stoked, turning the rain on our cloaks and hair and skin to steam.

Morette Yew paced in front of the hearth. I heard Fenir sigh, his brown eyes jumping between his wife and the long wooden bench pulled close to her, near the flames.

A boy with dark hair and a smattering of freckles across his copper nose rested on the bench. His eyes were closed, his arms folded neatly over the blankets across his chest, like a body at burial.

I stared, Emory Yew just as unnerving in repose as he had been Equinox night.

"His lips are still blue," Morette fretted, sitting at the head of the bench. "Elm, help me warm him."

Elm reached into his pocket for the Scythe and closed his eyes, the shadow of exhaustion prominent on his brow. Still, the red Card was at his command. He tapped it three times and placed a hand on Emory. "Feel the warmth, Em," he muttered under his breath. "Feel the fire."

"He walked all night," Morette said, her voice quiet. "I'm not sure if the King knows he's here."

"I'll deal with that," Ravyn said, kneeling at his brother's side. "How long has he been asleep?"

"An hour." Morette glanced at the door. "Where's Jespyr?"

Ravyn and I exchanged a glance. "There was an incident," he said. "She's with the Destriers."

Slowly, Emory's thin cheeks flushed. He opened his gray eyes, gazing first at his mother, then Ravyn and Elm. "I'm not dead," he said, smiling impishly. "Only asleep. For now."

Elm smacked the blankets. "This isn't a joke, Emory Yew," he said. "You can't travel alone. What if you'd fallen off the road—gotten lost in the mist? What then?"

"I wanted to come home." Emory wrinkled his nose. "But no one would take me."

"That's because you're not supposed to leave," Ravyn said, his voice harsh. When Fenir put a hand on his shoulder, Ravyn moved to the hearth, his eyes lost in the flames. "You could have died, Emory. How could you be so careless?"

"I'm already dying," Emory bit back. "At least this way, it's on my terms."

His words, though directed at Ravyn, hit me like a blow to the chest. Emory turned his head. He sank deeper into his blankets and stared at me, the corners of his mouth downturned. "Who is that?" he murmured.

The others looked at me, their faces drawn.

"Don't you remember her?" Elm asked.

"We—We've met before?"

"Yes."

The boy squinted. "I can't make out her face."

Morette bid me closer with a small, forlorn smile. Ravyn stepped aside to give me room, our bodies tensing as I passed him.

Emory watched me. I recalled what Elm had told me about Emory's degeneration—his changefulness, his loss of memory. My eyes widened, the Nightmare and I surveying the boy with morbid fascination.

"Hello," I said, my voice flickering. "I'm Elspeth Spindle."

"Spindle," Emory said. His gray eyes jumped between Elm and his brother. "Is she your friend?"

Elm opened his mouth, but Ravyn answered first. "Yes," he said, his voice softer than before. "Elspeth is a friend."

"Spindle," Emory muttered. "Shrub—no, tree. Both, perhaps? Seeded by birds and wind. Old, historic." Clarity filled his eyes and he sat up, his collarbones prominent beneath the neck of his tunic. "Spindle," he said again. "Small—seasonal. Oval, finely toothed leaves that yellow in autumn or, for some rarities, turn a deep blood red." He tilted his head as he surveyed me, so much like his older brother in looks and manners I might have been staring through time at Ravyn, ten years younger.

"I once came to a courtyard with an ancient spindle tree hewn betwixt stone," Emory said. "I saw a stern man cloaked in red and a little girl who carried a mirror with her, always." He blinked at me, as if trying to remember a long-forgotten dream. "Do you know this place?"

"Spindle House. I used to live there," I said, studying his face. "The girl did not hold a mirror—they are twins. The man in red is my father."

He ran a bony hand over his brow. "Spindle." He pulled the word out of his mouth as if he were unspooling yarn. "I'm sorry," he said. "My memory lives in a cloud these days."

"Please," I said, unsure if I was more relieved or disheartened that the boy's degeneration had wiped me from his memory. "Do not trouble yourself."

Emory held my gaze. "You're very beautiful," he mused. "Your eyes are so dark—so infinite." He paused. "Like a maiden in a storybook. As if the Shepherd King had penned you himself."

The Nightmare laughed, sending a shiver clawing up my spine. *Death at his door, and the boy still understands you better than the rest of these fools.*

I clenched my jaw, the horrors of Market Day still fresh upon me. *Shut up. If you ever cared for me, you will shut up.*

"Elspeth knows all about the Shepherd King and *The Old Book of Alders*," Morette said, smiling at her son.

"And about the infection," Elm said under his breath.

Emory leaned forward. "Did you also know, Miss Spindle, that we Yews are descendants of the Shepherd King?"

Ravyn and Elm sighed, rolling their eyes. "Not this again..."

"It's true!" Emory said. "The Shepherd King's history is gone, but Rowan histories are fascinating if you read between the lines. Stone was built by the first Rowan King, which means the Shepherd King dwelled somewhere else. There are no other grand castles in Blunder." His lips curled. "Save the one that sits in ruins here at Castle Yew."

Ravyn smiled. "The ruins are old—perhaps even the oldest thing in Blunder. Still, all that proves is that, hundreds of years ago, another castle stood here."

Emory shook his head. "But the ruins aren't the oldest thing in Blunder." He looked up at me, a glimmer in his gray eyes. "The trees are. If the Shepherd King did live here, he would have taken the name of the trees, the way everyone did. And what kind of trees are planted all along the estate, even near the ruins?" His smile widened. "Yews."

I froze. The ruins—the chamber. He had built them—he told me so. But he had never said his name, and there was no record of it. No one had uttered it in five hundred years.

This time, I clawed at him. *Your name is never given in* The Old Book, I whispered, my voice combing the darkness. *What is it—your real name?*

He snapped at me, vicious. *My name is ash,* he hissed, *lost to the winds.*

Elm snickered. "And now comes the part of the story where Emory reminds us all that *my* ancestors came and destroyed the Shepherd King's castle," he said, mussing his cousin's hair.

"It's a fair assumption," the boy replied. "The Rowan lineage is steeped in violence. After all, they were the first to exterminate those infected by magic."

"Yet they united the kingdom with Providence Cards, offering the people of Blunder a safer source of magic," Elm argued.

"By killing everything and everyone who didn't submit to their Scythes."

"That's enough, you two," Fenir said. "This never ends well."

Elm winked at his young cousin.

A knock sounded on the door. We all turned to see Thistle balancing several steaming bowls of food. "Anyone hungry?"

The fine smells of soup and meat and bread filled the library. Morette and Fenir bid Emory come to a nearby table. When the boy stood, we all let out a collective gasp, blankets falling away to reveal taut flesh and jagged bones. Even the Nightmare hissed his discontent at the sight of the boy, who had lost weight even in the last week since I'd seen him.

Don't they feed him at Stone? I said.

The Nightmare's tongue clicked against his teeth. *Food is not the trouble. He's degenerating. First his mind, then his body.* His voice quieted. *Quicker than I imagined.*

Ravyn stood and helped his brother to the table.

"Emory," he said, his jaw tight with strain, "I have to take you back to Stone."

Emory kept his gaze lowered. "Do you?"

Morette's eyes were wet. "He needs rest." Her voice hardened. "Let my brother worry."

Ravyn ran a hand over his brow. It was not Morette who would face the King's wrath when Emory Yew was found missing. It was Ravyn. But he said nothing of it. "He can stay tonight. But tomorrow I must return him to Stone."

"First, he eats," Elm said firmly, pulling himself into the chair next to Emory. "We could all use a little meat on our bones."

The food smelled delicious. But my appetite was gone.

"The garden," Emory said, his fingers shaking along the spoon as he took small sips from the steaming bowl. "I want to see the trees in the garden." His voice faltered. "Then you can take me back."

We sat at the table and watched Emory eat, the rest of us forgetting to feed ourselves. Next to me, his posture rigid, Elm glared daggers at Ravyn across the table.

After a full minute of biting silence, Ravyn slammed his fork onto his plate. "Trees, Elm. What?"

"I need to talk to you."

Ravyn gestured to the table, open palmed. "You have my full attention."

Elm shot me a narrow glance. "I doubt that."

"If you have something to say," Ravyn growled, "spit it out. I don't have time for one of your Princely tantrums."

Elm's voice deepened, hot with anger. "Fine. I think you're a fool, cousin."

Emory held his sleeve up to his mouth, smothering a laugh.

Ravyn's voice remained characteristically smooth. "How do you figure?"

"We could have been in Spindle House today, stealing the Well Card," the Prince declared. "But you insisted we go to Market Street because you wanted to be near *her*," he said. "Who, I might add, came this close to ruining our entire plan by flouncing about in front of Orithe bloody Willow."

I coughed into my wine. "I practically begged you to go into Spindle House with me and find the Well!"

Elm waved a hand in my face. "I didn't say it was a bad idea, only that it wasn't the right moment." He wrinkled his nose. "And I wasn't about to give you the satisfaction of having a semi-intelligent idea, Spindle."

I wanted to reach over and wring his long Rowan neck.

Ravyn, across the table, remained quiet.

"There will be hell to pay when we get back to Stone," Elm

said, his ire returning to his cousin. "She maimed a Destrier. My father won't take kindly to an assault on his guard, nor the botched arrest of an infected child." He paused, shooting me another unfeeling glance. "Whatever her magic, it's more than a penchant for spotting Providence Cards. I don't trust her."

"I do," Ravyn said, folding his arms over his chest. "That should be enough for you."

"Should it? Am I not allowed my own opinion? Or does everyone bow to the Captain of the Destriers?"

"You can have your own opinion," Ravyn said. "But just know, without all the facts, you sound like an idiot."

Elm's voice grew louder. "And what facts, pray tell, am I missing?"

"I wanted us all to go to Market Day so that if the Ivys stole the Well Card from Spindle House this morning, we would all be accounted for."

I blinked. Across the table from me, Fenir's and Morette's faces grew stern.

"The Ivys were in my father's house?" I said.

Fenir nodded.

"And when were you planning on telling me this?" Elm shouted. "Whenever it suited you, I suppose."

"I love when they argue," Emory said into his soup. "Keeps my weak little heart beating."

Fenir ran his hand over his beard. "I take it the Ivys didn't find the Well Card."

Ravyn shook his head.

"That's probably because they didn't know where to look," I cried, pushing out of my seat. "I could have helped them! I tried to go inside, but Elm—"

"Twenty people would have seen you march through that gate," Elm bit back at me. "Besides, the *Captain* bade we wait."

Ravyn looked on unapologetically. "I told only those who were imperative to the task."

"So everyone except me and the magically disturbed woman?"

"*Disturbed?*" the Nightmare and I called at once.

"We can't afford mistakes, Elm," Ravyn bit back. "What if we'd been seen? It's one thing to steal a Card behind a highwayman's mask. But entering a man's house—stealing in the light of day—is a risk we cannot afford. Unless you think you have the stomach to stand up to an inquest."

Elm's frown deepened, his mouth tightening in a long, unhappy line.

The air in the library felt suddenly thin. "Would there really be an inquest?" I asked. "Even if we were not caught in the act?"

Morette lips wrinkled into a scowl. "Card theft is unforgivable. My brother places full retribution in the hands of the wronged Card owner. Anyone, no matter their station, might be interrogated." She paused. "A Chalice Card is presented."

Ravyn cast Elm a pointed look. "And it is very difficult to cheat a Chalice."

Jespyr returned at nightfall. The infected boy and his parents had not been found. Linden was alive. Just. Her steps dragged, a noticeable limp in her gait. She wrapped her arms around Emory in a long, steadfast hug and bade us all good night.

Emory was next to claim sleep, Morette stationed in a large chair by his bedside, a night vigil. Fenir, Ravyn, Elm, and I moved to the parlor, Thistle popping in now and again to fill our goblets.

The wine put heat in my chest, and I stared at the fire,

fighting the urge to glance at Ravyn, who sat opposite me with practiced smoothness. When I caved and looked his way, he was watching me, his gray eyes unreadable, his hand scraping over the stubble along his jaw.

I didn't know where we stood, the Captain and I. The violence of Market Day had taken the fragile, unspoken thing budding between us and shoved it back into shadow. I held his gaze, searching for cracks in his unshaking smoothness. Longing for them.

Elm looked up from his second glassful, his green eyes flickering from Ravyn to me. "Bloody trees," he muttered, hoisting himself out of his chair. Without a good-night, he took the flagon of wine from the table and quit the parlor.

Fenir did not miss the cue. He cleared his throat. "Well, that about does it for me," he said, shuffling out of the room, leaving me and the Captain of the Destriers alone together.

Ravyn's eyes did not leave my face. But I could not read them. And it hurt, somewhere between my lungs and my sternum, knowing he was guarded around me once more. My fingers shook along the stem of my goblet. "Did you mean what you said?" I asked, matching his gaze. "You trust me? Or were you just making a show for your cousin?"

Ravyn thumbed the rim of his goblet. "What makes you think I was making a show?"

"No—don't do that," I said. Something burned behind my eyes. I pushed it away. "Don't answer a question with a question. I'm tired of that."

He cocked his brow, leaning forward in his chair. "How would you have us talk, Elspeth?"

I looked away, a lump rising in my throat. The muscles above my brow straining, holding everything I had not yet told him at bay. "I want us to be honest," I whispered. I pressed my hand to my face, but it was too late; he'd seen the tears in my eyes—the upturn of my brow. The fear.

The Nightmare slithered out of the darkness, his voice caressing my ear. *You needn't be afraid.* His voice was slick with oil. *Magic comes for us all.*

Go away! I cried.

You cannot undo what already begins. He paused, his voice serpentine as it flickered past my ears. *You cannot erase the salt from the din. But if you won't let me out...you must let him in.*

I closed my eyes. "I'm degenerating, Ravyn."

I heard his sharp inhale, then the clang of silver as his goblet hit the tray. He was out of his seat and kneeling beside me in a breath, one hand on the arm of the chair, the other on my knee. "Tell me," he said.

"It's why I attacked the Destrier—why Elm doesn't trust me. I'm changing. Not the way you are, and not the way Emory is, but just as sure." I felt for the Nightmare, but he had gone eerily quiet. "And I'm running out of time."

"Have you told Filick?"

"There's nothing he can do, Ravyn. Nothing anyone can do."

His hand on my knee tightened. "What kind of degeneration, Elspeth?"

I shook my head. "I've never spoken about it," I said. I covered my eyes with my hand. "I can't."

A hot tear slid down my cheek, dipping into the crease of my mouth. Ravyn wiped it away with his thumb. He leaned closer. "We all have secrets we're forced to keep, Elspeth," he murmured. He lifted my chin. When I opened my eyes, his gaze poured into mine. "I trust you. You're safe with me. Magic—or something else—is pulling us together. Only two more Cards," he said, the tips of our noses grazing. "And then you'll be free."

I wanted to believe him—to feel safe, like I had in his arms earlier that day. I wanted him to blot out the entire world, shielding me from everything and anyone who might do me harm. Still, even the vastness of Ravyn Yew's arms, the heat on his skin, the muscles beneath his clothes, could not keep me safe from myself.

But I was more than willing to lose myself to his touch, just to be certain.

I reached for him, my hand cupping the nape of his neck, pulling his mouth to mine. He let out a breath that slipped into a growl. The hand on my chin lowered to my neck, his thumb pressing lightly against the hollow of my throat.

The chair creaked in complaint as Ravyn pushed into me, our kiss almost frantic. His other hand traveled up my leg, his fingers digging into the fabric of my dress. When he gripped the soft skin of my thigh, I let out a gasp.

He pulled back, pupils wide, mouth swollen. "Is this—Do you want me to stop?"

"No," I said claiming his mouth again. Wine and firelight and the desperate need to escape my own fate blended in a heady draft. It struck a fire in me I had never tended, wild, unfettered.

I wanted it to burn me to pieces—for *him* to burn me to pieces.

A loud clatter sounded somewhere outside the parlor door, followed by the echo of rapid footfall, close, then far. Thistle, no doubt coming to refill our wine, scurried away in a hurry.

Ravyn swore under his breath. He gripped my hips, pulling me out of the chair. When we stood, he adjusted his jerkin, his voice a low rumble. "Come with me."

His room was at the end of the same corridor as mine, unlocked. He pushed it open and ushered me in, his hand grazing the small of my back.

The smell of clove and cedar and paper and leather reached

for me. His room was a flood of scent—drying herbs, shelves filled with books, freshly cut wood for the hearth, cedarwood in various forms scattered across the floor, some half carved, others whittled to perfection. Clothes were thrown without aim, crumpled in corners and flung over furniture spines. His bed was large and unmade, its heavy quilt shoved to the foot of the mattress, as if kicked there. Messy, warm—a gentle chaos. The kind of chaos that lived in stark contrast to the stony, controlled Captain of the Destriers.

And he was showing it to me.

Ravyn closed the door behind us and leaned against it, long shadows dancing across his face, the hearth the only light in the room. "I'd be a liar if I said it wasn't always this untidy."

"I like it," I said, my eyes lingering a moment too long on the bed.

It was jarring to go from having my hands full of him to this—him against the door, me in the middle of the room, unsure what to say or where to look. I put a hand to my cheek to steady myself, but it had the opposite effect. The touch of my own skin made me think of his rough, calloused hands, pulling at me.

Ravyn watched me, the invisible string tugging at the corner of his mouth. "Is this what you want, Elspeth?"

I leaned against the post of his bed frame. "What do you think I want, Ravyn?"

His eyes narrowed dangerously. He pushed off the door and came toward me. "I thought we weren't answering questions with questions."

It felt painful, saying what I wanted out loud, like flexing an underworked muscle. I wanted to make a joke of it—to play coy—to tease him—anything that would stop me from feeling vulnerable and exposed, the distance between us rapidly closing.

But I had kept too much of myself from him already. In this, at least, I could be truthful. I sat on the bed. With my good hand, I twisted my skirt, the fabric puckering as I pulled it up and over my knee, the quiver in my voice betraying me. "I want to be here. With you."

It was difficult, removing his jerkin with only one hand. He helped me, bowed over me, his mouth on mine. After the jerkin came his tunic, ripped over his head and tossed atop the pile of discarded clothes. I ran my hand over the taut muscles of his chest—his stomach—stopping just below his navel.

He shivered and pulled back, sliding his hands up my legs, pushing my dress until it sat in the crease of my thighs. His fingers caught on my wool leggings, easing them down from my waist over my curves, so slow I wanted to scream, his mouth a pace behind. His facial hair scratched against my inner thigh, my knee, my calf. When he slipped my leggings off and flung them onto the pile of clothes on the floor, his hands returned to my thighs.

My breaths came rapidly, far too shallow. I suddenly felt confined by my dress, my bodice too constricting, pinning me in all the wrong ways. I tore the lacings open, my fingers clumsy and wild as the long crimson cord released me.

The dress fell open. I took a filling breath, then another, my chest hurried as it rose and fell, covered now only by a thin chemise.

Ravyn's hands moved to my hips, his gaze traveling up the curve of body. He looked me in the eye, kissed me hard, and yanked me to the cusp of the bed. "Can I kiss you?"

My voice shook. "A bit late to ask, isn't it?"

"Not on your mouth, Elspeth." His eyes turned wicked as he lowered himself to his knees, kissing the inside of my leg, the tips of his teeth edging over my skin. With a sharp breath he pushed my thighs open, wide enough to accommodate his broad shoulders. "Here."

I put a hand over my mouth and fell back on the bed, my breath soaring out of me, caught between a sigh and a curse. The ache in my stomach moved lower, amber hot as it coiled, touch starved. I shut my eyes. "Yes," I said, dropping my fingers into his hair.

Ravyn sighed into me, his hands on my hips tightening, holding me to him. When he kissed me below my skirt, my ache responded, tendrils of heat knotting themselves over and over deep within me.

I had no practice living outside my mind. But here, pinned on Ravyn Yew's bed, his touch searing over my skin, I was alive only in my body, as if leaning out an open window in the tallest tower of Spindle House. I felt it in my stomach, the palms of my hands, the soles of my feet. And with every kiss, every flick of his tongue, Ravyn was crumbling the window's casement—pushing me toward an inevitable, ruinous fall.

He did not let me fall right away. By his sighs, the muffled, contented growls, he was taking his time with me. Laying waste to me.

"Don't stop," I uttered, squeezing my eyes shut.

I felt him moan and then I was falling, released from the casement, tumbling down the tower, every part of me caught in the fall. I cried out, pulling his hair, my legs flexing, toes curling.

He leaned over me and smiled, like he knew exactly how thoroughly he'd shattered me. His hand slid up my stomach to my chest, pressing over my breast, just above my heart. He bent down, his lips brushing mine. "Your heart is racing," he said with a smirk.

Somehow we ended up on the floor, heaped among his

belongings, tangled with one another. Clothes long discarded, I trapped Ravyn with my body, pinning him to the rug, taking my own time with him. He let me at first, ceding control, hands gripped tightly along my hips, brow strained.

But even he, with his abundance of restraint, could not hold back for long.

He flipped me onto my back in one fluid motion, never breaking our touch. His lips found my neck, and when he pressed into me, deeper than before, I let out an abrupt breath.

My name was a token on his lips, a barter, as if he was giving all of himself to me just to say it. "Elspeth." He pressed his forehead to mine, his breath coming quicker. "Fuck, Elspeth."

We lay, undone, on the floor and watched the fire with heavy eyes. Ravyn ran a finger down my spine and I traced the lines of his throat, his jaw, his brow, his hooked nose. When I could no longer keep my eyes open, he lifted me off the floor and carried me to the bed, wrapping us both in the thick quilt. I pressed my head to his chest, lost to the sound of his heartbeat against my ear. It stretched on and on, an eternal beat, a false promise.

As if all my woes would disappear if I remained there, naked, next to him.

As if I had all the time in the world.

Chapter Twenty-Eight

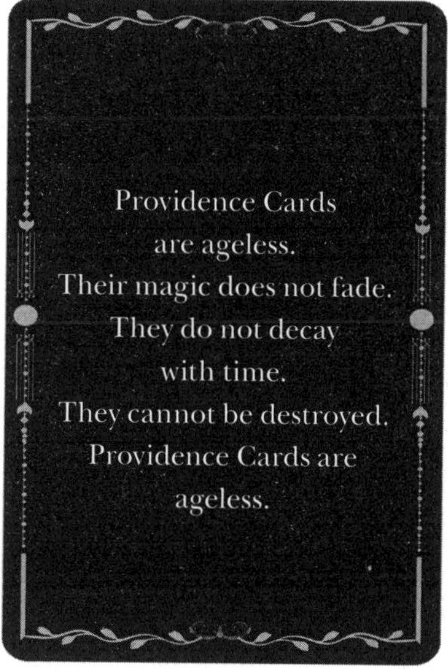

I slipped out of Ravyn's bed at dawn, careful not to wake him. I dug furiously at the clothes on the floor for my dress but found only my chemise. I might have searched longer had Ravyn not stirred behind me, muttering something in a low growl. I froze, but he was still asleep, resting on his stomach, his broad back rising and falling in long, easy breaths. I slid my chemise over my head and tiptoed through the labyrinthine mess on his floor.

His chamber door was old, heavy. The untrustworthy kind that so often screamed on its hinges. I held my breath and pulled gently, and the door rewarded me with only a low groan. I slipped into the hallway and shut it behind me, releasing a triumphant exhale.

"An enjoyable evening, I hope."

I whirled, my heart in my throat.

Jespyr stood a few doors down, already dressed for the day in Destrier black. Despite the dim light, the corridor torches not yet lit, there was no mistaking the wide, devious smile plastered across her face.

I crossed my arms over my chest, my chemise painfully sheer. "You startled me."

"Sorry," she said, not sounding sorry at all. She looked me up and down, her eyes landing on the mess of my hair. "You look…well rested."

"Thank you," I said, slipping past her. I stopped at my door. "You—you didn't hear anything, did you?"

She pressed her lips together. "Like what?"

"Nothing. Never mind. See you at breakfast."

I pushed into my room, the low rumble of her laugh following me.

The hearth in the great hall had been lit, breakfast on the table. Morette and Fenir sat with Emory, their voices low as they coaxed him with sweetbreads and bone broth. They greeted me with their usual friendliness, and I took my seat next to Jespyr, the apples of her cheeks rounding as I sat down.

"What?" I said through my teeth.

She smiled into her eggs. "Nothing."

Elm joined us next, his auburn hair catastrophic, flailing every direction like he'd slept in a windstorm. He landed in his chair with a plunk, yawning as he glanced up the table. "No Ravyn?"

Jespyr's fork scraped over her plate. I shot her a murderous glance.

Thistle entered the room with a fresh loaf of bread. Behind him, back in his Destrier clothes, came Ravyn.

Heat rose up my collar. Suddenly, I was very preoccupied with my plate.

"Smells amazing," Ravyn said, patting Thistle's back. He came up behind his parents and Emory, stealing a slice of bread off his father's plate. He passed Elm, mussing his cousin's wild hair before taking a seat.

Everyone was watching him, brows high. When I looked up, Ravyn's gaze was on me, his mouth upturned, his teeth tugging at his bottom lip. "Morning."

He looked stupidly handsome, smug to his boots. I hid behind my teacup. "Morning."

Next to him, Elm's face twisted in a grimace. "What the hell's wrong with you?"

Ravyn took a bite of bread and leaned back in his chair. "What do you mean?"

"You're *smiling*." Elm looked over the table. "Does no one else find that incredibly unnerving?"

Jespyr's shoulders shook. She pressed a napkin to her mouth, laughter seeping out of her. "We told him he should smile more, didn't we?"

I kicked her under the table, which only made her laugh louder. Across from us, Elm's eyes narrowed, jumping from Jespyr to Ravyn to me. When he noted the choke of red up my neck, paired with the unabashed grin on Ravyn's face, he made a crude *ugh* sound and dropped his fork on his plate. "And just like that, I've lost my appetite."

Down the table, Emory coughed. When he put a cloth to his mouth, it came back red. His coughs echoed through the hall, stealing our smiles, the mood immediately turning somber, all of us remembering at once.

Emory had to go back to Stone today.

Jespyr went to get the carriage ready while the rest of us walked in the garden, our steps heavy. The dawn rain had subsided to a gentle haze, but the grass was overgrown. It didn't take long before my boots and the hem of my green dress were dark with water.

Emory wanted to see the trees in the garden before returning to his gilded cage in the King's castle. He walked ahead of us, his gray eyes wide as he rambled through the mist. Behind him, Elm wrapped his horsehair charm around his knuckles, his gaze trained on his young cousin.

Ravyn and I followed a pace behind, far enough apart that we did not touch, but close enough for me to feel that invisible wire pulling us together. Salt stung my nose as the wind picked up, cold air brushing my cheeks as several strands of dark hair flew across my face.

The back of Ravyn's hand brushed against mine. "I'm glad you can see him as his true self," he said, nodding at Emory. "He doesn't have many days like this anymore."

Does anyone?

I jumped, the Nightmare's voice startling me. I had not heard him since the day before. Foolishly, I had let myself revel in his absence, pretending my mind belonged to me alone.

Rainwater dripped off the trees above us, wetting my head and shoulders. I could smell the water on Ravyn's wool cloak. He put an arm around me and pulled me beneath the same willow tree I had hid from him under. "Are you all right?" he asked, brushing my damp hair out of my face. "You were gone when I woke up."

I leaned into him. "I wanted to let you rest."

He kissed me, his fingers tangling in the hair at the nape of my neck. "I don't want rest, Elspeth," he murmured into my lips. "I want you."

I was in the warmth of him, his body shielding me from Blunder's autumn breeze as it caught along the reeds of the willow tree. My arms fit perfectly around his waist and I wrapped them there, content to be held and kissed and windblown.

A small, pointed cough echoed nearby. Emory peered at us through the willow's branches, his lips curled in a mischievous grin. "Found them," he called to Elm. "They were kissing."

I blushed down to my roots, hiding my face in Ravyn's cloak.

He smiled sheepishly, taking my hand and leading us back into the garden. Elm and Emory waited for us down the path, their arms crossed over their chests. Elm rolled his eyes. "Trees, we get it. No need to rub our noses in it."

"What a shame," Emory sighed, his eyes tracing me. "Here I was, thinking she'd come to kiss me. That's how the fairy tale goes, isn't it? Beautiful maiden saves sick boy with a kiss—boy miraculously heals and delivers the kingdom from dark magic."

"Almost," Elm said, his green eyes flickering to me. "Except, in this fairy tale, the maiden has blood on her hands."

I knew what I needed to do. Leaving Ravyn and Elm to bicker behind me, I hurried ahead, familiar bramble reaching out to snag my hair. "Emory," I called. "Wait."

The gray-eyed boy lingered beneath a wide yew tree, running his fingers across twisting branches. When he turned to me, the corner of his lip curled in a half smile. "Yes?"

I struggled with the words. Damp, my hair clung to the sides of my face. When I pushed it away, my nose filled with salt. "I need to ask you something," I said, peering over my shoulder.

"Something you don't wish my brother and cousin to hear?"

My eyes moved past him. Beyond the yew tree's branches, I

caught the looming shapes of the stone ruins. There, nestled in the mist below a great yew tree, sat the chamber, the darkness fixed in its window ensnaring me.

"I need your magic, Emory," I said, my voice quivering. "I need you to touch me again."

The Nightmare's voice ripped through my mind. *So this is how you unlock my secrets, Elspeth Spindle? You steal them?*

"Again?" Emory said.

You already know the truth. His snarl flooded my mind. *I've told you the story.*

I focused on Emory's face. "You don't remember, but you touched my arm at Equinox. You told me things about myself I'd never told anyone. You saw into my mind." My eyes stung with tears. "I want you to look again, Emory. Please. I need to know who—or what—he really is."

"He?" Emory asked, reaching out for my hand.

"You'll see."

When our hands clasped, Emory shut his eyes. His fingers flexed around mine, and when he spoke, his voice was strange, as if caught in a jar—close and far away at once.

"I see you, Elspeth Spindle," he said. "I see a woman with long black hair and charcoal eyes. I see a yellow gaze narrowed by hate. I see darkness and shadow." His lips quivered. "And I see your fingers, long and pale, covered in blood."

"What else?" I pleaded. "Do you see the Shepherd King? The man in gold armor?"

Emory shook his head, his brow creasing in concentration. "I see a creature, curled around your spine—as if woven into you."

A chill wrapped itself around my throat. "How long do I have until he takes me over entirely?"

Emory's eyes rolled behind his eyelids. "Not long, Elspeth Spindle. He is close."

I tried to pull my hand away, but Emory clung to it, his voice hitching. "He hunches, not animal, not man, but something between. He stands in the room he built for the Spirit of the Wood, perched upon a tall, dark stone." Emory's face twisted, his features contorted in fear. "He whispers something."

"What does he say?" I asked, my heart in my throat.

Emory's hand shook. When he spoke, his voice was strange—slippery. "There once was a girl," he said, "clever and good, who tarried in shadow in the depths of the wood. There also was a King, a shepherd by his crook, who reigned over magic and wrote the old book. The two were together, so the two were the same…"

He did not have to say the rest. I knew it by heart.

"The girl, the King…" I breathed.

The Nightmare's voice burned through my mind. *And the monster they became.*

Emory's eyes shot open, all the color blanched out of his face. "Your eyes," he gasped, tears streaming down his cheeks. "They're yellow."

I looked away, blinking furiously.

"What was that?" Emory asked, his voice still hitching. "It was like something out of a terrible dream."

"Oh, Emory," I said, suddenly wrought with guilt. He was so young, so burdened by his own degeneration. To put my own worries in his hands had been more than selfish—it had been wrong.

"I'm so sorry," I said. "I shouldn't have done that to you."

Beyond the yew tree, I heard the others rustling. "Emory," Ravyn called. "It's time."

I turned to Emory with a pleading look. "You won't say anything, will you?"

The boy tried to smile. "Don't worry," he said, wiping the tears from his eyes. "I'll forget by morning. That's the one mercy of my degeneration. I don't remember my nightmares." He let go of my hand, his gray eyes forlorn. "Goodbye, Elspeth Spindle. Be wary. Be clever. Be good."

When our fingers fell apart, my hand felt cold. I wanted to reach for him again, to tell him the fairy tale was true—that somehow, I could heal him. Not with a kiss, but with the Cards, all twelve collected, a means to save him—to save myself.

But I had grown tired of pretending. So I said nothing, my spine hunching as the Nightmare's claws curled around it.

PART III

The Blood

Chapter Twenty-Nine

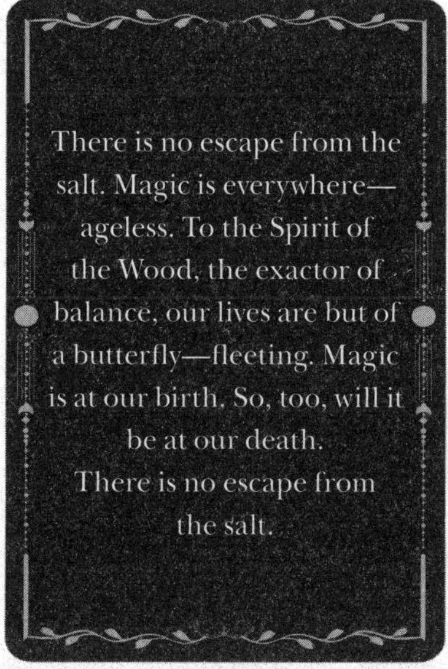

Children followed me, their eyes wide with fear. We ran, chased through brambles, our clothes tangling on the low branches of untrimmed yew trees. The sky was black, the crescent moon masked by smoke. When we came to the stone chamber at the edge of the woods, I lifted the children through the window one by one.

Someone was already waiting for me in the chamber, lit by the red light of his Scythe. Pain seared my every bone, and when I coughed, blood spattered across my long, pale fingers.

I fell—enveloped by earth. The sharp scent of salt stung my eyes and nose until the world around me had utterly disappeared into cold, isolating darkness.

I screamed, my fingers and toes growing blue with cold.

I woke from the dream, shivering on the floor of the crumbling chamber. Morning light peeked through yew branches down through the rotted-out ceiling. I coughed a cry, the sensation of being trapped in darkness still swimming in my mind.

I'd walked in my sleep again.

What is this? I demanded, my face damp with old tears. *Why are you doing this to me?*

The Nightmare echoed through my head, a specter on the wind—wordless, omniscient.

When I raised myself to a stance, I smothered a shriek, my hands and arms caked in dark, heavy soil that stretched from the beds of my fingernails to my elbows. My nightdress was ragged, the fabric sullied and torn. Around my feet lay loose earth, upturned around the base of the magical stone Ravyn had shown me.

"What happened?" I said aloud. "Why have you brought me here?"

I needed to see something, he said, untouched by my horror.

I shivered, my teeth chattering as I tried to shake some of the dirt from my hands. Above me, the trees rustled as three black crows took flight. A frosty wind cut through the chamber. Dirt slid beneath my feet, and I found myself looking down upon the upturned earth at the foot of the magical stone.

"What's there?" I said, kneeling for a better look.

It was obscured by dirt. I took the edge of my nightgown and brushed it clean. Even then, I could not understand it—the letterings worn down by time and decay. "Why write an inscription at the foot of a stone?"

His breath sent shivers up my spine. *Is that all you see?*

I stepped back, surveying the earth I'd upturned. It jutted away from the stone across the floor—a long, rectangular shape of choppy soil and grass. I blinked, then looked again.

It's not just a magical stone that hides Providence Cards, I realized, terror thick as mud as it crept across my heart. The chamber was at the edge of the cemetery. And the stone... the stone was a marker.

A gravestone.

I looked at my hands. *Whose grave?* I gasped, my breath coming in desperate, ragged gulps.

Don't you know? he whispered.

His laugh surrounded me. Suddenly the room darkened, the burn of salt so strong I coughed into my hands, choking on air. The last thing I saw before I lost my footing and fell into darkness was my dirt-covered fingers, long and stiff, covered in blood.

I tore the blanket away and gasped for air. The chamber had disappeared, morning light smothered by the thick walls and roof of Castle Yew. I was back in my room, abed—awake and free of the terrible dream.

I slunk to my hearth, last night's fire mere embers. I reached for the fire iron only to rear back, chills crawling up my spine.

"No, no, no," I cried, staring at my muddy arms—my broken fingernails. I glanced down at my nightgown, the white fabric dirty and ragged. "It was a dream!" I gasped. "How could—I couldn't—It was a dream, surely!"

He did not answer.

"*Enough,*" I cried out, my eyes prickling. "The Shepherd King is dead. Whatever you are—his soul trapped in the Nightmare Card—trapped in me—I beg you, please, leave me alone."

I cannot do that, dear one.

"This is my life, too, Nightmare. My mind you trespass upon. *My* soul."

A soul I protected, he said, a sharp edge to his voice. *When you were a child and the Physicians came to your uncle's door, who pulled you to shelter? When the High Prince stalked you like a deer through the wood, who protected you? When the Destrier came for your throat, who fell him to the ground? King Rowan has held you at the end of a noose from the moment the infection touched your blood, Elspeth Spindle. The only reason your neck did not snap was because I was there, holding you up by your legs.*

Tears of fury filled my eyes. *If I had died, so, too, would you have, Nightmare. Don't for a second pretend you did all this because you care for me. The Shepherd King is dead,* I said once more. *And you—you are a monster.*

That I am, he replied.

I put my hands over my ears and hissed through my teeth. "I won't do this—not today." I said, my fear eclipsed by rage. *There is too much at stake.*

A Well Card, he said, his voice mocking.

It's more than a Well Card. I took my basin and scrubbed the dirt from my hands. *It's the eleventh Card. We need it. I need it, so I can be rid of YOU.*

He sat in the dark, quiet while I cleaned myself. Only after I'd finished—when the maid had come to lace my black dress—did he speak again, his voice far away.

You have so little time, Elspeth.

What the hell does that mean?

But he was gone—retreated deep into my mind.

Elm and his red light waited for me at the foot of the stairs. When he saw me, his green eyes narrowed.

"What's wrong?"

"Nothing," I said, touching my hair. "Why?"

"You look... uneasy."

"I haven't been sleeping well."

"Separation from the Captain making it difficult to rest?"

When I ignored him, the Prince smiled, his face striking when it wasn't bogged down by its usual sullenness. "Ready to celebrate your sisters?" he asked.

"Half sisters."

It had been a full week since Ravyn, Jespyr, and Elm had left Castle Yew with Emory. The King, furious to learn of the Destriers' ineptitude on Market Day, had kept his guard sequestered to Stone, to "shore up their divisiveness," as Jespyr's letter called it.

Which simply meant the King would break their spirits with dawn-to-dusk patrols and backbreaking training sessions.

I had tried to keep a smile on my face for Morette and Fenir, who had been dismal since Emory's departure, but quickly learned it made little difference to them whether I smiled or not.

On the fourth day, Morette had received a handwritten note from my father, inviting me and the Yew household to Spindle House for a celebration that, like so many events at Spindle House, I had managed to avoid for the past several years.

Nya and Dimia's nameday.

But this time was different. This time, I would attend the gathering with the Captain of the Destriers, Jespyr Yew, and a Prince. This time, I would walk the halls of Spindle House with purpose and intent. This time, I would not cower beneath my stepmother's gaze.

This time, I would steal my father's Well Card.

Morette and Fenir joined us at the doors, their hands warm as they embraced me. "We'll be there shortly," Fenir said. He patted Elm's back. "Ravyn and Jespyr?"

"Finishing up with the Destriers. They'll meet us at the gate."

I said goodbye and followed Elm out Castle Yew's doors through the statuary. Above us the autumn sky darkened. A storm was coming. I could feel it in my broken wrist, the linen wrapping swelling beneath my black sleeve.

Crows cawed from the yew trees, sounding a warning I did not yet understand.

"How's Emory?" I asked when we reached the gate.

"Weak," Elm said. "The King wasn't happy about his jaunt home." He gave half a smile. "Nor was he keen to hear an infected child had escaped and a Destrier was attacked. Linden will boast some spectacular scars when he's back on his feet."

I flinched, my stomach turning.

Elm lowered his voice as we stepped out onto the street. "But my father's distracted. He's obsessed with finding the Twin Alders Card by Solstice. Only, he has no idea where to look."

"Be wary the green, be wary the trees," I said, my voice not quite my own, thin as thread. "Be wary the song of the wood on your sleeves. You'll step off the path—to blessing and wrath. Be wary the song of the wood on your sleeves."

Elm eyed me over his shoulder. "Been reading *The Old Book of Alders* lately?"

I hadn't. I hadn't meant to say anything at all.

In the darkness, the clicking of the Nightmare's claws beat a slow, ominous rhythm. I clenched my jaw lest I say anything else, my thoughts returning to the dark chamber and the grave therein.

Elm, who took my silence for apprehension, said, "Only two more Cards, Spindle. You'll soon have the pleasure of walking these streets free and clear." He grimaced. "And I'll soon have the pleasure of ridding Blunder of Physician Orithe Willow."

We were not the first guests to arrive at Spindle House. The torches had been lit, and a crowd gathered at the gate, their voices rushing like smoke up the street.

The guards lined up to open the gate, each fitted in a red cloak. Next to one stood Jespyr, and on her other side, leaned up against the stone wall like he owned the place, was Ravyn Yew.

My heart thrashed in my chest, as if it beat with dark, powerful wings. His jaw was freshly shaved, his black hair brushed back. But he looked tired—more tired than I'd ever seen him. The circles under his gray eyes were so dark they might have been bruises. There were scabs along his knuckles and a split in his bottom lip.

When he caught my eye, he pushed off the wall, slipping through the crowd on sure feet. His lips curled as he reached for me, one hand finding my waist, the other my cheek. When he leaned over me, a few strands of dark hair fell over his brow. "Elspeth," he said, kissing my mouth.

I swept his hair out of his face and looked him up and down. "Black suits you, Captain," I said. "All that's missing is the mask."

Ravyn smiled, almost boyish. "Same to you, Miss Spindle."

I trailed my finger above the half-healed split in his bottom lip. "What happened?"

"Training," he said with a shrug. "Haven't caught a break since Market Day."

Jespyr joined us, her eyes warm. "Everyone ready?"

"Yes, trees, yes," Elm said with a groan. "Anything to put an end to their *whispering*."

When the guards opened the gates, we stepped into the courtyard, the spindle tree at its heart surrounded by gold lanterns, red ribbons hanging from its branches. Ravyn draped his arm over my shoulders, and the four of us waited with the others as more of my father's guests spilled into the courtyard.

When the gong struck six, all eyes turned to Spindle House's great doors, now opening.

Applause swelled. Balian, my father's steward, announced my father, stepmother, and half sisters by name. I watched them step onto the landing, opening the house to their guests. Nerium's hand was tight in my father's, who did not smile, fixed with his usual austerity. There was no blue light in his pocket. Wherever he kept his Well Card, it was not on his person.

Nya and Dimia curtsied, basking in the applause. They wore red gowns and stood on either side of their parents, their faces mirrored in identical smiles.

I leaned into Ravyn and did not clap. They felt like strangers to me—young, striking strangers. For years, I had walked the same halls as Nya and Dimia, eaten the same food, enjoyed my own nameday celebrations, stared up at the same spindle tree. But the infection had changed everything. We were not the same, my half sisters and I. Life had sheltered them, like pearls kept in a velvet pouch. And I—I was not made of pearls.

I was made of salt.

"Twins give me the creeps," Elm muttered under his breath. His spine stiffened. "They're here."

The gong rang twice in quick succession. The crowd in the courtyard parted as the King passed through my father's gate. King Rowan stood tall in gold silk, his cloak collared by white fox fur. Next to him came Hauth, and at his side, Ione, who, though she did not carry it, was clearly still in the Maiden's clutch. My uncle trailed behind her, his clothes finer than those he'd worn at Equinox.

My aunt and young cousins were not with them.

My eyes narrowed as I watched Ione, my cousin's hand wrapped in the High Prince's grasp. Behind my gaze, the Nightmare shifted. *Yellow girl, beauty keen. Yellow girl, noticed—seen. Yellow girl, heart of stone. Yellow girl, cruel Queen.*

My father ushered King Rowan and his court into Spindle

House, signaling the start of the celebration. The rest of the guests followed, their voices high with excitement. Somewhere inside the house, a fiddle and flute struck a giddy harmony. Elm, Jespyr, Ravyn, and I lingered at the spindle tree.

The Prince let out a long sigh, bracing himself against the branches. "Let the festivities begin."

Chapter Thirty

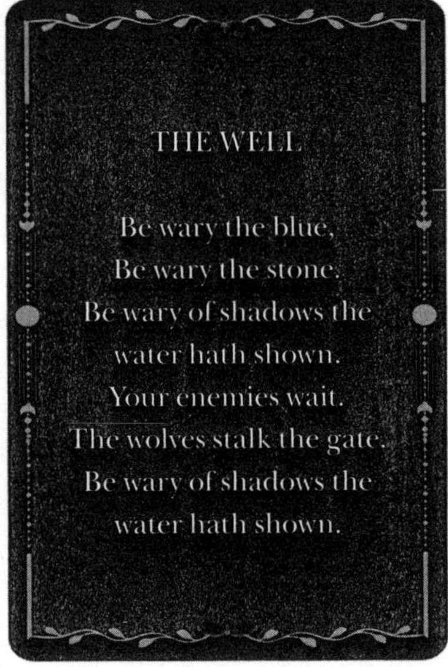

Everyone was in the great hall. No one saw me slip up the stairs with the Captain of the Destriers. Or, if they did, I was just a maiden, headed into shadow with a tall, handsome man. Not the first, nor the last, of my kind.

A moment later, Jespyr and Elm joined us, taking the stairs in shifts.

"We need to split up," Jespyr said, her eyes turned upward to the long, winding stairwell. "Each of us should take a floor."

Ravyn shook his head. "Better we go in pairs. It'll look less suspicious if anyone catches us snooping."

"Will it?" Elm tapped his finger on the banisters. His green eyes landed on me. "Fine. Spindle. You're with me."

I blinked. "You can't be serious."

"Oh, but I am."

Ravyn's voice was low. "She should come with me."

"Trees, Ravyn, you'll survive a moment without her." To his cousin's glare, Elm crossed his arms. "Unless, of course, your priorities lie somewhere beyond finding the Well Card."

Ravyn said nothing, his fingers flexing against mine.

"Oh, don't look at me like that. You have a Mirror, and Jes is our best lockpick. Out of the two of us, you're getting the bargain."

"I don't think it was lock picking that appealed to him," Jespyr murmured through her fingers. "Or, perhaps, that's exactly what—"

"All of you, shut up, we're wasting time." I slipped my hand out of Ravyn's. "Elm and I will search the library, then head up to the guest rooms on the third floor. You two start with my father's bedchamber—it's on the fourth landing—then go to the fifth." I glanced back at Ravyn. "If we don't find it, we meet back in the great hall and search the bottom floor."

Elm saluted me. "Yes, Captain."

"And if someone asks what you and the Prince are doing?" Ravyn said pointedly.

Elm flashed his Scythe in his cousin's face. "I'll send them on their merry way."

"What about the sixth landing?" Jespyr said, her eyes raised once more to the tall, spiraling stairs.

I shook my head. "My father doesn't go up there anymore."

"How do you know?"

"Because that's where my room is."

We didn't find the Well Card in the library. I'd have seen the blue light right away. But Elm insisted on digging through several old tomes and flinging open every drawer of my father's desk. I shadowed him, taming his chaos, making sure everything was put back where it belonged.

We moved to the next room, then the next. When there were no more rooms on the third floor, we hid in shadows, waiting for the stairwell to be clear above and below us.

What little patience Elm had, he was rapidly losing. He ran a hand through his unruly hair. "You sure you haven't missed it?"

I shot him a narrow glance. "If there's a Well Card here, I'd have seen it."

"Perhaps it's not here because your father used it." His voice lowered. "And saw us in it."

I chewed my bottom lip, nerves twisting my stomach. *To see one's enemies*, the Nightmare called. *Betrayed by a friend. Or in this case, his daughter, his successor, a Destrier, and a Prince.*

"Can I help you with anything, Miss Spindle?"

We both jumped, which made my father's steward jump in turn. Balian let out a small cough. "My apologies," he said. "Your father wishes to show the King one of his books—he asked me to retrieve it. I did not think anyone would be up here." He glanced over my shoulder, his eyes widening when he recognized Elm.

I did not often take pleasure in other people's turmoil. But in that moment, I relished Balian's utter shock as he surveyed me, the eldest Spindle—upon whom he had cast so much indifference and distrust—standing, chin high, in a fine black dress next to the King's son.

"Will you be joining us downstairs, Your Grace?" Balian asked, bowing low.

"Shortly," Elm said, gnawing at a fingernail, looking decidedly *un*-Princely.

"You may go, Balian," I said under a false smile. "I'm sure you have much to attend to."

When I spoke, Balian's eyes narrowed a moment, the pretense of civility dropped. It seemed it did not matter that I was with a Prince; he did not like taking orders from the eldest child—the infected child.

"Very good," he said, brushing past me.

Elm's hand lowered to his pocket, bathed in red light. "What, no bow for her?"

Balian hesitated. He looked at me, the lines in his face knit. Suddenly his eyes went bleary and he gave a low, stooping bow. A moment later he snapped upright, his eyes clearer, wider. He shot Elm a frightened glance and then hurried through the hallway before disappearing down the stairs.

Next to me, Elm chuckled, tapping the Scythe three times and twirling it between his long fingers.

"You didn't have to do that," I said, mounting the stairwell. "He's just a pompous little man."

The Prince's steps echoed behind mine. "What's the point of owning a Scythe if you can't have a little fun now and then?"

I had to lift the front of my dress, the stairs at Spindle House treacherously steep. "It doesn't always look fun. You seemed like you might fall over after the Market Day bedlam."

Elm's voice was dispassionate. "Everything has a cost."

"The Scythe Card higher than most," I said. "I've heard, if used too long, the pain is excruciating."

Elm feigned a gasp. "No one told me—I'll stop using it at once!"

I scowled. "It's a risk."

"So is treason," the Prince bit back. "And yet, here we are."

We reached the fourth landing off the main stairwell and took a sharp right, following a long, chilly corridor before reaching a spiral staircase, a servants' corridor to the fourth-floor bedrooms.

The Nightmare's gaze lightened the dimly lit stairs, and though he did not speak, I could hear his breath in my ears.

"What made you do it?" I asked Elm, winded as I climbed the stairs. "You're a Destrier—a Prince, second in line for the crown. Why risk it at all?"

"Emory's dying. I do what I have to do to save him. That's what family does."

"Aren't the Rowans your family, too?"

"Aren't they yours?" he said, gesturing to the walls of Spindle House.

I slowed my step. "My father could have turned me in when I caught the fever. But he didn't." I wrinkled my nose. "He broke the rules for me. And that's what he sees when he looks at me—a broken rule."

"What if he didn't?" Elm countered. "Suppose he, or someone else, risked their title—their life—for yours freely? Someone who saw all your secrets and sicknesses and did not fear you. Wouldn't you choose them over all the others?"

I tried not to think about Ione. I pictured my aunt—her tight, warm hugs, her wisdom. I thought of how she'd stayed up late with me those first few weeks, when the fever held me in its grip. I thought of her letter and how, should I come home, she'd embrace me once again.

I thought of the Yews, steadfast, loyal. Fenir, Morette, Jespyr—even Jon Thistle—who looked at me without fear and offered nothing but kindness.

And Ravyn.

Just like the bird of his namesake, there was pronounced intelligence in Ravyn Yew's gray eyes. When he looked at me, I felt seen, known. There was a line between us, drawn by fate and magic, that stretched out over space and time. Ravyn and I had walked that line our entire lives, unaware we were headed straight for each other. I saw myself in his cautious eyes and in the darkness that swam in my veins, and though I had not realized it until that very moment, there was magic between us that had nothing to do with blood or Providence Cards or anything in between.

"I think I understand," I said as we reached the top of the winding staircase. "And yes, I think I would do anything for someone like that. I truly would."

"And wouldn't you do anything to protect them?" Elm said, his words trailing me like a shadow.

I turned, caught by something in his voice. When our gaze met, the Nightmare stirred, watching Elm through my eyes. "You're worried about Ravyn," I said, already knowing the truth. "You think, because I have secrets, that I will betray him—betray all of you."

Elm did not deny it. Had I not been assured he carried only his Scythe, I might have thought there existed a Nightmare Card between us—a knowing, a reading of my mind. Just like in Ravyn, there lived a great intelligence behind the young Prince's gaze, and though they shone Rowan green, they were just as seeing, just as comprehending.

Only, Elm's eyes were filled with distrust.

"I would never betray you." When the Nightmare's laugh filled my mind like smoke, I flinched. "At least, not knowingly."

Elm raised his brows. "What does that mean?"

I turned away, a cool tear falling from my chin to the top stair below my feet. "Time will tell," I said, stepping into the first of several bedchambers. "One way or another, the truth will out."

An hour later we met Ravyn and Jespyr at the bottom of the stairwell at the lip of the great hall. My chest sank—there was no blue light coming from either of them.

Jespyr was gnawing at the hem of her sleeve. When she saw us, her voice was tight. "Please, tell me you found it."

I shook my head. Jespyr swore under her breath.

Elm ran a hand over his face. "What time is it?"

Ravyn turned toward the great hall, the muscles tense along his jaw. "They just sounded the ninth gong."

"The festivities won't end until late tomorrow night—we still have another day to search."

I could feel panic knitting itself into me. My jaw ached from clenching, my shoulders rigid, my hands locked in fists. "You three should go in—let the King and his court see you." Ravyn opened his mouth to disagree, but I cut him off, brushing against him. "I'll find you once I've spotted the Well."

Jespyr and Elm exchanged glances. "You sure?" Jespyr said.

"Yes." I gave a low laugh. "Trust me, no one in there is going to notice my absence."

Something shifted in my periphery, accompanied by the swell of a soft, birdlike voice. "Come now, Bess," it called. "You give me so little credit."

When I turned, Ione was there, clad in a deep violet dress I had never seen before. Its embroidered neckline was low, revealing her porcelain neck and the top swell of her breasts. She wore her hair in a loose braid, unadorned but for a single gold ribbon woven into her plait.

She looked like a moonbeam, mistress of the night, beautiful beyond measure. I stared at her, slack-jawed, captivated by every curve and edge of her. All but for her hazel eyes, which, even before the Maiden Card, had shone with their own special light, as if lit from within.

Only now they were clouded. Unfocused. Lost.

"Come sit with me," she said, nodding toward the great hall. She waved at Ravyn and Jespyr and Elm. "You too."

When she turned, I shot Ravyn a desperate glance. *The Well,* I mouthed.

He watched Ione turn into the great hall. When she glanced over her shoulder, he put his arm around me, and together we followed her. "Ten minutes," he said into my hair, nodding at Jespyr and Elm to follow suit. "Then you can continue your search."

Ione led us up the aisle of tables, the great hall clamorous, laughter and music warring for dominance as they bounced off the hall's looming ceiling. The King sat next to my father at the main table, their heads bent low in conversation. Down the line was Nerium, her lips tight as she surveyed her guests, and next to her, the twins, their cheeks rosy with drink.

Ione steered us past them to an empty table along the east wall. There, waiting on a silver tray, were six goblets of wine.

"Please, sit," she said, gesturing to the table. "Shall we make a toast?"

We lowered ourselves to the table, slow and rigid, as if our joints had all rusted over. I sat between Ravyn and Ione, Jespyr and Elm opposite us. Each of us took a goblet from the tray and held it up. "To Nya and Dimia," Ione said, taking a long, deep swill. "Many happy returns."

"Many happy returns," the rest of us repeated, our voices small. I drank from my cup and winced, the wine more bitter than I'd expected.

No one spoke. I shot Jespyr a glance and she shrugged, eyes wide. I turned to Elm—counting on him to say something—anything—to break the unbearable quiet.

But Elm was silent, leaning forward in his seat, his gaze

honed entirely on Ione. A moment later he reached across the table and gripped her face, his fingers pressing into her cheeks.

"Elm, what—"

"Shut up." He searched my cousin's face. "Miss Hawthorn," he said, his voice unusually soft. "Ione."

She did not respond, did not move his hand away, did not blink, her eyes just as unfocused as before.

Something was wrong. I gripped the table. "What's going on?"

"Look at her eyes," Elm murmured. "Someone's used a Scythe on her." He reached into his pocket, his eyes never leaving Ione's face. He tapped his Scythe three times, his voice gentle. "Tell me what you've done, Hawthorn."

She blinked. When she spoke, her voice sounded strangled. "Only what he bade me," she said.

I went cold. That's when I realized that there were five of us seated at the table. Five of us.

And six goblets.

I turned to Ravyn. But the Captain of the Destriers had gone still, his hand so tight in mine it felt like a vise.

Then, mouth twisted in a cruel smile, cloaked in Scythe red and the turquoise light of a Chalice Card, Hauth Rowan took his seat at the end of the table. He cast his gaze across the table and barked a laugh. "Come now," he said. "It's a nameday tradition. Surely you won't begrudge me a little fun."

He pulled his Scythe from his pocket and tapped it three times. "Thank you, my dear."

The light in Ione's eyes returned. Her gaze jerked from Elm to Hauth to her empty goblet. Not even the glamour of the Maiden could hide the pale in her cheeks.

Elm's fingers slipped from her face, his eyes burning as he turned to his brother. "You didn't," he snapped. He threw his empty goblet to the floor, rage broiling in the low notes of his voice.

"I did." Hauth smiled, draining the sixth goblet. "Now I have, too. Fair enough for you, brother?"

The Nightmare understood before I did. His anger burned through me, filling my thoughts with smoke.

I called out for him. *What's happening?*

The wine sat on my tongue, bitter, sour, unlike any drink I'd had before. The turquoise light in his pocket. The Chalice.

I stared open-mouthed at my goblet, my face reflected grotesquely in the last dregs of wine at the bottom of the cup.

No. My fingers shook. *He wouldn't.*

But it was written all over the High Prince's face, a smug, triumphant smile sewn across his lips as he slid the Chalice Card onto the table for us to see. "Only a few moments now," he said, his eyes turning to Ravyn. "Who wants to tell the truth first?"

Chapter Thirty-One

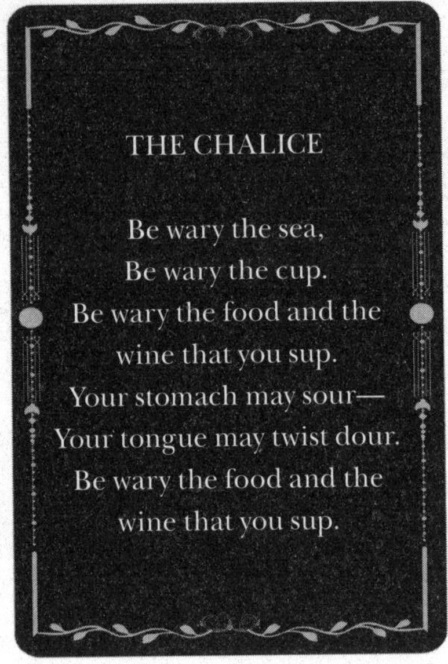

This was a game they'd played before. Only then, they'd all been younger and had a great deal less to hide. I stared at Hauth and he stared back at me, twisting the Chalice between his brutish fingers.

If you've a secret, the Nightmare called, *the Chalice will reveal it. The High Prince seeks truth. And now he will steal it.*

"Fine, then," Hauth said, opening his hands—as if to show he had nothing to hide. "I'll go first. You can ask only one question each, so make it count. Try to lie too much..." His lips curled. "Well, let's hope it doesn't come to that. Jespyr. Go first."

Jespyr looked as if she might be sick, her lips drawn so tight they seemed to disappear. "You didn't ask," she said, her voice low, shaking with anger. "It isn't a game if we never consented to the Chalice, Hauth."

Hauth leaned back in his chair. "Only someone with something to hide would refuse to play." His gaze flickered over the table, tracing our faces. "You don't have anything to hide, do you?"

Jespyr's eyes narrowed. She slammed her goblet back onto the tray. "Fine. I'll begin with an easy question, *cousin*," she said, spitting the word out like it were venom. "Are you jealous of Ravyn?"

Hauth's laugh did not touch his eyes. "N-n-n-n." He clenched his jaw and tried again. "N-n-n." But the wine—the Chalice—would not let him lie. "Yes," he said.

Elm was next. Pale as death, he managed to keep his head high. "Are you trying to turn the Destriers against him?"

Again, Hauth tried to lie. The veins bulged in his thick neck, fighting against the invisible leash tethered to his tongue. Finally, he conceded, shooting Ravyn a bitter glance. "Yes."

Ravyn held his gaze. "Will you challenge me for command?"

This time, Hauth did not try to lie. "Yes."

Silence spread across the table. It was my turn.

Be wary, the Nightmare whispered. *Be clever.*

"Have you used your Scythe Card on Ione more than once?" I said, my voice somewhere between a hiss and a strangle.

Hauth smiled, unaffected by my ire. "Yes." He turned to Ione. "Your turn, betrothed."

Ione's eyes, though brighter than before, conveyed nothing. "I don't want to play."

"You have to," Hauth said, patting her arm, a bit too rough to be affectionate. "We all do. If you don't, I'll think you have something to hide, my dear."

Ione gave him an empty glance. "I don't care what you think."

Something flared in Hauth's eyes. "Ask me a question, Ione."

I wanted to reach across the table and rip his face open again. Ravyn, sensing my rage, tightened his grip on my hand.

Ione propped her elbow on the table and rested her chin upon it, surveying Hauth as one might droppings stuck to the bottom of their shoe. "Have you been with other women since our betrothal?"

For someone who'd put up such a show, it seemed Hauth did indeed have a few things to hide. His face turned purple, as if holding his breath could seal in the lie.

But the Chalice Card held true.

"Yes," he admitted.

Elm snorted. But Ione sat under the shield of beauty, seemingly untouched by her future husband's infidelity.

"I'll go next," she said. She raised her hazel eyes up the table. "Ask me anything, Jespyr."

Jespyr's gaze was hard, but her voice softened. "Is Hauth treating you well, Ione?"

One of Ione's perfect brows arched. "As well as a brute like him knows how."

Elm leaned forward, quiet a moment too long, his green eyes measuring Ione. "Are you in love with him?"

My cousin held his intrusive gaze, measuring him in return. "No."

Jespyr let out a low whistle. It was Ravyn's turn. "What do you want out of your connection with the Rowans?" he asked.

"I want to be powerful," Ione said.

Her words frightened me, as did the lifelessness of her tone. The Ione I knew cared to laugh—smile—put wildflowers in her hair—ride her father's horse down the forest road barefoot. She drew strength from her own inner light.

A light that had been altered—darkened into something cold, hard. Unfeeling.

The Maiden had remade her.

It was my turn to ask her a question. "Is this what you really want, Ione?" I asked, my mouth downturned as my gaze drifted to Hauth. "To marry him?"

Her laugh rumbled in her chest, her perfect face smooth, her cheeks rosy pink. "You're just like Mother, Elspeth. Head in the clouds. You don't see how hard it is for a woman to be powerful—to be fearless—in Blunder, because you never cared about being more than exactly what you are. But I do." She folded her hands in front of her, her hazel eyes firm. "And if it takes a cold heart to be fearless, then so be it."

I was lost in her face. "But I did care about being more than what I was, Ione," I said, my eyes stinging. "I wanted to be like you."

My words didn't seem to reach her. "It doesn't matter now," she said, pressing a finger to her lips. "Now we are both sheep, nestled pleasantly in a wolf den. Or is it the other way around?"

The Nightmare's lips stretched over his jagged teeth. *I like this Ione.*

I thought I might be sick. I looked around, wondering if I could run, searching for an excuse that might free me from the table—from my changed cousin, from Hauth Rowan's brutal gaze.

You can't leave, the Nightmare said, tapping his claws with a swift, jarring rhythm. *You have to stay, just like the others, and pretend. Just as you've always done.*

"My turn," Elm said, pulling attention away from Ione and me. "Ask me your bloody questions."

The Nightmare Card below the table flashed in the corner of my eye. I looked at Ravyn, but he was somewhere else, his gaze focused entirely on Elm.

"Who do you think is the most talented Card user in Blunder?" Jespyr asked her cousin.

Elm propped his elbows on the table. "I am."

"That's his truth," Hauth muttered under his breath.

Ione leaned forward. "Why do you not live at Stone with your father and brother?"

What little color remained in Elm's face disappeared. His throat hitched, and I knew he was fighting to answer—trying to lie. But he could not cheat the Chalice. "I hate it there," he said, his voice so low it almost shook. "I'd tear it down if I could, set the whole thing to flame. Watch it burn to nothingness."

The Nightmare shifted in the darkness, flexing his claws, watching Elm.

Whatever Ione had expected him to say, it was not that. Her gaze shot to Hauth, who sat like a wall, unfeeling, unaffected. I wondered how much she knew—if Hauth had told her he'd brutalized his brother when they were children at Stone.

Ravyn broke the silence. "It's my turn." He looked at his cousin. Whatever was said in the silence of their minds, I could not tell. Their faces were blank but for slight shifts in their eyes. "Do you trust me, Elm?" Ravyn asked.

"Do I have a choice?" After a pause, the glass fading from his eyes, Elm sighed. "Yes. I trust you. I trust you with my life."

It was my turn. I wanted to ask if he trusted me as well, but it was too risky. "Does it pain you to use the Scythe for too long?"

Elm stared at me for a moment. The Scythe was a Card of power—control. To show pain was to forfeit that control. Pain was weakness. And, for a Prince of Blunder, weakness was an unforgivable trait.

But unlike his brother, Elm did not pretend he was beyond weakness. This time, he did not try to lie. "Yes," he said, straightening his back, his jaw firm. "It feels like glass cutting through my head."

Hauth watched his younger brother. "Do you think you are more fit to be King than I am?"

Elm turned to his brother. "Yes," he said, the depths of his green eyes and the hate behind them so strong I flinched. "But you already knew that."

I felt the table might snap for all the tension strung between us. *They play this game for fun?* I seethed into the blackness. *Wars have been started for less.*

This game is a war, darling, the Nightmare called. *And the Chalice—the truth—is the greatest weapon of all.*

"I'll go next," Ravyn said.

Hauth sneered. "What for? We both know you'll say whatever the hell you want, just as you always do."

Ravyn's features stilled—controlled. *He can't use the Chalice,* I recalled. *Nor can the Chalice be used against him.*

So the Captain of the Destriers does what he's best at, the Nightmare said. *Lie.*

Hauth made like he might object again, but Ione was already leaning in. "Do you care for Elspeth?" she asked. "Truly?"

Ravyn's fingers flexed along my hand. "From the moment I met her." He paused. "The second moment, perhaps."

I shot him a narrow glance. Ione watched me from her seat, a momentary smile painted onto her flawless porcelain face. Elm rolled his eyes, and Jespyr cracked a grin.

Hauth glowered. "What do you do when you are not with the Destriers?" he asked Ravyn. "Where do you go?"

"Only one question," Elm snapped.

Hauth slammed his hand on the table. "I could ask him a hundred questions and not get a thimble of truth. Such is his *gift*. Isn't that right, Ravyn?"

No one spoke. Ravyn's face remained even, untouched by his cousin's ire, free to lie at will. "I've been busy," he said, "with the King's biddings. What else would I be doing?"

Hauth's brow darkened as he sank back into his seat.

Jespyr's voice was quiet. "Do you wish that you had not become a Destrier—that you had a normal life?"

They shared a long glance, the lines along Ravyn's brow easing. "Only on days I don't have my sister there to steer me in the right direction."

It was Elm's turn. "Trees, Ravyn, I don't know." He ran his hand over his brow. "Do you think I'm better looking than you?"

The corner of Ravyn's lip twitched. "Decidedly."

It was my turn to ask a question. I looked up at Ravyn and he repaid me with a smile, his gray eyes just as clear as they'd been when he'd taken me by the hand and brought me into the deep underground of the castle—into a world of secrets and treason and purpose. A world of highwaymen and salt.

"Are you still pretending?" I said, reveling in his gaze.

Ravyn gave a surprised laugh and, in front of everyone, leaned in and kissed me. "I never was," he whispered into my lips.

When I looked up, Hauth's eyes were on me. He rested his hands on the table, lacing his fingers together, trapping the Chalice's turquoise light. "And now the one I've been waiting for. It's your turn to answer our questions, Miss Spindle."

Sweat pooled in my palms, and my breath came out in short, halting wheezes.

Easy now, the Nightmare called. *The Chalice is a Card of truth. But the truth must be framed—netted—caught. The question is just as important as the answer.*

I'd hardly had time to collect my thoughts before Ione began, her hazel eyes guarded, caught somewhere between curiosity and calculation. "Are you in love, Elspeth?"

I felt as if I might die. For the first time in my life, I almost hated my cousin. I wondered how a Maiden Card fared against a knocked-in tooth.

This is beastly, I groaned. *Help me.*

Help you?

YOU HEARD ME. Help!

The Chalice affects the blood, he said. *My strength—my magic—will not deliver you.* His laugh cut through the dark. *Unless you'd like me to rip the Card out of the High Prince's hand... and break all his fingers for good measure.*

That is entirely unhelpful.

Then you must find your own way around the Chalice's magic.

He was right—the Chalice's magic was strange. I did not feel it in my veins, nor could I discern the familiar scent of salt in my nose. It sat somewhere in my body, trapped, waiting for me to answer.

When I tried to lie, I coughed, the sensation of being strangled so acute my eyes watered.

"Come off it," Jespyr said. "She needn't answer if she doesn't want to."

"The rest of us had to," Hauth said, winking at Ravyn. "Let the girl finish."

But I couldn't. I wasn't ready to say it, even if I felt it. The truth was too new, so fragile it might break. I fought to find a way around the truth—but magic blocked my tongue at every pass, strangling me until I was left gasping for air.

Breathe, the Nightmare called, his voice a candle in the darkness.

Next to me, Ravyn stirred. "Elspeth." He squeezed my hand. "You don't have to—"

"Yes," I said, the word slipping out of me without resistance, so effortless it could be mistaken as nothing other than the truth.

I tried to pull my hand from Ravyn's, but he wouldn't let me, his thumb scraping over my knuckles. Still, I did not look at him. I cast Ione a bitter glance, her question a violation, ripping something from me I was not yet ready to say.

Hauth traced the discomfort on my face greedily, honing in on me. Hunting me. "Now, the question I've been longing to ask." He leaned in. "Tell me, Miss Spindle," he said, his voice full of false charm. "What happened to your arm?"

I did not have to glance up to know Ravyn, Jespyr, and Elm had all gone rigid in their seats. Ravyn tugged at my hand under the table, but I ignored him, frozen, grasping for words that would not betray me to the hangman.

The Chalice twisted my tongue, blocking the lies before they reached my tongue. Hauth had been smart. He could not steal secrets from Ravyn, a man immune to the Chalice.

But he could steal mine. And with them, condemn us all.

"I—" I said, choking on the word. "I—I was—"

Ione put a hand on Hauth's arm. "I told you, she fell—"

"Shut your mouth, Ione," Hauth snarled, swatting her hand away.

"Hasn't she endured enough of your spite?" Elm said through his teeth.

"What's it to you, brother?"

"Call me old-fashioned, but I don't think you should use a Scythe on the woman you're going to marry."

They argued. Jespyr joined in. But I didn't hear what they said. I felt like I was choking on my own bile.

Be calm, the Nightmare's voice called, close and far away at the same time. *Sooner or later, the truth will out,* he purred. *You said so yourself.*

I didn't mean like THIS!

I glanced up at Ravyn. He must have seen the fear in my eyes, because when he looked at me, there was a pain in his face I had not seen before—raw, protective. He grasped my hand,

and though his lips barely moved, I discerned four words from his mouth.

"Let me help you."

Tears filled my eyes. Next to me, Ravyn's Nightmare Card flickered again. Salt filled my nose and I froze, understanding only too late what Ravyn had meant.

Let me help you.

"Don't, Ravyn—" I gasped.

But it was too late. He had already broken his promise.

The intrusion into my mind felt like someone had splashed me with icy water. I felt it in my ears—my eyes—my nostrils, into the roof of my mouth. I coughed, gasping for air.

It's all right, Elspeth, Ravyn's voice echoed in my head. *You can do this—choose your words carefully. He asked you what happened—not how it happened.*

But I hardly heard him. I was too busy shouting, my fingers digging into the Captain of the Destriers' palm. *No, no, no! I told you, no, Ravyn!*

Breathe, Elspeth, he said, his voice calm above the din. *It's going to be fine.*

I told you NO, Ravyn, I said. *Get out.*

Ravyn stirred, confusion and hurt touching the corners of his face. *I'm sorry,* he said, *I only wanted to—*

The Nightmare lunged out of the darkness like a beast of prey. *You heard her,* he said, swiping his claws, a vicious snarl ripping up his throat. *Get out, Ravyn Yew. GET. OUT.*

Ravyn fell with full force out of his seat, the entire table shaking in his wake.

"Easy!" Jespyr called, jumping to her feet. The others stood as well, their gazes shifting from me to the Captain of the Destriers, who sat—dazed on the floor—his handsome face twisted in fear.

Elm rounded the table. "You look like you've seen a ghost."

Ravyn's gray eyes, wide and glassy, were tight on my face. "No... not seen."

"Sit down," Hauth barked. He reached forward, pushing past Ione, grasping for me. He caught my injured arm. "It's all right, Miss Spindle, you can tell me the truth," he said, his thumb pressing against my sleeve, into my broken wrist. "After all, it's just a game."

Jespyr lunged at him. "Get off her," she yelled, knocking him back, his fingers scraping against my wrist as he let go.

I saw stars, sick with pain. Hauth and Jespyr were at each other's throats. Elm was pulling Ravyn off the floor. No one but me saw Ione reach for the discarded Chalice on the table and, with the delicate tip of her finger, tap it, freeing me.

We shared a glance. I opened my mouth to say something, but she was already out of her chair, slipping away through the great hall.

Ravyn was on his feet, wolflike as he turned on his cousin. "This was an ambush, not a game," he snarled. "We've indulged you long enough." He offered me his hand and I took it, then nodded to Jespyr and Elm. "We're leaving."

I let out a breath of relief, scrambling to my feet.

But the world all around me buckled, and my knees, suddenly weak, bent under the weight of my body.

I fell, crashing to the floor.

Nausea gripped my stomach and I choked, a thick, oozing bile climbing up my throat, strangling me. When I coughed it out onto the floor, it was dark and grainy—heavy like the soil I'd dug up that morning. It slid down my fingers, hot and viscous, leaving long, angry trails that pooled darkly in my palms.

It wasn't until I'd coughed again that I realized it was blood.

Like a fool, I'd tried to beat the Chalice. I'd tried to lie too much.

In the brief moments before I vomited a sea of blood, I recalled the insignia of the Chalice Card: *Truth Serum*—the old writing hewn above an image of a cup filled with dark red liquid. On its opposite side, the cup turned on its head—the dark liquid spilling, unbidden…

Poison.

Chapter Thirty-Two

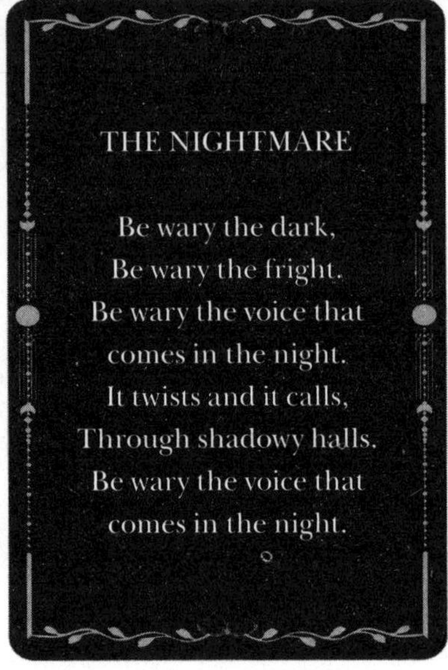

The room was dark when I woke, dawn still shy on the horizon. I stared at nothing, a dull ache throbbing behind my eyes.

I recognized the ceiling first. There were knots in the wood that, if my eyes remained unfocused, transformed into strange, grotesque faces that stared down at me. Before I'd any true concept of monsters, I used to imagine the shapes in the wood were creatures watching over me, neither benevolent nor evil.

But that was a long time ago.

I sat up in my childhood bed and scanned the room, pain thumping in the back of my skull. The room was exactly how I remembered it—the chest full of dresses, the wooden dollhouse. The pile of blankets, whose colors were now faded, moth-eaten, sat where I'd left them eleven years ago.

Nothing had moved, the room stilled, as if frozen.

The only thing out of place was the tall wooden chair and the man seated upon it, pulled from its home in the corner and placed beside my bed.

Ravyn was bent in sleep, his head bowed—as if praying. His face was smooth, all the strain and austerity washed away by sleep. In his pocket glowed the familiar violet and burgundy lights of his Cards, unblinking.

I watched him for some time, the light in my window growing brighter. I wondered how he'd gotten me up here, to the top of the house. I wondered how they'd cured me from the Chalice's poison.

Most of all, I wondered—my stomach dropping—if after last night, Ravyn Yew had irrevocably changed his mind about me.

A quiet hand rapped three times on my door. I closed my eyes, feigning sleep.

Ravyn jolted awake, jumping to his feet. "Who is it?"

"Elm."

I heard the latch release and the door squeak open, Elm's steps hurried as he came into the room and shut the door behind him. "How is she?"

"Still asleep," Ravyn muttered. "Filick left a few hours ago."

"Any more blood?"

"No."

"I could kill Hauth," Elm seethed.

"What's more alarming is why he wanted to use a Chalice in the first place," Ravyn said. "Your brother suspects it was us in the wood that night. He has no proof, but he suspects."

"We need to be careful, Ravyn."

"I'm well aware."

"Did you sleep?"

Ravyn's yawn was answer enough.

"Sit back down before you fall over," Elm said.

The chair creaked under Ravyn's weight. I kept my eyes closed, uncertain if or when I should speak.

Ravyn's voice lowered. "I used the Nightmare on her last night."

My muscles tensed.

Elm was quiet a moment. "You used it to help her—to talk her through the game. Just as you did me."

"I told her at the start I wouldn't use it on her. I gave her my word."

Elm snorted. "Last night was an extenuating circumstance, I'd say."

"I doubt she'll see it that way."

"Why not?"

Ravyn paused. When he spoke, his voice was quiet, doubtful. "I don't know how to explain it," he said. "It wasn't like anyone's head I'd ever been in before. I felt as if I'd been thrust beneath seawater. It was dark and shifting—a storm. When I spoke to her I could hear her voice, but it was far away." He paused, the sound of his palms rough against his face. "I don't know what happened, Elm. I must be losing my mind."

Are you going to let him suffer like this? the Nightmare whispered.

I shut my eyes tighter. *What will he think of me?*

Does it matter?

Of course it matters. He matters.

So don't lie to him.

My breath rattled in my chest. I opened my eyes, turning to Ravyn and Elm.

"Elspeth," Ravyn said, pulling his chair closer to my bedside. He reached for my hand. "How are you feeling?"

"Terrible," I admitted. "What happened?"

"After you spit up a lake of blood," Elm said, leaning against my bedpost, "Filick was able to get an antidote in you. You'll be weak for some time."

I rubbed my head, my eyes finding Ravyn's. "I asked you not to use your Nightmare Card on me," I said, my voice no more than a whisper.

Shame darkened the Captain's handsome face. "I know," he said. "I'm sorry. I thought I was helping." Then, as if fighting the words, he let out a sharp exhale. "What the hell happened, Elspeth? What was that voice?"

"Voice?" Elm said.

"A voice spoke to me," Ravyn said. "Like it was within the walls of my head. I heard it clear as day."

"What did it say to you?"

Ravyn looked at me, his gray eyes sharp. "It told me to get out of her head."

Tears fell from my eyes, betraying me as they washed down my cheeks. Ravyn reached for my face. "Elspeth," he said, my name a rose on his tongue. "Whatever it is, I'll help you. Just tell me."

I shook my head. "You can't help me, Ravyn."

"I can try, can't I?"

But I hadn't said the words—not in eleven years. I'd buried the truth so deep and for so long that I did not know how to dig it up.

I pointed to the burgundy light in his pocket. "Better if I show you."

Ravyn tapped his Nightmare Card three times, his eyes never leaving my face. The intrusion into my mind was just as abrasive as it had been last night—as if I'd been dunked beneath icy salt water. Behind my eyes, the Nightmare waited.

Be kind to him, I whispered.

It was strange, seeing Ravyn in front of me and feeling his presence in my mind at the same time. *Ravyn,* I said.

Elspeth.

The Nightmare's voice dripped like oil. *Ravyn Yew,* he said. *At least this time, you come invited.*

Ravyn jerked back, his eyes wide.

"What is it?" Elm said, placing a hand on his cousin's shoulder.

"There's something there," Ravyn gasped. "Someone else."

"Another person?"

"Not a person. I—I don't know." He searched my face. "What is it?"

I nodded to the Card in his hand. On its face, just below the burgundy velvet, a creature was drawn. A beast of darkness…

A Nightmare.

Ravyn blinked. "That," he said, holding the Card out between us. "That *thing* is in your head?"

Elm's face went pale, his green eyes glassy, his fingers a vise on Ravyn's shoulder.

Who are you? Ravyn demanded, shouting into the blackness.

The Nightmare was untouched by his distress. *The shepherd of the shadow. The phantom of the fright. The demon in the daydream. The nightmare in the night.*

Why are you in Elspeth's head?

My thoughts twisted before my eyes. Suddenly I was back in my uncle's library, the Nightmare Card splayed out on the cherrywood desk. I stared down at the monster on the Card. Yellow eyes—vicious claws—the slope of coarse fur trailing up his spine as he sat hunched, staring up at me.

I saw my small hands reaching for it, the library suddenly encased in the smell of salt.

Everything went black.

Across from me, Ravyn's face had turned to stone, terror visible only in his eyes. "I don't understand," he said. "How did he get in your mind?"

"I touched my uncle's Nightmare Card," I said. I glanced at Elm. "It's my ability—my magic. The moment a Providence Card touches my skin, I absorb whatever it was the Shepherd King paid to create it."

Elm choked on his words. "What do you mean, 'paid'?"

I gritted my teeth. "When the Shepherd King made the Deck, the Spirit required payment. So he bartered for each Card, paying in objects, animals—"

Elm shook his head. "Not the whole bedtime story, Spindle, the *essentials*, if you please."

"Let her talk," Ravyn growled.

I swallowed, the words sticky in my throat. "When the Shepherd King made the Nightmare Card, he bartered a part of himself." I closed my eyes.

Ravyn's voice was paper-thin. "His soul."

I nodded. "That is what I absorbed when I touched my uncle's Nightmare Card."

Ravyn and Elm stared at me, their eyes wide, as if they had never truly seen me. "But if he bartered his soul," Elm whispered, his eyes lowering to Ravyn's Nightmare Card, "and you absorbed it, then the voice in your head..."

The Nightmare's laughter filled my mind, making Ravyn flinch.

I looked up, the truth finally torn from me, piece by piece. "He's the Shepherd King."

There was not enough room in all of Spindle House to carry the burden of silence weighted over us. Elm looked as if he might scream, a hand on his mouth, his green eyes wide, his brow twisted by shock.

But Ravyn's reaction frightened me more. Stillness—his entire face frozen, as if made of stone. "What about other Providence Cards?" he said. "Can you really see them by color?"

I looked away. "I can't. But *he* can."

"Are you saying that creature," Elm said, pointing to the Card in Ravyn's hand, "is the Shepherd King? That *he's* been the one telling us where all the Cards are?"

"He doesn't speak for me." I bit my cheek. "Not often."

"But he does help you," Elm said. The Prince's voice grew stronger. "That's why you can fight—why you're strong, fast. How else could you have survived your father's attack that night on the road?" He turned to Ravyn, his shoulders tall with vindication. "It's how she injured Hauth—how she maimed Linden. *He* did it for her."

I didn't bother denying it. "He doesn't give me his strength unless I ask for it."

"Ethical, is he?" Elm snorted. "This just gets better and better. I suppose those are his yellow eyes we've all been seeing these last few weeks?"

I clenched my jaw, the ache in my head suddenly nothing to the overwhelming despair pooling in my chest. I wanted to cry—to fall back on the pillows and sleep for a hundred years—the pain of their scrutiny and the fear etched into Ravyn's face more than I could take.

Ravyn slid his hand up my arm. "Give us a moment, Elm."

The Prince balked. "This just confirms everything I told you about her. That she's been lying to us the entire time!"

Ravyn cast his cousin a sidelong glance. "Please. Go."

Elm's brow darkened. He turned from us, his shoulders low but his jaw tight. Beneath the shadow of his frown, I saw glass in his narrowed green eyes.

When the door latched, Ravyn turned to me, his brow knit and his mouth a tight line. "Why didn't you tell me, Elspeth?"

I twisted my neck and looked toward the window. "I know what I know," I said, tapping my teeth together. "My secrets are deep. But long have I kept them, and long will they keep."

Ravyn stared at me, his brows drawing together.

You saw, just as they did, the Nightmare purred. *You saw the yellow in her eyes the night you attacked her on the forest road. You've seen it a dozen times since.*

It wasn't my place to demand answers, Ravyn said. *How could I have known this was her secret?* He squeezed my arm. "He's been in your head eleven years?"

"Trapped," I said. "Just like I am. And he's getting stronger. That's my degeneration." I blinked, my mind weighted, as if underground. "Every time I ask for his help, he grows stronger."

"Has he ever hurt you?"

The Nightmare hissed. *Hurt her? I protect her.*

Then why are you growing stronger? Ravyn demanded.

The Nightmare's claws clacked against the dark floor of my mind as he paced, restless. *When Rowan stole my life, my soul remained, sealed in the Nightmare Card. I waited hundreds of years, consumed by fury and salt.* His voice clung to me, as if made of wax. *Elspeth pulled me from the Card, the darkness. So I protected her from a world that would see her killed. I spoke to her from* The Old Book. *She was already good, clever. But I taught her to be wary. I gave her my gifts—my strength. But nothing comes for free, Ravyn Yew. Especially not magic.*

Ravyn's voice was hardly a whisper. *What happens when you grow too strong for Elspeth's mind?*

But the Nightmare's only answer was the click of his teeth, everywhere at once.

My thoughts swam in darkness. I could almost feel the coarse fur along the Nightmare's spine, as if he were under my hand. His voiced sounded like a hundred thrashing birds through my mind. "It was his castle—the one in ruins. The first Rowan King burned it down, murdered him and his family." I looked up at Ravyn, my eyes damp with salty tears. "He's buried beneath the stone in the chamber at Castle Yew."

The door knocked three times again, this time urgent.

"Not now," Ravyn snapped.

"The King wants us downstairs," Jespyr's voice called through the wood. "Now."

"Tell him I'm busy."

"It'll look suspicious if you're not with us, Ravyn."

Ravyn dragged his hands across his face, the shadows beneath his eyes more pronounced in the morning light. "I'll be right there."

Jespyr's footsteps faded down the stairwell.

"What does the King want?" I said. "I thought everyone was staying here for another night of celebration."

"To discuss patrols, undoubtedly," the Captain said. "My uncle demanded more Physician inspections in town since the boy and his parents escaped. We escort them. I should be back before evening."

He pulled his hand from mine, tapping his Nightmare Card three times, severing our connection. I felt strain between us—hesitance.

But when I reached out for him, he was already at the door.

"We can talk more when I return," Ravyn said. "Get some rest, Elspeth."

I stayed in bed five minutes, so anxious my legs kicked the blankets off on their own accord.

You need to rest, the Nightmare said. *The poison has made you weak.*

I ignored him and swung my legs over the edge of my bed.

A tap on my door stilled me, and I sat frozen, waiting. "Hello?"

The door creaked open, and in stepped my father, awkward on tender foot, as if I were a slumbering giant. "I wasn't sure if you were awake," he said.

I did not reply. I was too caught up in the light that trailed from his pocket, blinding and sapphire blue.

The Well Card.

"Are you feeling better?" he asked.

I shot him a quick smile, forcing myself to appear calm. When my hands began to shake, my entire body aware of the Well Card, I sat on them. "Tired, but better."

My father stopped at the foot of my bed, legs planted shoulder width apart, hands clasped behind his back, ever the Destrier. "I caught Filick Willow on his way out. He told me you had been using a Chalice?"

"Prince Hauth, not me," I said, my voice cold. "I merely happened to be there."

"Hmm." My father's blue eyes traced my room. "I'd be wary of Prince Hauth, Elspeth. He's not...he's a very..."

"Horrid man?"

The corner of his lip twitched. "He's his father's son."

I didn't ask what he meant. I doubted he would tell me, even if I did.

"What of Ravyn Yew?"

My back straightened. "What of him?"

He winced, clearly uncomfortable. "The two of you seem to be enjoying your courtship."

Until he realized a King, five hundred years dead, occupied your mind, the Nightmare said.

I tried to smile. "I like him very much."

My father reached into his pocket, his fingers stiff, and

retrieved the brilliant blue light. He placed the Well Card at the foot of my bed and stepped back. Upon the Card, secured with a single piece of twine, was a dried yarrow stalk. "Your mother gifted me this Card when we wed," he said, his voice low. "Her father had given it to her, but she wanted me to have it. 'What need have I for a Well?' she'd said in her usual lighthearted way. 'Only a man would need a Card to keep track of his enemies.' "

He never talked of my mother. It splintered something in me, watching his eyes grow glassy.

"I wanted you to have it," he said, inhaling, standing straighter than before. "You don't have to give it to Ravyn Yew. You don't have to give it to anyone. I just thought..." He looked away from me, the light in the windows catching his eyes, his voice barely a whisper. "If I could go back and do it differently, Elspeth, I would."

He didn't give me time to answer. And it was best, for I had none to give. I was too surprised, too moved, too stung to know what to say besides the quiet "Thank you" I murmured as he slipped out my door.

My black dress lay in a heap on the floor. If I'd coughed blood into it, the dark fabric showed no evidence. I dressed and crept down the stairs to the galley, the King's voice loud as it billowed through the house, my father's guests still abed.

A cloud of darkness emanated from the bottom floor. The Destriers had not yet gone on patrol. I slid across the galley and perched near the top of the stairwell. When the Destriers passed, Ravyn and Elm were last to go. I watched them, red and violet and burgundy the only colors in a sea of black.

Drawn by my gaze, Ravyn turned, his gray eyes fast to find me on the stairwell.

His face was unreadable as he approached. I leaned over the banister, my long hair sweeping down between us. "The Well Card is in my room," I whispered.

Ravyn's eyes widened. "You stole it from Erik?"

"He gave it to me."

He cocked a brow. "Just like that?"

"Just like that."

A small laugh sounded in his throat. "I'll send Filick to check on you. He can take it with him back to Castle Yew."

I felt the same tightness between us from before, the same strain. I reached down between the stair's wooden balusters. I could only reach his shoulder. "I'm...I'm sorry, Ravyn," I said. "I'm sorry I didn't tell you. I didn't think you'd trust me. And I needed you to trust me if I was going to collect the Cards and cure myself."

He shook his head and reached up, the tips of his fingers grazing my cheek. "You don't owe me an explanation, Elspeth. I'm the one who broke my word."

"I should have told you sooner," I said. "I didn't know how."

Ravyn gave a small, sad smile. "I know."

Elm coughed, waiting at the door.

My eyes fell to Ravyn's mouth. "When will you be back?"

"Tonight," he said, his thumb grazing my lips as it fell.

His kiss was a ghost on my black hair. A moment later he stepped beyond the threshold of Spindle House into the courtyard, his boots treading upon the first red leaves to fall from the ancient tree.

The Nightmare's claws cradled my mind.

"Be safe," I whispered to the wind as Ravyn Yew disappeared beyond the gate.

Had I known they'd be the last words I'd say to him aloud, I might have chosen them differently.

Chapter Thirty-Three

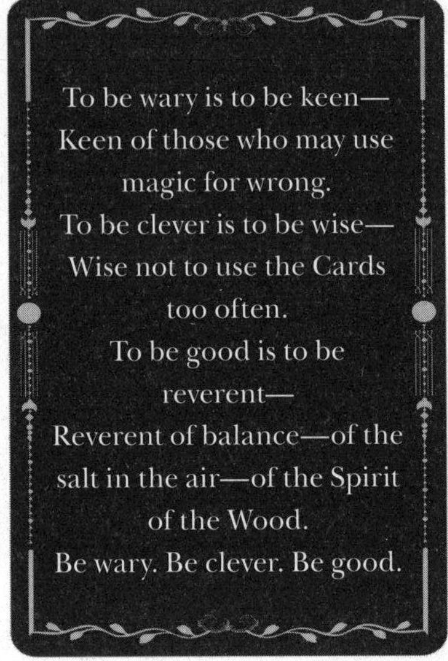

Filick came and went, the Well Card stashed deep in his white Physician's robes. I saw him to the door but did not have the strength to carry myself all the way back up to my room. I lingered in the parlor, near the fire. Balian brought me warm broth, and I sipped it as the house filled with noise from rousing guests.

I didn't see Nerium or my half sisters, and for that I was glad. But I did hope to see Ione, just as soon as I could summon enough energy to pull myself to my feet.

Don't, I said when the Nightmare stirred. *I want to be alone.*

Too bad, he called, slithering across my mind. *Someone's coming.*

I sank into my chair, praying I would go unnoticed. But when the parlor door pushed open, I froze, my uncle the last person I expected to see.

He was searching for something, his head whipping about. When I called his name, he jumped. "Elspeth." He coughed. "There you are."

I struggled to my feet. "Here I am."

"I heard you were sick. Are you feeling better?"

I nodded. "A fleeting illness."

My uncle did not seem to hear, his eyes distant, focused on the hearth, away from me. Then, after a severe pause, he said, "Your aunt is here, looking for you."

Warmth touched my chest, a smile, unbidden, curling my lips. "Where is she?"

"Waiting in your room. I told her I'd bring you." He pushed open the door, his mouth a pale, thin line. "If it suits you."

We walked up the stairs in silence. Weak with the aftereffects of poison, my muscles strained, and I was forced to take several rests. My uncle lingered behind me, his steps creaking as we climbed the stairs.

When we reached the fifth landing, my room just one flight away, he shivered.

I turned, but he looked away, a strained smile on his colorless lips. "I'm fine," he said. "Just cold."

Perhaps he was. It was always colder in this part of the house. Still, something about his expression gripped me, the lines of his face drawn—his skin ghostly pale, as if he'd been the one who'd ingested poison, not I.

And still, he did not look at me. The back of my neck prickled. I tilted my head. "Is everything all right, Uncle?"

He nodded stiffly, gesturing back up the stairs. "Opal is waiting."

He's hiding something, the Nightmare murmured.

I continued up the stairwell.

When I came to my bedroom, the wind whistled through the open window. Gray afternoon light cast long shadows across the creaky wood floor. Above me, a spider's web clung between the rafters, stirred by the draft. Had I not been there that very morning—the bed still upturned—I might have thought the room utterly abandoned, everything still and stale and cold.

My aunt was not there.

But Hauth Rowan, hidden in the shadow of the wardrobe, was.

The Nightmare hissed viciously, his claws slashing in the darkness. *Run.*

But it was too late. My uncle had already stepped behind me, forcing me into the room.

"Feeling better, Miss Spindle?" Hauth asked, his voice smooth.

I backed into my uncle, panic rising in my throat. "What are you doing here?"

The High Prince smiled. "I asked your uncle to bring you. So that we might talk."

I looked over my shoulder to my uncle. "You used your Scythe on him?"

Hauth smiled. "Care to answer that, Tyrn?"

My uncle's face said it all. His hazel eyes were downturned, his brow cracked by guilt. I stared at him, waiting for him to speak, waiting for him to tell me it wasn't real—that he had been forced to betray me and had not brought me, willingly, to the High Prince.

But he said nothing.

"What do you want?" I asked again, my voice shaking as I turned back to Hauth.

"I want the truth," the High Prince replied. "With Ravyn on patrol, I knew I'd finally have you all to myself. So answer me, Miss Spindle." His eyes dropped to my sleeve. "What happened to your arm?"

I was shaking, teeth on edge.

The High Prince looked at my uncle, his tone dismissive. "You may go now, Tyrn. If anyone asks, assure them Elspeth wishes to remain undisturbed, safe and asleep." He smiled at me. "If anyone bothers to inquire."

"Uncle!" I called, reaching for his arm. "Don't leave!"

He could not bring himself to look at me. My uncle jerked free, slamming the door in my face. I dove for the handle, but he'd already slid the key into the latch, locking me in with the High Prince.

"Father!" I screamed, banging my palms against the wood. "Someone! Ione! Balian! Help—"

Hauth was at my side in moments, his thick hand rough as he pushed it over my mouth, smothering my cries. "Quiet," he said in my ear. "I want to talk. No one need get hurt."

I reeled, turning fast enough to slap him across the face, my nails dragging across his cheek and jaw, ripping apart the old scabs I'd left a week ago.

Hauth swore and reached into his pocket, extracting his Scythe.

"Hold still," he commanded.

Salt stung my nose, the magic so potent my muscles cramped. I could not move, my mind at war with the Scythe's influence. I gnashed my teeth and balled my fingers into fists. When I looked up at Hauth, his lips curled in a smug grin.

"Don't fight it," he said. "You'll only hurt yourself."

I shut my eyes, my breath labored. He wasn't the first Prince who'd tried to make me cower with the red Card. *It's not real,* I said to myself, grinding my teeth together. *My mind has been tested, fortified. The Scythe's magic is merely a harsh rain—a storm to make me cower.*

And the Nightmare and I did not cower.

I broke through the wall of the Scythe's control with a guttural scream. Hauth's green eyes widened, his jaw agape. I struck out wildly, my fist colliding with the High Prince's hand—the hand Ravyn had injured. Hauth hissed and dropped the Scythe. I struck out again, the heel of my palm connecting with his chin. His head jutted back, his face contorted in pain. When he opened his green eyes, they were unfocused.

But only for a moment. The High Prince still had one more Card in his pocket.

The Black Horse.

A dark light flashed. I did not see him move, the Card granting him sudden, remarkable speed. I lashed out at the air, but he caught me by my injured wrist and twisted my arm behind me.

"Get off!" I screamed.

He pulled me across the room. When I tried to push him away, he slammed me into the wooden chair Ravyn had sat in that morning. He pressed his broad hand firmly against my throat. "I know it was you in the wood," he growled. "Scream again and I won't just snap your wrist this time. I'll break your neck."

He tore strips of bedding and tethered me to the chair, my hands knotted behind my back. I tugged against the binding, my broken wrist singing out in pain. "What do you want?" I seethed.

The High Prince picked his Scythe off the floor and tapped it three times. "Do you think I'm a fool—that I didn't wonder at your wrist, broken and bandaged, that day in the yard?" He flexed his injured hand beneath his glove. "I'd thought you'd had a weapon in the wood that night. The way you scratched me..." His fingers traced his scabs. "You're infected, aren't you, Miss Spindle?"

Life drained out of me, replaced by a forge of seething hatred.

Hauth continued. "Why else would Ravyn protect you so ardently?" He smiled, cruel. "Your uncle confirmed it."

It felt as if he'd choked me. When I tried to speak, my voice was uneven. "My uncle—he told you?"

Hauth nodded, touched by a cold, heartless humor. He tucked the Black Horse into his pocket, his eyes lingering on the afternoon light outside my window. "To be fair, Tyrn tried not to give you up. But harboring an infected child is treason and a terrible, terrible death. All his hard work finding that Nightmare Card—negotiating a place on the royal court—gone. And for what?" His green eyes narrowed. "An infected niece forced upon him eleven years ago?" He shook his head. "Tyrn can keep his land, his title—his life. I'm not after his livelihood. But I needed his help. Or rather, yours."

I didn't know what made me sicker, the fact that my uncle—my own family—had betrayed me to the likes of Hauth Rowan or that, somewhere deep down, I was not surprised. "Help with what?" I said.

Hauth folded his arms across his chest. "Ravyn," he said, his lips curling. "I want you to help me with Ravyn."

I remained silent, the Nightmare's snarl radiating through me, burning my tongue.

"He's been absent lately," Hauth continued. "He and Elm and Jespyr. They disappear during patrols and keep to themselves, thick as thieves." His jaw flexed. "And, of course, they kept your infection secret. Why would they do that, unless it was a part of a greater deception?"

It was a trap—a snare for Ravyn, Elm, and Jespyr. Hauth had provided the cage, my uncle had set the trigger, and I was the bait.

I felt like I was going to vomit. "Ravyn's not going to tell you anything," I said, searching for courage I did not feel. "You're wasting your time."

"Am I?" The High Prince bent só that our faces were even. "I've seen the way he looks at you. Was he there in the wood with you that night you attacked me?" He smiled. "If he wants me to keep your infection from my father's listening ears, Ravyn's going to tell me everything he's been up to. He'll step down as Captain." He took me by the face, cupping my jaw roughly in his palm. "After that," he said, his teeth on edge, "if I'm satisfied, I may consider letting you both live."

Darkness pooled in my head like smoke off a kiln. I stared into Hauth's green eyes, the same wrath I'd felt that day I'd maimed the Destrier swelling in my chest.

I spat in the High Prince's face.

My vision snapped, Hauth's knuckles like stones as they collided with my cheek. I let out a low moan, my face hot where he'd struck it. *Help*, I cried out into the blackness, my injured wrist burning as I twisted against the sheets that bound me. *It can't end like this.*

The Nightmare coiled in the corner of my mind. *I don't know what will happen, Elspeth,* he said. *Your degeneration is almost at an end.*

I could see the spindle tree in the courtyard from my bedroom window. Its crimson branches swayed, ever gallant, in the autumn breeze. I whispered a goodbye no one would hear and closed my eyes, shutting out the spindle tree and my childhood room until there was nothing but shadow. Shadow, and the Shepherd King.

I'm asking for your help, I said, my voice clear. *I understand the price.*

Darkness plumed, smothering my senses. The Nightmare sat in the heart of it, waiting—watching. When the door rattled with a menacing knock, he slid over my eyes, his voice so clear in my head it might have been my own.

You'll need to free your hands.

Hauth moved to the door. "Who is it?" he barked.

A voice sounded on the other side of the wood.

I yanked my uninjured wrist with all my might. The sheets dug into my arms, rubbing the skin raw. I heard a key slide into the lock, the latch clicking.

Focus, the Nightmare snarled, sending burning magic down my arm.

I clenched my teeth and shut my eyes. The Nightmare's strength enflamed my muscles as I focused on the binding around my right wrist. I pulled so hard my skin tore. When I opened my eyes, dozens of little white spots flecked across my vision.

Pain seared, hot and wet, across my arm. Fresh blood slid down my fingers to the floor beneath, staining the wood.

But my hands were free.

The door opened with a slam. I heard the clang of metal, and when I looked up I saw him—tall, pale, garbed in white. On his long fingers rested the glove-like contraption with looming, brutal spikes reaching out from each digit.

A metal claw.

"Hello," Orithe Willow said, looking down at me through unfeeling eyes. "A pleasure to finally meet you, Miss Spindle."

Chapter Thirty-Four

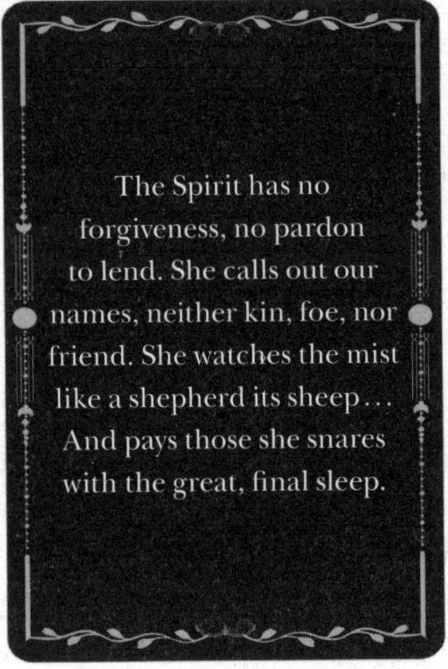

I watched the spindle tree from my seat on the floor. Its shadow grew long against the stonework, autumn light quick to fade as evening came on.

They'll be back from patrol any moment, I whispered to the dark. *We're almost out of time.*

Above me, Hauth and Orithe spoke in hushed voices. Every so often, Orithe looked my way, his unnaturally light eyes clouded.

It had taken him only moments to confirm my magic, my blood all over the floor. After that, he and Hauth had left me alone. Huddled together, they discussed Ravyn and Jespyr and Elm, what their duplicity—their treason—might entail. For a time I was almost forgotten, my arms dripping blood where I'd torn myself free.

Tears streamed down my cheeks, my teeth gritted against what I needed to do. *It's all ruined,* I called into the darkness, my voice breaking. *Even if Ravyn doesn't admit to stealing Cards or being a highwayman, they know he hid my infection. No matter how you parcel it, he's condemned. They'll kill him.*

Ravyn need not die, the Nightmare said, his voice eerily smooth. Then, so quiet it might have been the wind whistling through the window, he said, *Do you trust me, Elspeth?*

I blinked through the blur of tears. *Do I have a choice?*

My darling, you've always had a choice.

I opened my eyes wider, the sound of Spindle House's gates echoing from the courtyard to my open window.

"Ravyn," I breathed.

The Destriers were returning.

Hauth and Orithe watched from my window, a small, menacing smile sliding onto the High Prince's mouth. "Douse the lantern," he instructed Orithe. "Stay close to the girl. I want to make it abundantly clear to Ravyn, should he try to fight his way out of this, that you'll gladly send a blade through his pet's pretty neck."

Orithe glanced at me. "Shouldn't we alert the other Destriers, sire?"

"Not yet," Hauth said. "Ravyn is clever. By the time my father arrests him for harboring her, he'll have thought of a dozen lies, immune to any inquest levied at him." He cast me a sidelong glance. "But he won't give us any trouble. Not with her life at stake."

The footsteps grew louder and louder in the courtyard below. I saw the dark cloud of Black Horses pass beneath the spindle tree, lightened only by a small cluster of color that, when placed together, emitted the same dark red hue as the leaves falling from the tree above them.

Red. Violet. Burgundy.

They were almost here.

The Nightmare's voice cut through my thoughts. *It's time.*

I screamed. Even through the gag, my shriek ripped through the room—the howl of an animal caught in a snare. I closed my eyes and released the fire in my lungs, my vocal chords scratched raw as the scream carried on in a long, tireless call.

Orithe reached me first, but I sent a foot shooting out, clipping him at the knee. He fell to the floor with a hard thud. I screamed again, my teeth tearing against the gag.

"Enough," Hauth said, slapping me across the face as he reached into his pocket for the Black Horse. "I swear I'll break your jaw if you don't—"

I sprang out from my chair, reaching for him.

Hauth jolted aside, his reflexes quick. I reached out a second time, my fingers slick with my own blood. This time, the heel of my palm collided with Hauth's chin.

He hit the floor with a bang.

Next to me, Orithe found his feet, his eyes wide as he rushed to Hauth's side. "Sire!" he said. "Are you all right?"

My body felt strange—weak and strong at the same time—the Nightmare's strength spinning within me like a wheel stuck in mud. I sprang for the door, but Hauth was on his feet again, levying all his weight into his fist as it collided with my stomach.

I coughed and doubled over, all the air knocked violently out of my lungs.

"Help me hold her," the High Prince called, his hand tangling in my hair as he forced me to stand.

I cried out as the tips of Orithe's claw dug into my arm, my black dress quick to absorb the blood as the tips of his blades tore through my skin.

"Put her in the corner," Hauth called, "away from the door."

They dragged me across the room and threw me against the wall. I lay dazed, my body twitching as magic burned through it.

Get up! called the voice in the dark. *Get up, Elspeth.*

The King's Physician lowered to a crouch above me, his eyes wide and ghostly as he pulled up my sleeve. "Your veins grow dark, child. What is your magic?"

I did not reply, my body shaking.

"The King will not be pleased if I kill you before presenting you to him," Orithe murmured. "So please, for both of our sakes, stay still."

I hissed, spitting blood onto his perfect white cloak.

He almost smiled—if smiles could be bitter and filled with pity. "Those eyes," he said. "So dark." He stared at me without blinking. "The same eyes I saw behind the black mask on Market Day, before the boy disappeared into the mist."

Hauth's head jerked up. "You helped him escape?" he spat at me.

I set my jaw and said nothing, forcing all the hate in my heart into my eyes as I glared up at the heir to the throne.

Hauth watched me, his brow twisting. Suddenly, he barked a laugh. "It was you Linden came upon in the mist, wasn't it? He had the same marks," he said, gesturing to the broken scabs on his face. "Only, his were practically to the bone."

When I remained silent, he looked toward the window, straightening his tunic. "You've wasted your energy, Spindle. Just as I've caught you, I'll catch that boy again. Whether tomorrow, a fortnight, or a year from now..." He smiled to himself. "He'll burn just the same."

A moment later Hauth was on the ground coughing, the force of my entire body weighted on his chest as I sent blow after blow into his face, the Nightmare's strength so powerful Orithe had not even seen me move.

Hauth bucked his hips, knocking me onto the floor, though not before I'd split one of his eyelids. I scurried to my feet, my reflexes keener than I'd ever felt. Hauth wiped furiously at his face, blood dripping into his eye. His Scythe had fallen to the ground between us.

He dove for it, tapping it three times.

"Stay still!" he commanded.

A strange, animalistic laugh ripped through me, my eyes drifting to the Card in the High Prince's hand. "It cannot help you, not against me," I said, my voice dripping oil. "And what are you, without it?"

Orithe's claw rang through the air, the tips of his blade a whisper from my face. He came at me again and again, and each time I dodged him.

The Physician's pale eyes grew wide as I twisted away, my movements unnaturally fast. "What's her magic?" he called to Hauth, striking the air, only to miss me again.

I could see the whites of Hauth's eyes. "Tyrn said she had none."

I reached for the door—my fingers grazing the latch, escape a mere breath away. But before I could open it, salt water filled my eyes and nose. I coughed, choking, stunned.

The intrusion of a Nightmare Card.

Elspeth? Ravyn's voice called. *Are you there?*

I was dazed only a moment. But a moment was all Orithe needed to wrap his brutal claw around my neck and tug.

I froze, a single flex of his muscle the difference between life and death. "Your father would want to know about this straightaway, sire," the Physician panted. "We need to call the Destriers."

"She's a bloody waif," Hauth snapped, stepping forward. "I'll make her hold still."

Elspeth? Ravyn called in my head, concern touching the edge of his voice.

I didn't have time to answer. A moment later I was seeing stars, Hauth's hand brutal as he took me by the hair and, with the full force of his strength, slammed my head into the stone wall.

I slumped, my body crashing like dirt into a grave.

Everything went black.

Wetness trickled down my neck and pooled on the floor around my hair, hot and sticky—a dark halo of blood.

"You cracked her head," I heard Orithe say above me.

"She'll live," Hauth said, leaning over me. His rough hands shook my shoulders. When I did not move, he slapped me across the face. "Spindle," he barked. "Spindle!"

But I was far away.

Panic tipped the edge of Ravyn's voice. *Elspeth! Can you hear me?*

The world was slipping, my toes sinking deeper and deeper into dark soil.

I saw my aunt's face as she crouched over me beneath the alder tree, my hands dirty from clawing my way to safety. I saw Ione—the wild, sweet Ione—reaching out to me as we walked through crowded cobbled streets. I saw a bouquet of yarrow in my father's hand, then yellow in my eyes in the looking glass, the monster in the dark watching me.

I saw Ravyn Yew looking down at me. But there was no fear, no resentment in his clear gray eyes. Only concern—concern and wonder.

Ravyn, I called, my voice tearing away from me, distant, heavy with resolve. *Don't come for me. Hauth and Orithe. They know what I am. They're waiting for you.*

The control in Ravyn's voice was gone, his words tight with worry. *Where are you, Elspeth?*

They'll see you hang, Yew, the Nightmare said. *You cannot save her.*

You can still find the Twin Alders, Ravyn, I called into the dark. *You can still save Emory.* I bit my lip, my voice trembling. *But not with Hauth and Orithe hunting you.*

"Trees." Hauth sighed from above, jerking my head as he gripped me by the chin. "Spindle! Wake up!"

Elspeth, the Nightmare cooed, my name like honey on his tongue. *Get up.*

I reached out in the darkness for him, and when my mind scraped against the coarse fur on his back, he did not flinch away. *I can't,* I said. *I can't get up. Not this time.* I felt heavy, buried. *But you can.*

Elspeth.

It was going to happen anyway, Nightmare. You're strong. And I'm... I'm so tired. My head...

His voice was no more than a whisper. *Let me help you.*

I sank deeper into the blackness. New visions crossed my mind—places and people I did not recognize—strangers with yellow eyes. They smiled at me, and the world around me swayed, as if on the tide.

But as quickly as it came, the vision vanished. I saw a man run through the mist, children behind him, their faces pale with terror. They fled the burning castle on the top of the hill, disappearing into the chamber beneath tall yew trees.

A gray-eyed boy stood at the edge of the mist, facing down the red light of a Scythe and a mountainous man whose cloak bore the Rowan insignia.

I saw the castle aflame, reduced to ruins. Suddenly my mind was filled with visions of hundreds of children—their veins dark as ink—screaming as they were thrown into an inferno. I saw the mist darken, its tendrils reaching deeper and deeper, choking Blunder off from the rest of the world.

Centuries of rage boiled in me, time marked by neither sun nor moon. Hatred poisoned my blood and I lost myself to the dark, my body twisting—bones snapping—claws scraping—eyes narrowing, until my body, monstrous, mirrored the hate in my heart.

Animalistic, a creature of the dark—powerful, vengeful, and full of fury.

The last thing I saw before I opened my eyes was a small girl, timid as she peered into a looking glass, her black eyes glazed with fear.

"Do you have a name?" she whispered.

I smiled at her, memory tugging at the corners of my ancient mind. The strange magic, the same beautiful wonder, of the children I once knew. *They called me a King's name once,* I said, my tail flickering. *But that was a long time ago.*

"What shall I call you, then?"

Nothing, child, I said, crawling back into the blackness. *I'm just the wind in the trees, the shadow, and the fright. The echo in the leaves... the nightmare in the night.*

I snapped awake with a cough, my mind filled with Ravyn's voice.

Elspeth! he shouted. *Goddamnit, Elspeth, hold on. We're on the stairs.* His voice was shaking. *You don't have to do this alone.*

Hauth Rowan stood above me, gripping my chin. "There you are," he said. "Not dead after all." Confusion crossed his face. He furrowed his brow, leaning closer to me. "What's wrong with her eyes, Orithe?"

"Her eyes, sire?"

"They've gone yellow. Like some kind of cat."

Orithe approached, his metal claw tracing my cheek. “Strange,” he said. “They were dark only a moment ago.”

We looked up at Orithe, the corner of our lips curling, as if tugged by invisible string. When Ravyn tried to call out to us, we clenched our teeth, banishing him from our mind. *Don’t try to save us, Ravyn Yew,* the Nightmare and I said, our voices melding in a strange, echoing dissonance. *We cannot be saved.*

We struck without fear.

Orithe’s eyes bulged and he recoiled. But it was too late. The Nightmare used all our strength to rip the bladed glove off the Physician’s hand—bone snapping and skin sloughing.

Then we shoved it, full force, into his throat.

Orithe let out a gurgling scream, blood spraying onto his white robes. He slumped to the floor, shock and fear the last things to pass across his milky eyes before he was taken by the great stillness, his blood the final sign of life as it dripped, unbidden, from his veins—dark, magical, and final.

Hauth jerked back. “Stop!” he commanded.

We smiled, and when we stood, the world around us faded, time and space, Prince and King, child and spirit. All that remained was magic—black as ink.

Powerful, vengeful, and full of fury.

Our voice dripped oil, Hauth fixed in our gaze. We stalked him, pinning him in the corner of the room. “They came in the night,” we said, “the black and red horde. They burned down my castle, put my kin to the sword. The usurper was crowned, though my blood had not dried. But he did not account for the turn of the tide. For nothing is safe, and nothing is free. Debt follows all men, no matter their plea. When the Shepherd returns, a new day shall ring. Death to the Rowans…

“Long live the King.”

Hauth’s cheekbone shattered beneath our hand. He crashed

to the floor and moaned, his face leaching color, blood spilling out his mouth.

I looked down at him, pitiless. *This is the end, isn't it?* I murmured, darkness creeping across my vision. *I go now. And you—you remain.*

It was inevitable, the Nightmare said, his voice louder and louder. *This is your degeneration, Elspeth Spindle. Nothing comes free.*

The air around me thinned. I blinked, trying to stave off the darkness, like a child fighting sleep. *Promise me you'll help Ravyn. Promise me you'll save Emory.*

It's time, dear one, he purred, lulling me to rest.

Promise!

He sighed. *I promise to help the Yews in all their endeavors.*

I closed my eyes, a final whisper escaping my lips. The story—our story. The Nightmare's and mine. "There once was a girl," I said, "clever and good, who tarried in shadow in the depths of the wood. There also was a King—a shepherd by his crook, who reigned over magic and wrote the old book. The two were together, so the two were the same..."

The last thing I heard before I was buried in darkness was the Nightmare's silky laugh, wicked and absolute. *The girl, the King... and the monster they became.*

Chapter Thirty-Five

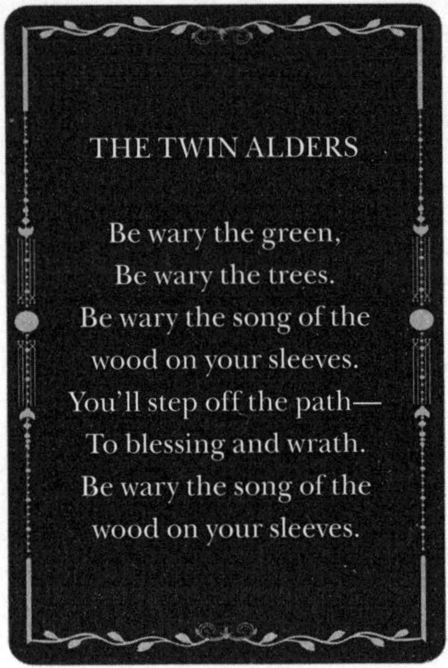

The dungeon was the coldest part of the castle.

The Captain of the Destriers and the Prince waited together in silence, the hour not yet dawn. Ravyn tapped his boots on the stone floor to keep his toes from losing feeling.

"Have you slept?" Elm asked, his breath pluming out his nostrils as he paced the antechamber. A piece of crumpled sandstone lay on the floor. Elm kicked it back and forth, his eyelids heavy.

Ravyn gritted his teeth, the knot in his stomach tightening. "I keep having nightmares," he said, rubbing his eyes with the heel of his palms.

A moment later he ripped his hands away, yellow eyes flickering across his vision. Even now, three nights later, they were bright in his thoughts. He could not escape them, that night at Spindle House burned into his mind with painful clarity.

It all had happened so fast.

Shadows chased them like demons up Spindle House's winding stairs. Ravyn pushed ahead, his heart aflame in his chest. When they got to the small door on the sixth landing, he slammed his hands into the wood, calling with his Nightmare Card.

But he was met by only silence.

"Elspeth!" he shouted, dread tightening like a rope around his neck.

Elm's knuckles were white on the latch. "It's locked."

"Break it down," Ravyn snapped, turning to Jespyr and the Black Horse in her hand.

It took three kicks to flatten the wood, splinters flying like pine needles in a windstorm. "Elspeth!" Ravyn called, pushing into the room, his boots slipping on dark liquid pooled across the wooden floor.

"Holy…" Elm breathed. "What happened here?"

Ravyn's eyes scanned the room, passing over Orithe's lifeless body until he spotted the maiden slumped against the far wall, wind from the open window blowing in her long black hair.

"Elspeth," he called, lurching toward her. "Elspeth!"

Her skin was cold to the touch. Ravyn ran his hand across her cheek, his stomach turning. Her face was beaten and bloodied. Her dress was torn at the sleeve, and her arm—stiff with dried blood—was punctured by harsh, distinct claw marks.

"He's dead," Elm called, leaning over Orithe. "Decidedly."

"Elspeth," Ravyn called, his fingers sliding to the skin below her pale jaw, searching for a heartbeat. When she stirred, coughing out a low, violent breath, he felt weightless.

"Elspeth." His hands shook against her jaw. "Are you all right?"

"Hauth's still alive," Jespyr called from the other side of the room. "Barely. His legs... there's something wrong with them."

But Ravyn was too engulfed by Elspeth Spindle and her long, deep breaths to pay mind elsewhere. He ran his shaking fingers through her hair, relief so sweet he could almost taste it. "I thought you were dead," he whispered.

"I'm not dead," she said, her voice oddly even. "I'm just... waking up."

"Don't sit up too fast," Ravyn cautioned, the hair at the back of her head heavy with blood. "Take your time."

"I've had enough time," she said. "More than you could ever know."

She kept her eyes closed as Ravyn brought her to a slow, supported stance. "What happened?" he said, taking in the mayhem around him for the first time.

"They were going to turn you in," she said plainly. "Everything you'd worked for, gone in a moment."

"You—you killed him?" Jespyr blinked, her eyes fixed on Orithe's lifeless body.

Elspeth looked down at her hands, her fingernails dark, embedded with blood. "His claw began the slaughter of dozens of magical children," she said, flexing her fingers like talons. "He deserved to die by it."

Elm's voice was lifeless. "We were going to use his blood to save Emory. And you've just spilled it all over the floor."

Elspeth acted as if she had not heard him. When she spoke, her voice was quiet. "You should call the Destriers. Better they know it was me and me alone."

Ravyn and his sister exchanged glances. "What are you talking about?"

"She's bleeding," Elm muttered. "Look at her head."

Ravyn reached for Elspeth, desperate to pull her close—feel her, tight and safe, in his arms—but when his fingers touched her shoulder, she pulled away, a snarl on her lips.

"Don't touch me," she said, her yellow eyes flaring.

Yellow.

Yellow, like the flames of a torch. Yellow, like the coins he'd collected as a boy.

Yellow, not black.

Relief turned to dread in the pit of Ravyn's stomach. *Elspeth,* he called into the blackness. *Elspeth!*

But all was silence.

Then, like a snake slithering out beneath rocks, the Shepherd King spoke. *She's quiet now, Ravyn Yew. Let her rest.*

What the hell have you done? Ravyn cried, probing deeper into the darkness.

She set me free, he said, his voice filling Ravyn's mind like smoke. *I'm here to help you.*

Ravyn stepped away from the creature wearing Elspeth Spindle's skin. *Let her out,* he shouted, his voice cut by fear and rage. *Let her out right now or I swear to god I'll—*

You'll what? Elspeth's lips curled. *How could you hurt me without hurting her?*

Elm stepped forward, his eyes wide as he surveyed Elspeth's face, her yellow, catlike eyes. "What's happening?" he said, glancing at Ravyn. "What's she done?"

"It's not Elspeth," Ravyn said, his hands shaking. "It's *him.*"

But the monster behind Elspeth's eyes merely looked ahead, Elspeth's fingers trilling an invisible rhythm as she placed her hands—wrists touching—out in front of her. "I've killed the King's Physician and maimed the heir to the throne," she said. "I'm infected with magic." She ran her teeth over her bottom lip, her mouth curling into a twisted grin. "I surrender myself to the Captain of the Destriers and await an inquest by the King."

Elm kicked the stone against the dungeon door, its bang clamoring in the din. Ravyn flinched, wrenched from his thoughts. "Shepherd King or not," he said to his cousin, his voice rusty with disuse, "he made it clear he wanted to help us."

Elm looked up. "You can't seriously consider trusting him."

"I don't," Ravyn bit back. "Still, without him, it might be us in that cell."

Footsteps echoed from the stairwell above, yellow torchlight climbing the walls all around them. "They're here," Elm said, his spine straightening.

King Rowan led the Destriers into the dungeon, his steps loud on the stone steps. His brow was low, furrowed and resolute. Still, he could not hide the evidence of his own sleeplessness; dark shadows nestled beneath his green eyes.

Anger cracked his voice. "Well?" he demanded.

"Ready when you are, Uncle," Ravyn said.

Jespyr and a second Destrier pulled twin keys from their cloaks. When they turned the locks, first one, then the other, the antechamber echoed. "Here we go," Jespyr said, opening the door.

It was dark on the north side of the dungeon. Worse still, it was quiet. The King had ordered the rest of the cells emptied three days ago, afraid Elspeth Spindle might poison the minds of the other prisoners with her dangerous, dark magic.

When they got to the last cell on the block, they stopped and lit the torches on the wall, yellow light illuminating the body, curled in sleep, upon the icy floor.

Ravyn's hands were fists at his side, the knot in his stomach moving to his throat, choking him. She looked so peaceful, so still, so much like the woman he'd held in his arms...

But she wasn't. She was something else now. And it hurt more than he'd ever imagined it could to think she might be gone forever.

But he couldn't show it—wouldn't think it. Ravyn stood with the rest of the Destriers, forcing all the fear and pain and longing deep behind the cracking wall of stone he'd built over his heart. His features stilled, as if frozen, and he watched her through the iron bars with the rest of them, determination setting his jaw.

He would find the last Card. He would lift the mist. He would save Emory's life.

And he would free Elspeth Spindle from the darkness that consumed her.

"Why isn't she chained?" the King growled.

The Destriers stirred. "We couldn't restrain her, sire," Gorse said. "The risk was too great."

"Risk? She's but a girl."

"Her magic..." another called, the fear in his voice palpable. "Several of our men were sent to the Physicians with deep lacerations."

King Rowan's shoulders tightened. "Get her up."

The dungeon echoed as two Destriers unsheathed their swords, knocking the steel across the iron bars of the cell. The noise clanged through the dungeon, its sinister echo clamoring down the corridor.

Elspeth stirred and sat up. Her long black hair was stiff with dried blood. Breath plumed like smoke out her nostrils, but she did not tremble, seemingly untouched by the cold.

Ravyn watched the long black pupils of her yellow eyes widen—like a cat's in the dark.

"My Captain tells me you won't speak to him," the King called. "That you agreed to speak to only me."

Elspeth twisted her neck and stretched her arms one at a time.

"He tells me you carry the infection," the King continued. "That you can see Providence Cards."

The corner of her mouth twitched as she gave a stiff nod.

"And that you have an offer for me, in exchange for your miserable life."

Another nod, accompanied by the sound of her teeth clicking as she opened and clamped her jaw. *Click. Click. Click.*

"But you killed my Physician," the King said, his voice dripping venom. "And my son—should he survive—will never be the same. You are an enemy of the vilest quality." He leaned into the bars. "There is nothing you could offer that would bring me more satisfaction than watching you die a slow, horrible death."

Elspeth tilted her head to the side, her yellow eyes narrowing. "You came all this way into your frozen underworld to tell me that, usurper?"

King Rowan slammed his palms on the bars, his gold rings clanging against the iron. "I came to tell you you're an abomination." His control leached to a hot, unrestrained rage. "A disease. And I'll see you and everyone who ever sheltered you gutted like animals."

Ravyn and Elm exchanged desperate glances.

But Elspeth merely smiled. "Even without hearing my offer?"

The King's fury tangled in his mouth. "There is nothing you have that I want."

Elspeth unfolded herself from the dungeon floor. When she stood, her spine curled, as if bent. "Then kill me," she murmured. "That is no matter. Even dead, I will not die. I am the shepherd of shadow. The phantom of the fright. The demon in the daydream." Her yellow eyes flickered to Ravyn. "The nightmare in the night."

King Rowan made to speak—to slam his hands on the bars once more. But something in Elspeth's eyes stilled him, his anger frozen in his throat.

She slunk across the cell, her movements so fast some of the Destriers stepped back.

A long, unnerving grin parted her lips. "But kill me, usurper, and you will never collect the Deck, never heal the infection. The mist will continue to spread. The Spirit of the Wood will consume Blunder and everyone in it. I may be gone, my body mortified by violence and time, but in a hundred years, it is you, Rowan, who will be forgotten. Your castle will be reduced to dust. Destrier bones will clack in the wind, strewn by children between windows to frighten crows. Your name will turn to rot, your Providence Cards lost. I have seen it all before, Rowan. And I smell it upon us now. The salt of magic in the air…the turn of the tide."

Silence cut through the dungeon. King Rowan stared at the creature tucked behind Elspeth's skin, and the creature stared back, its yellow eyes cunning.

"What is it you want?" the King whispered.

Elspeth ran her fingers against the bars, dried blood caked under her fingernails. "Same as you," she said, stalking the length of the cell. "I want to collect the Deck. But first, you must release Emory Yew to his parents."

Ravyn felt the breath leave his chest. Next to him, Elm and Jespyr had frozen, their faces trapped between fear and wonder.

"Why would I do that?" The King took a step back. "You must know I need his blood."

"You'll find you don't," Elspeth said. "Not when you have mine."

"You'd trade your life for the boy's?"

"That is my offer."

Ravyn tapped his Nightmare Card beneath his cloak, reaching out in the darkness for any hint of Elspeth. He needed to hear her voice—needed to know she was still there...

But there was nothing. The Shepherd King had blocked him out entirely.

"And what do I get in return for prolonging your wretched life until Solstice?" the King demanded, uncertainty darkening the corners of his voice.

Elspeth continued to pace the cell, stopping only when she stood directly in front of the King. "You get the Twin Alders," she said, drawing the words out of her mouth like spider silk. "The Card you seek but cannot find. The last Card."

King Rowan nearly choked on his words. "The Twin Alders has been lost for hundreds of years," he said. "What makes you think you can find it?"

Elspeth lowered her voice to a whisper, her spine twisting as her yellow eyes narrowed, wicked and infinite. "The Twin Alders is hidden in a place with no time. A place of great sorrow and bloodshed and crime. Betwixt ancient trees, where the mist cuts bone-deep, the last Card remains, waiting, asleep. The wood knows no road—no path through the snare. Only I can find the Twin Alders...

"For it was I who left it there."

The story continues in…

Book Two of The Shepherd King

Keep reading for a sneak peek!

Acknowledgments

I stepped into the book world on tiptoe. And while my steps have become surer, my footprints remain soft, because there are people with me, shouldering me.

To John, my husband, who brags about me, holds and feeds me, who always has the correct answer of "Sounds spooky!" whenever I'm doubting myself—thank you. I love you. This book was possible because of your encouragement and tireless work as a partner and father.

To Whitney Ross, my agent, whom I will never stop gushing about—you are the dream. Thank you for seeing the heart of *One Dark Window* through the brambles and working with me to carve it into the story it is today. None of this would have been possible without you!

To my family, large and small. To Mom, Dad, and Ben. My imagination, my love of stories, began with you. Thank you for loving me and always buying me books. To Molly, whose help with Owen made my revisions and countless other book tasks manageable—my thanks and love.

To my friends. The ones who always ask about my writing with unadulterated joy and keep asking, even when I am too shy to answer. Leah, Grace, Shannon, Lena, Laura, Katy. You are my shining suns. Thank you for always asking.

To my editor, Angeline Rodriguez—thank you for helping me give these characters the proper angst they deserve. And to the team at Orbit, a mountain's worth of gratitude. It's been a pleasure to work with you and an honor to watch my story transform into a book.

To all the readers and authors who've cheered on *One Dark Window* with feral excitement—thank you! My stories were always for me, until I came into the book community. Now they're for *us*. I can't wait to share future stories with you; thank you for helping make this my dream job.

To Sarah Garcia—I know this book will be too scary for you, and I know you'll read it anyway. Thank you. For *everything*.

Finally, because, though on tiptoe, I still walked, I'd like to acknowledge myself. My hard work. My strange, sensitive, imaginative spirit. Somewhere quiet and deep down, I knew I'd get here.

extras

meet the author

Photo Credit: Rachel Gillig

RACHEL GILLIG was born and raised on the California coast. She is a writer and a teacher, with a BA in literary theory and criticism from UC Davis. If she is not ensconced in blankets dreaming up her next novel, Rachel is in her garden or walking with her husband, son, and their poodle, Wally.

Find out more about Rachel Gillig and other Orbit authors by registering for the free monthly newsletter at orbitbooks.net.

if you enjoyed
ONE DARK WINDOW
look out for
BOOK TWO OF THE SHEPHERD KING
by
Rachel Gillig

Chapter One

Ravyn

Ravyn's hands were bleeding.

He hadn't noticed. He couldn't see them. With three taps on the velvet edge of the Mirror, the purple Providence Card, Ravyn had erased himself. He was utterly invisible. Which made it easier to abuse his fingers, knuckles, the heels of his palms on the hardened soil at the bottom of the ancient chamber at the edge of the meadow. But he could still feel the pain, see the blood—warm and viscous—slide down his fingers and fall onto the dirt he upturned.

It hardly mattered. What was another cut, another scar? Ravyn's hands were but blunt tools. Not the instruments of a gentleman, but of a man-at-arms—Captain of the Destriers. Highwayman.

Traitor.

Mist seeped into the chamber through the window. It slipped through the cracks of the rotted-out ceiling, salt clawing at Ravyn's eyes. A warning, perhaps, that the thing he dug for at the base of the tall, broad stone did not wish to be found.

Ravyn paid the mist no mind. He, too, was of salt. Sweat, blood, and magic. Even so, his calloused hands were no match for the soil at the bottom of the chamber. It was unforgiving, hardened by frost and salt and time, ripping Ravyn's fingernails and tearing open the cracks in his hands. Still, he dug, enveloped in the Mirror Card's chill, the chamber he'd so often played in as a boy shifting before his eyes into something grotesque—a place of lore, of death.

Of monsters.

He'd woken hours ago, sleep punctuated by thrashing fits and piercing yellow eyes, Elspeth Spindle's voice an echoing dissonance in his mind.

It was his castle—the one in ruins, she'd told him, her charcoal eyes wet with tears as she spoke of the Shepherd King, the voice in her head. *The first Rowan King burned it down, murdered him and his family. He's buried beneath the stone in the chamber at Castle Yew.*

Ravyn had torn himself from his bed and ridden from Stone like a specter on the wind to get to the chamber. He was restless—frantic—for the truth. Because none of it seemed real. The Shepherd King, with yellow eyes and a slick, sinister voice, trapped in the mind of a maiden. The Shepherd King, who promised to help them find the lost Twin Alders Card.

The Shepherd King, five hundred years dead.

Ravyn knew death—had been its exactor. He'd watched light go out of men's eyes. Heard final, gasping breaths. There was *nothing* on the other side, no life after death. Not for any man, cutpurse or highwayman—not even for the Shepherd King.

And yet.

Not all the soil at the base of the stone was hard. Some was loose, upturned. Someone had been there before him—recently. Elspeth, perhaps, looking for answers, same as he was. She'd dug at the base of the stone. There, hidden a hand below the hardened topsoil, was a carving. A single word made indecipherable with time. A grave marker.

Ravyn kept digging. When his fingernail ripped and the raw tip of his finger struck something cold, sharp, he swore and reared back. His body was invisible, but not his dripping blood. It trickled, a striking crimson red, appearing the moment it left his hand and scattering over the hole he'd dug in the soil, the earth thirsty for it.

The sound his blood made over dirt was muffled, delicate. *Thud. Thud. Thud.* Then, a sharply pitched *ting!*

Ravyn looked down.

Ting! Ting! Ting!

Something was hidden in the earth, waiting. Sharper than stone, colder than soil. Ravyn swiped at the topmost layer of dirt, guessing—dreading—what it was.

Steel.

Heart in his throat, he dug until he'd unearthed the entire surface of a sword. It lay crooked in the earth, soil caked on it. But there was no mistaking its make—castle-forged steel—with an intricately designed hilt, too ornate to be a soldier's blade.

He reached for it, the salt in the air piercing his lungs as he took short, fevered breaths. But before Ravyn could pry the sword from the earth, he caught a glimpse of something else hidden deep within the soil, beneath the sword.

It rested perfectly, undisturbed for centuries. A pale, knobbed object. Human. Skeletal.

A spine.

Ravyn's body seized, every muscle locked. His mouth went dry and nausea rolled up from his stomach into his throat, bile coating his tongue. Blood continued to drip from his hand onto the soil. And with every drop he gave away, he earned a fragmented, biting clarity: Blunder was full of magic. Wonderful, terrible magic. The Shepherd King was dead.

But his soul carried on, buried deep in Elspeth Spindle, the only woman Ravyn had ever loved.

He tore from the chamber.

Bent over himself beneath the yew tree outside, Ravyn coughed, fighting the urge to be sick. The tree was old, its branches unkempt, its canopy vast enough to keep the morning rainfall off his brow. He stayed that way for some time, bent over himself, chilled to his bones, his heartbeat reluctant to steady.

"What business have you to dig, raven bird?"

Ravyn whirled, the ivory hilt of his dagger in hand. But he was alone. The meadow was empty but for long dying grass, the slender path back to Castle Yew unmanned.

The voice called again, louder than before. "Did you hear me, bird?"

Perched in the yew tree above Ravyn's head, legs dangling over the edge of the aged branch, sat a girl. She was young—younger than his brother Emory—a child no older than twelve. Her hair fell in dark plaits over her shoulders, a few stray curls framing her face. Her cloak was undyed, gray wool with an intricately hemmed collar. Ravyn searched for a family insignia, but there was none.

He did not recognize her. Surely he'd recall such a striking face—such a distinct nose. Such vivid, yellow eyes.

Yellow.

"Who are you?" Ravyn said, his voice scraping his throat.

She watched him with those yellow eyes, tilting her head to the side like a falcon. "I'm Tilly," she said.

"What are you doing here, Tilly?"

"What I've always done," she said. For the briefest moment, she looked like Jespyr had as a girl, with those wide eyes and unruly curls. "I'm waiting."

Rain fell in earnest, carried on a swift wind. Droplets pelted the side of Ravyn's face, and the wind caught his hood, pulling it off his brow. He raised a hand, shielding his eyes from the sting.

But the girl in the tree remained unmoving, though the branch beneath her trembled and the yew tree's leaves whistled in the wind. Her cloak did not shift, nor did a single strand of her hair. Water and wind seemed to pass entirely through her, as if she was made of mist, of smoke.

Of nothingness.

Only then did Ravyn recall he was still using the Mirror. This had been his purpose—the answers he sought. He'd dug with blunt fingers, met bone with blood, but the Mirror was his greatest tool. A window into the past—to see beyond the veil.

Ravyn cleared his throat. The Mirror was a Providence Card he used sparingly—he had never encountered a spirit before. He knew nothing of their temperaments—if they were as they were when they died, or if the afterlife had…remade them.

He raised a shaky voice against the wind. "Who do you wait for, Tilly?"

The girl's eyes shifted to the chamber's one, dark window.

"Do you know the man who is buried there?"

She laughed, her voice sharp. "As well as I know this glen, bird. As well as I know this tree, and all the faces that have tarried beneath it." She twisted her finger in the tail of her plait. "You've heard of him, I suppose." Her lips curled in a smile. "He's a strange man, my father. Wary. Clever. Good."

Ravyn's breath faltered. "The Shepherd King is your father?"

Her smile faded, her yellow eyes distant, unfocused. "They did not give him a King's burial. Perhaps that is why he does not…" Her gaze returned to Ravyn. "You haven't seen him in the Mirror, have you? He promised he would find us. But he has not come."

"Us?"

The girl turned, her eyes tracing the woods on the other side of the meadow. "Mother is over there, somewhere. She does not come as often as she did. Ilyc and Afton linger near the statuary. Fenly and Lenor keep to your castle." Her brow furrowed. "Bennett is somewhere else. He did not die here. Not like the rest of us."

Die. Ravyn's throat tightened. "They are...your family? The Shepherd King's family?"

"We're waiting, bird," she said, crossing her arms over her chest. "For Father."

"Why does he not return?"

The girl did not answer. Her gaze fluttered across the meadow to the ruins. "I thought I heard his voice," she murmured. "Night had fallen. I was alone, here in my favorite tree." Her eyes flashed to Ravyn. "I saw you, raven bird. You came as you always do in your black cloak, your gray eyes clever, your face practiced. Only this time, you were not alone. A woman came with you. A strange woman, with eyes that flashed yellow gold, like mine. Like Father's."

Ravyn's insides twisted.

"I watched you both leave, but the maiden returned." Tilly held out a finger, pointing to the chamber's window. "She went inside. That's when I heard it—the songs my father used to hum as he wrote his book. But when I entered, he was not there. It was the woman who hummed as she raked her hands through the soil above Father's grave."

"Elspeth," Ravyn whispered, the name stealing something from him. "Her name is Elspeth."

Tilly didn't seem to hear him. "Twice the maiden visited and dug at his headstone. She wandered through the meadow, the ruins, humming my father's songs." Her lips drew into a tight line. "When dawn came, her yellow eyes shifted to a charcoal color. My father, if he was with her, vanished. So I came back here, to his grave. To watch. To wait."

Ravyn said nothing, his mind searching for answers it did not have. He remembered that night he'd brought Elspeth to the chamber. It was burned into him. He could still smell her hair—feel her cheek against his palm. He'd kissed her deeply and she'd kissed him back. Every part of him had wanted every part of her.

But she'd torn herself away, her eyes wide, a tremble in her voice. She'd been afraid of something in the chamber. At the time, Ravyn had been certain it was him she'd feared. But he knew now it was something else—something far greater than him—something she carried with her, always.

His eyes snapped back to the girl in the yew tree. "What happened to your father?"

The girl did not answer.

Ravyn tried again: "How did he die?"

She looked away, her yellow eyes lost. Her fingers danced a silent melody on the yew branch. "I do not know. They caught me first." Her voice quieted. "I passed through the veil before my father—before my brothers."

It wasn't the Mirror's chill that was seeping into Ravyn. It was something else. A question that, in the dark corner of his mind, he already knew the answer to. "Who killed you?" he said.

Those yellow eyes flared. They landed on Ravyn, measuring him. "You know his name," she said. Her voice went low, a deep, scraping whisper. "Rowan."

The King's insignia flashed in Ravyn's mind. His uncle's flag—the unyielding rowan tree. Red Scythe, green eyes. Brutes, conquerors.

Family.

Ravyn's bleeding hands shook.

"We've waited a long time for Father," Tilly said, her gaze turning upward, as if she was speaking now to only the yew tree. Her voice grew firm, her fingers curling like talons in her lap. "We will keep waiting, until his task is done."

A chill clawed up Ravyn's neck. He thought of the creature in Elspeth Spindle's body—of yellow eyes and twisting, silky words spoken in the dungeon. A promise to help find the lost Twin Alders Card.

But Ravyn knew better. No promise comes without payment. Blunder was a place of magic—barters and bargains. Nothing was free. "What does the Shepherd King want?" he asked the girl-spirit. "What is he after?"

"Balance," she answered, head tilting like a bird of prey. "To right terrible wrongs. To free Blunder from the Rowans." Her yellow eyes narrowed, wicked and absolute. "To collect his due."

if you enjoyed

ONE DARK WINDOW

look out for

WILD AND WICKED THINGS

by

Francesca May

In the aftermath of World War I, a naive woman is swept into a glittering world filled with dark magic, romance, and murder in this lush and decadent debut.

On Crow Island, people whisper that real magic lurks just below the surface.

Magic doesn't interest Annie Mason. Not after it stole her future. She's on the island only to settle her late father's estate and, hopefully, reconnect with her long-absent best friend, Beatrice, who fled their dreary lives for a more glamorous one.

Yet Crow Island is brimming with temptation, and the most mesmerizing may be her enigmatic new neighbor.

Mysterious and alluring, Emmeline Delacroix is a figure shadowed by rumors of witchcraft. And when Annie witnesses a confrontation between Bea and Emmeline at one of Crow Island's extravagant parties, she is drawn into a glittering, haunted world. A world where the boundaries of wickedness are tested, and the cost of illicit magic might be death.

Chapter One

Annie

Rumour had it that Crow Island was haunted by witches.

As I saw it for the first time, I understood why. People said the witches who had first discovered the island lived on in the bodies of the crows that flocked on every street corner and bare-branched tree. They flew high above as the boat drew closer to the shore, a constellation of black stars against the bright summer sky.

Tucked away beyond the murky water off the east coast, the island's crescent-moon shape gave it the appearance of a curved spine, a body curled secretively away from the mainland. Yet up close the properties, built to resemble American plantation houses and crumbling Georgian manors, dispelled this illusion of secrecy. They loomed large, like spectral grey sentries guarding their land.

On Crow Island, people had whispered to me back home, real magic lurked just below the surface. Wealth seeped from the place like honey. They said that it had a reputation, that here the law looked the other way.

My mother hadn't wanted me to come, but I had pleaded, surprising both of us. It was my father's final request, which felt vital somehow, and I was compelled in a way I never had been before. He had wanted me to do this, to travel to a place I had never been, to sort through and sell his belongings, although I had hardly known him. And I had thought I could do it. I thought, at least, I should try.

I was no longer sure. I had never been away from home, had never slept anywhere but the squat back bedroom in the little stone terrace house I shared with my mother. The thought was both light and sharp. I inhaled a lungful of the salty ocean air, which tasted different here than it did back home, and reassured myself that I could be brave. Crow Island might be haunted, but it couldn't be much different than the rest of England had been since the war, life trudging on despite the ghosts. I would be fine.

In the harbour the final traces of Whitby drained away: here was no Mam to guide me; there were no familiar street corners to remind me of sunny afternoons with Sam and Bea; there was not even to be the routine of the shop, of cosy evenings by the fire or Sunday afternoons visiting the gallery in town. It was an unwritten story. I had never had so much freedom, or felt so timid.

There was a car waiting for me by the harbour office, a swanky hayburner unlike anything I'd ever dreamed of driving, with a paper slip bearing my name tied to the steering wheel. I approached hesitantly, placing my palm flat against the sun-warmed metal. It felt, for a second, like I could feel the heartbeat of the island, the same thundering under my skin I sometimes swore I could feel when I scavenged shiny polished stones on the beach back home. I pulled my sweating palm back and glanced around nervously.

The harbour had long since emptied and I couldn't see another soul. The office loomed ahead, its windows mirrored by the sun. In the letter I had received before leaving I'd been told I would have to go inside to collect the key for my father's car, but some force held me locked in place. It wasn't the office itself that scared me, more the idea that once I had the key—what then?

I stood for a minute watching the occasional cloud scud across the dark glass of the office windows. Two minutes. Five. My thoughts trickled towards my father. I should be more upset by his death, but I was almost indifferent. Perhaps I was being harsh, perhaps he *had* loved Mam once, but she had never said. She had shed his surname as if even the suggestion of his love was painful for her. I almost preferred to think that he had never loved her. After all, what kind of man would abandon his wife and newborn daughter for an *island*? Still, this was my inheritance—money that could mean everything for Mam and me.

The sun beat down on my shoulders and I was hot and impatient with myself. Sam would have thought I was silly. Bea would laugh if she saw me. But Sam wasn't here and Bea was probably still angry with me. My irritation grew. A roaring sound began inside my ears, the same sound I always heard when a panic came on—like ocean waves. Like drowning. I closed my eyes, squeezing them tight, blocking out the sensation of swirling water that clogged my mind.

"Are you…well, miss? Do you need a doctor? Papa says it looks like you might faint."

A girl of no more than ten had appeared, red-haired and freckled, wearing a grey smock. Concern etched her forehead. I must have been standing here for longer than I'd thought.

"I'm—a little lost," I said, fumbling for an excuse. "I think this is my car but I don't have the key…?"

The girl's face sagged in relief and she snatched at the handwritten slip tied to the wheel plus the paper I handed her, my own messy scrawl in the margins of the note my father's lawyer had sent me. When she returned them, it was with a small key ring, which she thrust at me.

"Thank you," I managed, finally able to breathe.

The girl disappeared as quickly as she'd come. I gazed at the car for a moment more, remembering the illicit runabouts in Sam's dad's jalopy. I'd hated them at the time but was glad now, although I was worried that it would be harder here than roaring along the winding, empty country roads at home.

I didn't want to think of Sam, or of home, and that spurred me into action. I threw my meagre belongings into the car, and once I was on the road it came back to me little by little. It was easier than I remembered, or perhaps the car was simply better. The air tasted of tree sap, the future shimmering ahead like a mirage in the heat.

The reality of Crow Island stretched and grew around me as I drove, lavish houses making way for smaller dwellings as I headed away from the harbour, and quiet, crooked streets peeling off the main road through the town known as Crow Trap. I took in the freshly whitewashed shops and the bright, shiny windows. I hadn't seen such a lush air of festivity since the parties we'd thrown after the armistice. The bunting was fresh and neat, fluttering between lampposts, and the children who ran in circles outside the small bakery wore clean aprons and shoes.

It was beautiful, and yet I couldn't help the nervous way my palms itched at the sight of the wooden boards outside shops peddling *Genuine Palm Readings* and *Holidaymakers' Charms for Good Fortune*, and at the windows that offered a glimpse of trailing greenery, framing small signs that proclaimed the vendors' license to advertise faux magic.

It had been this way since the prohibition began after the war. Licenses, posters, and provisos, silly games that danced on a knife-edge as far as the law was concerned. Back home I hardly thought about magic except to avoid the advertisements at the back of the newspaper where faux mediums passed public messages to the great beyond. In Whitby there wasn't much cause for meddling with magic, real or otherwise; most people barely had enough money to put food in their bellies, never mind extra to waste on trifles.

And it wasn't worth the risk.

Mam always said that real magic was cunning and it was best to steer clear. Fake magic was a joke, a party trick for rich people who had nothing better to do, so it was best to steer clear of that too. Her most well-worn bedtime caution over the last two and a half years was the story of a girl in York, Bessie Higgins, who'd been hanged for selling poppets that turned out to have dried monkshood in them, although she'd sworn she had simply picked the weeds near the river.

There must be more to Bessie's story, but talking about magic had always made Bea act foolish, so we never did.

Magic seemed different here. The licenses and advertisements were light, funny. These signs offered a glimpse into the future instead of the past. Perhaps the rich could better enjoy the soft scares of make-believe fortune-telling, since they hadn't lost as much as the rest of us.

I counted seven of the island's famous crows as I headed

back towards the coast. They were perched on rooftops and in trees, one more on the pinnacle of a lamppost, her beady eyes and sharp little beak shining in the May morning sun. I acknowledged each one under my breath like a prayer, the hazy words of a half-remembered poem in the back of my mind.

One for malice,
Two for mirth...

The stretch of coastline where I'd rented a house for the summer was a jungle of grand houses and sprawling estates, the odd cottage like mine annexed from wealthy land a long time ago. I drove down roads shaded by hedgerows growing verdant and wild and speckled with dark thorns. It was a relief to easily find the cottage, nestled less than five minutes' slow drive away.

It sat atop a sloping lawn, surrounded on three sides by so many trees you could hardly see the sky, or the ocean, or anything but tangles of green. At the back of the cottage the lawn dipped until it fell away into a sandy stretch looking out to the North Sea. I'd used some of my new inheritance for the privilege of being able to see water. That was why outsiders came to Crow Island after all, wasn't it?

There was a man waiting for me outside the cottage when I arrived. He was tall and broad shouldered with greying rust-coloured hair and a cheerful, ruddy face. He smoothed the jacket of his immaculate herringbone suit and smiled.

"You must be Miss Mason," he said, shaking my hand warmly as I climbed out of the car. "Your father spoke very highly of you. My name is Jonas Anderson—it's a pleasure to finally meet you. I'm very sorry about your father. Such a shame to have lost him so unexpectedly."

This was my father's lawyer. The man he'd left in charge of

his estate. He was the one who had written after my father's heart attack and begged me to come. *It's what your father wanted. The only thing he asked for.* He was the one who had given me an advance on my father's money—for the cottage. I hadn't expected him to be here, and his presence made my muscles bunch nervously.

"Mr. Anderson," I said, smoothing my hair flat under its scarf. I didn't like the idea that my father had spoken about me at all when it hardly seemed like he'd remembered I existed, but I tried to keep that from my voice. "How nice to see you in person—but I'm here so early. I thought we weren't scheduled to meet until next week."

"No, but I wanted to, ah, welcome you to the island," he said, still smiling. "I wanted, really, to make sure you found the car without trouble, and the cottage..." He pointed vaguely. "I was surprised you chose one over here, but I can understand why. It's lovely, isn't it? Anyway, I know it can be daunting to find your feet in a new place. Especially one like this." He gestured at a single crow that had perched itself comfortably on the bonnet of my car. "So, if you need anything, you mustn't hesitate to let me know. Particularly if it's about your father or his things. We were good friends, you see. I'm sure you must have questions, though I understand if you're too overwhelmed today. I thought perhaps that was why you came early. I can try to speed through the necessary paperwork, but I'm more than happy to give you this week to get settled if that's preferable."

I blinked away the unexpected tightness in my throat at his kindness and nodded as he talked, allowing myself to settle into this new world and agreeing gratefully to keep in touch. Once he was gone I slipped into the cottage, shutting out the sunny warmth to set about unpacking my few belongings.

Now that I was alone, the cottage seemed big and rambling.

Frivolous. It wasn't like it was even my money I was spending yet. It was strangely quiet too, the sound of my footsteps muffled by the distant rush of the ocean and the caw of a crow. And there was a different quality to the quiet; it felt like the blackest part of a shadow, coiled and waiting.

I had never been alone like this before. I had spent all my early years with a gaggle of other neighbourhood children, Sam and Bea and a snotty girl called Margot at my heels as we ran and played in the streets behind my mother's chocolate shop. Later, when Sam was gone, I had Mam and Bea, and then Mam. What would I do with all this space? I could walk from one side of the cottage to the other without tripping over Mam's knitting basket or having to slow for Tabs and her kittens. I could swing my arms and not hit a single thing if I wanted to. I didn't want to.

I wasn't sure I wanted to be here.

Until Sam was deployed I'd never thought about leaving Whitby. After he left I thought about it constantly. I was still trying to convince my mother to let me sign up to nurse when we found out he'd died. Just—died. Gone.

It felt like a warning. *This is what happens when you dream.* This is what happens when you get ahead of yourself. For two years Bea and I hardly spoke of him, and when we did we pretended that he was still away, travelling the world and collecting experiences he would bring home to share with us. He never came home. And when Bea had left last spring—when she'd come to this very island—without saying goodbye to me, it felt like I was doomed to lose everything, each part of me slowly chipped away until there was nothing left.

I stayed with Mam, pretending I was content. I did what it felt like I should do, going through the motions like no war had ever happened. How was my loss any different from anybody else's? My life became a pattern of dance halls on the weekends, more out of obligation than anything else, and the shop during the week. Trips to the gallery and the dull excitement of a new sewing pattern. Mam never said so, but eventually she expected me to marry. It had been four years since Sam died, and my inevitable future grew closer every month. I couldn't put it off much longer.

And then...?

That was the part that scared me. The picture of a life already lived, so predictable I could write it point by point in my journal and tick it off. Marriage, babies, hard work, and never enough money to stretch... The problem was, as much as my father's death felt almost like a windfall, coming to the island scared me too.

Standing here, in this cottage that wasn't mine, I told myself it didn't—*couldn't*—matter that I was afraid. This felt like my last chance to change my path; I needed to grasp it with both hands, pull the opportunity up at the roots, and carry it with me, ready to plant, or else the life back home was all that waited for me.

It seemed like fate that Bea was here. I'd been thinking of her a lot since I set out on the ferry, wondering if she'd truly missed me like her letters said. Whether she was still angry with me. The hole she'd left in my chest ached. If only we could be friends again—true friends—maybe I wouldn't feel so lonely.

Bea and I had been so close, once. Both of us had grown up without fathers, although hers had died when she was just a baby, and we often joked that we were fierce enough not to need them. It felt strange, after all our jokes, all the secret longing we'd hidden behind our bluster, that I was here today because of my father.

Perhaps he had hoped coming to the island would be good

for me. Perhaps he had hoped that the island would jostle my soul and wake me from a slumber he recognised—that it would cut this stunted part of me free. Perhaps he hadn't thought of how it would affect me at all. I wasn't sure which possibility I liked the least.

The late-afternoon air in the cottage was loaded with my questions. I wanted to know about his life, about his friends, his work, and his hobbies. I wanted to know why this place had captivated him so much that he had left us without a second thought. And most of all, I couldn't stop the small voice in my head that asked the same thing I'd been returning to for weeks—at home, on the boat, seeing that shiny car for the first time…

Why now? Why had my father only wanted me to come to Crow Island once he was dead?